REDEMPTION OF THE SWORD

THE CHRONICLES OF ARKADIA

J. JONES

Chapter 1

Kane Devan, Prefect of Vangor, stood upon what remained of the southern gatehouse and stared out over the shattered battlements at the mass of men forming up on the plain below. Many a time he had climbed to the top of the gatehouse just so he could gaze in wonderment at the view below. Stretching out before him would be league after league of sprawling fields and meadows all of them alive with a myriad of colourful and aromatic flowers. Now the flowers were all dead, crushed mercilessly beneath thousands of anonymous boots or suffocated by the bodies of the dead. The air no longer smelled sweet and perfumed. Now it smelled of decay. The stench of death hung heavy in the air choking those still alive.

A little over an hour ago he had stood in that same position with Teren Rad, Ro Aryk and Queen Cala trying to decide whose troops it was appearing over the ridge far to the south. They had hoped that it was the Remadan relief column the messenger had assured them was on its way, but it had soon become apparent that it was yet another detachment of enemy soldiers.

Teren and his son Eryn, had departed shortly afterwards hoping to pick up the trail of the Narmidian raider who still held Eryn's fiancée, Tayla, captive. The others had remained in Vangor intent on mounting a last determined defence in the hope that the relief column would soon arrive. However, when the true strength of the enemy had become clear, they had decided that a serious defence of the city was tantamount to suicide and had changed their plans. There was not enough time to evacuate the whole city, but what remained of the men-at-arms might be able to escape if a small force of volunteers remained behind to buy them some time. It would be a brief and ultimately futile defence, but it might just be enough to enable the soldiers to escape.

Approximately thirty minutes after Teren and Eryn had left, the wagons blocking the city's eastern gate had been rolled out of the way and all but a handful of the remaining men had marched silently out. Watching Teren depart had been hard on the city's population, but to then also have to watch the remaining soldiers leave had been almost unbearable. All hope marched with them and they knew it.

For reasons which now escaped him, Kane had volunteered to remain behind and lead the defence of his city. He imagined that it had been out of some misplaced sense of loyalty or duty, but it all seemed rather pointless now.

Still, here he was and he was just going to have to make the most of it. He tore his gaze away from the enemy fanning out in front of him and stuffed his trembling hands deep inside his pockets.

Wouldn't do to let the others see how scared I am.

He glanced around at the men who now formed his paltry defence force. For the most part they were the soldiers who were too badly injured to be moved let alone taken on a long arduous journey across rough terrain. Ordinarily these men would have been in the infirmary receiving treatment for their wounds, but these weren't ordinary times. The only people left in the wreckage of the infirmary now were those close to death.

Alongside the wounded stood civilian men who had not wanted to evacuate the city as it would have meant leaving their families behind. Instead they had chosen to remain in Vangor and share the same uncertain fate as their loved ones. Dotted here and there was the odd able-bodied soldier who for their own reasons had also chosen to remain in the city. These were mostly men from Vangor's own garrison who had been given the chance to leave with the others, but had declined, opting instead to remain with their captain, Jer Matalis.

Positioned in-between the defenders, were the bodies of some of the men who had fallen in the earlier battles. Propped up against the battlements it was hoped that their presence would make it look like the city was far better defended than it actually was. It was an unpleasant state of affairs and Kane would much rather have seen the men buried or cremated, especially as most of them were starting to attract the flies, but it was a necessary one, or so Ro Aryk had assured him. It was a simple ruse and one that would be found out very quickly once the Delarites started climbing the walls and realised that most of the defenders were not fighting back. Every minute bought, however, was another one Ro and the others could use to put some distance between them and the city.

Kane glanced to the east and could just about make out the small column of men disappearing in the distance.

Good! If they can't see them, perhaps the Delarites won't realise that anyone's escaped, at least for a while.

It was a comforting thought and Kane suddenly found his wavering resolve start to return.

A series of bugle calls drew his attention back to the plain below where the Delarite army was forming up into a number of blocks. Kane supposed that someone like Ro or Teren would be able to draw some conclusions from the way the Delarites were deploying, but he was not a soldier, just an administrator and their disposition meant nothing to him.

Kane heard somebody approaching him from his left before stopping and snapping smartly to attention. He turned expecting to see Colonel Baptiste's calm and reassuring face, but was surprised to see Baptiste's second-in-command, Captain Matalis, instead. Then with a heavy heart, Kane remembered how his friend had been killed almost in that very spot earlier in the day.

"Yes, Captain?"

"The men are drawn up as we planned, sir," replied Matalis.

"Very good, Captain." The man made no effort to move and Kane wondered what else he was expecting from him. "Was there something else, Captain?"

Matalis looked a bit embarrassed and after surreptitiously glancing round, he stepped in closer to the prefect. Kane hated people violating his personal space and desperately wanted to take a pace back, but resisted the urge. The captain had to have his reasons for coming so close and Kane decided that despite his discomfort he would have to endure it.

"I think it would be a good idea if you addressed the men, sir," said Matalis in a hushed tone.

"Address the men? Me?" asked Kane incredulously.

"It's expected of the commander in situations like this, sir."

"I'm a quill pusher, Captain, not a general; what am I supposed to say?"

"Nothing much, sir as I don't think we've got a lot of time anyway; just a few inspiring words to stiffen their backbones. You'll think of something I'm sure."

Having evidently said his piece, Matalis took a couple of steps back, much to Kane's relief.

The prefect glanced round him at the pockets of expectant faces and knew that the captain was right. Straightening his tunic and doing his best to smile and exude confidence, Kane stepped forward to the inner battlements so that those standing in the courtyard below would also be able to hear him.

"Defenders of Vangor, once in every man's life will come the opportunity to do the right thing and to make a difference; today is our time." A half-hearted cheer rose up from around the gathered crowd. "The enemy is once again at our gates and he is many whilst we are few. I am not going to stand here and try to convince you that we can win this battle, because we can't; you know it and I know it. What we can do, however, is deal the enemy a bloody nose, giving our comrades the chance to escape and fight again. You will have all heard by now that a relief force is on its way and for all we know it might just be over the ridge. The longer that we can hold out here, the greater the chance of them arriving in time to save the city.

"The enemy do not know how many we are and because of the beating we gave them earlier they are likely to hit us with everything that they've got. I know that you are all tired and wish to be with your families, but I'm begging you, when the Delarite storm breaks against our walls, stand firm and fight like Tanith himself."

The prefect's words were greeted by another cheer, louder this time and more widespread.

"Fight for your families, fight for your country and fight for your freedom and make those Delarite dogs pay tenfold for every single son of Remada who has perished on these walls," bellowed Kane warming to his task and raising his sword in the air.

This time the cheer was taken up by everybody who had heard the prefect's speech and despite their depleted numbers, the cheering boomed out across the plain to the assembled Delarite soldiers.

Kane stepped back from the battlements and glanced at Captain Matalis.

"So how did I do, Captain?"

"You're a natural, sir, very inspiring. Perhaps in the future when you tire of being Prefect you could become a speech writer," replied the captain smiling.

"That's very kind of you to say, Captain, but I don't think so. Besides, that rather presumes that we've all got a future beyond the next hour or so."

The captain nodded knowingly. "That being so, sir, I fully intend to make the most of what time I've got left, by killing as many of these Delarite whoresons as I can."

Kane smiled at the captain's use of Teren's favourite insult; the man's influence was everywhere. He was about to make a comment along those lines when another series of trumpet notes, different to the ones earlier, drifted across the plain to the city's walls.

"Here they come," someone standing behind Kane shouted unnecessarily.

The prefect and Captain Matalis stepped to the forward battlements and stared down at the mass of men rapidly approaching the city walls. Archers had been sent out ahead of the others to provide a screen, whilst behind them ran two rows of men carrying sturdy looking long shields. Behind them were dense ranks of men bearing ladders and grapples. The Delarites apparently meant business this time.

"What are your orders, sir?" said Matalis turning to face the prefect and standing to attention.

The prefect looked at the captain and smiled, pleased to notice that the trembling in his hands had ceased.

"My orders are simple. Stay alive as long as you can, Captain and kill as many of those fellows as possible. When all hope is lost I will wave a white flag and order what remains of our force to lay down their arms. What happens after that will very much be down to our conquerors. I pray to Sulat that they are merciful, at least to the civilians."

"Let us hope so, sir. May Sulat watch over you," replied the captain.

"And you too," replied Kane.

They shook hands briefly before the captain turned and dashed down the steps to take up his battle position.

Kane glanced eastwards again and was pleased to see that Ro's column was nowhere to be seen.

Good luck, my friends. Avenge us.

When he turned again, the first ladders were already appearing against the city walls.

"Tip them over, tip them over," Kane shouted at the men nearest him as he raced towards the southern battlements.

Two of the men nearest to Kane rushed forward to help, but one suddenly dropped to the floor clutching at an arrow through his throat. The other man, a soldier from the city garrison whose name the prefect didn't know, reached one of the ladders just as a Delarite was preparing to clamber over the parapet. The Remadan soldier punched the man hard in the face. The Delarite instinctively let go of the ladder and reached for his injured nose before toppling backwards taking the man directly below with him. The Remadan soldier tried to push the ladder away from the wall, but laden with men it was just too heavy.

Seeing that he was struggling, Kane shouted for a couple of the civilians to hurl rocks down onto the men climbing the ladder before rushing over and helping the soldier push the ladder back. At first it seemed that even their combined strength wasn't going to be enough to push it back from the wall, but then it gave way.

For the briefest of moments the ladder remained upright and the prefect locked eyes with the man nearest the top. Then slowly it toppled backwards. Some of the men on the ladder jumped thinking their chances of survival better that way whilst others clung on, desperately hoping for a soft landing. None of them survived. The ladder crashed into the mass of men below, killing those still clinging to its rungs and those unfortunate enough to be beneath it.

Kane stared down at the carnage below and smiled. When

the battle for Vangor had first started he would have been horrified at the loss of life he had just caused, but now he took it all in his stride.

It's you or them.

Teren Rad's words echoed in his mind.

An arrow suddenly ricocheted off the battlements to his left, its head viciously grazing his left cheek as it flew by to land harmlessly behind him. Kane winced and touched his cheek, quickly withdrawing his blood covered fingers when their touch caused a stinging pain.

The top of another ladder appeared in the same place as the last one and without thinking Kane leant over to see what was happening below. The upward sword thrust missed the underneath of Kane's chin by a hair's breadth, some form of self-preservation making him move his head just at the last moment. Enraged by his own stupidity and frightened beyond all belief, Kane swung his own sword downwards intent on slicing open his attacker's head, but the Delarite had anticipated the assault and had raised his own sword to parry the blow.

Kane hesitated giving the Delarite soldier the time he needed. Quick as a flash he shoved the prefect back before clambering over the parapet. Then he started to advance on the prefect who was slowly backing away. The head of another Delarite soldier had already appeared at the top of the ladder. The first Delarite soldier swung his sword at Kane who just managed to block the man's blow, the force of the strike jarring the prefect's arm. Somehow the prefect then managed to anticipate the next stroke, though it was all he could do to hold onto his sword, but the third stroke, a powerful horizontal slice, knocked the prefect's sword clean out of his hand.

Terrified, but determined to die with all the dignity he could muster, Kane straightened his back, stared into the other man's eyes and waited for the killing blow.

I just hope our deaths are not in vain.

If Kane had been hoping that his show of bravery in the face of imminent death would curry pity from his attacker, he was wrong. Grinning with delight, the Delarite was raising his sword ready to strike when something struck him on the head. Although the man rocked backwards, the iron helmet he was wearing absorbed most of the force, though he appeared somewhat dazed. The Delarite glared in the direction from which the object had been thrown and appeared to be on the verge of saying something, when another missile struck him squarely in his unprotected face.

Kane looked on in shock as the man's nose literally exploded into a bloody pulp in front of him. The Delarite soldier instinctively dropped his sword and clasped his ruined face with both hands, wailing in pain as blood seeped through his fingers. It took Kane a few seconds to realise that this was his opportunity, but when he did he quickly bent down and retrieved his sword. Then with a shout of triumph he drove the point deep into the man's belly giving it a final twist as he withdrew it.

When the man had crumpled to the ground either dead or dying, Kane had turned to thank whoever had just saved his life. Standing a few paces to his left with three arrows protruding from his upper body, was a young boy of perhaps fourteen years of age. Kane recognised him as the one of the boys who had joined him in coming to Ro's help a couple of days earlier when the defenders had been on the verge of being overwhelmed. After rounding up every young boy and old man he could, the prefect had led a last desperate charge onto the battlements, an action that had ultimately saved the day.

The boy, who Kane remembered was called Thom, stumbled to his knees, a shocked expression on his face. His right arm stretched out reaching for Kane and his mouth moved as he tried to say something, but above the roar of battle Kane couldn't hear him. He made to approach the boy, but suddenly felt a red-hot pain in his back. Kane glanced down and for the briefest of moments couldn't figure out what it was protruding from his stomach. When the Delarite soldier who had attacked him from behind wiggled his sword blade from side to side before withdrawing it, he knew for certain.

Kane collapsed to the ground in front of Thom and stretched his own arm out desperately trying to reach the boy's fingertips. All around him the sounds of battle raged on though they somehow seemed to be becoming more subdued and distant. Kane's peripheral vision was also starting to go. The pain in his back and abdomen was unbearable, but he was determined to reach the boy's hand and offer some small comfort in his last moments on Chell. With one last excruciating effort, Kane wriggled forward and just managed to grasp the boy's fingers, but instead of smiling the boy just stared back at him from lifeless eyes. Tears of frustration formed in the prefect's eyes, but he never even felt the downward thrust from the Delarite sword which ended his life.

***

From his position some thirty or so paces away, Captain Matalis had watched in horror as first his sister's son had been cut down by several arrows and then the prefect had been killed. His pride in his nephew was boundless. Armed with nothing more than a few rocks the boy had stood his ground when others had run, even briefly saving the prefect's life when a well-aimed missile had struck the Delarite soldier squarely in the face.

The prefect had said that they would fight on until their position was hopeless and then he would signal for the white flag to be run up. Matalis was pretty sure that their position had been hopeless from the outset. When the prefect's position had been overrun he had fully expected the man to signal the surrender, but he hadn't. Whether he had forgotten or perhaps simply changed his mind, Matalis didn't know. Nor did he care. No surrender had been signalled. So be it. He glanced round briefly taking stock of the situation. The battlements were now virtually overrun and he had to search hard to find any Remadans still alive, though isolated pockets fought on. The end was near though, very near.

Two Delarite soldiers suddenly came charging towards him and Matalis braced himself. The soldier on Matalis's right chopped down with his sword, slicing through the air where Matalis had been standing. Anticipating the man's attack, Matalis had crouched and spun completely around, slicing his own sword across the back of the other man's thighs, hamstringing him. The first soldier whose momentum had carried him forward had just about turned when Matalis launched into him with a series of blows the Delarite did well to block. Matalis raised his sword high as if preparing to chop down at the man's head, his opponent instinctively raising his own weapon to block the impending blow.

It was the opening Matalis had been hoping for and quick as a flash he raised his left leg and pushed the man over the edge with his foot sending him crashing to the stone courtyard below where he landed with a sickening thud. Matalis turned and quickly despatched the man he had hamstrung, driving his sword point deep into the Delarite's chest.

Already though his existence had been spotted by a small knot of Delarite soldiers and they were now picking their way across the body strewn battlements towards him. It was time to go. He would make a last stand in the courtyard under the Remadan flag. He turned and as quickly as he could, made his way down the steps towards the courtyard.

The captain's departure was noticed by a few of the remaining defenders and thinking that he was running and trying to save his own life, some of them panicked and turned to follow. Others threw their weapons down and pleaded for their lives. Everyone who tried to surrender was slaughtered where they stood.

Realising his mistake, Matalis stopped in the courtyard and turned to face the battlements. The first time he tried to shout, his voice was hoarse and barely audible. He swallowed hard a couple of times trying to lubricate his constricted throat before trying again. This time his voice boomed out across the courtyard and up to the battlements.

"Remadans to me, Remadans to me."

Some, notably the few remaining regular soldiers, instantly disengaged where they could and made their way towards the officer. Others, however, became distracted by his call and were cut down in their hesitation.

It was a pitifully small force of about twenty men that finally congregated around Matalis. A few yards in front of them in a dense semi-circle several men deep, the Delarite attackers massed ready to deliver the killing blow.

A Delarite officer slowly pushed his way through the crowd and stood before the Remadan defenders.

"Who is in command here?"

Matalis took a step forward and pinned the officer with his hardest stare. "I am."

The Delarite officer looked at Matalis with a mixture of amusement and disgust.

"I think, Captain, the time has come to discuss surrender."

Captain Matalis nodded and turned to look at his exhausted and wounded men. They all looked back at him with a grim determination that made him feel proud, prouder than he'd ever felt before. Matalis smiled as he turned back to face the Delarite officer.

"I thought you'd never ask. If you and your men are prepared to lay down your arms and surrender, I am willing to let you return to your own lines on the understanding that you will not attack the city of Vangor again."

The Delarite officer stared at Matalis incredulously, the young captain's deadpan expression making him wonder whether he was joking or not. When some of the Remadans started laughing his expression turned from one of bemusement to anger. Even some of his own men were smiling at the Remadan's audacity.

"Then you have chosen death, Captain and death you shall have," the Delarite officer finally said as he stepped to one side.

Matalis turned to face his men once again. "It has been an honour fighting alongside you, men, but now the Chariot of Souls approaches. I say we make it wait a little longer." The handful of Remadans cheered enthusiastically one last time, but when Matalis turned to face the enemy for the last time, the cheering stopped. The Delarite soldiers who had been surrounding them had quickly been replaced by two ranks of men armed with crossbows and they were all pointed at Matalis and his men.

"You cowardly bast..." Matalis never got to finish his sentence as dozens of bolts suddenly tore through the air and slammed into him and his men. A few seconds later Matalis and his men all lay dead.

The Delarite officer stepped forward and nudged the

Remadan captain's body with his foot, but he was clearly dead. The Remadan's arrogance had been unbelievable yet the Delarite officer also secretly admired the man's courage, however futile. Now he was just one more corpse in a city of thousands. The stench of death was everywhere. The killing, however, was not yet over. General Malik had given express orders that once the city was taken, either by force or through surrender, everybody was to be put to the sword; men, women and children. There was no honour in such a thing, but there was nothing he could do to stop it. His men were going to tear through this city and wreak a terrible vengeance on its remaining inhabitants. The women would be raped and then killed, the men and children tortured and butchered. His men would act like a pack of wild dogs and all with his commander's blessing. The families of the gallant defenders deserved better.

A junior officer strode up alongside him and snapped smartly to attention after glancing disdainfully at the Remadan bodies around his feet.

"What is it?" asked the senior officer.

"The men want to know if they can begin to...carry out the general's orders, Colonel?"

The colonel sighed. It was no good; there was nothing he could do to stop it. If he tried to his men would more than likely kill him and then run amok anyway and if they didn't, General Malik would have him killed painfully for disobeying his orders.

"Yes, tell them the city is theirs, but remember, both Teren Rad and Ro Aryk are to be taken alive at all costs; the Silevian monk too if at all possible."

The junior officer nodded and marched off to give the orders, a loud cheer greeting his announcement before the men dispersed throughout the ruined city to satiate their carnal desires and bloodlust.

The Delarite colonel watched them go. If Teren Rad and his companions were still here they would have been on the battlements fighting, but they weren't. Instead his men had been confronted by wounded soldiers, civilians and dead men; a clever ruse. Something told him that Rad and his men had managed to slip away unnoticed. He smiled to himself.

They were honourable men, more so than those who commanded the Delarite army. He hoped that they were far away by now. General Malik would be in a foul rage when he heard the news and he pitied the man who had to deliver it. It was then that he realised that he was probably the last ranking officer left alive out of the assault force and as such, that duty would fall to him.

A sinking feeling in his stomach suddenly made him feel quite nauseous and he hurried away. He needed a stiff drink and quickly. All around him the screams and crying of the men and women of Remada began to permeate the streets of Vangor. It was going to be a long and terrible night.

Chapter 2

Kern Razak was not a happy man. Everything was falling apart. The expedition had started out fine and they had managed to capture a good number of young girls to sell as slaves back home, but then things had turned sour. It had all started to go wrong at the Remadan village the locals called Lentor. It should have been a routine raid like so many others before it. They had attacked at dawn with the sun at their backs and had taken the village completely by surprise.

The Remadan traitor, a loathsome little man called Bratak, had given him the location of all the young girls in the village in return for a handful of coins and they should have been in and out of there in no time. Instead his men had found themselves embroiled in a vicious fight. Some of the Remadan villagers had fought like demons and Kern had lost seven men as a result. Bratak had omitted to tell him that the village was home to a couple of Remada's greatest warriors, albeit old ones. He didn't ever expect to see the Remadan traitor again, but if he did, he would make him pay dearly for his omission.

Unbeknown to Kern the disproportionate loss of life they had suffered attacking the village had sown the seeds of rebellion amongst his own ranks, culminating in an open challenge to his leadership. One night, shortly after attacking the village of Tarle, against Kern's express orders, Beren, one of his closest friends and a number of other men from his party, had taken some of their girl prisoners into the woods intent on rape. A man loyal to Kern had woken him and alerted him to the treachery and together with a handful of men he thought loyal, they had slaughtered the mutineers. The battle had decimated their numbers however, making the return journey to Narmidia at best perilous and at worst suicidal. But the treachery had not ended there. Whilst Kern and his remaining loyal followers had been in the forest putting down the mutiny, one of the two men he had left guarding the girls had killed the other guard, freed their horses and then made off with one of the girl captives.

Kern had been left with a handful of men, no horses and too many girls to guard. Their options now limited, they had struck out east towards Narmidia, hoping to sell their captives on route through Salandor. Even that one small recompense had been denied them though. They had not travelled far when they had run into a troop of Remadan cavalry. Unlike all the other Remadan soldiers they had set eyes on, these men were actually riding north towards their Delarite enemy. They had either been very brave or very foolish.

On foot and with a score of women prisoners to watch over, his party had been an easy target for the patrol. Luckily there had been a small copse no more than a hundred paces away and Kern and just three of his men had made it to the relative safety of the trees. The Remadan cavalry had not pursued them and had instead freed the hostages and ridden off north towards the city of Vangor, taking the girls with them.

With no girls to sell and too few of them to even consider raiding another village, Kern and his three companions had been left with no choice but to strike out for home.

They had been walking for several hours and darkness now covered the land, when the sullen man Kern had sent ahead to scout, came hurrying up to him.

"What is it?" asked Kern barely disguising his irritation.

"Zalis!" replied the scout.

"Zalis! What about him?" Zalis was one of the men Kern had left guarding the girls whilst he put down the mutiny, but who had also betrayed him and made off with one of the captives after killing the other guard. Kern had been hoping to see him again.

"He is camped just over that ridge," replied the man grinning. "He sleeps."

Kern grinned and nodded knowingly. "Does he now?"

Sulat be praised. Finally some good luck. Now someone is finally going to pay for the misfortune which has befallen me.

"What is it, Kern?" asked Varil, his most trusted man, as he sidled up alongside Kern.

"Nebu says that Zalis is camped just over that ridge and sleeps like a baby." Kern was pleased by the malicious look that crossed Varil's face at the mention of the traitor's name. Clearly no love was lost between the two men and he knew then that he could count on Varil, at least for the time being.

"I trust we are going to pay him a visit?" The question had been rhetorical, but Kern chose to answer anyway.

"Of course."

After filling Talik, the other member of his party in on the plan, the four men quietly made their way to the top of the ridge before spreading out. As promised, Zalis appeared to be fast asleep next to the small camp fire that was just beginning to die out. His sword and bow were lying on the ground next to him and he undoubtedly slept with a dagger concealed beneath his blanket as Kern himself did. Nevertheless, Kern fully expected the four of them to still be able to take him by surprise without casualties. Even if there were casualties it didn't matter so long as he wasn't one of them.

Kern scanned the camp drinking in every relevant detail. The girl he had taken when he fled the camp was tied against a tree, but did not appear to be asleep. They had no idea how she would react if she saw them enter the camp and didn't want to risk her waking Zalis. There were two horses, including Kern's own one. The sight of his beloved horse both pleased and incensed him. Zalis would truly pay for his treachery especially if his horse was injured in any way.

Kern glanced round one last time making sure that his men were in position. When he was happy that they were, he quietly drew his sword and raised himself to a crouched position. He was just about to signal the others to make their move, when the girl, who had evidently been struggling against her bonds, suddenly stood, freed herself of the rope and darted towards the ridge. Kern signalled for Nebu to intercept her and then gestured for the others to make their way into the camp and converge on where Zalis slept. Three of them should still be enough.

The girl had clearly not seen the men surrounding the camp, so when Nebu stepped out from behind a shrub and made to grab her, it came as a total surprise. Nebu had been quick and efficient but the girl had still managed to squeeze out a scream loud enough to wake the dead.

Zalis was instantly awake, his hand instinctively reaching for his sword even before he had sat up. Talik, who had been the nearest to Zalis had run full pelt towards him and was unable to slow up in time once he saw that Zalis was awake. Kern watched in horror as the man's momentum carried him onto the point of Zalis's sword, the blade emerging from the man's back. Talik dropped his own weapon and clutched at the sword blade buried deep in his abdomen, a look of shock on his face.

Zalis, now aware that he was under attack by more than one person, was on his feet and desperately trying to free his blade from his former comrade's guts, but the dying man's body was in no hurry to release it. Zalis had just put a boot on Talik's stomach to try and push him off the blade, when a sharp crack on the back of his head sent a shockwave of pain coursing through his body. He instantly lost consciousness and collapsed to the ground.

Kern stared down at the inert body of the last remaining traitor and smiled to himself, as he sheathed his sword. The sound of heavy footsteps behind him and the crying and wailing of a young girl caught his attention. He turned to see a grinning Nebu carrying the girl who had tried to run, slumped over his shoulder.

"Well done, my friend. Tie her up again, better than this fool did," said Kern spitting on Zalis. Nebu dropped his captive unceremoniously to the ground before kneeling down next to her and starting to bind her hands with rope. The girl screamed and yelled and kicked out with her feet, clearly not happy at the prospect of swapping one jailer for another. "And gag her before we have every soldier for a hundred leagues paying us a visit."

"What do you want me to do with this dog, Kern; the same as we did with Beren?" asked Varil gesturing at Zalis's still motionless body.

Kern stroked his beard as he contemplated the question. "Stake him out, but do not place the dagger underneath him; I do not want his passing to be so quick."

Varil nodded knowingly and set about his task. Kern went over to where Talik laid, dark blood seeping through his fingers which were clasped over his stomach. Kern knelt down and felt the man's neck for a pulse, but couldn't find one. He lightly brushed his fingers over the man's eyes closing them.

"Enjoy Paradise, my friend and as you ride on the Chariot of Souls know that your death will be avenged."

When Kern stood and turned around, Varil and Nebu were just finishing tying Zalis's feet to the small wooden stakes they had driven into the hard ground.

"He's coming around, Kern," said Varil as Zalis began to groan and whimper.

"Excellent! I wouldn't want him to miss his own funeral," said Kern turning and looking down at Zalis's prone body. "Wake him fully."

Varil glanced round, his gaze finally falling on a flagon. He picked it up, uncorked it and emptied the contents over Zalis's face. Zalis coughed and spluttered as the lukewarm water splashed against his skin. He instinctively tried to wipe his face with his hands and looked frantically from side to side when he realised that he couldn't move them. When he found that his feet were bound in the same way, a small cry of panic escaped his mouth. As Kern's grinning face loomed over him, that panic threatened to overwhelm him.

"Welcome back to the land of the living, Zalis, though I'm afraid it's only going to be for a very brief and painful time," said Kern crouching down by his captive's right side.

"What do you want, Kern?" spat Zalis. He was glad to feel the cold hard ground under his back knowing that one of Kern's favourite tortures was to tie a man above the point of a knife buried in the ground beneath him.

"What do I want? That's easy. I want revenge, satisfaction and to watch you pay for your betrayal by dying slowly." Kern reached out and grabbed the man's right ear and then very slowly and deliberately began to slice it off. Zalis's warm blood trickled through Kern's fingers as he held it up to show the screaming Zalis. Then with a cruel grin he tossed it onto the dying camp fire.

The girl who was tied up and propped against a nearby tree quickly closed her eyes and willed herself not to be sick, suddenly grateful for the gag in her mouth.

Kern let the knife tip linger menacingly under Zalis's right eye for a few seconds, enjoying the look of terror reflected there, before eventually getting up and slowly walking round to his other side.

Fearing what was coming and terrified beyond the point of reason, Zalis struggled against his bonds but was unable to even slightly loosen them.

Kern crouched down to Zalis's left and grinned, prolonging the torment. "Why did you betray me, Zalis?"

Zalis didn't immediately answer. He was alarmed at the amount of blood he could feel running off his face and was preoccupied with wondering what he could say to Kern that could possibly save his life. Nothing had come to mind.

"I don't think he hears too well, Kern," said Varil grinning. He was clearly enjoying the man's pain.

"I think perhaps you're right, Varil," replied Kern grabbing Zalis's remaining ear.

"I was scared, that is why I ran, Kern; I was scared." The words tumbled out of Zalis's mouth, the words of a frightened and desperate man.

"Why?" asked Kern without releasing his grip of the man's ear.

"I thought Beren and the others would kill you. I hate Beren and he hates me. If I'd stayed around and he had killed you and the others like I feared, the first thing he would have done upon returning to camp was to kill me."

"So you fled like a woman in the night taking one of my captives with you?"

"I needed a way to raise money; it wasn't personal."

"And what of Akila; was that personal?" Akila had been the other man left to guard the girls whilst Kern and the others had gone to confront Beren and his traitors.

"No, I liked Akila, but he would not come with me nor would he just let me go. I panicked and stabbed him. Is he with you?" Zalis cast his eyes about the camp.

"He is dead and died cursing your name. Even now he looks down from Paradise urging me to kill you," replied Kern.

"Please, in the name of Sulat, Kern, have mercy. Let me rejoin you."

Kern sat back a little as if contemplating the man's request and for the briefest of moments Zalis dared to believe there was hope.

"I could possibly have forgiven your cowardice, Zalis and your pathetic pleading, maybe even your treachery. What I cannot forgive, however, is the fact that you stole my horse."

Zalis was about to say something further when Kern suddenly reached forward and viciously sliced off Zalis's other ear. Zalis screamed and wailed with the pain.

"Kern, for the love of Sulat kill him or his screaming will bring every soldier within twenty leagues down on us," said Nebu suddenly alarmed.

A look of anger flashed across Kern's face and for a moment or two he considered using the knife on him as well but then he seemed to gain control of his emotions and the moment passed. He ripped part of Zalis's tunic and stuffed it into the man's mouth stifling another scream before it came to fruition. Then he tossed the knife to Varil.

"Have your fun, but don't kill him too swiftly; I want him to die slowly and full of regrets."

"It will be my pleasure, Kern," said Varil smiling as he took the knife and strode towards a petrified looking Zalis.

***

Varil had gone about his business with an enthusiastic zeal and Zalis's body was a bloody and ruined mess when the three men and their female hostage left camp a short while later. Kern had liked Akila and wanted Zalis to suffer and at first he had been annoyed with Varil for hurting the man too badly. Varil had assured him, however, that although Zalis was a mess, he would live a while longer and his suffering and pain would be great. That had brought some comfort to Kern.

They were all tired and badly in need of some sleep, but Kern had insisted that they should move on for a while longer. The stink of death surrounded the area, but there was also the possibility that Zalis's screams had been heard by nearby soldiers. The three of them, the state they were in, were no match for anybody at the moment, Remadan or Delarite.

There were only two horses in the camp. Kern had been reunited with his, whilst Varil had taken possession of the other one, leaving Nebu to walk alongside them with their hostage. Kern had recognised the girl as a friend of the one called Keira. Keira had been the one who had given him the most trouble, yet had also been the one he had found most alluring. It was a pity that she had escaped; he had wanted her for himself. This one would have to suffice.

Her loss had been an embarrassment for him and to cover his failure, he and the others had told the remaining girls that she had been captured and that her throat had been slit. Having already witnessed him kill one girl in that fashion they had been more than ready to believe him. However, just to be sure he had instructed one of the more traumatised girls, Bella, to say that she had seen Keira's dead body. If she did, he had promised her that she would receive good treatment on their journey and would only be sold to one of his more civilised clients. If she didn't, things would be very difficult for her. Even if she somehow managed to escape or was rescued, he promised her that he would track her down and do unspeakable things to her if she ever told anyone that Keira had in fact escaped. The young girl had been so utterly terrified that she had agreed. Kern had no reason to believe that even now that she'd been rescued by that Remadan cavalry patrol, she would have told the truth.

After a last glance back into camp, Kern could just about make out in the diminishing glare of the camp fire the silhouette of Zalis as he pathetically continued to struggle against his bonds. His movements were slower now, much weaker, probably due to the loss of blood. Kern silently prayed to Sulat that the man's suffering would be long and arduous. The last thing he wanted was for him to be rescued from his pain by the blessed relief of passing out.

Smiling at the notion of a satisfied Akila grinning down from Paradise as he was attended by a score of virgins, Kern nudged his horse eastwards and towards home.

Chapter 3

After leaving Vangor, Teren and Eryn had initially headed north before finally turning east and hoping to pick up the raider's tracks. The Remadan cavalry patrol that had arrived in Vangor shortly before they left had reported seeing a large body of enemy troops forming up to the east. It had therefore been necessary for them to detour north before swinging east again, hopefully safely behind enemy lines. Neither one had spoken much since leaving Vangor, each lost in his own thoughts about the rights and wrongs of their departure.

They hadn't gone far, however, when Eryn's keen young eyes had spotted a dense column of men and horses approaching Vangor from the south. Eryn had smiled immediately assuming from its direction of approach, that it was the Remadan relief column, but Teren had not shared his excitement. It had been another couple of minutes before Teren could finally make them out and Eryn had noticed the worried expression which had crossed his father's face. Teren had asked Eryn what colour uniform the men were wearing and although he couldn't be sure from that distance, Eryn had replied that it was dark coloured, blue or perhaps black. Teren had grunted and resumed his journey east a confused Eryn hurrying after him.

Eryn had suspected that his father thought that the army approaching Vangor was Delarite, but he had still found it necessary to ask the question. Now as he silently walked alongside him, his every step taking him further away from the city and his friends, Teren's answer echoed in his mind.

If those boys are ours then we've nothing to worry about, but if they're Delarite our two swords wouldn't have made much difference if we'd stayed.

Eryn had taken little comfort from his father's words and his thoughts had constantly returned to the friends they had left behind like Ro, Arlen and Queen Cala. His guilt at leaving, even though it was for the noble cause of trying to rescue his fiancée, suddenly became too much to bear.

"We've got to go back," Eryn suddenly announced coming to a stop. Teren glanced at his son but kept walking. "Father, did you not hear me?"

Teren sighed and came to a halt as Eryn walked up alongside him. "I heard you, Eryn; I just chose not to answer you."

"Why?" asked Eryn, his tone clearly demonstrating his irritation at his father's apparent disinterest.

"Because we've been over this already, that's why."

"I know, our two swords won't make any difference, but at least we will have died alongside our friends and not run out on them."

"Firstly," said Teren leaning on his axe handle, "we did not *run out* on them and secondly you should not be in such a hurry to lay down your life, especially when you have so much to live for."

"Like what?" snapped Eryn. "Keira's dead and so is Tav."

"I know, lad, but Marta isn't and neither is Tayla."

"We don't know that."

"No, we don't, but until we see proof with our own eyes we've got to believe that Tayla is alive," replied Teren. "Now, enough of this self-pity understood?"

Eryn suddenly looked very shamefaced and nodded almost imperceptibly. "It's just that it doesn't feel right leaving them behind."

"I know," replied Teren scratching his beard, "and your loyalty does you credit, but sometimes you can walk away with honour and this is one such occasion. Do you understand?"

"Yes, I think so," replied Eryn glancing back in the direction of Vangor though it was no longer in sight.

"Good, then let's hear no more of it. Besides, by the time we got back there it would be all over one way or another. Now come, there isn't a moment to lose if we are to have any hope of catching up with the man holding Tayla," and with that Teren turned and resumed his journey, hefting his axe over his right shoulder.

Eryn watched his father stride off and after a few

seconds more of wrestling with his conscience, he hurried after him.

* * *

They had continued for several hours heading in an easterly direction, Teren stopping every now and again to inspect the ground, though Eryn could never see any tracks or anything else that could suggest the raider and Tayla had passed by that way. Eryn was beginning to suspect that his father didn't actually have a clue whether they were headed in the right direction and was about to challenge him on the subject, when the sound of someone approaching caught his attention. Teren silently signalled for Eryn to take cover as his father darted behind a shrub and Eryn hurriedly found cover of his own.

A couple of minutes later an old man in civilian clothes came wandering along the track leading a mule pulling a small cart. What Eryn took to be the man's wife and all his worldly possessions seemed to be stacked on the cart. They did not appear to have noticed Teren and Eryn. When the fearsome looking man with the unkempt beard, huge sword and fearsome looking axe suddenly stepped out in front of them, that all changed. The woman had seen him first and had immediately shouted a warning to her husband and once he had got over the initial shock, he had turned and reached for something in the cart. As Teren closed on his position the old man stepped forward brandishing a rusty scythe.

"That's far enough, stranger unless you want me to cut you down to size."

Teren stopped and smiled to himself. The old man had more guts than a lot of men Teren had come across. "Easy there, old timer, we mean you no harm."

"We?" asked the old man suddenly not feeling so confident.

Teren half glanced over his right shoulder. "You can come out now, Eryn, but do it real slow." When Eryn appeared from behind the old man and not where Teren was expecting, he nodded in appreciation of the boy's stealth. The boy had obviously taken it upon himself to sneak round

28

behind what could have been an enemy and had done so without being noticed even by Teren. Apparently there was a lot more to his son than he realised.

"Seems you're all alone, stranger and I'm not easily going to fall for the old 'I've got more men hiding in the bushes' ruse," said the old man relieved that the fearsome looking man was apparently alone. "So you'd best be on your way."

"He's not alone," said Eryn from behind him. "I just wasn't where he was expecting me to be."

The old man looked crestfallen and frightened.

"Put your scythe down before you do yourself a mischief; we are not a threat to either you or your wife," said Teren risking a couple of paces forward.

"That maybe, but what do you want, because we've nothing of value; the damned Delarites have it all and everything I now own is on this cart?" said the old man spitting on the ground.

"An exchange of information and to share a cup of water that's all," replied Teren smiling at the wife. She stared back at him with a neutral expression.

"Fair enough," said the old man evidently satisfied with Teren's explanation. "I could do with a break. Climb down off that cart and get our new friends some wine and cheese, woman; that's something we have got plenty of."

"That's extremely civilised of you," replied Teren.

Eryn had sheathed his sword and had now walked over to the side of the cart and was in the process of helping the man's wife down to the ground.

"Come let us sit for a while," said the old man almost collapsing at the side of the dirt track.

"Father, is this wise? Soldiers could come galloping along here at any moment?" asked Eryn as he strode over to where Teren had sat next to the old man.

"They could, but we haven't seen anyone since we left Vangor and unless our friend here has seen anyone, we should be safe at least for a while," replied Teren.

"We haven't seen any Delarites for some time," said the old man, "and then it was only from a distance. My name is Darik by the way and this is my wife, Alyce."

Teren shook hands with the old man and nodded at his

wife. "I am Teren Rad and this is my son Eryn."

"Teren Rad?" said the woman clearly startled.

"Yes," replied Teren glancing at Darik who appeared to be choking on his wine after hearing Teren's name.

"And you've come from Vangor?" asked Darik.

"We left it earlier today," replied Eryn.

"What news of the city?"

"It still stands and was still in Remadan hands when we left, though for how much longer I cannot say. It looked like another Delarite army was arriving as we left," said Teren.

"And you left?" asked Darik, his tone slightly accusatory.

"We have other business to attend to."

"I see," said Darik, but clearly he didn't.

An awkward silence descended over the small party for a minute or two and it fell to Alyce to break it by offering more wine and cheese to everyone even though she had only just refilled their mugs a short while ago.

"Where have you come from?" asked Eryn.

"Our family's farm is right on the border of Delarite. We run it with our two sons. When the Delarites invaded our sons sent us away and promised to follow, but we haven't seen them for a few days. We're heading west. We've family in Briden," replied Alyce glad of the change in topic.

"And you haven't seen any other Delarite soldiers apart from the column you saw far in the distance?" asked Teren.

"Nope. We haven't seen any other soldiers, Delarite or Remadan. Come to think of it, we haven't seen anyone else at all," said Darik.

"Yes we have," said Alyce looking at her husband. Darik stared blankly back at her. "There were those eastern looking men we saw earlier."

Darik suddenly nodded as he recalled the incident.

"Eastern looking men?" prompted Eryn.

"Yes, I remember now," said Darik as he stuffed another large lump of cheese into his almost toothless mouth.

Teren and Eryn looked at him expectantly, but he merely pointed at his mouth indicating that he was going to be some time. He gestured for Alyce to tell the story in his stead.

"Earlier today, just north of here, we had stopped for a rest when we saw a group of four eastern looking men enter a wood on foot. Luckily they didn't appear to see us. We should have moved on once they had disappeared into the trees, but Darik's knee was hurting badly and he was unable to stand on it until he rested a while. Anyway, turned out to be a good decision, because a short while later they came out again, the same way they'd gone in, but then turned due east. Going home I suppose, though what they were doing here in the first place beats me."

Teren and Eryn exchanged a hopeful glance, which Darik who had now finished chewing and had washed the cheese down with several large gulps of wine, picked up on.

"Friends of yours are they?"

"Not exactly," replied Teren.

"No, but they might know the whereabouts of someone we're desperately trying to find," added Eryn.

"Really?" prompted Darik fishing for more information.

"Well I don't know if it matters or not," said Alyce as she corked the wine and began collecting the mugs, "but when they went in to the woods there were four of them and they were on foot. When they came out again there were only three and two of them were on horses. Oh, yes and they had a girl with them."

"A girl," exclaimed Eryn lightly grabbing Alyce's wrist. "Are you sure?"

"Yes, I'm sure," replied Alyce.

"What did she look like?" asked Eryn excitedly.

"I couldn't say, dear, they were too far away and my eyesight isn't what it used to be."

"I take it this other business that tore you away from Vangor involves a girl, possibly this girl?" said Darik.

"It does," replied Teren.

Eryn quickly filled them in on what had happened over the last few days.

"That's terrible," said Alyce.

"And you think that the girl with these men is the one you're looking for?" Darik said turning to face Teren.

"It's certainly a possibility. Sounds to me like these other fellas caught up with the man who ran out on them and exacted their vengeance, losing one of their number in the process, which from our point of view isn't a bad thing. The only thing that has worked against us is that now at least two of them are on horseback. When they manage to acquire another couple of horses they're going to be able to put some distance between us."

"Which is exactly why I think we should be going," said Eryn getting to his feet.

"Yes, I suppose we'd better be on our way too; we've a long journey ahead of us and Rosie's not as young as she used to be," said Darik.

Teren glanced at the man's wife looking confused; he was sure that he'd introduced her as Alyce. When Teren looked back at Darik, he had a bemused expression on his face and he was pointing at something. Teren looked in the direction indicated and his gaze fell upon their mule grazing quietly at the roadside.

Teren noisily cleared his throat and got to his feet hoping to mask his embarrassment. "Yes, well, I think the lad's right, we'd better be on our way. Thank you for your hospitality." After shaking Darik's hand and nodding his thanks to Alyce, he strode off muttering about the stupidity of giving animals human names. Eryn smiled knowingly and after thanking Alyce and Darik, hurried after him.

***

It took them a little under an hour to find the copse Darik and Alyce had told them about and after spending a few minutes scouting round to make sure they were alone, they finally entered. The trees were sparse and it didn't take them long to find the raider's camp site. After again briefly checking that there was no one lurking in the undergrowth, Teren and Eryn entered the camp. Teren wondered how the camp owner had allowed himself to be taken by surprise given the lack of cover available to attackers and concluded that the man must have been asleep. It was the only plausible explanation. He was still debating the possibilities when they stumbled across a man staked out on the ground.

"Well what have we got here then?" said Teren coming to stand alongside the man's prone body.

Eryn came and stood on the man's other side, but when he

saw the full extent of the mutilation that had been visited upon the man, he promptly turned and vomited into what had once been the camp fire. As he stared down into the ashes trying to control his retching, Eryn was sure that he could see the remains of what looked like an ear. A fresh convulsion wracked his body, but he didn't bring anything further up.

Teren looked at his son, but said nothing. Sights like this would be hard on the boy, but Teren had seen it all before. Compared to some of the things he had seen during the Northern Wars, this was a picnic. The man was a bloody mess. Both of his ears had been savagely cut off and his body was a tapestry of cuts and abrasions. None of the wounds had been a killing one. Whoever had done this was skilled in the art of torture and had wanted this man to suffer greatly as he slowly bled to death. There was no honour in what they had done.

Teren's mind flicked back to a few days earlier when he himself had strung a man upside down from a tree and tortured him in a not too dissimilar way. The man and his comrade had been assassins sent by the king's adviser to kill Ro Aryk. They had inadvertently stumbled across Teren's mountain home and had sought to kill and rob him. That had been a mistake. After learning everything there was to be had from the assassin, Teren had chosen not to kill him outright. Instead, Teren had left the man hanging there where the smell of his blood had no doubt attracted the local wolves. Teren winced at the thought that perhaps he was no better than the men who had perpetrated the brutality lying in front of him, but then rationalised that the man he had killed had been an assassin, sent to commit murder. No, he had no need to feel guilt; that man and his comrade had deserved to die.

"Why would anyone do this?" asked Eryn standing straight and forcing his gaze back down onto the man's dead body.

Teren chewed on his bottom lip and then scratched his beard as he thought about his answer. "Revenge most probably."

"Revenge! Why?"

"The way that girl back at Vangor ...erm."

"Bella?" suggested Eryn.

"Yes, that's right, Bella. The way Bella told it, a few of the raiders mutinied against their leader for whatever reason and during the fight this one ran taking Tayla with him. I would say that a few of his friends caught up with him today and this was pay back," replied Teren.

"Why not just kill him?" asked Eryn, clearly horrified by the pain one man could joyfully inflict on another just for the sake of revenge.

"Because that would be too easy, probably and they wanted their pound of flesh. This man betrayed another's trust and loyalty and for that the other man wanted him to suffer. Have a good look, Eryn, because it's not likely to be the last time that you ever see such barbarity. It's a cruel world, full of cruel people and you've got to be able to deal with it dispassionately."

"I'm not sure that I want to," replied Eryn.

"We all feel like that at the start, but you'll come around, trust me."

Eryn glanced from his father back down to the man's body. He wasn't convinced that he'd ever be able to endure grisly sights like this one, let alone be prepared to readily accept them.

"So what do we do, bury him?" asked Eryn.

"No, there isn't time for that. Besides this is one of the men who attacked your home and killed and abducted your neighbours; do you really want to waste your time and energy on scum like that?"

Eryn's heart said that no matter what the man had done he deserved a burial, but his head said to leave him rather than waste valuable time. "No, I guess not."

"Good. Then let's push on for a little while longer and then we'll find somewhere for a few hours' rest. Maybe tomorrow we'll catch up with them," said Teren as he started to walk about the camp looking down at the ground.

"You really think so?" asked Eryn happily.

"It's possible. Now let's continue your education. Come and look at these tracks and tell me which way the others went when they left," said Teren.

"That way," said Eryn without moving. His finger was pointing east.

Teren looked surprised. "How did you know that? Did you notice the tracks on the way in?"

"No," replied Eryn. "Darik and Alyce told us they left the same way they entered before turning due east when they exited the woods."

Teren felt his face flush and was suddenly grateful for the bushy beard which was helping to mask his embarrassment. He'd forgotten that Alyce had already told them which way the raiders had gone, just like he was forgetting a number of things these days. Just part and parcel of getting old he supposed.

"I know that, I just thought we ought to check in case the old woman was mistaken."

"And was she?" asked Eryn trying to hide a small smile as he enjoyed his father's discomfort. It was something he imagined didn't happen very often.

"As it happens she wasn't," replied Teren and before Eryn could add to his embarrassment further, Teren turned and headed off out of the woods the way they had come.

Smiling broadly now that his father's back was turned Eryn shook his head and hurried after him, trying not to look down at the mutilated body as he did so. The thought of perhaps catching up with the raiders tomorrow and being reunited with Tayla, gladdened his heart and he increased his pace. There were three of them, but he had the mighty Teren Rad at his side. What could possibly go wrong?

Chapter 4

Leaving the city the way they did had been an unhappy affair and the small column had marched in almost virtual silence for the best part of an hour since slinking out of the eastern gate. They had headed east for a while before turning due south parallel to the Delarites attacking the city, but far enough away not to be seen. Marching two abreast with the Lydian cavalry screening their flanks, each man had walked quietly lost in his own thoughts. Some were grateful to be escaping the slaughterhouse which was Vangor, some were angry, others were ashamed. The men who had remained behind to try and stall the enemy whilst their comrades escaped, knew that their act was likely to be a suicide mission. So did the men who marched sullenly out of the city gates unable to meet their eyes.

The small garrison that remained behind was largely comprised of the men too badly wounded to march, men who weren't prepared to leave their families and a handful of brave volunteers, such as Captain Matalis of the city garrison. Despite their protestations, Prefect Devan had also remained behind. If they wanted him out the Delarites would have to carry his dead body out in a box, he had said. As Ro Aryk marched quietly alongside his new friend, Arlen Meric, a priest of the Golden Tree in Silevia, he had a terrible feeling that Prefect Devan's proud boast might well come to pass.

"Do you want to go back?" Ro heard the words but didn't acknowledge them. "Ro! Shall I halt the column?" asked Arlen.

"What? No, it's too late now anyway, even if I wanted to. We made our decision and now we've got to live with it."

"That we have," replied Arlen staring off into the distance.

"I just hope that with the majority of the fighting men either dead or with us, the Delarites show mercy to the remaining city inhabitants. The courage they have all shown these last few days deserves nothing less," said Ro earnestly.

Arlen nodded thoughtfully, still not looking at his friend. "Maybe they will," he replied, though he seriously doubted it; they both did. Their unexpectedly resolute defence of the city had cost the enemy dearly both in terms of men killed and time wasted. The Delarite general was likely to be in a rage and would probably try and satiate his anger by letting his men loose on the city's occupants. Arlen momentarily closed his eyes and tried to force the thought from his mind.

Although Ro had been stripped of his rank and no longer commanded the Royal Bodyguard, the senior officer left alive from the 9th Ligara, Captain Baradir, had been more than happy for Ro to take command of the column. Although his bravery during the defence of Vangor had won the respect of his men, they had still not completely forgotten or forgiven his part in the flight from Torogora; it would be a while before they completely trusted him. There was work still to be done. He was a good officer though and Ro had no doubt that eventually his men would follow him out of loyalty rather than duty.

Worried that the Delarite general would realise that a force of Remadan and Lydian soldiers had managed to slip through his grasp and would despatch a pursuing force to hunt them down, Ro had pushed the column hard. Nearly two hours had elapsed since leaving Vangor before he finally gave the signal to halt and rest.

The column came to a weary stop and without waiting for the order to fall out, most of the men collapsed to the side of the road. Some took the opportunity to force some food and water down their tired throats whilst others were too exhausted to do anything other than lay back and close their eyes for a few precious moments.

"Riders approaching, Ro," said Arlen as he peered ahead of the column.

Ro spun round alarmed.

"It's all right, they're mine," said Queen Cala of Lydia recognising their uniforms. "Probably scouts just coming to make their report."

The two riders reined in a few paces in front of Ro's party and quickly dismounted, unwilling to make their report from a position higher than their queen who was walking alongside Ro and leading her horse by the reins. The officer, who Ro recognised from the battle outside Vangor city, snapped smartly to attention and waited patiently to be granted permission to speak.

"Report, Captain," said Cala, dignity personified.

She is going to make a fine queen, thought Ro, *if she ever gets her kingdom back.*

"There is a large body of men approaching, my queen. We should make contact in less than an hour."

Cala nodded. She was clearly worried by the news, but realised that she had to remain calm and give the impression that she wasn't unduly concerned.

"Delarites?" she asked warily.

"We were unable to get near enough to make a positive identification, my queen before one of their cavalry patrols ventured too close and we had to withdraw."

"How many men, Captain?" asked Ro.

"There could be as many as two or three thousand. Most of them soldiers, but there also appeared to be a number of irregulars in civilian clothing."

"What about cavalry?" asked Arlen.

"We never saw any other than the patrol that chased us off, but that doesn't mean they don't have any," replied the captain.

"You're right it doesn't," said Ro thoughtfully.

The sound of approaching footsteps drew their attention and they all turned to see Captain Baradir striding towards them. The captain had wanted to remain at Vangor, but Ro had ordered him to accompany the column.

"What news?" he asked when he was close enough not to be overheard by the men who were only now beginning to relax a little and converse with their comrades.

"We have a large force of men bearing down on us apparently," replied Ro.

"How large?"

"Best guess is two to three thousand comprising troops and irregulars. Possibly cavalry as well, but we can't be sure."

"Irregulars!" said Captain Baradir sounding surprised. "Sounds like the relief column to me."

"What makes you say that?" asked Arlen.

"Well it stands to reason that although our new government has mobilised all of its regular armies, it still needs to raise the militias. Sounds like whoever's leading this force is raising a levy as he passes through the various towns and villages," replied Baradir.

"What do you think, Ro?" asked Arlen.

Ro scratched the stubble on his chin and suddenly wondered what sort of a mess he looked in front of a queen; it was something he would have to address at his earliest opportunity. "I think Captain Baradir is probably right. It does sound like a Remadan army that's come north at a forced march picking up conscripts and volunteers as it goes."

"Then this is a good thing is it not?" asked Queen Cala.

"Yes and no. Don't get me wrong I'm delighted that it's probably a Remadan army heading our way, but if a significant number of its men are irregulars, its fighting capability will be greatly reduced."

"And what if they aren't Remadans?" asked Arlen.

"Then we've got big trouble. The men are too tired to put up any sort of fight and even if they weren't, there aren't enough of us to stand any chance of withstanding an attack by a force that size. That said we'd better make preparations. Have the men form a defensive square over there please, Captain Baradir," said Ro pointing. Then he turned and smiled at Queen Cala. "If you don't mind, your majesty, perhaps your cavalry could once again cover our flanks?"

"It will be our pleasure, Captain Aryk. Give the order, Captain."

The young Lydian officer who had delivered the news about the approaching army saluted once again before remounting his horse and riding off to disperse their men as instructed.

Moaning and cursing the small force of infantry had wearily formed the defensive square, whilst the larger force of Lydian cavalry took up positions on either side of them. A little after thirty minutes later the first troops appeared from the south. A small cavalry patrol had suddenly crested the ridge just out of bow range, watched them for a couple of minutes and then ridden back in the direction from which they had appeared. Ten minutes later the first skirmishers had shown up and begun to fan out in front of Ro's men.

"Time to show the colours I think, Captain Baradir," said Ro smiling.

"They've seen better days, sir. They're not quite the stirring sight they used to be."

"Neither are we, Captain. Now the colours if you please. Quick as you can."

Captain Baradir strode off to give the order and a couple of minutes later the battle flag of the Ninth Ligara, torn, dirty and partially scorched, flapped defiantly at the centre of the square.

Ro nodded approvingly. He could feel the nervousness of his men. They had been through much, too much and he could sense that some of them were ready to run. Whilst he could understand their fear, to do so would be to invite certain death for all of them.

"Steady men, this is nothing we haven't seen and beaten before," said Ro without turning round to face the men. They were empty hollow words and he feared that they would see the truth of it in his face.

When the first banners appeared over the ridge ahead of the following columns, the chattering behind him intensified. If one broke they'd all run.

"Steady, hold your positions."

The dense columns of men were streaming over the ridge towards them now.

"Stand fast. Stand fast, damn you." The words had been bellowed by a man who was evidently used to being obeyed.

Ro glanced round and saw Sergeant Renus grinning back at him, his pike held vertically in his right hand. Ro nodded his thanks and turned back to face the approaching men. Then he laughed.

Some of the soldiers kneeling in the front of the square near Ro looked at him as if he'd gone mad. They exchanged nervous glances with their neighbours when his laugh became even more raucous. When Captain Baradir joined in they were ready to bolt.

"At ease, men," shouted Ro, an order taken up by the few

remaining officers and sergeants. "They're our lads."

As Ro's words slowly sunk in the Remadans and their Lydian allies stood and began to cheer and yell, waving their swords in the air.

"That was a close one, my friend," said Arlen as he sidled alongside Ro and sheathed his sword. The relief of the men was almost palpable.

"It was never in doubt," smiled Ro as he strode forward to greet the clutch of officers approaching them from the larger force. Arlen fell in beside him as did Captain Baradir and Queen Cala.

The senior officer of the other group was a fearsome looking man with a shaven head and a long droopy moustache. Despite his advancing years his body looked lean and fit. Arlen had no doubt that this was a man who led by example and who suffered when his men suffered. Different to Teren Rad but of the same generation and no doubt made of the same hard resolve. He was a man to be taken seriously. Arlen suddenly found his thoughts drifting to Teren and Eryn and wondered how they were doing.

"I hope we're not interrupting, Captain Aryk, only it looked like you were expecting company," the big man suddenly said his face breaking into an enormous grin.

Ro clasped the man's arm in the traditional warrior's embrace. "Always pays to be ready, Jeral, you know that." Ro made a point of staring at the other man's uniform before adding, "My apologies, *General* Tae. It does the heart good to see you back in uniform."

"Aye, but they seem to be letting smaller lads into the army now, judging by the size of the uniforms; this one barely fits."

"Nothing to do with you going soft and flabby as a civilian then?" said Ro smiling.

"Nothing at all," said Jeral sternly before breaking into a hearty laugh. "Now tell me, who were you expecting?"

"From what I understand Delarite armies are wandering all over the countryside so I simply assumed that you were one of them. I can't tell you how pleased I am to be wrong," replied Ro.

"Indeed. Your boys look like they've been through it. We

have a lot to catch up with, but before that I suggest that you introduce me to your companions, particularly the pretty young lady at your side."

Ro turned and caught the first sign of a blush on Cala's face.

"Forgive my rudeness. Queen Cala of Lydia, may I introduce you to General Jeral Tae of the Remadan Army?" said Ro.

"It's all right, Ro, we know each other," said Cala smiling.

"Cala? Dear Sulat how you've grown since I last saw you," said Jeral beaming. "I didn't recognise you. I was sorry to hear about your father."

Cala briefly cast her eyes down to the ground. "It is lovely to see you again, General; it has been far too many years. As for my father, he was killed defending his people and his country. His death will be avenged."

"Of that I have no doubt, your majesty. Together we will right some of these wrongs."

"That would be good, General, though what use me and my small force will be to you I don't know."

"You are not alone, your majesty. I ran into a friend of yours a while back."

"A friend?" asked Cala, her face brightening. "Who?"

"General Tain," replied Jeral.

"General Tain lives?" Aside from her father, there wasn't another man she loved more. It was more than she could have hoped for.

"He does."

"But we thought him killed holding up the Delarites outside Tahira," said Cala.

"Apparently he and a number of his men managed to escape. He tells me that other groups of Lydians have escaped the carnage of your country and are regrouping in the west. General Tain is heading there now and asked me to tell you should our paths cross; Lydia fights on, your majesty."

Cala could feel the pride begin to swell in her chest.

"This is excellent news, General, my thanks."

"It is my pleasure, your majesty. Now, Ro, are you going

to tell me who these other two gentlemen are who accompany you?"

"General Tae this is Captain Baradir lately of the Ninth Ligara out of Torogora and this is my friend, Arlen Meric of Silevia."

Jeral clasped arms with both men and smiled. "I am pleased to make your acquaintance gentlemen." He glanced up at the lowering sun and nodded. "Captain Abel!"

An officer rushed over to stand in front of General Tae where he snapped off a smart salute. "Sir."

"I think we'll make camp here for the night, Captain. Send a cavalry patrol out now and arrange a rota so that we've got men out patrolling all night please. The rest of them can set up camp and get something to eat; they deserve it after the long march today."

"Yes, sir," replied the captain as he turned to leave.

"Oh and Captain?"

"Sir."

"Tell the men to be vigilant. The enemy aren't that far away," said Jeral.

"I will, sir," replied the captain before hurrying off to carry out his orders.

"Right your majesty, gentlemen. I think it's time we exchanged news over a cup of wine don't you? If you'd all like to follow me," and with that Jeral walked off followed by Cala and Arlen.

After telling Captain Baradir to inform the men that once they'd set up camp they could rest and get something to eat, Ro followed after them, calling back to Baradir that he should join them when everything was in hand.

* * *

"Then things are much worse than I feared," said Ro as he downed the last remnants of the wine.

Captain Baradir had started the meeting by telling Jeral Tae and his senior officers about the debacle at Torogora, although he never mentioned that under orders from his then commanding officer, they had shamefully left the majority of their wounded behind. He had then told them about the subsequent retreat and their meeting with Teren Rad. Then Ro had stepped in and described the defence and retreat from Vangor, heaping praise on the prefect and the men who remained behind. After that Jeral had filled the others in on what had been happening in the rest of Remada and his tale had not been a happy one. Much if not all of northern and eastern Remada was now in Delarite hands and they were slowly making inroads into the hinterland. Western and southern Remada around the capital still remained in Remadan hands, but for how long Jeral didn't know. The Cardellans had also invaded and although they had initially been repulsed sheer weight of numbers meant that they too were now in control of vast swathes of Remadan territory in the north-west.

"Maybe, Ro, but we're not out of the fight yet. With a military council temporarily in control of the government, we at least know we're going to make a fight of it, but that fool of a king has let our armies deteriorate to such an extent that some of them aren't even battle ready. Some are so short of weapons and provisions that all they'd be able to do is blow kisses at the enemy for all the good it will do them. We should have put him under house arrest much sooner and then things might have been different."

"What of our allies; do any flock to our assistance?" asked Ro hopefully.

"I think the speed of the Delarite attack has caught people out, Ro. None have come to our aid yet but envoys have been sent to some of our neighbours. I am hopeful that at least the Laryssans will march to our defence. I think most fear that their country will be next and prefer to keep their armies close at hand."

Ro nodded thoughtfully. "And you were heading to Vangor?"

"Still am," replied Jeral as he stroked his long moustache.

"Surely you aren't still going there?" asked Cala surprised.

"There are still some of our people there that need our help."

"Maybe, but if you go there you'll just be putting the lives of your men in danger," pleaded Cala.

"Perhaps, but that's what we do. We're soldiers after all."

"I admire your courage, General, but as Cala says, to go there now would be tantamount to suicide. The whole area is crawling with Delarites and even if you make it through, the force we saw arriving as we left was considerably larger than your own and may well have been reinforced further. We left the city in the hope that the Delarites would show the remaining occupants mercy now that the majority of the combatants had gone. If they have done as we hoped the sight of another Remadan army showing up might provoke them into taking further reprisals against the citizens," said Arlen.

"You might well be right, Arlen, but my orders from the Council were to try and assist the people of Vangor and that's what I intend to do."

"Is there nothing we can say to dissuade you?" asked Ro. "It is entirely possible that there is no one left alive there to help and all you'd be doing was throwing away the lives of your men."

"No, I'm afraid not. Actually I was hoping that you might join me."

"That's very kind of you, General, but I've lived through that Kaden once; somehow I don't think I'd survive a second time. Besides, the priest and I have a promise to keep," replied Ro smiling.

"We do?" It was clearly news to Arlen.

"I promised Teren that as soon as we were done at Vangor we'd follow after them and try and help find Eryn's fiancée."

"That means you'll be travelling north-east; hardly safe territory either," said Jeral.

"I'm not convinced that anywhere is truly safe anymore, General."

"Well if I can't convince you to join me then I wish you the best of luck on your quest. Bring the girl and Eryn back safely; the old man too if you can manage it." Jeral had been pleased to hear that Eryn was safe at least for the time being and that a reconciliation of sorts had taken place with his father. The news about Tav Rhem had saddened him though.

"After watching Teren in action on the walls of Vangor I really don't think we'll need to watch out for him," said

Arlen, as he recalled the way the old warrior had stood virtually covered in blood swinging his axe into the terrified enemy.

"No, you're probably right. I should have liked to see the old fool in action one last time," said Jeral ruefully.

"Cheer up, General; this war's only just starting. Something tells me there's plenty more work for Teren's axe yet," said Ro.

"That's provided that he doesn't go traipsing around the east for another five years, yes." Jeral turned to face Cala. "And you will be leaving us in the morning as well I take it, your majesty?"

"Please, General, call me Cala when my men aren't around; you've known me since I was a child after all. And yes, I'm afraid I must. I am eager to see General Tain again. I hope that when word spreads of my escape, more Lydian soldiers will flock to my banner. I am determined that Lydia still has a part to play in this war."

Jeral nodded in appreciation of the young woman's determination to do the right thing by her nation. "Oh, one last thing, Ro. When you catch up with Teren be sure and tell him that Tanya and Alun send their love and say they will be waiting for him at Calatra."

"You've met them?" asked Ro surprised.

"Yes, we ran into them a while back with the wounded convoy. They all made it you'll be pleased to hear, though I was surprised by how few wounded there was." His gaze fell on Captain Baradir who had not said much since beginning the briefing. He had looked sheepish at the mention of the wounded and Jeral imagined that the flight from Torogora was still an open wound on the young man's body. "And what of you and your men, Captain; what will you do now?"

Baradir glanced over at Ro as if looking for guidance from the man he had been regarding as his senior officer. Ro smiled warmly at the young officer and gestured for him to answer Jeral.

"If you'll have us, General, I would respectfully request that what remains of the 9th Ligara joins your command," said Baradir.

"We'll be glad to have you, Captain. I need every battle

experienced man I can get right now. Will your men follow you back to Vangor?" asked the general.

"Yes," replied Baradir with more confidence than he actually felt.

"Captain Baradir is a fine officer, General and will be a useful addition to your staff I'm sure," said Ro still smiling.

Jeral noticed that Baradir averted his gaze and suddenly looked somewhat embarrassed by this praise.

Was there more going on here than either man was letting on?

There was no time to find out and besides Jeral trusted Ro's judgement in these matters.

"Right well if there's nothing more I'd better go and inspect the sentries," said Jeral standing.

"Can't one of the junior officers do that for you?" asked Cala.

"Of course they can, but I like to keep them on their toes. I wish everyone a safe journey and good fortune and pray that one day we can all meet again to share some wine under happier circumstances."

Those with any wine left in their cups duly raised them and saluted his toast. Then after one last glance round at his erstwhile companions, Jeral Tae strode off to inspect the night's watch.

Chapter 5

Teren and Eryn had been travelling east for the last twenty-four hours and during that time they'd managed to catch the odd tantalising glimpse of their quarry as they disappeared over a ridge or behind a hill. The raiders had done their best to cover their tracks and Teren had lost their trail on more than one occasion only to pick it up again further on. Although he'd never admit it to Eryn, this was usually by chance.

When the raiders had finally realised that they were being followed, they had doubled up, two to a horse and had tried to put some distance between themselves and their pursuers. The horses had tired quickly though and the raiders were forced to take frequent breaks allowing Teren and Eryn to close the distance only to see it widen once again when the horses were refreshed.

Eventually, however, the raiders must have wearied of the pursuit and decided to turn and make a stand, perhaps aware that they were only being followed by two men. The raiders had entered into a narrow pass that dissected a barren mountain. On either side of the pass were small ledges and rocky outcrops, all of which made perfect cover for anyone who might be planning an ambush.

Teren signalled for Eryn to stop just outside the entrance and studied the path before him. If the raiders were going to stop and make a fight of it as he suspected they might, here would be a likely place.

"What is it, why do we stop?" asked Eryn his irritation barely masked.

"Because they're planning on ambushing us in there," replied Teren his eyes never leaving the pass in front of him.

Eryn looked from his father to the pass and nodded. Eryn didn't know much about these things, but his father was right; if he'd been planning on ambushing any pursuers here is where he'd do it. The pass ahead of them was narrow and windy, with steep inclines either side. Whilst there weren't any trees or bushes for the ambushers to hide behind, there were plenty of large rocks and concealed ledges. Still, they had no choice. The raiders had Tayla and were not far ahead of them. They had to follow them.

"We must go in there," Eryn suddenly said. "This is the closest we've been; we can't let them escape now."

"I know," replied Teren irritably, "but *we're* not going in there, I am."

"What? No way. If you're going in there, then so am I. Tayla is my fiancée."

"All the more reason for you to stay out here," said Teren.

"I'm coming and that's all there is to it," snapped Eryn.

"You're not and *that's* all there is to it." Father and son locked eyes, neither one flinching under the other one's scrutiny. Teren sighed. This was one battle of wills he possibly wasn't going to win. Eryn was as stubborn as a mule. Like father like son apparently. He was going to have to try another tack. "Look, Eryn, you can see for yourself this pass is a death trap. If those lads have got bows or crossbows, we'll be dead before we even realise they're there. Our only hope is if they can be drawn into a sword fight."

"That being so, you'll need me; there are three of them," said Eryn feeling that he had found the decisive justification for him to accompany his father.

"There is, that much is true, but one will have to remain with Tayla which means I'll only have to face two of them. If I can draw them to a spot where the pass is narrow, they may only be able to face me one at a time."

It sounded sensible to Eryn, but he still didn't like it. "But what if they do have bows or crossbows?"

"Then I guess you'll be free to make your own decisions, but my advice to you should that happen would be to find another way round the mountain and try and pick up their trail again on the other side. Do not repeat my foolery."

"By the time I've found another way round this wretched mountain they'll be long gone and I'll never find them again. I don't wish to disappear from my family for seven years on a futile search." Eryn regretted the words as soon as they had left his mouth. He watched anger flare in his father's eyes and the tightening of his neck muscles as he stared at Eryn, but then he seemed to regain control of his emotions. "I'm sorry, Father, I did not mean that."

"Yes you did and you had every right to. What you say is true. Never apologise for telling the truth. Now hear the truth in my words. There is no sense in us both going in there and possibly being cut down by arrows; what purpose would that serve? Who would come to Tayla's aid then? Let me go in and if I don't come back out again within twenty minutes, find another way and resume the chase. Don't throw your life away in some reckless folly. Do you understand?" Eryn nodded. "Good, then let's get this done before they tire of waiting for us and ride off."

Teren drew his short sword and then took his axe in his other hand leaving his huge two-handed sword with Eryn.

"Why am I not taking that?" Teren asked Eryn nodding towards his larger sword.

Eryn straightened his back as if he was about to impart some important information. "Because you're planning on trying to draw them into a narrow space where they will only be able to face you one at a time. In such a situation that sword is likely to be too big and cumbersome to wield."

Teren grunted his approval and then without commenting further, strode off towards the narrow pass. "Wait here for my return."

Eryn stood and reluctantly watched his father go. He was not happy to be left behind, but his father's reasoning did make sense. Besides, if he did manage to draw them into single combat there was only going to be one winner and it wouldn't be the raiders.

Eryn glanced behind him just to make sure nobody was creeping up on them, but the approach was clear. When he looked back at the pass, his father was nowhere to be seen.

***

Teren cautiously edged his way along the ever narrowing path trying to keep his back as close to the rock face as possible. At any moment he expected a man with a bow to appear on one of the many ledges lining the pass, but so far none had.

Every now and again he would stop and listen for any sound that would suggest he was being watched or stalked, but the mountain was eerily silent. It was also virtually devoid of any smells. With no vegetation and just covered in rocks and dust, the air was clear save for the smell of stale sweat on his own body. He couldn't remember when he had last bathed and briefly found his mind wandering to his mountain cabin and the nearby cool stream that meandered down the mountainside.

Concentrate or you're likely to end up wearing an arrow or missing your head.

Teren momentarily closed his eyes and tried to focus. He was beginning to consider the possibility that the raiders had passed up the opportunity to spring an ambush and had instead pushed on. It would have been a clever ploy as they knew that their pursuers would have to cautiously pick their way through the mountain pass. It would also give them the opportunity to once again widen the distance between themselves and their pursuers.

That thought irritated Teren, but he had no choice but to continue. He inched on, his palms becoming sweaty, loosening his grip on the weapons. About ten paces ahead of him, the path turned sharply left. The rock wall on its right was steep with nowhere for anyone to hide as far as he could tell, but the left side looked more favourable to any would-be ambushers. If Teren had been one of the raiders it would be here that he would set the ambush. He wiped his palms on his trousers as best he could and started forward, his heightened senses searching for any sign of the enemy.

He reached the corner and stopped, once again adjusting the grip on his weapons. Then he took a deep breath and stepped round the corner, his sword held high above his shoulder ready to slice down at the first person he saw.

The sound of quick light footsteps, not in front, but behind him surprised Teren. He turned quickly, his sword already slicing down, but it failed to connect causing him to stumble slightly from the momentum. He quickly regained his footing and instinctively brought his axe up into a defensive position and waited for the jarring impact as whoever was behind him delivered their own blow, but none came.

Teren straightened and was surprised to find a mountain goat staring back at him with an almost amused expression on its face. After a few seconds it bleated at him and then turned and scurried off in the opposite direction.

Teren shook his head in dismay and allowed himself a small smile of amusement. It was then that he heard the sound. It was indistinct, but nothing to do with the goat as it hurried away. More importantly, Teren was sure that it had come from behind him, just around the corner he was about to turn when the goat had surprised him. He could also smell the faint but distinct aroma a man gets when he's been riding a horse for several hours.

Teren hoped that it was the raiders because his arm was starting to ache from holding the heavy axe and his fingers were giving him pain, making his grip hard to maintain. With a mighty roar Teren spun round, swinging his axe through the air at head height. In a blur of movement, someone had just managed to duck at the last moment and Teren's Carliri war axe clattered into the rock wall to his right.

Even as he realised that his axe swing had missed his quarry, Teren was raising his sword horizontally to try and fend off any incoming blows. His arm jarred as the dark-skinned man in front of him swung his own sword at Teren as he tried to stand, its blade clashing noisily in the still mountain air with Teren's own blade. Both men took an instinctive step back and eyed each other warily. The man facing Teren was tall and well built with a hard look to his eyes. He was strong and had the look of a natural fighter. His sword looked razor sharp Teren noticed, but it was also too big for the confined area in which they were now facing off. He was going to have to try and use that to his advantage.

Teren was still deliberating how he could do so when the man suddenly lifted his sword above his head and clasping it with both hands, brought it thundering down towards Teren's head. Teren raised his Carliri war axe with its reinforced handle just in time to save his head being split in two, and the force of the blow sent a painful jolt coursing down his arm and into his shoulder making him cry out.

Before the other man could bring another swing down on

him, Teren thrust forward with his sword aiming for the man's midriff, but he swivelled at the last second and Teren felt the sword point glance off the man's body armour.

Seeing that Teren was momentarily off balance the raider kicked out and caught Teren just behind the left knee sending him sprawling to his knees. Sensing victory, the raider again raised his sword ready to bring it slicing down into Teren's unprotected head, but Teren reacted quickest and powerfully swung his axe at the other man's right leg, severing it just above the knee.

The raider fell to the ground howling with pain, landing heavily on his right side, his sword dropping harmlessly from his grasp.

Teren struggled to his feet still holding on to both of his weapons. The other man was cursing at Teren in Narmidian as he tried to back away from him leaving a bloody trail in the dusty path as he did so. Teren glanced around expecting at least one of the other raiders to suddenly rush at him, but they didn't. He slowly started to walk after the fleeing man placing his sword tip at the man's throat when he eventually caught up with him.

"Where are the others hiding?" asked Teren increasing the pressure slightly. The man's eyes were wide with fright and probably shock and Teren couldn't make head or tail of what he was saying. "In the common tongue if you please."

"I'm telling you nothing. You'll be a dead man in Kaden in a minute," the raider suddenly spat in words Teren could understand.

"Maybe, but you'll be there before me." Teren drove the point deep into the man's throat and quickly withdrew it.

There was a few seconds of unpleasant gurgling as the raider who was now clasping his wounded throat with both hands, started to choke on his own blood and then he was still.

Another raider was almost upon Teren by the time that he looked up, his approach both swift and silent and this time it was Teren who just managed to duck in time. As the other man drew his sword arm back ready to strike again, Teren backed off a couple of paces, shaken by the way the man had very nearly managed to take him by surprise.

This one though was in no mood for sizing up his opponent like his comrade had and immediately came at Teren again; his sword swings powerful, but measured. Teren matched all of the man's swings with blocks and counter-strokes of his own with neither man managing to land a blow on his opponent.

Still the other man came onto Teren and what he perhaps lacked in finesse he more than made up for with sheer power and determination. Whilst Teren could read practically every stroke the other man was going to make and therefore didn't consider himself in any great danger, neither could he find a way through the other man's defences. Of greater worry to Teren was the pain in his fingers which was getting worse with every passing second. He had to bring the fight to an end whilst he was still able to grasp his weapons.

Thinking that he was probably better off with just his sword, Teren went to drop his axe, but then changed his mind at the last moment. The raider seemed momentarily distracted by Teren's aborted attempt to lose his axe and quick as a flash Teren launched a ferocious assault on the other man, swinging and probing first left then right, forcing the other man onto the back foot. The raider again managed to parry most of Teren's blows although a couple of thrusts nicked him, one on the forearm and the other in the thigh. Teren was driving him back though, back towards the narrowest part of the path where he hoped the raider would be restricted in what he could do with his larger sword.

The raider must have sensed what Teren was trying to do and began to fight even more furiously, but Teren continued to back him into the narrow gap. Unable to swing his sword horizontally anymore, the raider clasped it with both hands and raised it high above his head. He would slice this scruffy Remadan clean in half and be done with it.

Teren smiled realising that the fight was about to end one way or another. He had the raider where he wanted him, but now he had to find a way to kill him before he had a chance to slice his head in two like a juicy melon.

Teren raised his axe horizontally above his head blocking the raider's powerful downward slice. The force of the blow again jarred his arm and shoulder sending fresh waves of pain through his body. Sensing his time had come Teren suddenly thrust forward with his sword and grunted with satisfaction when he felt the slight resistance of firstly the man's body armour and then his skin as the blade thrust deep into his abdomen.

The two men locked eyes, their faces no more than a couple of hands distance apart. Teren could smell the raider's spicy breath hitting his face as he thrust his sword ever deeper into the man's guts. After the initial shock had sunk in, the raider surprised Teren by finding the strength and willpower to again try and force Teren's axe out of the way, but Teren was too strong for him and the attack fizzled out.

When he was satisfied that the fight had finally left the man, Teren quickly yanked his sword out of his body, giving it a final twist as he did so, before swiftly stepping back, his sword still pointing towards the enemy.

The raider's face was a mask of pain, his eyes wide and bulging. He dropped his sword which landed harmlessly behind him before collapsing to his knees clutching at the gaping wound in his stomach through which his glistening intestines now struggled to escape. After one last look of disbelief at Teren he silently collapsed face first into the dirt.

Teren stood ready and alert for the sound of the third raider rushing towards him, but there was no sign of him. He wiped his sword blade on the back of the second raider he had killed and then sheathed it. If the other raider did appear at least he still had his axe to hand.

The sound of someone approaching him from behind caught Teren by surprise and he whirled round, his axe raised high ready to strike. Eryn stood a few paces behind him staring at the two dead raiders a look of satisfaction on his young face.

He is too young to witness such carnage, thought Teren as he watched his son, *and far too young to be taking pleasure in another man's death. But then he has already seen more death in his young life than most men will see in their entire life.*

"Any sign of Tayla?" asked Eryn breaking Teren's train of thought.

"None. These men were waiting in ambush as I feared,

but I suspect their leader has already pushed on with Tayla once he saw that his men would not be joining him again."

"Then we must get after him before he gets away," said Eryn pushing past Teren.

"Will you not give an old man a few minutes to regain his breath, Eryn?"

"But if we don't get going we risk losing his trail," pleaded Eryn.

"That will only happen if we are complete idiots. There is but one way he can go for now and that is to follow this mountain path until it leads down the other side," said Teren.

"And what is on the other side?" asked Eryn feeling exasperated.

"Salandor." Teren seemed to spit the word out as if he had no respect for the country or its people.

"Salandor? We are that far east already?"

"So it would seem."

"What's it like?" asked Eryn, his curiosity suddenly piqued at the thought of his first excursion into a foreign country.

"Dangerous. It is an inhospitable land, full of largely inhospitable and deceitful people. One minute you are crossing a vast stretch of desert and the next you are riding through a deep rocky valley or a huge meadow. It is like no other country as far as that goes," replied Teren.

"And what of its people and cities? You said they were deceitful."

"The Salandori are a nomadic people; they don't live in cities or villages as we do. There are many tribes and they wander the land setting up camp wherever they choose and living off the land. They tend to be distrustful of other tribes and even more so of outsiders. They are constantly fighting one another, which is one of the reasons that Narmidian raiders and the like can just ride through their country almost unchallenged. They just pay a small toll to whichever tribal chief happens to be occupying the land they need to travel through and then the Salandori leave them alone."

"Are the Salandori friends with the Narmidians?" asked Eryn.

"The tribes to the east and south are their allies, but those to the west and north despise them, or so they say. The Salandori are distant cousins of the Narmidians. When our ancestors first arrived in Arkadia the whole continent was home to the Narmidians, but over time they drove the Narmidians east and out from Arkadia. Remada, Lydia, Angorra, all used to be the Narmidians' ancestral lands but our ancestors drove them out. It is why the Narmidians refer to people from the west as usurpers.

"Some of the Narmidians who were tired of running decided to settle in the lands now known as Salandor, but the rest pushed further east looking for more fertile ground. After a series of conquests they eventually settled in the lands to the east of Salandor and called it Narmidia. Over the years the two factions drifted apart until eventually the Salandori assumed their own identity.

"So to answer your question I think they tolerate the Narmidians more than anything because they're too weak to stop their powerful neighbours. Whilst the Narmidians have flourished in their fertile and rich lands, the Salandori as a people have stagnated and are jealous of their neighbours' prosperity. I'm sure they regret their ancestors' decision and cast envious eyes eastwards, but like I say, they're too weak to do anything about it. Maybe if the Salandori united one day they'd be able to stand up to them, but I can't see that ever happening; they're too busy fighting each other.

"Right that's enough of the history lesson, let's be getting after the raider before he gets too far ahead of us." Then without waiting Teren strode off down the narrow path towards the last raider.

After a last satisfied look at the two dead men and wondering whether either of them had been responsible for initially abducting Tayla, Eryn followed.

***

From his vantage point on a small ledge fifty or so paces away, Kern Razak had watched as the giant Remadan had killed first Nebu and then his best friend Varil, both of them with consummate ease. He had known as soon as the Remadan had managed to trap Varil in the narrow path that his friend's fate was sealed. He had then watched in horror as he was run through with the Remadan's sword before dropping to the ground trying to retain his entrails. As soon as the Remadan had delivered the killing blow Kern had left his place of concealment collected the girl and continued on down the path and out of the accursed mountain towards Salandor.

He had no idea who the two men were or why they were following him, though he supposed it might have something to do with the girl. At first he had thought that perhaps they were just a couple of civilians trying to flee the war, perhaps even deserters, but as time wore on, it had become pretty obvious that they were following Kern and his men. Just to be sure though Kern had deviated from his intended course adding unnecessary time to their journey, but every time they had turned or double-backed, the two men mirrored their movements.

Not so much two men as a man and a boy, thought Kern. *One was a grizzled old warrior who could clearly look after himself, the other a young boy of perhaps seventeen or eighteen, not yet versed in the ways of the world. They are strange companions indeed.*

The way the older man had confronted Nebu and Varil alone could only mean one of two things. Either he did not trust the boy's fighting ability or he was trying to protect him. *Perhaps the boy is his son.* That was an interesting thought and one he might be able to turn to his advantage. Still contemplating how he could use this new information, Kern hurried on down the path, Tayla walking in front of him leading one of the two horses. He was sure that the girl was deliberately walking as slowly as she could and wanted to whip her into some urgency, but decided against it. She had seen the two men following as much as he had and was obviously going to do everything she could to delay Kern and give the pursuers a chance to catch up. Still, the path widened again soon and then they would be able to ride. When they were on the vast plains of Salandor they'd soon be able to lose their pursuers.

After muttering a brief prayer for the souls of his two fallen comrades, Kern hurried on.

Chapter 6

After bidding Queen Cala good luck in her search for General Tain and the other free Lydians, Ro and Arlen had left Jeral's camp early and immediately headed in a north-easterly direction. They had travelled across country for the most part in an attempt to avoid the Delarites, but had still been forced to hide on two occasions when small cavalry patrols had been spotted.

They'd also run into the odd refugee here and there, all of whom had their own tale of woe to tell. If what they had to say was true, the whole of northern and central Remada was now under Delarite control meaning that Jeral Tae and his small relief force was an island in a sea of enemy troops.

Once more Ro silently questioned whether he'd made the right decision and repeatedly looked back over his shoulder to where he knew Jeral's small force would be preparing to march on Vangor. Ro was getting tired of feeling guilty and vowed that the next time he was put in a position where he had to decide between staying and going, he would stay. Still a promise was a promise and he had given Teren his word that as soon as the danger at Vangor was over, he and Arlen would join him on his quest to rescue Eryn's fiancée.

"It's bad for you apparently, all this guilt and remorse," said Arlen smiling.

The way the priest could seemingly read his mind was almost uncanny. "Perhaps."

"Seems to me that it's almost becoming a habit for you."

"I was just thinking the same thing."

"You've heard what the refugees have been saying, Ro; the countryside is overrun with Delarites. What possible difference could we make?" asked Arlen.

"Not much in a fight I grant you, but perhaps we should have done more to persuade Jeral not to march to Vangor. I fear that all he is going to find there is sorrow and his own demise."

"Something tells me that Jeral Tae, like our friend Teren,

is a hard man to convince once his mind is made up," said Arlen.

"A stubborn ox of a man you mean?"

"Yes, I believe that is what I just said," said Arlen deadpan.

"You're probably right."

"Oh, I know I am and in fact I..." Arlen's words trailed off as something in the distance caught his eye.

Ro, who had been thoughtfully gazing down at the dirt track as they walked along, looked up at his friend when Arlen's voice had trailed off. When he saw that his friend had been distracted by something in the distance he shielded his eyes and followed his gaze.

"What is it, Arlen, what do you see?"

Arlen didn't immediately reply wanting to make sure his eyes weren't playing tricks on him before he unnecessarily alarmed his companion.

"Trouble," replied Arlen eventually as he unhooked his crossbow and began to load a bolt.

"Are you sure?" asked Ro still unable to make much out in the bright sunshine other than a clutch of what looked like refugees further up the road. However, the priest's excellent eyesight had proved to be right on several occasions already in the short space of time Ro had known him and he had no reason to doubt him this time.

A piercing cry rang through the still morning air.

"Pretty sure, yes," replied Arlen as he kicked his horse into a gallop and raced off down the road towards the people.

"Wait," cried Ro surprised by Arlen's swift reaction, but the priest was already some distance away. Cursing Arlen for his impetuousness Ro reached down and drew his shorter sword before finally chasing off after his friend.

As Arlen neared the gaggle of people standing in the road he could see that a group of refugees were being harassed by half a dozen Delarite cavalry. Three bodies lay in the road, presumably cut down by cavalry swords. Arlen felt his anger well up inside him. These were just ordinary people trying desperately to flee the war with their families and meagre possessions, but the Delarites had still chosen to hound them.

There were approximately twenty civilians including three or four children from what Arlen could make out as he raced towards them. The men, mostly old men, were desperately trying to plead with their attackers to leave them alone, whilst the women ran around screaming and crying trying to protect their distraught children.

Three of the Delarites suddenly jumped down from their horses and dragged two young men out from one of the flat backed carts before hacking viciously into them with their swords laughing cruelly as they did so. One of the old men tried to stand between the Delarites and the two young Remadans, but a grinning Delarite soldier merely swung his sword and decapitated him. He then laughed as he kicked the old man's head as hard and as far away down the road as he could.

One of the Delarite soldiers who had been watching the proceedings suddenly toppled forward from his horse hitting the dirt road face first in a cloud of dust. His comrades stared open-mouthed at their friend's lifeless body for a few seconds unsure what was happening. When a horseman barged into the two remaining mounted men, swiftly cutting the head from one before slicing the other one deeply across the back, they finally reacted.

Two managed to mount their horses, but the third was only half in the stirrups when a small metal object buried itself in his throat. As dark red arterial blood began to bubble out of his mouth, the man fell backwards into the dirt clutching at his wound.

Arlen who had by now turned his horse and was making ready to launch himself at the remaining men, nodded to Ro as he rode alongside him and then charged at the remaining Delarites who were preparing to flee. Arlen began exchanging sword blows with one of the two men, but it looked like the other was going to escape. Ro readied another *jemtak* ready to hurl at the man, but stopped when the Delarite was suddenly dragged unceremoniously from his horse by an assortment of old men and women. When the Delarite hit the ground they immediately began hacking at his body with a variety of tools and weapons. The man's cries were pitiful, as the refugees took their vengeance. Ro pocketed his *jemtak* and went to intervene, but a blood splattered Arlen gently grabbed his arm and shook his head slowly.

"Leave them. They need this vengeance. Besides, he is already as good as dead."

Ro nodded and sheathed his sword, glancing behind Arlen at the other Delarite soldier his friend had just despatched. In a matter of seconds his friend had killed four enemy soldiers seemingly without regard for his own safety. His respect for Arlen was growing with every passing day. So too was his curiosity. He knew little about the man's history, but that would have to wait for another time.

Eventually the Delarite soldier's frantic screaming died away and shortly after the small mob ceased their stabbing and hacking and slowly backed away from what was now just a bloody carcass. Ro looked away in disgust, but the sight didn't seem to affect Arlen.

Three or four of the civilians sidled up alongside the two riders before one of them, an old man with just a few teeth spoke.

"We owe you men our thanks."

"You are most welcome," said Arlen.

Ro just nodded and the old man seemed to pick up on his apparent disgust at what had happened to the last Delarite soldier.

"Don't feel any pity for him, stranger. He and his mates killed three of our number before you got here just for sport before killing those two boys who were lying in the cart."

"Who were they?" asked Ro nodding towards the two bodies.

"Wounded Remadan soldiers we picked up along the way. They were both badly injured and were no harm to anyone. These Delarite pigs still murdered them in cold blood, so save your pity for those who deserve it," said the old man glaring fiercely at Ro.

Ro nodded and looked away unable to hold the man's gaze.

"Where are you headed?" asked Arlen.

"South, anywhere away from the Delarites."

"You're too late I'm afraid; they are already ahead of you.

If you keep on this road sooner or later you're going to run into more Delarites," said Arlen.

"Well I guess that's a chance we'll have to take because we sure as Kaden can't go back. Besides I doubt there's anything to go back for. What the damned Delarites haven't stolen they will have burned to the ground."

"True. Well at least try and stay off the main roads as much as you can. I know that it will slow you down, but at least there's less chance of running into the enemy that way."

"Perhaps we'll do that, stranger. Anyway, where are you two fellas going?"

"North-east," replied Arlen. "We're trying to catch up with some raiders who abducted a girl."

The old man wiped the sweat from his brow with the back of his hand and seemed momentarily shocked when he saw fresh blood smeared across the back of it. "Seems to be a lot of that going around."

"What do you mean?" asked Ro.

"Ran into another couple of fellas yesterday who were chasing after raiders; friends of yours are they?"

Ro and Arlen exchanged a hopeful look. The old man knew more than he was letting on, perhaps protecting whoever it was until he was certain of the strangers' intentions.

"Tall man, shaggy beard, built like an ox with a fierce countenance and a young boy of about seventeen. They were travelling on foot," said Ro hopefully.

"Like I said, friends of yours are they?" asked the old man suspiciously.

"They are," replied Ro. "They left to pursue the raiders before we could, but we promised that we'd catch them up as soon as we could. If you've seen them, you must tell us."

"Well I'd say you just gave me a pretty good description of Teren Rad and his son, Eryn. Yes, we ran into them yesterday and they told us pretty much the same story about the raiders as you just did."

"Where did you see them?" asked Arlen.

"A few miles back down that road," said the old man pointing behind him. "We saw the raiders too and pointed

Teren and Eryn in their direction. Last I heard they were headed after them."

"Where exactly was this?" asked Ro.

The old man pursed his lips as he considered the question. "Maybe six or seven miles back there is a small woods, you can't miss it if you stay on this road. We told them that we'd seen the four raiders enter the woods, but that only three had come out although they were now accompanied by a girl. Then they rode eastwards. Whether Teren and Eryn have gone after them I can't say, but it seems likely."

"Then we must be after them. Farewell old man and stay safe," said Ro. He was about to gallop off when a young boy walked up to the side of his horse and extended his hand. Ro reached down and took whatever the child was offering him which turned out to be the *jemtak* he had used to kill one of the Delarites. He put the *jemtak* safely away, smiled at the boy and ruffled his hair before urging his horse forward and down the road.

The old man watched him go for a few seconds before turning to face Arlen. "Not much of a talker your friend is he?"

"Don't be too hard on him friend, it's been a rough few days and he has much weighing on his mind," replied Arlen.

"It's been a rough few days for all of us and I can't see that changing for some time," replied the old man suddenly looking his age.

"There is always hope. Now I must be after my friend before I lose sight of him too. It was a pleasure meeting you..."

"Darik, my name is Darik. If you meet up with Teren and Eryn again, remember me to him will you?"

"I will," said Arlen shaking the man's hand and after waving at the other refugees, he nudged his horse into a trot and followed Ro.

Not wishing to exert their horses in case they needed them to suddenly evade another Delarite cavalry patrol, Ro and Arlen rode gently in companionable silence arriving at the small woods in less than an hour. It had not taken them long to find the two bodies, though both had been partially eaten by some of the wood's scavengers. It wasn't a pretty sight, but it was an informative one.

"So what happened here do you think?" asked Arlen trying not to let his gaze linger on the grisly scene.

"The old man said four raiders rode in, but only three came out although now they had a girl with them. Sounds like they caught up with the last traitor and disposed of him, but only after he'd managed to take one of them with him. Then they've ridden out of here with the girl. These fresher tracks here are from a heavily built man and another lighter man and they seem to backtrack the way they came."

"Teren and Eryn?" asked Arlen.

"Seems likely. They've followed the raiders' tracks in here and then followed them out again. I'm sure when we look outside we'll see that they've headed east."

"How far behind them would you say we are?"

"Not far and they both appear to still be on foot. We should catch up to them soon all being well," replied Ro.

"And what is to the east from here?" asked Arlen.

"The mountain pass to Salandor," replied Ro and behind that a land of deserts, meadows and barren mountains."

"It does not sound very appealing, my friend; most inhospitable in fact."

"So too are its people for the most part," said Ro.

"It is becoming more and more appealing by the minute. Couldn't we just go back to Vangor; I was happy there?" said Arlen grinning. "Three square meals a day, lots of visitors and things to do."

Ro smiled at the priest's attempt at humour. "Something tells me, Arlen that before this is over we're going to be wishing we were both somewhere else. Come, let's be on our way," and with that Ro began to retrace his steps out of the small woods coming to a stop a few paces outside.

"What is it?" asked Arlen coming alongside Ro who was looking down at the ground again.

"It's as I suspected I'm afraid, look. They've all headed directly east."

Arlen looked down at the ground, but all he could see was dirt, dust and weeds. If there were discernible tracks there he couldn't see them. "So I see."

Ro looked at Arlen unsure whether he was teasing him or really could make out the tracks on the ground. Not wishing to offend his friend he chose not to ask. "Mount up, Arlen, we best be on our way. We've a lot of hard riding ahead."

***

The ride eastwards was generally uneventful, neither man setting eyes upon a Delarite patrol and it was late in the afternoon when they eventually reached the entrance to the mountain pass.

Tracks had been hard to come by in the hard ground as they approached the mountain, non-existent in Arlen's mind, but somehow Ro claimed to have seen some anyway.

"So what's the path like?" asked Arlen staring nervously at the track that wound its way slowly up the mountainside.

"Okay at first, but then it gets quite narrow with ledges on both sides and little cover," replied Ro.

"Charming! It sounds like it's the perfect place for an ambush," said Arlen.

"From what I can recall and I haven't been this way for some years, it has many spots ideally suited for executing an ambush."

"Perfect. Remind me why we came this way again?"

"Because to go around the mountain would have meant adding many hours to our journey and we might never pick up their trail again," replied Ro earnestly.

"Instead we've got to pick our way through a barren landscape where our enemy could be hiding behind any rock or on top of any ledge," said Arlen bitterly.

"That sounds about right. It should be fun should it not?" grinned Ro. He gently nudged his horse forward.

"Has anyone told you that you have a warped sense of fun my Remadan friend?"

"Only you," Ro called back.

"Then I am the only one who tells you the truth," replied Arlen urging his tiring horse after Ro.

It wasn't long before Ro's warning about the path becoming extremely narrow was proved right forcing both men from their horses and soon after that that they came across the two dead bodies.

"And then there was one," said Arlen looking down at the second man's body an unruly coil of his intestines piled up beside him.

"Looks that way," said Ro thoughtfully.

"I'm not absolutely sure that Teren needs our help now, Ro. He appears to be making a pretty good fist of it by himself, assuming this isn't Eryn's handiwork."

"Well there's no sign of a third body so presumably the last remaining raider escaped whilst Teren was busy here. Even so, they can't be far behind."

"What about us?" asked Arlen glancing about.

"It'll be dark in a couple of hours so I think we should look for somewhere to make camp, but not here. Sometime during the night the stench from these bodies is going to attract every wolf and mountain lion for some distance."

"Mountain lions?" asked Arlen looking nervously about.

"Relax, Arlen, the wolves will have you long before the mountain lions get here," smiled Ro.

"That is truly a comforting thought and I thank you most sincerely," grumbled Arlen. "Shall we move on? The scene around me is turning my stomach yet I plan on eating my share tonight."

Ro laughed. "Come then, let's find somewhere where both you and your stomach will be happy."

***

Teren and Eryn had just managed to climb down the mountain before the darkness had descended, bringing with it the cooler night air. Just before Teren had called a halt to the day's proceedings they'd caught a brief sight of two riders disappearing over the horizon and into Salandor.

Eryn had demanded that they go after them straightaway, but Teren had refused saying that they both needed rest and that they could lose their way in the dark. Eryn had been livid and had threatened to go on without his father, but instead of reacting to the boy's histrionics Teren had merely invited Eryn to go ahead.

Teren's reaction had surprised Eryn and given him pause for thought. After glaring at his father for the best part of a minute he eventually slid his pack from his shoulders and started to prepare for the night ahead. He had then sulked for an hour or so only speaking again when the smell of fresh meat roasting on a spit became too irresistible.

When it became clear to Teren that his son wasn't going to apologise for his behaviour earlier or even mention it, he decided to raise the subject himself.

"I know you're keen to get after them, lad, I understand that, but haring after them in the near dark when you're exhausted, wasn't the smart play. Besides my feet are killing me; I'm not as young as I used to be."

For a second or two anger flashed across Eryn's face and Teren readied himself for another bout of verbal jousting, but then the boy seemed to get hold of his emotions.

"I know, but it's just so frustrating when we've been tracking them for so long that they're in spitting distance yet still out of our reach."

Teren smiled wryly to himself. The lad had been tracking Tayla and the others for a matter of days and was already making it sound like it was an epic journey worthy of songs and legend. Compared to his own fruitless search for his wife it was a drop in the ocean. He tried to shake his mind clear of such thoughts; they weren't healthy.

"I know, but they won't have gone on much farther themselves; their horses must be spent as well. We'll resume the hunt at first light."

"You promise?" asked Eryn.

"I said I would and I meant it. Now get some food inside you and then bed down for a few hours. I'll take the first watch and then you can take over whilst I grab some sleep," said Teren.

"You think the raider might double back and try to kill us in our sleep?" asked Eryn surprised.

"What? No! But Narmidian raiders aren't the only danger around here and it pays to be vigilant."

"Who else then?" asked Eryn his hand snaking out searching for his sword.

"The Salandor border is just over there and they're not

above venturing onto our lands for a quick raid either, especially as the army, or what's left of it, is a little preoccupied at the moment. There's also the Delarites to worry about although I doubt they're this far to the east."

Eryn nodded and tried to relax a little. "Oh, yes and the mountains around here are full of wolves and lions apparently. Sleep well."

There was a glint in his father's eye and Eryn wondered whether the old man was perhaps just having some fun with him. When the first wolf howled about twenty minutes later he knew that he wasn't and pulled his sword close to hand. He closed his eyes and tried to sleep, but something told him sleep was going to be hard to come by that night.

In the end Eryn slept like a log and he woke feeling refreshed and annoyed. His father had not woken him to take his turn standing guard and whilst he felt good his father looked understandably fatigued.

"Why did you not wake me?" snapped Eryn.

"Because your body obviously needed the sleep and we've a big day ahead of us," replied Teren. He was trying to put a brave face on though in truth he partly regretted letting the lad sleep on as he now felt worse than he had anticipated.

"That's all the more reason why we should have shared the watch. What use to me will you be if you can't keep up because you're so tired?"

"Don't you go worrying about me, lad, I'll be just fine, you'll see. Now get yourself something to eat and drink and then we'll be on our way. Our friend may already have moved on," said Teren.

"You think so? We need to get after them right away."

"Not until you've had something to eat and drink we don't. Besides, they won't have gone far and they'll be easy enough to track across this terrain," said Teren reassuringly as he shielded his eyes against the early morning sun and stared eastwards. For a second or two he thought he caught sight of two dots in the distance, but then they were gone.

Despite his father's reassurances about being able to track and catch them, Eryn still ate as little as he thought he could get away with, forcing it down quickly. They were soon on their way.

Chapter 7

They'd been walking for a little over two hours and Eryn's mood was beginning to sour when he suddenly caught sight of two riders in the distance. The riders had stopped and Eryn shouted with joy and quickened his pace. By rights Tayla and her captor should have been out of sight by now, but obviously something was wrong with one or both horses or perhaps Tayla was doing her best to delay them. Eryn didn't know or care. The fact that she was still in sight was all he needed. He glanced over his shoulder and saw that his father was languishing behind him and had not increased his own pace to match that of Eryn's.

"What are you doing? This is the chance we've been waiting for," snapped Eryn angrily. Teren didn't reply and instead seemed to be staring at something in the distance which Eryn assumed to be the raider and Tayla. "Come on! If you don't have the strength to go after them I do."

Teren continued to stare ahead of him and eventually nodded in the direction of some riders. "We've got company, or rather they have."

Eryn's anger was such that at first he didn't register his father's words and continued glaring at him, but then slowly but surely the words sank in and he turned in the direction his father had indicated. Galloping towards the two riders ahead of them, were approximately twenty other men on horseback, who when they caught up with the others, immediately surrounded them.

"Who are they?" asked Eryn nervously, his anger suddenly replaced by fear, not so much for them, but for Tayla. He dreaded his father's answer.

"Men from the local Salandori tribe I should imagine."

"But where did they come from? There's almost nowhere to hide out here," said Eryn looking around. Their appearance had come as a complete surprise to him.

"They've been travelling this land for hundreds of years and have learned to blend in with the landscape; they've probably been tracking them for some time," replied Teren.

"Do you think others are following us?" Eryn nervously glanced around once again.

"Probably not, but they'll be aware of our presence of that I've no doubt."

"What will they do to them?"

"I don't know," Teren lied. In actual fact he expected that any second now they would slaughter the Narmidian raider and make off with Tayla and once again the task to rescue Eryn's fiancée would become that much harder. There was nothing he could do but wait and watch. The distance between them was too far and even if he did manage to close on them, there were far too many for a tired old man and a young boy to take on; they'd be slaughtered. The next move was not his. "Promise me you won't go tearing off over there on some fool's errand. We must wait and see what happens."

Eryn wasn't happy, but nodded anyway, his gaze never leaving the gaggle of people a short distance in front of them. Satisfied, Teren glanced around trying to formulate a plan for every scenario that was playing out in his head. None of them ended well.

Already the parley had gone on longer than he expected. Things were not turning out how he had anticipated and he was not sure whether that was a good or a bad thing. When most of the riders turned and seemed to look in their direction he was pretty sure it must be a bad thing. When they suddenly started racing towards them he was certain of it.

"Damn it," said Teren drawing his larger sword. "Eryn there is no time to argue. Run as fast as you can towards that woods and do not stop for anything."

"No way! I'm staying and helping you fight them," said Eryn drawing his own sword.

The Salandori riders were closing fast.

"Eryn, for the love of Sulat do what I say. Save yourself so that you can continue the search for Tayla; there is no sense in us both dying here."

"But..."

"But nothing," roared Teren. "Go now," and with another

mighty roar he raced towards the oncoming riders, praying as he did that Eryn would run.

Eryn hesitated for a few seconds as he watched his father race off to confront the Salandori riders, but even as he watched six of them peeled off and started to ride towards him.

Eryn desperately wanted to stay and help his father fight, but he knew to do so was in all likelihood to condemn them both to death and who would go after Tayla then? His presence would also handicap his father as he would constantly be trying to protect him and in doing so would make himself more vulnerable. His mind briefly flicked back to the attack on his village a few days earlier and the death of his uncle, Kam Martel. Had he caused his uncle's death? Would he still be alive if he'd remained hidden behind the lumber wagon like he'd been told? He didn't know and it probably didn't matter now. His beloved uncle was dead, but his father was alive and the best way that he could help to make sure he remained that way was to run. With a last desperate glance towards his father who was now just a few paces away from the Salandori, he turned and ran towards the relative safety of the trees. Behind him the Salandori started to close in.

***

As Teren had raced towards them, the Salandori horsemen had fanned out into a crescent shape clearly intent on enveloping him once contact was made. Teren didn't care; they could come at him from whatever direction they liked because he wasn't going to die cheaply and many would feel the bite of his axe and sword before he succumbed. What he did care about was the fact that a number of the riders had peeled off and presumably gone after Eryn.

Teren hadn't looked round to check that Eryn had fled because what was the point? He couldn't stop and go back even if he wanted to. The boy was on his own now. He had done his best to give him a fighting chance of survival, now it was up to him. If he had left as soon as he was told he should make the safety of the trees and then it would be up to him to conceal himself. If he'd hesitated then he was likely to be caught and it was improbable to think that he'd be able to defeat five or six riders. Teren's only regret as he raised his sword and prepared to slice down at the nearest Salandori warrior, was that he and Eryn were just starting to get on better, perhaps even to bond and now it was all going to be taken away from him by these Salandori dogs.

He was still seething about that when his sword bit deep into the side of the first warrior to approach him. Before the man had even hit the ground Teren had swung again, this time in the reverse direction. This time the blade dug deep into the unprotected head of a warrior who had leaned down to try and slice at Teren. Teren had hit the man with such force that he was unable to pull the blade free and instead he let go and began swinging his axe in all directions whilst bellowing at the top of his voice.

Three more Salandori were cut down within a matter of seconds, but the riders were so tightly intermingled that only one body toppled from its horse the other two lying slumped across their saddles.

Teren continued to wield his axe like a maniac turning this way and that, parrying, chopping and cutting the enemy who by now had learned to give the mad Remadan a wide berth unless they wished to die.

A young Salandori perhaps not much older than Eryn, forced his way through the throng to confront Teren and after throwing a series of wild swings all of which Teren easily parried, he seemed to run out of ideas and hesitated. In that instant Teren launched an attack of his own the last swing of which was intended to remove the boy's head. Somehow though the young Salandori had anticipated the swing and managed to sway back in his saddle far enough to prevent his head from being cleaved from his shoulders. It was not far enough, however, to prevent the top of Teren's axe from tearing a huge gash in his throat spraying bright red blood everywhere.

Teren's swing had been a powerful one, but because the axe head never made proper contact with the boy's neck the momentum of the swing caused him to tilt dangerously forward. It was the opening that the more experienced warriors had been hoping for. Whilst Teren was trying to regain his balance, six or seven of the Salandori crowded into him raining blows down onto his head, back and shoulders. At any moment Teren expected to feel his skin pierced by a blade driving for his heart, but instead all of the blows he had taken were from blunt instruments, sword handles and the like. They obviously wanted him alive for some reason. He was still considering that fact when he finally lost consciousness.

***

Eryn felt like his lungs were going to burst such was the burning sensation, but he still kept running. It was going to be close, but he figured that he should just make the cover of the trees before his pursuers caught him. Whether he'd have enough time to find somewhere to hide or whether the trees were even dense enough to consider doing so, he didn't know. Seconds later he burst into the woods, his face getting scratched by a low hanging branch as he did so. The cooler air brought momentary relief from the almost oppressive heat outside and his nostrils were suddenly filled with the smell of rotting vegetation.

Eryn could hear the Salandori riders as they reined in just outside the tree line and began to talk animatedly. Eryn didn't understand or speak Salandori, but he guessed they were probably trying to decide which way he'd gone and whether they should follow. He desperately hoped that they would decide against it as he frantically searched for somewhere to hide. His hopes were dashed a few seconds later when three riders slowly emerged into the woods, leaving another three outside in case he managed to give them the slip.

Eryn had managed to find a fairly dense clump of trees within the woods and had crouched down among them, but whether it would be enough to avoid detection by the Salandori he had no idea. He slowly and quietly unslung his bow and nocked an arrow. The line of sight would be terrible and he was only going to be able to fire when one of the riders was practically upon him, but it couldn't be helped. He would take any advantage however slender. He quietly and carefully settled into a more comfortable position and raised the bow ready. His hands were shaking and despite the cooler air in the woods, his forehead was running with perspiration. The tension was almost too terrible to bear. If they found him he was going to have to act fast and decisively or he was dead.

Not for the first time recently he wished that his father was by his side. Then he remembered his last sight of his father had been of him charging headlong towards the enemy and he was in all likelihood, now dead. He felt a great sadness wash over him yet at the same time he felt proud. The man hadn't run from the twenty riders, but had run towards them. He was truly the brave warrior everyone had said he was.

Well if he is dead as seems likely, I am not going to join him, not yet, not today, thought Eryn as he tried to relax and ease some of the tension in his shoulders. One of the Salandori riders had started to edge closer to his hiding place. Eryn waited trying to regulate his breathing. The rider was moving ever nearer and unless something distracted him, Eryn would soon be discovered. The other two riders had slowly started to fan out to Eryn's left and right and again if they went too far they would eventually flank him.

The Salandori in front of Eryn was just a handful of paces away now and Eryn wondered how the man had not yet seen him. The effort in keeping his bow raised was starting to make his arms ache. Just when Eryn thought that he might cry out from the effort, a shout from his right startled him; he had been outflanked and discovered. The rider in front of Eryn suddenly appeared from behind a large tree and with a grunt of relief Eryn loosed the arrow. The arrow struck the rider in the throat with such force that the tip and a considerable bit of the shaft emerged from the back of the man's neck. He tumbled from his horse hitting the hard ground with a thump.

The remaining two riders were both closing in on him from different directions, though it looked to Eryn like the man to his left would reach him first. Realising that he probably didn't have time to nock another arrow and even if he did that he'd be leaving his back completely exposed to the remaining rider, Eryn dropped his bow and drew his sword. The stinging pain on his left cheek where a branch had scratched him on the way into the woods suddenly gave him an idea and he quickly stood and grabbed a low lying branch which he then proceeded to pull back. He had no idea whether his plan was going to work or even whether it would make a difference, but it was all he had. It was going to need perfect timing though.

The rider on his left was virtually upon him, but the one to his right was further away having more difficulty in trying to pick his way through the foliage towards Eryn. When the man to his left was no more than four or five paces away, Eryn released the branch he had pulled back. He watched in satisfaction as the branch slammed into the man's midriff. Eryn had hoped that the branch would knock him out or even maybe kill him somehow, but all it seemed to do was knock the man from his horse and leave him momentarily winded on the ground. It was better than nothing and had temporarily evened the odds. Eryn immediately turned to the right just as the third rider sliced his sword towards Eryn.

Eryn's sword was up in a moment blocking the swipe, the clattering of metal against metal startling some birds from the nearby trees. He immediately tried a slice of his own but the Salandori managed to block his stroke by reversing the angle of the blade. Both men then launched a series of thrusts and cuts all of which were blocked by their opponent. Eryn was already tiring against the other man's strength however. Although he daren't risk taking a look, Eryn sensed that the rider he had unseated was slowly getting to his feet and would soon be ready to resume the fight; he had to act quickly or he was dead for certain.

He sliced down with his sword knowing full well that his opponent would move to block it, but at least it would help him to position his arm for what he had planned. As soon as he felt the other man's sword block his own blow, Eryn followed through with his right elbow making perfect contact with the man's mouth and sending his head snapping backwards. Although the Salandori's sword was still blocking Eryn's, the force that was previously holding it in place was no longer there as he had been distracted by the blow to his mouth. Using all of his strength Eryn rolled his wrist and came up underneath his opponent's sword sending it flying from his grasp and into some nearby shrubbery. The Salandori immediately started to reach for a dagger, but before he succeeded Eryn had dragged his sword point across the man's throat.

The two men stared at one another for a moment and Eryn began to worry that he had not put enough force behind the slice. Then almost as if on cue, a thin red line appeared across the man's throat and a dozen streaks of blood began to race each other down his neck. The warrior continued staring at Eryn for a couple of seconds and then silently dropped from his saddle.

A noise behind Eryn caught his attention and he managed to turn just as the third Salandori hacked down with his sword. The man had decided to attack Eryn on foot thinking that it would be easier to manoeuvre that way. Eryn managed to block the chop just in the nick of time, but the man's second stroke caught Eryn a glancing blow across the left thigh. It stung like Kaden and had instantly started bleeding quite heavily, but there was no time for Eryn to feel self-pity.

Instead he immediately swung his own blade in a horizontal arc trying to cut his attacker's legs off at the knee. The warrior though had anticipated the move and nimbly jumped over the blade immediately launching a series of blows once his feet were back on the ground. Eryn drew on all the training his uncle had given him as well as the battle experience he had gained at Vangor and managed to block all of the man's strokes, but he was tiring badly. The Salandori warrior could see that Eryn was hurting and blowing hard and closed in for the kill, grinning and beckoning Eryn towards him as he approached the young Remadan.

Eryn knew that unless he did something to even the fight he would in all likelihood soon be dead. He was just glancing about him searching for something which might give him an advantage when his opponent suddenly stumbled forward and hit the ground. He had fallen over an exposed root. Eryn realised that this was his opportunity and threw himself at the other man raining blow after blow down on him. Despite being on the ground the warrior who was clearly not without skill, managed to somehow block and parry all of Eryn's strokes, but Eryn had no choice but to persevere. There was no skill or finesse in his strokes, just raw power and rage. Blow after blow smashed into the Salandori's sword until eventually the man could no longer hold his sword aloft and collapsed onto his back.

Eryn rushed forward and placed his sword point at the man's throat, whilst treading on his right wrist, forcing him to release his grip on his own sword. Eryn knew that if his father had been there he would be telling Eryn to drive the sword point into the man's throat and end it, but as he looked into the warrior's eyes he hesitated.

One of the three riders who had remained outside the trees, was calling what sounded like someone's name, though Eryn couldn't be sure, so strange was their tongue. If the others entered the woods now he was finished. Eryn held his breath and waited, his sword still pressing against the other man's throat.

One of the men outside called again, a different name this time. When there was no reply Eryn could hear the three men discussing something and then the sound of swords being drawn. He closed his eyes briefly and prayed to Sulat that he would die quickly and painlessly. Even as he shut his eyes he realised his mistake and opened them again just as the man on the ground reached up and grabbed his wrist and tried to force the sword away from his throat. Without hesitation Eryn thrust down as hard as he could driving the sword point deep into the warrior's throat. The man continued to struggle and flail at Eryn's wrist but the outcome was certain. Eryn drove the sword in further to cut off the man's pitiful noises and then pulled his sword free, a sudden gush of blood spurting up and spraying his trousers. The Salandori warrior was still.

The three warriors outside sounded like they were about to enter the woods when another shout from further away drifted through the trees. Again Eryn had no idea what had been said. One of the three men just outside the trees called back sounding angry and annoyed. When the distant voice answered again the three men outside muttered angrily to one another. Eryn listened intently and thought that he could hear what sounded like weapons being sheathed and then the sound of several horses riding away. He breathed a sigh of relief unable to believe his luck; they had left, at least for now; he still had a chance.

He cautiously made his way to the edge of the tree line taking care to remain in the shadows should any of the riders suddenly look back over their shoulder towards him. The three riders were galloping towards the other riders who had already turned and were riding eastwards. Eryn could just about make out that there were a number of bodies lying on the ground, but couldn't see if any of them were his father. If he had been killed, he had not died alone. It was a small comfort.

Eryn watched them ride off as he decided what to do. If he were to walk out now and leave the safety of the trees to follow the riders there would be nowhere to hide if any of them suddenly turned round and decided to give chase. He would be ridden down and killed just like his father most likely had. His bravery in trying to buy Eryn time and his subsequent death would have been for nothing and he owed the man more than that. No, he would wait here until they had travelled some distance and would then follow them. His father had said that tracking the solitary raider and Tayla across the Salandori terrain would be easy so tracking a much larger group should be no trouble.

Eryn slumped down against a tree and quickly bandaged his wound with a strip of cloth he tore from the tunic of one of the dead Salandori, his own too dirty to use. Then he helped himself to a long drink of water not realising how parched his throat had become. Suddenly feeling very hungry he reached into the pouch around his waist and pulled out some cheese and a few dried biscuits which had clearly seen better days. He didn't much fancy any of it but he had nothing else and didn't have time to hunt for any fresh meat. Reminding himself that his old friend Tav who had been killed during the defence of Vangor, would have eaten the cheese and biscuits without complaint and probably then asked for more, Eryn started to eat.

When he had eaten as much as he could face, Eryn walked back into the woods and retrieved his bow from where he'd dropped it, trying not to look at the grisly sight of the man with an arrow, *his* arrow, protruding from both sides of his neck. After slinging the bow back over his shoulder, he turned and headed for the tree line again. The Salandori riders were no longer in sight, but he knew in which direction they had gone. After taking a long fortifying breath he was about to emerge from the trees into the bright sunlight, when he heard the slightest cracking sound behind him. Fearing that the Salandori had either doubled-back or had indeed been following him and his father as well, Eryn quickly drew his sword and whirled round. He instinctively brought his sword slicing down, but the stroke was met by an equally strong parry.

Eryn quickly withdrew his sword and slashed twice more, both strokes being easily parried by one of the two men behind him, the nearest of which was saying something to him.

"Eryn! Eryn, stop, it's us."

Eryn raised his sword again, but didn't follow through. His eyes were wide with fear and he was shaking violently. It took a few more seconds for their faces to register but eventually Eryn managed to control his rage as he recognised Ro Aryk and to his left, with a small crossbow pointed at his chest, Arlen Meric.

"Ro! Arlen! I've never been so pleased to see you," said Eryn laughing, no longer caring who might hear him.

"So I see," said Arlen as he lowered his crossbow and nodded towards Eryn's sword, which was still raised above his head.

"Oh, sorry, I thought you were more of these men."

"Lucky for us that we weren't by the looks of it," said Ro as he sheathed his own sword. "You killed all of them?"

"I did," replied Eryn proudly.

"Impressive," added Arlen. "Sorry about sneaking up on you like that, but we had to be sure. All we could see was the dark silhouette of a man; we had no idea it was you until you turned round."

"That's okay," replied Eryn.

"Where is your father, Eryn?" Ro asked after glancing round.

Eryn swallowed nervously and glanced down at the ground. "We had almost caught up with the last raider and Tayla when about twenty Salandori riders suddenly appeared and surrounded them. We thought they were going to kill the raider and take Tayla, but then they all came charging towards us. My father told me to go and hide in here and he charged into them. Some of them followed me here whilst others waited outside. Just when I thought the others were going to come in here and kill me they suddenly rode off with the main party. There are a number of bodies lying just over there and I am expecting to find my father amongst them." Eryn looked his two companions in the eye. "I didn't want to run and hide in here; I wanted to help him. I'm no coward."

Arlen reached over and placed a hand on Eryn's shoulder. "We know you're not, Eryn and so did your father. He knew that he was probably going to die and didn't want you to suffer the same fate. This way you can continue your quest to rescue Tayla and keep your promise. There is no sense in throwing your life away in some misguided notion of honour."

Eryn glanced over at Ro who was nodding earnestly in agreement with his friend.

"But what if he is lying over there, but was only wounded and his life has been ebbing away whilst I skulked and drank in here?" asked Eryn bitterly.

"They would not have left him alive, Eryn, of that I am sure. Trust me you did the right thing and your father would have been proud. If you'd shown yourself too soon, they could have circled back and attacked you before you could make it to the trees again and where would Tayla be then? Come, let us go and see if your father is among the dead and how dearly he made those Salandori pay for his life," and with that Ro edged out of the trees to where the bodies were lying. High above in the azure sky, the vultures were beginning to circle.

Chapter 8

They were too late. Jeral Tae had known it the minute he clapped eyes on the once mighty citadel of Vangor, long before his scouts had come galloping back to tell him the bad news. That there had been a battle of some magnitude was obvious, with the city's southern gate destroyed and much of the surrounding walls either damaged or demolished. Pillars of dark billowing smoke still ascended into the clear morning sky and the stench from the decaying dead was everywhere. Then there were the bodies; hundreds of them lying strewn across the vast plain leading up to the city's southern entrance. Food for the scavengers of which there were many.

As he picked his way slowly through the broken bodies lying scattered across the battlefield, Jeral glanced around him at the myriad of different uniforms worn by the dead. There were many different Delarite uniforms, some of which he recognised like the Datani Regiment and Gremlin Corps and many he didn't. Then there was the bodies of the dead Remadan soldiers some wearing the uniform of the esteemed 9th Ligara others the over-elaborate uniform of Vangor's city garrison. Further into the battlefield lay the pitiful sight of dozens of dead horses, the bodies of their proud Lydian riders never far from their beloved mounts. Saddest of all were scores of dead civilians; old men, young boys and those who were already carrying a wound before they were killed, none of whom should have been on the battlefield in the first place. Ro Aryk and Queen Cala had said that it had been a vicious and terrible battle and they had not been exaggerating. It had been a fight to the death.

There was more to it though, Jeral could sense it. His scouts had reported that from what they could tell the city was abandoned, but that could just be a ruse. Hundreds of Delarite archers could be hidden inside just waiting to unleash their fury on the unsuspecting Remadans.

Jeral Tae was a brilliant general, but he was also a cautious man. He had arranged the vanguard of his army into attack formation and was approaching the city in the proper manner, with skirmishers out front and his limited cavalry on the flanks. If Delarite soldiers were waiting for them in the remnants of the city his men would be ready for them. If they weren't, well then they'd lost nothing but a little more time.

When they were no more than fifty paces from the destroyed southern gate, Jeral gave the order to halt. Then he signalled for the skirmishers to enter the city. The few archers he had at his disposal were ordered to spread out and cover the walls.

Ten agonising minutes later, a junior officer from the skirmishing party came hurrying over to make his report, snapping smartly to attention before he did so.

Jeral indicated for the man to speak.

"The city is empty of enemy combatants, sir."

"Very good," replied Jeral, but it was obvious from the way the other officer didn't move off that he had something further to say. "Is there something else, Lieutenant?"

The lieutenant looked nervous clearly not relishing the prospect of having to impart this further news. "The people, sir...they've all been...butchered."

"What?" asked Jeral not sure that he'd heard the young officer correctly. Some of Jeral's other officers had gathered round, initially to collect their new orders, but now keen to learn of the city's plight. "Explain yourself, Lieutenant."

The lieutenant took a deep breath and briefly glanced at the huddle of senior officers expectantly awaiting his response. There was no getting out of it.

"The city square, sir is full of bodies, a few garrison soldiers, but mostly civilians."

"That's to be expected, lad. Captain Aryk said that there was a bloody battle in the courtyard," said Jeral.

"That may well be the case, sir, but these people, men, women and children have been executed, not killed in battle and executed most foully."

The small group of officers started to mutter angrily amongst themselves, but Jeral held up his right hand and they immediately fell silent.

"How so?" The lieutenant didn't immediately respond. "Lieutenant?"

"They've been mutilated and dismembered, sir."

"Dear Sulat! The women and children as well?" asked Jeral outraged.

The lieutenant merely nodded.

"The Delarite dogs will pay for this," muttered one of Jeral's senior officers a sentiment apparently supported by all of his comrades.

"What of the prefect; did you find him?" asked Jeral.

The lieutenant nodded. "He has been nailed to a door, sir, but only after they'd cut off his hands and feet."

Jeral felt his face flush as a great anger welled up inside him. "Are there no survivors at all?"

"We found a few, sir, no more than a handful. They're traumatised as you'd imagine, but at least they're alive."

"Thank you, Lieutenant. Return to your men and start to gather what survivors you can. Once I've secured the perimeter I'll be in with the rest of the men."

"Very good, sir," said the lieutenant saluting and then turning to leave. He then seemed to have second thoughts and turned back to face Jeral. "What shall I do about the prefect, sir?"

Jeral stroked his droopy moustache as he thought about the lieutenant's question for a minute. "Leave him where he is for the moment; I want the lads out here to see what sort of enemy we're fighting so that when the time comes they will harden their hearts and remember to show no mercy."

The lieutenant nodded and as he turned away again Jeral thought that he caught sight of a small smile tugging at the corners of the lieutenant's mouth.

Obviously the lieutenant approves of my last order. That's good. If they're all burning with indignation and clamouring for revenge they'll fight that much harder when the time comes.

As he watched the lieutenant walk away Jeral suddenly became very aware that his other officers were looking at him expectantly.

"Major Lorn, I want a perimeter set up about the city and I want cavalry details patrolling the nearby countryside. If a mouse so much as sneezes I want to know about it, you understand?"

A middle-aged man in an immaculate uniform nodded his understanding to Jeral before striding off to carry out his orders. Major Lorn was ostensibly a staff officer who had been hoisted onto Jeral as part of the deal that granted Jeral a field command. In their march north he had proved to be an efficient and steady officer if a little pompous and Jeral had no doubt that the man had never seen any action.

Well he will soon and plenty of it I dare say.

Jeral turned to the other officers. "Come gentlemen, let's go and bear witness to what these Delarites have done to our people," and with that Jeral started towards the city closely followed by his officers and the men not detailed to guard the town's perimeter.

The lieutenant had not been exaggerating Jeral was sorry to see. If the battlefield outside had been dreadful with its deep carpet of death, the inside of Vangor and the courtyard in particular, was Kaden itself. The fighting inside the city had been brutal and personal and there was evidence of a terrible slaughter everywhere except on the battlements.

Probably tipped the bodies over the side to make more room, thought Jeral. *It's what I would have done.*

By contrast the courtyard floor was strewn with bodies, many of whom had clearly died in battle and some, more than he had feared who had clearly been tortured and mutilated before being sent to the afterlife. Others had clearly been mutilated after death, apparently just for the fun of it. Jeral felt a surge of revulsion wash over him. Worst of all, however, was the sight of the city's former prefect, Kane Devan, nailed to a wooden door, the ends of his arms and legs nothing more than bloody stumps.

Jeral had spoken to the surviving civilians, seventeen out of a city of thousands. Some had been too frightened or traumatised to talk to him or anyone else for that matter, but a handful had been willing to tell their story. Whilst each story was slightly different, depending on where the person had been during the attack and subsequent atrocities, the general theme was consistent. The prefect had led a gallant and desperate last defence of the city whilst Ro Aryk, Queen Cala and the bulk of the remaining soldiers slipped away. With nothing but wounded men, civilians and the odd brave soldier who had volunteered to remain behind, the prefect had led an inspired defence of the city for as long as he could until he was finally killed. Then Captain Matalis of the city garrison had called the remaining men to him in the city courtyard where he and no more than a score of men had faced off against several hundred Delarites.

One of the witnesses spoke with tears in his eyes at how the Delarites had called on Captain Matalis and his men to surrender. When they'd refused they had been cut down in a hail of crossbow bolts. Then the Delarite soldiers had run amok rounding up and torturing every last civilian they could lay their hands on.

Even that had not been enough for the Delarites and incensed by the casualties the brave defenders had inflicted on his army, the enemy general had given orders for the dead Remadan soldiers to be mutilated and his men had gone about their task with relish.

Jeral had listened to the stories in horror, desperately trying to mask his true feelings and sense of indignation. The only saving grace in all of this had been that the prefect was already dead by the time they nailed him up and cut off his hands and feet. Jeral prayed that the same had been true for all the other poor souls who had suffered a similar fate, but he knew that was not the case.

A little after an hour of entering the city, the first patrols Jeral had sent out returned and reported no sign of the enemy army, which generated a mixed response from Jeral. Whilst he desperately wanted to get at the men who had committed these atrocities he wanted it to be on his terms and at a place of his choosing. Now was a time for cool heads and not rash action. When he had finished listening to the stories of all those able to recount them, Jeral had ordered his men to mass in the courtyard and on the battlements so that he could address them.

Most had been quick to assemble keen to learn the news, but others notably the men who made up the civilian levy accompanying his force had been slow to respond. Many of them, often peasants or simple farmers, had been found wandering the side streets rummaging through the pockets of the dead or looting abandoned shops. Jeral had not been surprised to learn that Pular Bratak and his gang of ruffians from Jeral's home village of Lentor had been among them.

He and Bratak had clashed a number of times over the last couple of years culminating in a confrontation during a village meeting the night the village had been raided and the girls abducted. He had tried everything he could that night to undermine Jeral's authority and disrupt the meeting. Jeral had sworn then that one day he would have his revenge and that oath still held true.

Yet there was more to his loathing of the man than a simple clash of personalities. It had troubled him every day since the raid how the Narmidian raiders had seemed to know which houses to attack to find the young girls. It had been more than good fortune he was sure of it, almost as if the raiders had received help from inside the village though the very thought turned Jeral's stomach. Still he had his suspicions and those suspicions revolved around Pular Bratak. His suspicions would have to wait though, as there were more important matters to deal with. It was not the first time Bratak had escaped Jeral's wrath for that reason.

After ordering some of his regular troops to round up Bratak and any other men loitering in the streets, Jeral addressed the troops whilst stood just in front of Prefect Devan's still pinned body. It made a grisly backdrop for the men listening to Jeral, but then that had been his intention. He wanted them angry and he wanted them vengeful. He had spoken for a little over ten minutes about what had happened to Vangor, imparting a lot of the information the surviving civilians had told him. Then he'd told his men to have a good look at the prefect's dismembered body and those of the others lying around particularly the women and children. He told them to try and imagine how they'd feel if that was their family lying on the ground next to them.

Jeral could tell by the angry muttering that his message had hit home and he let them continue for a couple of minutes stoking their rage. Then after giving a discrete pre-arranged signal, somebody at the back of the crowd, one of Jeral's loyal sergeants, bellowed the word "Remada" over and over getting louder with every rendition. Soon the chant was taken up by more and more of the men until eventually just about everybody was shouting it at the top of their voice at which point the sergeant changed the chant to "death to Delarite". The noise as hundreds and hundreds of men took up the new chant was deafening and encouraging.

Jeral Tae had his men where he wanted them. As he cast his eye over the sea of smiling faces, his gaze uncannily fell on Pular Bratak, who unsurprisingly was not chanting. The man and his cronies had been conscripted into the levy and had no wish to be there or anywhere near the fighting. As always his thoughts were no doubt about money and protecting his own worthless hide. Jeral found himself silently wishing that Bratak would say something controversial or try and undermine Jeral's authority. If he did Jeral had no doubt that the vast majority of the men would support their general and Bratak would suddenly find himself wearing a knife in the small of his back. Regrettably, Bratak was showing unusually good sense and kept his mouth shut although he did stare back at Jeral his eyes brimming with hate.

So be it. We will have our day you miserable little maggot.

Jeral was about to say something else to his men when he caught sight of one of his cavalry officers forcing his way through the crowd in front of the demolished gate. He was clearly in a hurry to find the general and perhaps carried some important news to impart.

The officer eventually forced his way through the throng and up the steps to stand in front of the general. The chanting and shouting of the soldiers had gradually died off until the courtyard was virtually silent save for the odd cough and the sound of the officer's footsteps.

He stopped a couple of steps below Jeral and saluted, but instead of lowering his hand once Jeral returned the salute, the man stood still his gaze fixed on a point behind Jeral. Jeral slowly turned suddenly realising that it was the prefect's mutilated body which had caught the officer's attention.

He cleared his throat noisily. "You have something to report, Captain?"

For a moment or two Jeral wondered whether the man had

heard him or even registered his words, but then the officer seemed to get a hold of himself, lowered his hand and straightened to attention.

"Yes, sir. Patrol reports enemy army sighted, heading south-west, but slowly wheeling south about twelve leagues away, sir."

"Thank you, Captain, you may return to your men."

"Sir," replied the captain before saluting and hurrying off down the steps and back towards his horse.

"Major Lorn."

The major came striding over to Jeral and once again executed an exemplary salute. "Sir?"

"Detail the men to start burying the dead and inform the senior officers there will be an officers' meeting over there in ten minutes, if you please."

The major made a note of where Jeral was pointing to and then nodded, before saluting and marching off to carry out his orders.

The news that the Delarites were moving south wasn't that much of a surprise to Jeral. With most of the north and a good portion of the east of the country already in their hands and the west subject to a Cardellan invasion, south was the only way open to them. Had the enemy immediately travelled south Jeral's force would have never had the opportunity to catch them, but because they had apparently initially headed south-west, there was a chance that with some forced marches, they might. What Jeral needed to do was pick where and when would be best to intercept them. His mind full of plans and possibilities he strode off to the designated meeting place as all around him the troops and civilians began the grisly job of burying the dead.

Chapter 9

The meeting had been a constructive one and most of the senior officers had agreed with Jeral's interpretation of the situation. After poring over a series of maps and receiving briefings from soldiers who came from the areas in question, they finally decided that they would try and intercept the Delarites a few miles north of the town of Ederik. It would be close and would require a series of forced marches, but they calculated that they should arrive there in enough time to deploy their army in the most favourable terrain. Their plan was dependent on a number of factors working in their favour, something the usually cautious Jeral wasn't comfortable with, but he was left with little choice. It was either that or waste the next few days or even weeks chasing the enemy up and down the country, discovering more death and destruction in their wake.

Only Major Lorn had openly spoken out against the plan drawing a series of withering looks from most of his colleagues and subordinates. He had argued that the men were already exhausted from their long hard march north and that by the time they reached Ederik they would be in no fit state to fight, especially the civilian levy that accompanied them.

Not just a pompous prig then; he does have a backbone, thought Jeral as he considered the man's words. In all likelihood he was right. The men were tired from their march north, as Jeral himself was and to ask them to immediately march south again and then fight a battle in which they were likely to be hopelessly outnumbered, was perhaps expecting too much. He was also probably right about the civilian levy too as they would struggle most of all. They would undoubtedly lose quite a few men during the march. Nevertheless, it was unavoidable; their options were limited.

The major had accepted Jeral's explanation with good grace, at least outwardly and a little under an hour later the men were again on the march, this time south. There had been some mumbling and grumbling in the ranks, but nothing to really concern Jeral. From his own time as a foot slogger he knew that soldiers loved nothing better than to moan when they were on the march as it helped to pass the time and take their minds off their sore feet. Their sense of anger at what the Delarites had done to the citizens and soldiers of Vangor was also still fresh in their minds. Yes, they would moan and gripe, but they would also fight and fight hard. It was all Jeral could ask for.

Before leaving, Jeral had met with the remaining citizens of Vangor and offered to take them with him to Ederik where they'd be left to sort themselves out, but they'd all declined. As one of them had said looking Jeral straight in the eye, what more could possibly happen to them? Jeral wasn't sure he agreed with their decision but he did respect it. He was also secretly relieved not to have another seventeen civilians to worry about.

***

The march south had been every bit as arduous as Jeral had feared though thankfully they hadn't run into any Delarite patrols or cavalry. One of Jeral's patrols reported seeing a column of Delarite cavalry in the distance, but in accordance with his orders they had remained concealed and just observed the enemy.

It was not until late afternoon on the third day when Jeral's men finally arrived at the location he had in mind a few miles north of the town of Ederik. Scouts had reported that the enemy had sighted them and were now swiftly marching to intercept the Remadans. He estimated that they had but a few hours before they arrived.

The men were exhausted and hungry and whilst Jeral didn't think that the Delarite general would attack during the night, he couldn't take that risk. Before the men were allowed to rest and grab something to eat, work details were set up. Some men were set to digging ditches whilst others prepared barricades. The rest were ordered to sharpen wooden stakes which were then driven into the ground at an angle to deter enemy cavalry.

Jeral's men had not been happy and this time the moaning was very real. Nor was the moaning just confined to the civilians with many of the soldiers suffering as much as their civilian counterparts. Jeral himself was exhausted and despite the insistence of his officers that he should rest, he had made a point of walking round the camp and encouraging his men, calling many of them by their name. Here and there he would stop to help the men digging a ditch or erecting a barricade. Witnessing their commander-in-chief sharing their suffering did wonders for morale and by late evening the work was done and most men had had something to eat. Jeral retired to his tent satisfied that the camp had a happier feel to it.

It was just before midnight when the first torches could be seen arriving on the small hill about a league and a half away. Most of the Remadans had fallen into a deep sleep by then, the day's exertions finally catching up with them. Those who were still awake or on guard duty slowly got to their feet and watched in trepidation as column after column of Delarite soldiers appeared on the hill side.

Jeral Tae watched their arrival with a growing sense of dread. He'd known that the Delarite force far outnumbered his own, but the sheer magnitude of it now was astounding. Doubt began to gnaw away at his stomach. Had his own arrogance and ego condemned his men to certain defeat?

What was I thinking? How could I ever believe that we could defeat such an army?

"Should I stand the men to, General?" said the voice to his right.

Jeral tore his gaze away from the myriad of pinpricks on the dark hill side and glanced to his right where Major Lorn stood bolt upright and looking at him expectantly.

"No, let them sleep, Major, they won't attack tonight."

"What makes you so sure, General?"

"Because their general will want to make use of their overwhelming numbers and they haven't all arrived yet. He knows what the gradual arrival and deployment of his troops is doing to the morale of our men, those awake anyway, and he'll want to prolong that. Besides, they're probably as tired and hungry as we are. No, we've got to dawn at least. Just remind the men on sentry duty to be vigilant though I doubt they'll be anyone falling asleep on duty tonight."

The major turned and walked off in the direction of the sentries and it took Jeral a few seconds to realise that the usually disciplined major had forgotten to salute him.

That's good, thought Jeral. *If he's preoccupied that means he's probably scared and if he's scared he'll be more likely to follow orders without question.*

Jeral yawned, suddenly feeling every bit his age. Had he done the right thing coming out of retirement and leading the coup against the useless young king or should he have stayed back in his home village of Lentor with the other village elders? There was no sense in double-guessing himself now he realised because he was there and there was no going back, not yet anyway. With that sobering thought at the forefront of his mind he took a last glance at the hill side opposite where the pinpricks of light had significantly multiplied, turned and headed back to his billet intent on grabbing a few hours' sleep. He didn't know what the morning would bring or how it would end, but it would certainly look better after some sleep.

***

Sleep had for the most part eluded Jeral during the night, though he was aware that he had briefly dozed here and there, snippets of dreams flitting in and out of his mind. It had not been the deep and refreshing sleep he had hoped for, but then to the best of his failing memory, it never was the night before a big battle.

By the time that Jeral had dressed, eaten a chunk of bread and tried to wake himself up with a couple of mugs of cold water, one inside him and one poured over his head, it was already fully light and most of the men were already up and about. Jeral stared out across the plain towards the hill top where the early morning light revealed the full extent of the Delarite army. Whilst it wasn't as formidable as Jeral had feared in the small hours of the morning, it was still more than enough to crush his force.

A small group of his officers stood waiting for him with a

bugler and they all greeted him with cheery smiles as he approached. Only Major Lorn appeared to be missing from his senior staff which Jeral found odd.

"Good morning, gentlemen."

"Morning, sir," the officers replied in unison.

"Looks like it's going to be a lovely day, eh, but perhaps not so much for our Delarite friends over there?"

The officers all laughed as they gathered round the small table across which a roughly drawn map had been spread and held down by stones.

A young soldier suddenly appeared at Jeral's right looking nervous. He saluted and then without waiting to be invited to speak, addressed the general.

"Major Lorn apologises for his tardiness, sir and says that he will be with you shortly."

"Is that right? Well I'm sure the Delarites will be happy to wait on Major Lorn's convenience." The other officers laughed. "And just what is it that delays our smart young major from attending the meeting at the allotted time?"

"He didn't say, sir."

"No, I bet he didn't. All right, trooper, you're dismissed." The relieved trooper saluted and then hurried off glad no doubt to be away from the scrutiny of every senior officer in the army. "Well we'll start the briefing anyway; Major Lorn will have to quickly adapt to the battle plan or find himself in charge of the baggage train like a newly minted lieutenant." Jeral was making light of the major's lack of attendance, but inside he was seething. He looked down at the map in front of him and began to once again go over the battle plan for the coming day.

The plan was daring, particularly considering that Jeral was normally far more cautious. It was also well-thought out, but there were still any number of things that could go wrong. The other officers gathered round the table were invited to voice their honest opinions about the plan and the few worries that his men had were easily addressed. Jeral was relieved to see that they believed in the plan. There was nothing he could do about the enemy's overwhelming numbers, except retreat and there was no way he was going to do that. Besides, he didn't think his men would stand for it. They were tired, they were sore but above all they were angry and spoiling for a fight.

Well today they're going to get one.

The sound of someone walking quickly towards them drew Jeral's attention and he looked up to see the normally unflappable looking Major Lorn striding towards them, a worried look upon his face.

"Major Lorn! How good of you to join us," said Jeral standing erect and doing everything in his power to intimidate the young officer. "Decided to sleep in did you?"

"My apologies, sir, but I had an urgent matter to attend to."

Jeral looked at him in disbelief. "I don't know whether you've noticed or not, Major Lorn, but there are several thousand Delarite soldiers camped over on that hill side awaiting the order to kill us. Now before I clap you in irons for dereliction of duty perhaps you'd be as kind as to tell me what in Kaden's name is more important than that?" Jeral's voice had grown louder with each passing word, drawing the odd curious look from some of the troops sat around eating their morning meal.

To his credit the major didn't flinch, Jeral noticed.

"Sir, I have to report the murder of four of our sentries."

"What?" boomed Jeral, raising a hand to silence the mutterings of the other officers in attendance. "How did this happen?"

"Deserters, sir."

"Deserters?" spat Jeral. "How many?"

"We don't know for certain, sir, but somewhere in the region of a hundred to a hundred and twenty," replied the major.

"How the Kaden did one hundred and twenty men sneak past you, Major Lorn?" Jeral Tae was roaring now, no longer concerned who was listening.

"Sir, the civilians were camped on the fringe of our camp and once they'd killed or knocked out the sentries it was easy for them to just melt into the darkness," replied the major trying his best to hold Jeral's fierce stare. "If the general recalls, I did suggest billeting the civilians in the centre of the camp to prevent something like this occurring?"

Jeral's face flushed crimson and he sensed one or two of his older officers seething with indignation at the major's perceived insubordination. "That you did, Major and it seems you were right. So how did this happen? Was it a spontaneous thing or had they been planning it for some time? More to the point, why am I only hearing about it now?"

"Sergeant Marix brought it to my attention as soon as he discovered what had happened whilst he was doing his inspections. I immediately gave chase with a squad of lancers, but by then most of them had done a disappearing act. As for not informing you, sir, I apologise, but in the circumstances I thought it best to immediately give chase rather than delay and make my report."

Jeral was shaking with rage. Not so much at the major, although he was still mystified how so many men could simply vanish without anybody noticing, but at the fact that he had been betrayed. He took a long deep breath and tried to calm himself.

"You said that most of them had disappeared. Does that mean that you've recaptured some of them? Please tell me it does," said Jeral coldly.

"None alive I'm afraid. We managed to run down a small group of them, but they weren't willing to give themselves up for military justice and some of the men with me were ...over-zealous in their retribution," replied the major.

Jeral nodded knowingly. The regular troops obviously felt as betrayed as he did and he could therefore understand their reaction. "I see."

"However, I did manage to question one man before he succumbed to his injuries, General."

"And what did the whoreson have to say?"

"That it was a ruffian by the name of Pular Bratak who organised the desertions. He isn't one of the few we killed unfortunately," said the major apologetically.

"Of course he isn't. Scum like that always seem to get away whilst others pay for their crimes." *I'm going to get you Bratak and I'm going to kill you and what's more I'm going to take my time over it.*

"What do you want me to do about the lancers who killed

the deserters, General?" asked the major breaking into Jeral's train of thought.

"What?" replied Jeral still distracted.

"The men who killed the deserters; what do you want me to do with them?"

"You can give them a medal as far as I'm concerned, Major, just don't do it in front of the remaining civilians." The major stared at Jeral unsure whether the general was being serious or not. Jeral sighed at the man's naievity. "You do nothing, Major and return them to their unit. Whilst I don't condone their actions I do understand them. Besides, when the Delarites have had enough of trying to scare us to death and decide to try and do it the old fashioned way, we're going to need every man we can get. Now..." Jeral's words were cut short by the sound of one of his other officers noisily clearing his throat, who once he'd gained the general's attention, pointed towards the hill opposite.

"The enemy is on the move, General."

Jeral spun round and stared at the hill which now seemed to be alive with columns of black dots as hundreds of men slowly began marching forward.

"To your positions if you please, gentlemen. Major Lorn, you missed the briefing but essentially I want you and your men on my left flank as a strategic reserve, understand?" said Jeral.

"Yes, sir, but I was rather hoping that I'd be allowed to lead the attack."

"Damn it, Lorn this is no time to be arguing with me; do as you're told. You'll get your chance to fight don't worry," snapped Jeral.

"Yes, sir, of course," replied Lorn looking a little abashed as he marched off to rejoin his men.

"Bugler!" bellowed Jeral.

A young lad of perhaps no more than nineteen or twenty hurried over to his side.

"Sir?"

"Sound the stand to, son and make it loud and clear. I don't want any of these ladies sleeping in and missing all the action."

The bugler smiled at the general's joke and continued

standing there looking at him. Jeral gave the lad another couple of seconds to figure it out before eventually bellowing at him to get on with it.

The call to arms and stand to rang out across the camp, the sound drifting lazily towards the oncoming enemy and within a couple of minutes the Remadan force was deployed in battle formation.

It's going to be a long and bloody day, thought Jeral as he took two steps in front of his men before raising his sword and roaring at the oncoming enemy. Like a well-rehearsed play, the officers took up the roar and then the men until the fast approaching Delarites found themselves marching towards a wall of noise.

A very angry and determined wall of noise.

Chapter 10

Everything was dark, but he could hear voices, muffled and undistinguishable. They might have been speaking in a foreign tongue, but he wasn't sure. If this was Kaden as he feared it was, then he was in for a rough time.

The voices grew steadily louder and eventually he was able to discern that they were speaking in some eastern language though he wasn't sure which. They appeared agitated and angry. His head hurt like crazy but for some reason he was unable to move his hands to check for injury.

Am I paralysed? Is this what it means to die and go to Kaden?

He lay there for a while concentrating on blocking out the babble of noise all around him and tried to remember what had happened. At first he'd been sure that he was dead, probably killed fighting in some glorious battle or other, but now he wasn't so sure.

If I'm dead surely I wouldn't be able to feel the thumping pain in my head?

When the bucket of warm liquid splashed his face shocking his eyes open, he knew that he wasn't dead. What he didn't know was whether that was a good or bad thing.

Dear Sulat, please let that only have been water.

The excited chattering voices around him had been replaced by much laughter and he had a dreadful feeling that whatever had just been thrown over him wasn't water. He took a deep breath and nearly gagged. Incensed he roared with rage, somehow finding the strength to roll firstly onto his side and then onto his knees. He smiled with satisfaction when the people around him quickly backed away despite the fact his hands were apparently bound behind his back. Then the pain in his head returned with a vengeance followed by several waves of nausea. He briefly closed his eyes as he tried to regain his balance and as he did so, someone rushed up and pushed him back to the ground with their foot, causing another outburst of laughter.

Teren lay there with his face in the sand trying to gather his thoughts. Slowly recent events began to coalesce in his mind: Vangor, the raiders, the fight with the Salandori, Eryn.

Eryn! Where is Eryn?

Teren remembered charging at the Salandori after telling Eryn to run as fast as he could towards nearby woods. He also remembered looking on in despair as half a dozen Salandori riders had peeled away and gone after Eryn. There had been nothing Teren could do. He remembered fighting like a maniac and killing several of the Salandori riders before some whoreson had struck him on the side of his head. That was the last thing he remembered until now. Teren offered Sulat a silent prayer that Eryn was safe somewhere far away from there.

"Ah, the mighty Remadan warrior who single-handedly slew four of my finest warriors is awake at last; that is good." The voice had spoken in the common tongue but with a heavy eastern accent. Teren went to try and kneel up again, but whoever was talking to him quickly stepped forward and put their foot on the side of his head pinning him down in the sand. "Stay there, Remadan, it is where you belong." The man's companions of which, there sounded many all laughed.

"You're first," snarled Teren as he tried to avoid swallowing any sand.

"First what, Remadan?"

"You're the first one I'm going to kill when I get out of here, but you won't be the last."

The cold and confident tone in which the Remadan had spoken briefly seemed to unnerve the man, but then his bravado rallied.

"Brave words from a man covered in Ulak piss and face down in the dirt." The man looked round for support and on cue his companions all dutifully laughed.

"Aye, I might be covered in it, but at least I wasn't raised on it like you whoresons."

The Salandori removed his foot from Teren's head and kicked him hard in the ribs making Teren cry out.

"I would choose my words more carefully if I was you,

Remadan; your life is nearly over, don't make it unnecessarily painful as well."

"You think it will always be this way, do you, whoreson? If I were you I'd kill me now because if you don't, I promise you that one day it will be your face down in the dirt with my boot holding it in place," said Teren defiantly.

"Trust me, Remadan there is nothing I'd like more than to separate your ugly head from its shoulders, but my father in his wisdom has other plans for the great Teren Rad." The warrior slowly backed away from Teren.

Teren wasn't surprised that they knew who he was, after all he'd killed enough Salandori in his time, though at that moment in time it didn't feel like anywhere near enough. What he was surprised about was that having recognised him they hadn't immediately put him to death, a painful one. The Salandori were known for being quite inventive when it came to inflicting pain.

"Then you have both sealed your own fate," said Teren matter-of-factly, as he once again knelt up and smiled.

***

The Salandori had led Teren eastwards for several days through an ever changing countryside. One minute they were walking across a poker hot desert with seemingly endless sand dunes, the next through barren and harsh looking mountain passes. Then just when Teren thought that he would never set eyes upon another tree or blade of grass, they'd suddenly emerge into a lush green valley full of game. The Salandori tribal lands were indeed a mishmash of landscapes. Teren had been through Salandor before of course, but then seven years ago, he had been travelling as fast as he could in pursuit of the men who had abducted his wife and he had had no interest in the countryside.

As he'd been dragged along behind a particularly irritable Ulak that clearly had digestive issues judging by the number of times Teren had to nimbly jump out of the way before he was covered in Ulak mess, his thoughts had turned to Eryn. Had the lad managed to avoid being captured or killed by the Salandori? Had he turned round and gone home or was he even now tracking the Salandori caravan? Occasionally Teren's thoughts would turn to Vangor and the friends he had left there. Had the city fallen? Were Ro and Arlen still alive and if so were they now coming after Teren and Eryn like Ro had promised? Teren certainly hoped so. If Ro and Arlen caught up with Eryn the boy's chances of surviving would have increased greatly. It was a cheering thought and one Teren was determined to hold onto whatever fate his own future held.

It was not until noon on the sixth day since he was captured that Teren set eyes on another person outside the caravan in which he had been travelling. The Salandori people were tribal and distrustful of other people, he knew that, but not to see anyone else in six days of travelling was unusual. When they did eventually run into another group of Salandori, it seemed to Teren that the meeting had been arranged and wasn't coincidental.

After a few minutes of performing their ritual greetings, the man who had put his foot on Teren's head led one of the newcomers, an older man perhaps in his fifties, over to where Teren sat eating the scraps of food they had chucked to him. The older man wrinkled his nose in disgust and the other man said something in their language causing them both to laugh heartily. Teren had no idea what they'd said but he had a feeling it involved Ulak piss.

They talked for a couple of minutes more, before money seemed to exchange hands. Then the younger man suddenly shouted something to one of his men who immediately yanked Teren to his feet and untied the rope that had bound him to the Ulak. The Salandori dragged Teren over to his leader who in turn passed the rope end to the older Salandori.

"Goodbye, Remadan. I hope that you will be content in your new family. I'd wish you a long and happy life, but I'm glad to say that it will be neither."

Teren merely stared into the other man's face as if burning his features into his memory. Clearly unnerved, he slapped Teren in the face with the back of his hand, drawing an angry response from the older Salandori who was now dragging him away.

"Why do you stare at him so, Remadan? Do you not know

that is the easiest way to offend a Salandori?" said the older Salandori who now apparently owned Teren. He had spoken in the common tongue.

"That's exactly why I stared at him. Besides, I just wanted one last good look at his ugly face so that I don't forget it," replied Teren.

"And why is that?"

"Can't kill a man if I don't remember what he looks like."

The Salandori laughed as he handed Teren's rope over to one of his men who fastened the other end to the saddle of another brutish looking Ulak.

"You may as well forget Perok, Remadan, because you will never see him again, not where you're going."

"Oh, I'll see him again, don't you worry and now that I know his name he'll be that much easier to track down."

"I admire your courage and determination, Remadan; that is good. You are going to need it where you're headed." Then without saying anything further, the Salandori leader strode off barking orders to his men and pretty soon their small caravan was on its way.

After another day of travelling east, they eventually turned south-east. In the oppressive heat with little food or water and tired almost beyond the point of recovery, Teren had no idea how far they'd travelled or how far he now was from the Remadan border. The previous day he had briefly caught sight of some other prisoners trailing behind their own Ulak. From what Teren could see there were three men and a couple of women. In their dirty and bedraggled state and without being able to speak to them, Teren could not tell from which country they came.

The caravan suddenly came to a halt and Teren tried to peer round the side of the Ulak to see why they'd stopped. They were on top of a small hillock looking down into a long valley through which a stream slowly meandered. The water looked cool and refreshing. The valley was filled with canvas shelters; this was without doubt the biggest gathering of Salandori Teren had ever seen. On the far side of the stream was some sort of clearing lined with rocks and large stones though what its purpose was Teren had no idea.

"Welcome to your new home, Remadan." Teren had not

103

heard anybody approach him and was momentarily startled.

"What is this place?" asked Teren.

"I told you; this is your new home. This is where you are going to live and very shortly die," replied the Salandori who had purchased Teren a few days earlier. "It is the camp of Alith, High Teah of the southern tribes."

The name Alith meant nothing to Teren, but before he could ask anything further he felt the Ulak moving forward as the caravan began to make its way slowly down the hillock into the camp.

***

Teren and the other prisoners were treated surprisingly well over the next couple of days, being allowed to bathe in the stream and receiving better and larger helpings of food. They were housed in large wooden cages, one for the men and one for the women. There were already other prisoners in the cages when Teren and his group arrived and from what Teren could make out they came from just about every country in Arkadia. There were some whose language and dress he didn't recognise and Teren guessed that they must have come from the lands to the south or east.

Although conversation amongst the captives was frowned upon, the guards soon got tired of continually shouting or prodding the prisoners, so every now and again Teren was able to speak to some of the others. The problem however, was getting them to talk back. Some clearly didn't speak the common tongue, but others in the group, who did, were openly hostile to his approaches to engage them in dialogue, none more so than a Delarite. Teren was on the verge of abandoning his attempts at conversation, when a tall blond man with a heavy northern accent suddenly spoke to him.

"Do not waste your breath, my friend, as you are going to need it."

"Thank Sulat! I was beginning to think that none of you knew how to speak or that perhaps the Salandori dogs had cut out your tongues."

A fierce poke in the back with the blunt end of a spear

told Teren that one of his guards had heard his insult and taken exception to it. As he rubbed his back he turned and glared at the guard, burning his face into Teren's hall of revenge; it was becoming very crowded. Still, at least he had learned that some of the guards spoke the common tongue. It meant that he had to be careful of who was around when he spoke.

"Careful, Remadan, do not provoke them or your turn will come quicker than was intended," said the blond man.

"My turn at what?" asked Teren flexing his aching back as best he could in the cramped conditions.

"You really do not know?"

"I only just got here remember and I don't plan on staying long, however pleasant our hosts are," said Teren.

"Your stay here might be much shorter than you think, though I have a suspicion you can look after yourself in a fight," said the blond man.

"That I can, sonny, now why don't you stop dancing around whatever it is you're trying to tell me and just spit it out?"

The man nodded and tried to shuffle closer to Teren. "This is the camp of Alith, High Teah of the southern tribes."

That apparently was meant to be explanation enough, but Teren was none the wiser.

"And what of it?" asked Teren feeling a little exasperated.

"You have never heard of him?" asked the blond man incredulously.

"No, can't say that I have. One Salandori pig leader is very much like the next if you ask me."

The wince that briefly flickered across the blond man's face warned Teren what was coming, but he was still unable to avoid the painful blow to the small of his back that told him that the guard had once again been listening. This time Teren whirled round and tried to grab the retreating spear shaft, but was too slow.

"The next time you do that you whoreson I'm going to shove that stick point first down your throat, understand?" snarled Teren.

The Salandori uttered a threat of his own and was quickly joined by another guard and they both proceeded to try and poke Teren through the bars of the cage, but he and the blond man had moved too far away.

"Yes, I think your stay here is going to be a short one, Remadan," said the blond man smiling and shaking his head.

Teren glanced over at the man and returned his smile, starting to warm to the northerner.

"My name is Teren Rad." He extended his arm and after a few seconds hesitation, the blond man clasped it in the traditional warrior's greeting.

"Brak Todash."

A few of the other prisoners looked on with only a passing interest. The Delarite merely sneered and then looked away.

"What's his problem?" asked Teren.

"Aside from the fact that he's a Delarite you mean? He's one of the many in here who believes that it's stupid to get to know your fellow prisoners when you might be forced to kill them tomorrow," said Brak.

"Why would anyone want to kill their fellow prisoners?"

Brak took a deep breath before continuing. "Teah Alith likes to gamble, but not on horse or chariot racing, but on men's lives. He captures and buys slaves and then forces them to fight to the death for his and his companions' amusement, whilst they bet on who will win and who will die. All of us here are destined to fight for his pleasure at some point. I hear that his brother's caravan is due to rendezvous with us the day after tomorrow at which point some of us at least will be forced to fight."

"I remember my grandfather once telling me that our ancestors who first settled this land came across a tribe who used to make prisoners fight for their amusement, but I assumed the practise had died out hundreds of years ago," said Teren incredulously.

"For the most part it has, but in lawless lands like this, men like Alith can get away with it."

"There are others?" asked Teren.

"Oh, yes. Alith might be the most notorious, but there are other Teahs who enjoy the same entertainment. Sometimes we are forced to fight men from another tribe or camp and sometimes if Alith is bored he will make a few of us fight each other. I watched my younger brother, Andrik die at the point of a Datian's spear."

"I'm sorry about your brother, Brak. What happened to the Datian?"

"It didn't end well for him I'm afraid. He died bloody a few days later in another contest."

"Who killed him?"

"I did," replied Brak proudly.

Teren nodded approvingly. He was starting to like this northerner more and more.

"If they put a sword in my hand then I'm going to carve my way out of here," said Teren arrogantly.

"Fool!" It had not been Brak who had spoken and Teren glanced round to see who was responsible. His gaze finally fell on the large Delarite who was glaring at him with obvious loathing.

"Well what do you know; it speaks. Would you care to elaborate on that insightful remark, sonny, or was that the full extent of your vocabulary? You are after all a Delarite I suppose," said Teren in a derisory tone.

The Delarite made to get up and go for Teren, but the two Salandori guards were watching him menacingly and so he eased himself back down.

"There's a good dog, you just sit there and do what your Salandori masters tell you," sneered Teren.

"I am going to kill you, Remadan, and I'm going to do it slowly to the cheers of the crowd," hissed the Delarite.

"If I had a coin for every time somebody had said they were going to kill me, I'd be a rich man. Besides, you're going to have to wait in line."

"You're here for a couple of days and talking about escape as if the thought had never crossed our minds; typical arrogant Remadan. Do you think any of us want to be here? Yes, they give us weapons in the arena, old sometimes almost blunt weapons, but stationed all around us watching our every move and twitch are a number of archers with instructions to shoot if they suspect we're about to try anything," said the Delarite quietly so the guards couldn't hear.

"Doesn't mean that it can't be done," said Teren.

"Arrogant fool! No wonder my people hate yours and will one day rise up and crush you."

That's interesting, thought Teren. *He obviously doesn't know that war has already begun, which means he's been here some time.*

"I see you make friends fast, Teren. If you want your stay here to be more than fleeting might I suggest that you try and be a little more inconspicuous?" said Brak.

"Not my style I'm afraid."

"I had a feeling you'd say that. Now get some sleep. You're likely to need it over the next few days."

Teren nodded. "One last thing, Brak; what's the most fights anyone's ever won?"

"To the best of my knowledge, six," replied Brak as he settled down on the hard ground and closed his eyes.

"Six, eh! How many have you fought in?"

Brak rolled onto his side facing away from Teren and as he did so Teren thought he heard him say six.

Teren lay back and closed his eyes though he doubted very much that sleep would come that night. He had got himself in some situations before, but this perhaps was right up there with the worst of them. It was going to need some careful planning to extricate himself from this one. The only saving grace in the whole sorry mess he realised was that Eryn did not appear to have been captured. True he might be dead, but at least then his suffering would be over. Teren once again offered a silent prayer to Sulat that Eryn was alive and safe and preferably with Ro and Arlen. A couple of minutes later Teren fell into a deep sleep.

Chapter 11

After waiting long enough to be sure that they weren't being watched or followed, Eryn, Ro and Arlen eased out of the tree line and made their way over to the small group of bodies lying on the sand. Eryn had steeled himself for the very real prospect that one of those bodies was that of his father, whilst silently praying to Sulat that he'd somehow survived. His father had constantly referred to the Salandori as an untrustworthy and deceitful people, but to Eryn's mind being their captive had to be preferable to being food for the predators, some of whom were already circling the bodies.

"Do you want me to go first and take a look?" Arlen asked Eryn.

"No, it's fine, I'll come," said Eryn.

"If your father is here, Eryn, it may not be too pretty."

"I know, but I'm prepared."

Arlen seriously doubted it, but decided not to push the matter any further. The three companions edged forward, their approach scaring the vultures into a panicked flight. When they were no more than a dozen paces away it became clear that there were four bodies lying in the dirt.

"He's not here," said Eryn smiling, the relief obvious.

"That is good," said Arlen. "But then where is he?"

"In the absence of a body I think we must assume that he is a prisoner of the Salandori," said Ro.

"Well wherever he is, he didn't go lightly," said Arlen glancing at the four bloody and partially consumed bodies lying around them.

"Indeed not," said Ro who was now busy studying the ground.

"What do you see, my friend?" asked Arlen.

"There are two sets of tracks leading away from here. One consists of many horsemen and the other just two horses. They did not ride off together."

"Tayla and her captor?" asked Eryn.

"It would seem so. My guess would be that the Salandori

were bought off somehow by the man holding Tayla and persuaded to attack you and your father. Whilst that was going on, he made good his escape."

"That leaves us with a dilemma does it not?" said Arlen.

"How so?" asked Eryn.

"Which do we follow; the man who still has Tayla or the men who are now holding your father?"

Eryn's expression suggested that he had not yet considered that particular problem.

"We can worry about that problem when it arrives. For the moment both sets of tracks are headed in the same direction and I suggest that we get after them whilst the tracks are still clear," said Ro.

Eryn nodded. He was glad that he didn't yet have to decide who to try and follow, particularly when the wrong choice might lead to one of their deaths. Something told him, however, that his luck would not hold out and that eventually he would have to make that call. With a last look down at the bodies as the bravest of the vultures returned and started to hop about a few paces away, Eryn turned and headed east. After exchanging a brief knowing look, Ro and Arlen followed.

***

The companions had followed the tracks east for a few days until late on the fifth day they were suddenly assailed by a sandstorm which lasted several hours. When the storm lifted the tracks which they had been following had all been blown away. They continued to head due east hoping to pick up fresh tracks outside of the storm's path, but none were found. Despondency was fast settling in when quite by chance they ran into a small band of Salandori. Arlen and Eryn had immediately reached for their swords, but Ro had assured them that the men were from the peaceful Crytani tribe.

After exchanging greetings Ro had been able to ascertain that a large band of Salandori had been spotted heading south-east earlier in the day. The Crytani claimed not to have seen a woman amongst their number, although they did concede that it was possible that her appearance had been disguised. They did, however, confirm that a large scruffy looking Arkadian had been a captive of theirs. After thanking them for their help and questioning them about the likelihood of running into any other Salandori nearby, Ro's group had ridden on a bit further until they found the tracks heading south-east.

"It is as we feared, Eryn. Two sets of tracks continue east, whilst the rest head south-east. The time has come to decide whether to try and rescue your father or your fiancée," said Ro.

Eryn climbed down from the horse he had been sharing with Ro and stared east. Then he glanced from Ro to Arlen and then back to Ro as if willing one of his two companions to make the decision for him. They, however, had clearly come to the decision that it was Eryn's choice and nobody else's.

Eryn's mind was in turmoil and his heart was breaking. Should he go after the girl he loved and intended to marry before she disappeared into the east never to be found again or should he go after his father who after an absence of seven years had come back into his life just when he needed him to? Eryn reasoned that if either of them was in danger of losing their life then it was his father. If the raider was going to kill Tayla he wouldn't have dragged her halfway across Arkadia before doing so.

Just when he thought that he'd made up his mind to ride to his father's aid another part of his mind would scream at him that his father could look after himself, but Tayla was alone and vulnerable.

"Eryn?" Eryn looked up to see Arlen smiling down at him. Eryn had no idea how long he'd been stood there trying to decide what to do but evidently it had been some time. "In which direction do we ride because my skin is burning sat out here in the open?"

Eryn glanced south-east and then nodded eastwards. "That way. We finish what I set out to do and that's rescue Tayla," and with that he climbed back onto Ro's horse. He had no idea whether he'd made the right decision or whether Ro and Arlen agreed with him, but he'd made the decision from his heart. If Ro and Arlen did disagree they didn't say so.

"So be it," said Ro as he nudged his horse forward and once again the three companions were heading east.

***

They'd ridden on for as long as they could that afternoon through an ever changing terrain. By late afternoon they were just facing up to the likelihood of having to make camp out in the open, when totally by chance they stumbled over a small almost secluded oasis. The sparse trees and bushes provided scant cover, but it was better than being totally out in the open in a hostile land. They also had a ready supply of water for them and the horses.

Taking it in turns to keep watch in three hour blocks, they rested there until a little after dawn the next morning, when after filling everything capable of carrying water, they finally moved out. The sun was already high in the sky and the temperature was steadily climbing. It was going to be another long, hot and tiring day.

Two sets of tracks had led to the oasis where Tayla and her captor had obviously stopped to gather water before moving on. Eryn found himself wondering where they'd spent the night and how close they'd been.

He had not slept well during the night. At some point whilst he had lay there huddled against the cold thinking about Tayla, his mind had started to torment him with the possibility that the Narmidian might use Tayla's body to keep warm. The thought had made him both uncomfortable and angry. After that, try as he might, the thought would not leave his mind and sleep would not come. Finally, a couple of hours before dawn, Arlen had come over to tell him it was his turn to stand watch giving his mind something else with which to occupy itself.

They did not set eyes on anyone until a little after midday when a short distance in front of them they stumbled across a group of men fighting. At first they feared that Tayla and her captor had been attacked by a group of passing Salandori, but as they drew nearer they saw that all the combatants were Salandori.

"What do you think?" Arlen asked Ro.

Ro studied the scene before him for a while before answering. "Tribal dispute I should think. See they have two different colour sashes around their waists."

"They all look the same to me," said Arlen.

"What should we do?" asked Eryn.

"Nothing," replied Arlen sitting back in his saddle and watching the fight. "Let them all kill themselves, what do we care?"

Already one side in the fight had the upper hand with six of them left against two from the other tribe.

"We ride in and scatter them and try and take one hostage to question. They may have seen Tayla and her captor," said Ro.

"Or we could do that," said Arlen sarcastically.

"Since when have you turned down the chance of a good fight, my Silevian friend?" asked Ro as he drew his sword.

"Never I suppose. Can't stand to watch an unfair fight anyway."

Whilst they'd been discussing it three more men had fallen leaving four of the purple sash wearers against just one wearing red and even as they watched, the red sash wearer was suddenly knocked to the ground.

"Time to go," said Ro as he kicked his horse into a charge and moments later, Arlen and Eryn did likewise, though they were considerably slower sat upon the same horse. Their presence had not been noticed but now as the three friends came shouting and roaring towards the small group of Salandori, that all changed. Trying to take advantage of their momentary distraction, the Salandori wearing the red sash tried to escape the ring of horsemen, but his attempt was spotted and he was knocked to the ground again.

One of the other riders suddenly fell to the ground clutching at his chest from where a crossbow bolt now protruded and shortly after another one followed suit. This one had a small metallic object with spikes, lodged in his neck.

Suddenly confronted by less favourable odds and with three unknown riders bearing down on them fast, the remaining two purple sash wearers tried to kick their horses into a gallop and head north, but the approaching riders had anticipated their move and cut them off. There was a brief clash of swords and a few seconds later the last two purple sash Salandori riders were laying dead in the sand.

The red sash wearer who was also unsure of the intentions of the newcomers tried to back away towards his horse, but the youngest of the newcomers and a strangely dressed fat man with a crossbow, stepped between him and his horse.

"Who are you? What do you want with me?" spat the warrior in broken common tongue.

"Be at peace my friend," said Ro smiling and sheathing his sword, "we mean you no harm."

Arlen and Eryn looked at him in surprise and Ro gestured for them both to lower their weapons.

"Then what do you want?" repeated the Salandori.

"A little gratitude for saving your neck wouldn't go amiss," Arlen muttered under his breath, but still loud enough for the others to hear.

Ro shot him an exasperated look.

"I did not need your help."

"No, why were you on the ground then? Perhaps you were planning on tickling their feet until they submitted?" said Arlen.

The Salandori glared at Arlen, but Arlen merely grinned back, amused by his own humour and not in the slightest perturbed by the aggressive little Salandori warrior.

"Arlen, back off. *Please!*" implored Ro.

Muttering something under his breath that this time no one could hear, Arlen eased his horse backwards. Eryn slid from the horse as he did so.

"Keep your eyes on the Salandori, Eryn, I don't trust him," whispered Arlen as he sidled by.

Eryn nodded and his hand surreptitiously slid towards his sword. As his fingers slowly curled around its hilt his thoughts momentarily turned to his father somewhere out in the desert and he prayed that he was safe and would forgive him for not coming after him.

Ro put on his warmest smile. "We meant you no disrespect, my friend, but we saw that you and your comrades were outnumbered and thought you could use our help. If we'd known that you had it under control we would never have insulted you by coming to your aid uninvited."

The Salandori's expression seemed to change from one of hostility to embarrassment.

"No, the fault is mine, Remadan. You and your friends showed great honour and courage coming to our aid and to my shame I repay it with hostility and ingratitude. Please forgive me."

Ro nodded. "Let us speak no more of the matter."

"You are most gracious," replied the Salandori, "although I would feel happier if your young friend here would release his hold on his sword; it is making me feel most uncomfortable."

Ro gestured to Eryn to let go of his sword and after a quick glance towards Arlen who merely shrugged in response, Eryn did so.

"Thank you. Now tell me, what are three usurpers doing in the middle of Anvak's Forge, so far from their homelands?" asked the Salandori.

"We are seeking a couple of friends of ours. One is a young girl who is travelling with a Narmidian who holds her against her will. They were last known to be travelling east. The other is an older man, a warrior, with long hair and an unkempt beard. He was last known to be heading south-east with a group of Salandori warriors who were persuaded to attack him by the Narmidian holding the girl." For the briefest of seconds Ro thought that he saw a flicker of recognition register on the man's face, but then it resumed its neutral expression. "Have you set eyes on either party?"

"I wish I could tell you that I had, my friend, if only to repay some of the debt I owe you for coming to my aid. Sadly I haven't set eyes upon anyone else all day, not until we were attacked and you showed up that is. I am sorry."

Ro nodded but continued staring at the man as if weighing up the truth of his words.

"No matter, I had to ask."

"Of course you did. Now as I cannot provide you with the information that you seek, please allow me to repay my debt by offering you the hospitality of my father's camp tonight.

You can eat, drink and have a good night's rest before resuming your search tomorrow," said the Salandori.

"What do you think, Arlen? Salandori cooking is said to be exquisite," said Ro.

Arlen was hungry, fed up with cheese and dried biscuits, but he was truly distrustful of these people and this man in particular. "I don't know, Ro, tempting as it sounds we really ought to be going."

Ro had been thinking along the same lines and was about to decline their invitation when the Salandori spoke again.

"My father, the tribal chief has many pretty wives and is sure to want to lend you some to keep you warm tonight," said the Salandori smiling.

"On the other hand, Ro I think it would be incredibly rude of us to just leave and ignore the man's hospitality," said Arlen winking. "Besides, I think it'll do the boy good to take his mind off Tayla for a while."

"If you think I'm going to be unfaithful to Tayla with some tribal girl, Arlen, you're mistaken," said Eryn indignantly.

"Have you lain with Tayla yet?"

"What? No, of course not," said Eryn as his cheeks began to flush.

"Well then you wouldn't be being unfaithful to her then would you?" said Arlen.

"Maybe, but it just wouldn't feel right."

Arlen shrugged. "Oh well, more for me then I guess."

"It looks like we are accepting your kind offer, my friend," said Ro turning to face the Salandori. "My name is Ro Aryk, this is Arlen Meric and the young man over there is Eryn Rad."

There it was again, that flicker of recognition. Is this man lying to us? Ro was suddenly full of doubts.

"Excellent. My name is Perok, son of Nestor, Chief of the Muhabi. Tonight you will feast and drink like you have never done before. Now quickly follow me, because there might be more of these dogs around here looking for their friends."

The Salandori nimbly mounted his horse and without looking over his shoulder to check that the others following him, he rode off north.

"What happened to not trusting these people?" said Ro as he passed Arlen.

"I don't, but it doesn't mean I can't eat their food and drink their wine," and with that Arlen galloped off after the Salandori followed by Ro.

Eryn gazed one last time in the direction he knew his father had been taken and then climbed upon one of the dead warriors' horses and followed them.

***

It had taken them less than an hour to arrive at the camp of the Muhabi and whilst Ro wouldn't have described their welcome as hostile, he had known friendlier greetings. The small party had been greeted at the entrance to the camp, their approach obviously noted some time before by sentries no one in Ro's party noticed. Perok had briefly argued in his own language with an older man who Ro took to be Perok's father and although Ro didn't speak their language, it was obvious to him that their presence in his camp was not welcomed.

Still it was customary for the Salandori to welcome visitors and with a great deal of barely disguised reluctance, Nestor had welcomed Ro and his party to his camp in his best attempt at the common tongue.

After being shown where to attend their horses, Ro, Arlen and Eryn were led to a small tent made of skins where they were encouraged to rest whilst the Salandori made preparations for the evening feast and festivities.

A mean looking Salandori covered in scars made no attempt to disguise his disgust at the usurpers' presence and tried to confiscate their weapons, but after Perok intervened they were allowed to keep them.

A couple of hours or so after they'd arrived, Perok came and collected them, leading them through the rows of tents to the centre of the camp, where a huge fire roared and everyone sat around drinking and eating. Most of the camp dwellers stopped talking as the small group approached, but after what Ro took to be a rebuke from Perok, the babble of conversation resumed. Arlen noticed how everyone's gaze remained firmly fixed on the newcomers however.

"Feeling welcome yet, Ro?" asked Arlen as he sat down where indicated.

"Not especially, Arlen, no, but might I remind you that it was your base desires that forced us to attend in the first place? Talking of which, I thought Priests of the Golden Tree were forbidden to couple with women?"

"Ever thought that might be why I left?" said Arlen smiling before popping some of the food that was being offered to him by a pretty young Salandori, into his mouth.

"Yes, I am aware that we still haven't had that conversation," said Ro also helping himself to some of the food. "I believe I have asked you several times how you came to be in Remada in the first place, but you have not yet answered."

"Nor will I now I think. It is neither the time nor place," replied Arlen.

"Another time then?"

"Indeed." Arlen turned to say something to Eryn, but the boy's gaze was fixed firmly on the six young scantily dressed girls who were dancing and swaying around the fire as several old men played strange looking instruments. "They're a sight for sore eyes are they not?"

"Err, yes I suppose they are," replied Eryn distractedly.

"I think that one's got her eye on you," said Arlen nodding to a young black haired beauty who kept glancing over at Eryn. "I think your luck might be in lad. Better eat something; looks like you're going to need all your strength one way or another."

Eryn didn't reply and Arlen found himself wondering whether the boy's eyes could stretch any wider. Arlen chuckled and helped himself to some more food, which was surprisingly tasty.

For the most part the three friends were left on their own, only Perok making any effort to speak to them. Whether that was because no one else spoke the common tongue or whether they couldn't bring themselves to converse with the despised usurpers, Ro wasn't sure. Aside from the scarred warrior who Ro learned was the chief's champion, no one was openly hostile to them, most adopting an attitude of tolerance, but nevertheless Ro and from what he could see, Eryn, couldn't wait for the evening to be over. In fact Ro couldn't wait to be on his way out of the camp never to return. Arlen by contrast seemed to be heartily enjoying himself, apparently oblivious to the Salandori's indifference towards him. Arlen had eaten enough for ten men it seemed to Ro and had washed it down with enough wine to fell a giant, but the jovial priest seemed totally in control of his faculties.

When he could finally take no more, Ro had stood and bowed towards the chief and indicated for Eryn to do the same, which he did. Then he asked Perok to thank his father for his hospitality saying that they were tired now and were going to retire. Perok had seemed relieved at the news, but the chief merely nodded as if he wasn't bothered whether the strangers were there or not. The chief's champion, however, glared menacingly at them as they stood and walked away.

Ro had suggested Arlen come with them, but enjoying the attentions of two of the dancers as he was, Arlen merely waved Ro away and said that he'd be along shortly. Ro didn't like the idea of leaving Arlen alone, but the priest had made it patently clear that he had no intention of leaving just yet and Ro had no authority over him. Watched by the chief's champion and a handful of other warriors who had gathered around him, Ro and Eryn made their way back to their tent, carefully retracing the route they had taken a couple of hours earlier.

Several times, both Ro and Eryn had glanced over their shoulders suspicious that they were being followed, but when they looked there was never anybody there. They were either imagining it or their pursuers were very adept at hiding. They eventually arrived back at their tent and were both relieved and surprised to find that all of their gear and possessions, including their weapons, were still there.

Perhaps I am worrying over nothing and their intentions are honourable, thought Ro.

After a final check outside, Ro suggested to Eryn that he try and get a few hours' sleep whilst he waited up for Arlen; Ro was desperate to be away from the Salandori village at the rising of the sun. Eryn had not been happy and wanted to keep Ro company, but after assuring Eryn that when Arlen returned he would get to take watch whilst Ro slept, Eryn finally acquiesced and was soon fast asleep.

Ro sat facing the tent entrance, his sword close at hand and the pouch holding the *jemtak* open and ready. He even took the precaution of loading a bolt in Arlen's crossbow. If they had to leave in a hurry, they were going to need every weapon primed and ready, although even then their chances of survival would be slim. With a deep sigh an anxious Ro tightened the grip on his sword and waited for the return of his friend. He hoped that he wouldn't have to wait too long.

Chapter 12

Even as he'd watched his friends walk away Arlen had kept up the pretence of being drunk. How anyone could believe that the pigswill they'd been serving them all evening could render anyone inebriated was beyond Arlen, but those around him appeared convinced. *If this had been Barg ale or even Pirix wine, then the desired effect might have been achieved for real*, thought Arlen.

For most of the evening Arlen had suspected that the whole thing was a trap and had wanted to alert Ro to his suspicions, but had been unable to do so without alarming Eryn and had therefore refrained from doing so. Therefore, to prevent drawing unwanted attention to himself he had pretended to get steadily drunk whilst making a big show of enjoying the attentions of a couple of the young dancers. In hindsight he decided that part of the charade hadn't been too onerous.

All evening the chief's champion had been throwing venomous looks at the three friends and the fact that a small group of warriors had gravitated their way towards the champion had also not gone unnoticed by Arlen. Once or twice he thought he saw Ro glance their way and hoped that his friend was alert to the possibility of trouble. Not long after, Ro and Eryn had made their excuses and prepared to retire for the night and Ro had all but begged Arlen to come with him. However, instead of telling his friend about his suspicions he had kept up the act. Eventually, looking more than a little annoyed, Ro had left with Eryn. That was good and was what Arlen had wanted. He would be in a better position to help his friends if he was temporarily separated from them.

About a minute or so after Ro and Eryn had departed the four warriors who had been standing and whispering with the chief's champion, suddenly melted back into the crowd. Arlen knew instantly that they were going after his friends. After staggering to his feet, stumbling around and slapping both girls on their behind, causing them to giggle, Arlen had waved to the chief and then lurched after them, drawing much amused laughter from those around him. Out of the corner of his eye, he saw the champion lean down and whisper something in the chief's ear before he too melted back into the crowd. Arlen would have to deal with him first.

When he was sure that he was out of sight of just about everyone who had been watching him at the feast, Arlen began singing drunkenly before deliberately stumbling to the ground where he immediately rolled out of sight behind one of the tents. Quick as he could he crawled round behind the tent and waited. A few seconds later, as he'd expected the chief's champion came striding past with his sword drawn. Arlen glanced at the ground around him, his gaze finally falling on a rock small enough to be lifted in one hand, but big enough to do what he planned. He quietly reached over and picked the rock up and after checking to make sure nobody else was following, he silently hurried after the champion.

Arlen prided himself in his stealth an attribute that had helped to save his life on many occasions, but either he was more inebriated than he thought or the man he was following had extraordinarily good hearing because all of a sudden he came to a dead stop. The champion stood there for a few seconds listening, perhaps sensing that someone was following him and then slowly began to turn. Quick as a flash Arlen closed the distance between them, raised the rock high above his head and then brought it crashing down into the man's face.

If he had sensed somebody behind him the champion still looked shocked at the sudden appearance of the priest and consequently he hesitated. In that split second of hesitation the priest had brought something he was holding in his hand crashing down into his head.

There was a sickening crunch as the rock made contact with the man's face, shattering bone and muscle and reducing the champion's face to a bloody pulp. The man's blood splattered Arlen's face and clothes as the rock struck home. Arlen had hoped to sneak up behind the man and knock him out with a blow to the back of the head, but it was not to be.

This way had turned out to be much messier, but just as effective.

Once again checking that no one else had decided to follow them, Arlen got hold of the man under his arms and dragged him into the nearest tent, praying as he did so that the owners were at the feast and not having an early night. He was in luck. Puffing from the exertion of dragging the large warrior into the tent, Arlen hoped that the delay had not endangered his friends. Ro was a brave and sensible man and would have taken precautions to prevent them from being taken by surprise, but if Arlen was right in his suspicions, there were four men coming to kill them. Although Eryn was improving with the sword, he would probably be no match for any of them and four was too many for even Ro. He had to hurry.

Arlen was about to leave the tent and hurry to his friends when something in the corner of the unusually large tent caught his eye. He quickly walked over and nodded in recognition when he got close. Leaning up against a crate of some sort was Teren Rad's large sword. There was no doubt. Arlen had seen the sword up close at Vangor and would recognise it anywhere. The Salandori had lied. Despite having claimed not to have seen Teren, they clearly had. Worse still, they might even have killed him. There was of course the possibility that he was being held hostage somewhere in the village in one of the many tents, but they did not have the time to search them all. Sooner or later the champion would be missed and more men, a lot more men, would come looking for him. His priority was to get to Ro and Eryn as soon as possible, deal with the men following them and then figure out what to do about Teren.

Lifting Teren's sword Arlen was shocked to find out how heavy it felt and wondered how his friend ever found the strength to wield it. Then after a cautious look outside the tent flaps, Arlen hurried out, but only after picking up a couple of ornate looking daggers he saw lying on a makeshift table.

These are more like it, thought Arlen as he slipped Teren's sword through his belt and took a dagger in either hand. He hoped that he wouldn't be seen because there was no way he would be able to run with the weight of Teren's sword dragging him down.

By the time that he had made his way through the almost deserted village back to their tent, the four Salandori warriors had already arrived and were standing quietly outside gesturing to each other. Arlen's mind was in turmoil. If he raced over there yelling a warning, Ro and Eryn might be able to react in time and save themselves. However, such an action risked alerting other people in the village in which case their fate was sealed. If he tried to quietly sneak up on them he was likely to be too late and unless these men were unusually ponderous at least two of them were likely to have breached the tent by the time that he got there. That was still the smart play though he decided.

Moving as quickly and as quietly as he could, Arlen crept across the ground towards the four warriors adjusting his grip on the two daggers as he did so. Just when he thought that he was going to make it in time, two of the men suddenly crouched down slightly and quietly entered the tent.

Arlen was almost upon the remaining two warriors when one of the men who had entered the tent came tumbling out backwards. As he hit the ground Arlen who was now right behind the others was able to see the small crossbow bolt lodged deep in the man's forehead. Ro had not only been awake, but he'd also been ready for them. When the second man came stumbling out of the tent weapon less, both hands clutching at his sliced stomach in an attempt to keep his entrails inside him, the other two turned and made to run. For the briefest of seconds their faces registered fear and then shock as Arlen forced both daggers up catching each man under the throat. The blades sliced through the soft tissue burying themselves deep in the roofs of their mouths, killing them instantly. Both men dropped silently to the ground at Arlen's feet revealing a grinning Ro behind them, his sword bloody.

"Once again it seems I owe you my life, Arlen."

"Erm, no, I think you had this one pretty much covered; these boys were about to run after all," replied Arlen smiling.

"Still, I am grateful for your timely return to sobriety."

"Oh, that was just an act. I had a feeling our hosts had no

intention of letting us leave. Staying behind and pretending to be drunk so I could watch your back was the only thing I could think of."

"A good deception, my friend, but probably a futile one. Their absence will soon be noticed and they will come looking for us in greater numbers led by their champion," said Ro frowning.

"Oh I wouldn't go worrying about him. He's stoned," said Arlen grinning widely.

Ro felt sure there was more to the explanation than the obvious, but now was not the time. "Then perhaps you have bought us enough time after all." Ro suddenly noticed the sword handing from the priest's belt. "Is that...?"

"Teren's? Yes. Our hosts have not been completely honest with us it seems."

"Is he here do you think?" asked Ro.

"No, my guess is that they've either sold or passed him on, or he's ...dead."

"Who is?" asked a bleary-eyed Eryn, his expression turning to one of shock when he clapped eyes on the four dead Salandori.

Ro and Arlen looked at each other weighing up what to tell the boy. Ro decided on the honest option.

"Arlen has found your father's sword, which means that they are either holding him prisoner or have passed him on. We also have to consider the possibility that he's..."

"Dead," finished Eryn.

"Yes, but neither Ro nor I think that is likely."

"We've got company," said Ro turning round to face Arlen and Eryn.

"Get your gear, Eryn, it's time to leave. I think remaining in this village will be detrimental to our health," said Arlen before suddenly lunging forward and burying his sword deep inside a Salandori warrior who had appeared through the rows of tents. His place was soon taken by another three.

After a few seconds hesitation, Eryn reached for his own sword, a sword given to him by his uncle and which had been wielded by his father in many famous battles over the years. Now it was Eryn's and it was time for him to live up to its history.

The fight was brief and in a very short space of time, another three Salandori warriors lay dead at their feet, each of the three friends having accounted for one, though Eryn had taken longer to despatch his adversary than his friends. More were coming though; many more.

"Do you remember where they put the horses, Ro?" asked Arlen slowly backing away towards his friends as a large crowd of Salandori closed in on them.

"I do," replied Eryn. "Unless they've moved them since, they were tethered just over there." He had nodded with his head to indicate the direction, but neither Arlen nor Ro had looked, both unwilling to take their eyes off the large group of warriors edging their way ever closer.

"You go and get the horses ready whilst Ro and I try to hold them off, Eryn, but watch your back," said Arlen.

"That's our plan?" asked Ro without looking at his friend.

"Best I could do in the circumstances. You have a better one?"

"As it happens I do." Even as he was talking Ro had quickly sheathed his short sword and was now quickly drawing his large broadsword. "Ready?"

"For what?" asked Arlen anxiously.

"For this." Ro suddenly raced towards the Salandori, his sword raised high over his right shoulder in both hands.

Some of the Salandori, but not all Arlen noticed, stepped forward to meet Ro's attack. One of them, a large man dressed almost entirely in black save for his white sash, moved ahead of the others, his sword poised to strike. Using every ounce of strength that he had, Ro brought his sword down in a diagonal sweep, brushing aside the other man's sword before continuing its journey on into flesh and bone.

For the briefest of moments everything seemed to stop as all eyes turned to the large warrior who was gazing at Ro in wide-eyed disbelief, his expression frozen on his face. Then ever so slowly the top half of his body began to slide away before toppling to the sand in a mass of entrails and blood. The man's legs remained grotesquely upright for a few seconds longer, blood spewing out in a couple of bright red jets, before they too eventually toppled to the ground.

The Salandori standing behind their dismembered

comrade looked on in horror first at the dead warrior then at the blood splattered Remadan who had wielded the terrible weapon. When his gaze turned to them their resolve began to weaken. When he suddenly roared and raced towards them with his sword poised to strike again, it broke and as one they turned and fled, trampling one another as they did so.

Arlen picked up his friend's cue and launched himself at the fleeing men, slicing and hacking at their backs as they ran. The Salandori were petrified, dashing everywhere and anywhere in an effort to evade the blade of the huge sword. Both Ro and Arlen knew that the effect would be short-lived and that eventually the Salandori would come to their senses and rally. Then secure in the knowledge that overwhelming numbers would win the day, they would fight back, but for the moment, fear clouded their judgement.

Ro was already tiring from swinging the huge sword, but it had had the desired effect and as he finally came to a stop and called over to Arlen to do the same, he noticed something on the ground. Lying curled up and favouring his right arm which had presumably been trampled on when he was knocked over, was Nestor, chief of the tribe.

Ro quickly sheathed his larger sword and once again drew his smaller one. He placed the point at the chief's neck and gestured for him to get up, which after a moment or two's hesitation he did. About thirty or so paces away, another warrior dressed almost entirely in black, seemed to be rallying the men around him with the liberal use of shouts and blows from the back of his hand. Slowly but surely and with a varying level of enthusiasm, the Salandori were re-forming.

"It was a nice try, Ro, but unless Eryn's located our horses, we're in a bit of trouble," said Arlen his eyes never leaving the Salandori who were starting to reluctantly inch forward.

"And you say that I'm the master of understatement," replied Ro.

Arlen glanced at his friend only then noticing that he had a prisoner by the scruff of the neck. "What've you got there, Ro? This is no time to be collecting souvenirs."

"What this? Just a little something I picked up."

"Is that the chief?" asked Arlen incredulously. The Salandori had closed to within ten or twelve paces and had noted that Ro's mighty sword had once again been slung across his back. Some of them looked relieved.

"It is."

"Do you not think that you holding a sword point to his throat is likely to upset them a little?"

"I'm counting on it," replied Ro smiling wryly.

"Then we are truly dead."

The tribesmen had inched even closer and were eyeing the two men menacingly.

"No, I don't think so. He's our bargaining chip out of here."

Perok, the chief's son suddenly appeared at the front of the crowd and bellowed for his men who had become increasingly voluble as their bravado rose, to be silent. Then he glared over at Ro and Arlen.

"I invite you into my camp and offer you our hospitality and you thank me by killing my people and taking my father hostage? You usurpers are dishonourable scum."

"Do not speak to me of honour, Perok. Your father and his men tried to have us murdered in our sleep," replied Ro.

Perok looked genuinely surprised. He glanced at his father and spoke rapidly in his own tongue and then his father nodded apparently confirming Ro's allegation.

"I did not know of this and offer you my apologies. You are after all my guests."

"I think it's a little late for apologies, Perok, don't you? Or are you going to deny that Teren Rad was here? We found his sword," said Ro.

This time Perok looked annoyed. "Yes, he was here and my father sold him on to another tribe for a good price. I thought it better you did not know the truth so you didn't go getting yourselves killed on some fools' errand to rescue him."

"I think that was our decision to make, not yours." The sound of horses approaching from behind momentarily distracted Ro and he hoped that they were with Eryn and not more armed Salandori on horseback. "Is that you, Eryn?"

"It is," replied Eryn from his position upon one of the horses. The situation below did not look good.

"How many horses have you got with you?" asked Ro.

"Three."

"We're going to need another one. The chief here is coming with us for a while."

"You cannot be serious, Remadan?" said Perok glancing nervously between the three friends.

"Deadly serious," replied Ro.

"If you let my father go now, Remadan, you can leave the same way you arrived – as a guest, but if you try and leave with my father we will hunt you down and your deaths will not be pleasant."

"Now that's the Salandori I know," said Arlen beaming.

"Tell your men to fetch another horse, Perok and not a lame one," ordered Ro.

"No," replied Perok.

Ro sighed and very slightly increased the pressure at the end of his sword drawing a pinprick of blood from the chief's neck. "Are you sure about that?"

Perok's face was one of pure anger and hatred. He locked eyes with the Remadan, but all he could see in them was a steely resolve. This was a man who would be good to his word. Perok barked an order to one of his men and a minute or so later he reappeared leading a fine looking white horse, whose reins he handed over to Arlen.

"You will die for this insult, Remadan. All of you," said Perok.

"So be it." Ro gestured for the chief to mount one of the spare horses and then hurriedly bound his hands first together and then to the pommel of the saddle. When he was secure, he mounted his own horse whilst Arlen watched the chief with a loaded crossbow pointed at his chest. "I guess it is futile to tell you not to follow us, Perok, but know this. If any of your men stray too close, my rotund friend here will use your father for crossbow target practise. Understood?"

Perok nodded sourly. "We will meet again, Remadan."

"You'd better hope not." Then with a last glance round to make sure none of the chief's warriors were preparing to do anything stupid, Ro eased his horse forward followed by

Eryn and then the chief with Arlen alongside him, the crossbow pointedly fixed at the chief's chest.

Despite his threats and apparent confidence, Ro still expected someone to try and attack them as they made their way out of the camp and it was all he could do to gently stroll out when every fibre of his being was screaming at him to run. That would have been a bad move he knew, as it was dark and the Salandori knew the terrain; they'd soon be run down. No, their only hope of survival, of making it out of there alive, was through a show of bravado and confidence.

Praying to every god he knew, Ro forced himself to slowly walk out of the camp and into the all encompassing darkness. Behind him he could hear the sound of men racing to their own horses.

Chapter 13

Jeral Tae hadn't cried since the day his father had beaten him for touching his sword without permission, nearly fifty years ago, but now he felt like sobbing. The hero of so many battles in Remada's recent history, he now found himself skulking in the bushes with a handful of his men, the only survivors as far as he was aware, of the recent battle.

He had known that they were seriously outnumbered by the Delarites, especially after a large number of the civilian levy had been encouraged to desert by that maggot Pular Bratak, but still his pride had insisted that they stand and face the enemy. Now that pride had led to the virtual destruction of his army and the death of many of his friends and neighbours. Worse still, as far as he knew, his had been the only Remadan army left in the northern sector, which meant that the marauding Delarites now had a clear run at the country's hinterland.

The handful of men with him now was all that remained of the small force that had managed to disengage and then retreat from the battle. That they were able to do that was only thanks to the sacrifice of a small force of men who had volunteered to remain behind and hold the enemy off. The bravery of Sergeant Renus and the other volunteers brought a lump to his throat making it hard to swallow. The guilt and shame were almost too much to bear, but Jeral found himself smiling when he remembered Sergeant Renus's last words.

I'm too damned fat and old to go running about the countryside, so if it's all the same to you, General, I think I'll stay here with a few of the lads.

Well he had minded. Jeral had wanted to stay behind and lead the rearguard troops himself, but Renus and the remaining officers had insisted that he leave. He was too important to the overall war effort to die in some northern field in what would be a futile gesture they had said.

Reluctantly he had acquiesced and had led the retreating troops, but even that had not gone as planned. Just when they thought that they'd managed to successfully disengage from the battle and would live to fight another day, they'd run into an advancing Cardellan cavalry unit. The last Jeral had heard the Cardellans were content to just invade and hold the west of the country and weren't supposed to be this far to the east or north, but there they were. It had been a chance encounter, but a costly one. Strung out in a line the Remadans had been an easy target for the armoured cavalry and Jeral's men had been cut to pieces. Worse still, the Cardellans had made off with the Ligara's standard; the ultimate shame for a commanding officer.

Jeral sighed as he relived the moment the young lad to his left had been run through with a lance before the Cardellan had snatched the standard from the his dying hands. The look of shock and sadness on the boy's face would live with Jeral forever.

"What do you think, General?" Jeral's brain registered the words but not their meaning. "General?"

Jeral finally turned to face whoever had spoken and saw a young man of no more than twenty years of age looking expectantly back at him. He wore the stripes of a captain and had obviously graduated from the Officer Academy with flying colours to have made the rank of captain at his age. Still, Remadan army officers seemed to be getting younger all the time.

Or perhaps it's just that you're getting older all the time, his mind taunted.

There was no substitute for battle experience in Jeral's opinion. True, the lad had just lived through one murderous conflagration, but he still undoubtedly had a lot to learn.

"Sorry, what did you say, Captain?" asked Jeral.

"I was just wondering whether you thought we should enter the town, General, or whether we should skirt round it."

Jeral turned from the young captain and stroked his long moustache as he stared down at the town below. As far as he could tell from his position concealed in the trees just to the north of the town, Ederik had not yet been touched by the war, despite the presence of enemy soldiers, both Delarite and Cardellan all around it.

It wasn't a military town and didn't possess a garrison or

even a local militia and consequently didn't pose a threat to the invading armies, but Jeral was still surprised that the Delarites had not moved to occupy it.

Perhaps they are aware what a cesspit of humanity the place is and don't think it's worth their time bothering with.

The town was well-known to be infested with every type of lowlife there was, from thieves, rapists, to smugglers and murderers. It was also home to a large number of whorehouses. If someone wanted to hide out without fear of being bothered by the authorities, then Ederik was where they went. It was a haven for the worst kind of scum.

Pity the Delarites don't come here and kill the whole rotten lot of them.

Jeral instantly regretted that thought. Not everyone in the town could be bad. In fact most would probably be decent law-abiding citizens given the chance, but whilst the town was virtually run by the thugs and the scum, they would never be given that chance.

Jeral suddenly realised that the young officer was still staring at him expecting an answer.

"We're going in, Captain. There doesn't appear to be any sign of enemy troops, at least from what I can see from here. We'll go in, commandeer some horses and ride south until we come across some friendly faces."

"Ederik is a Remadan town, sir. Surely we'll find friendly faces in there?"

"Remadans yes, friendly, no. You've a lot to learn, Captain," said Jeral glancing around him at the small group of survivors. "We'll need to get out of these uniforms too otherwise we'll stick out like a virgin in a whorehouse."

"Surely when the people of Ederik see our uniforms they'll want to help us?" protested the captain.

"Where are you from, son?" asked Jeral.

"Cardoza, near the Laryssan border," replied the captain.

"That probably explains your naivety about Ederik then. That town is full of the worst scum in the known world. Yes it is a Remadan town, but it is home to men from many countries but who hold allegiance with none. Their only loyalty is to themselves and they would sell you out as quickly as look at you. When we get in there, hopefully we won't have to interact with too many people and those that we do, we'll probably have to kill. Trust no one but the man by your side. Understand?" The young captain nodded dutifully, but looked shocked. Obviously the thought of having to kill some of his own countrymen did not sit well with him. "Prepare the men to move out, Captain."

The captain still looked worried, but to his credit he immediately shuffled off to carry out his general's orders. Jeral stared down into the village and offered a silent prayer to Sulat. The captain was right, the sensible thing would be to skirt round the town and avoid running into any Delarite soldiers, but to do so would mean continuing to travel on foot and in their uniforms, neither of which was very appealing. On the other hand a group of armed men in army uniforms was also going to draw unwanted attention when they entered the town.

"The men are ready, sir," said the captain as he slid in alongside the general again.

"That's good, Captain, but there's been a change of plan."

"We're going to go round the town?" asked the captain hopefully.

"No, but neither are we all going to go in there. A small party comprising me, you and three men you trust, will go in, acquire some clothes and horses and then get the Kaden out of there. Then we'll give the town the wide berth you're craving."

It was a compromise and probably the best he was going to get the captain realised. "Choose your men and meet me back here in a few minutes. I'll brief Captain Baradir on the plan as he'll be in charge of the remaining men whilst we're away," said Jeral.

The captain nodded and for a moment Jeral thought the young officer was going to bother saluting, but then he seemed to think better of it and slipped away to choose three men for the mission.

Perhaps there's hope for him after all.

It was mid-afternoon by the time they were ready to make their move. To try and hide their identity a little they'd all removed their tunics and those who still possessed them had taken off their caps, but their trousers still marked them down as army men. Unfortunately, there was nothing that could be done about that. As a further precaution, the men had been ordered to leave their swords behind and instead were only allowed to carry concealed daggers. None had been particularly happy with that order, but they did understand the logic. Bad enough five strangers turning up wearing army trousers, but if they were all seen carrying army swords, the game would be up for sure. The cover story they'd decided on was that they were deserters from one of the northern garrisons and had killed their officers before slipping away in the night. Jeral hoped that they wouldn't have to explain themselves to anyone, but if they did that was the kind of cover story which the people of Ederik would buy.

One by one and from different directions, the five men tried to sidle into the town unnoticed, some more successfully than others They had identified and agreed upon a rendezvous point before setting off and now without trying to draw too much attention to themselves, they all made their way towards it.

"Any trouble?" asked Jeral as he arrived at the meeting point, noticing that it had turned out to be some sort of disused barn.

"One or two inquisitive looks, sir, but other than that, no bother," replied the captain. The three other men all nodded their agreement.

"Excellent. There seemed to be some sort of store just back that way a bit and I'd guess we'd be able to get our hands on some civilian clothes in there. We might also find some other provisions, which could come in useful on our journey, so keep your eyes open."

"Me and Jared will go and... borrow some stuff from there, sir," said one of the three soldiers. Jeral remembered that his name was Roviliak and was a career soldier. Not an exemplary soldier, but a career soldier who knew how to live off the land and how to make the most of a bad situation.

"Very well. Did anyone notice the stables?" asked Jeral.

"I passed them on my way in, General; they're just over there and they looked like they were chock full of horses," said the third soldier whom Jeral didn't recognise, as he pointed down the road.

"Good. Captain, you and Trooper...?"

"Otix, sir," replied the soldier.

"You and Trooper Otix go and ready as many horses as you can. There may not be enough for all the men, so we might have to double up, but do what you can," said Jeral beginning to feel like they might actually get away with their little foray into the town after all.

"Where will you be, sir?" asked the captain.

"I'm just going to poke around a little to see what I can find out. We'll meet over at the stables in what, fifteen minutes?"

The others all looked at one another silently debating whether that would be enough time to perform their allotted tasks. Eventually they all nodded their agreement, before slipping away as discretely as possible.

Jeral watched them all depart making sure that they weren't being watched or worse still followed. A disinterested middle-aged woman hurried past without so much as looking up at him and then a drunk stumbled by. Jeral gave him a cheery wave and the man stared at him briefly before returning the gesture and continuing on his way.

When the man had disappeared out of sight, Jeral began to cautiously make his way down what he took to be the town's main street, ducking into doorways and shadows whenever the sound of approaching footsteps or conversation reached his ears.

The town was pretty much as he had expected, full of drunks, miscreants and whores. As far as Jeral was concerned it was also full of young Remadan men who should have been wearing a uniform. Although there didn't seem to be much in the way of commerce in the main street, save for the general store he had seen earlier and a blacksmiths, it was a bustling town. What the place lacked in terms of shops and tradesmen, it more than made up for with taverns and whorehouses. If you were looking to trade your goods or perhaps stock up for winter, you were probably out of luck in Ederik, but if you were looking to get blind drunk and then rut to your heart's content, you'd definitely come to the right place.

When he was convinced there was nothing more to be

learned by loitering there any longer, Jeral made to leave when suddenly two men wearing Delarite uniforms, rounded the corner.

Jeral melted back into the shadows and watched them. For a moment or two it looked like they were making their way over to the stables, but an invitation from a particularly buxom redhead dressed in next to nothing seemed to lead to a change of heart. Jeral let out a breath he hadn't realised that he'd been holding onto.

He watched the two soldiers enter a nearby house, each one walking arm in arm with the redhead. Then when he was sure they were safely preoccupied and unlikely to appear again for a while, he absent-mindedly stepped into the street and started to make his way over to the stables. He had not gone very far when somebody called to him from behind. It wasn't a voice he recognised and Jeral froze debating what to do.

"Can you spare a few coins for a thirsty traveller, friend?" asked the voice.

The way the words had been slurred Jeral doubted very much that the man was thirsty. He had no doubt, however, that the man was not his friend. He didn't turn round.

"Hey, I'm talking to you." The man's tone had turned decidedly aggressive. "If you don't turn round and answer me I might just decide to take all your money, old man."

Jeral's anger was rising and every fibre of his being screamed at him to turn round and teach this loudmouth some manners. His head, however, told him that such an action would serve no purpose other than to draw unwanted attention. Instead, he bit back his retort, fixed a smile to his face and slowly turned. The other man was grinning with triumph but as recognition slowly dawned through the haze of drunkenness, the grin dropped away. Now he stood open-mouthed and staring at Jeral, first with a look of surprise and then with a look of terror.

Jeral's own smile had vanished as he recognised one of Pular Bratak's cronies from the village of Lentor. Jeral didn't know the man's name, but his face was indelibly etched in his memory. This had been the man who had drawn a knife and threatened Jeral during the village meeting the night after the raiders attacked their village. Jeral had been trying to inform the villagers about the casualties and damage and all Bratak and his cronies had done was to heckle him. It had finally erupted into a confrontation where this man had drawn a knife and gone for Eryn, but the village blacksmith, Rom Tagral had stepped in and disarmed him. Jeral had vowed that night that one day he would have his revenge on Bratak and his men. It seemed that day had finally come, at least for one of them. To make matters worse as far as Jeral was concerned; he was also one of the deserters who had fled from Jeral's camp on the eve of the recent battle.

"You?" stuttered the man as he slowly started to back away from Jeral, the virtually empty flagon of ale he was holding, dropping from his shaking hands and smashing on the ground below.

"Come here you cowardly scum," snarled Jeral, as he closed on the man, all thoughts of needing to remain inconspicuous being pushed to one side by his need for justice. Justice for the men who had stayed at their post and died. Men like Sergeant Renus, Jeral's friend.

The man continued to back away, continually glancing over his shoulder in the hope that Bratak or some of the others might be around. Jeral was so angry he too was hoping that Bratak and the rest of them would show. Today was as good as any other for a reckoning as far as he was concerned.

The look on the old general's face left the other man in no doubt that Jeral intended to kill him. With no sign of anyone coming to his aid, the man turned to make a run for it, but was suddenly floored by a blow to the back of his left knee. The man hit the ground hard, but knew that he couldn't languish there. He tried to struggle to his feet but suddenly found himself being dragged there instead. For a brief second he found himself almost dangling in mid-air staring into the general's face, but then Jeral jerked his head back slightly before bringing it hurtling forward to connect with the bridge of the man's nose.

There was a sickening cracking noise and Jeral felt something wet splatter his face. A split second later Jeral let go of the man and recoiled holding his head, suddenly wondering whether his head butt had done more damage to himself than his adversary. When he finally managed to cope with the sharp pain and the feeling of nausea, he opened his eyes and saw the stricken man kneeling on the ground clutching at his bloody face. The man was howling with pain and the noise was starting to draw the curious attentions of a few passers-by. His anger not quite satiated, Jeral took two large strides over to where the man was kneeling before planting a hefty kick to the side of the man's face.

The deserter instantly collapsed to the ground silent. Jeral looked down at the prostrate man and wondered whether he'd just killed him. He certainly hoped he had. If he hadn't, one thing was for certain; he wasn't going to look pretty any time soon and was going to wake up with the mother of all headaches. That was a pleasing thought and Jeral suddenly found himself considering the possibility that he would actually prefer that outcome.

Some of the onlookers were starting to cautiously make their way over to where the stricken man lay. With a last grunt of satisfaction, Jeral turned and began to make his way down the street towards the stables, a small crowd of people gathering around the other man as he went. Jeral cursed his luck. Out of all the people to run into it had to be one of Bratak's men. Well now they needed to get out of town and quickly in case some of the man's friends came looking, or worse still, a squad of Delarite troopers.

The stable doors were open as he approached them, but there was no immediate sign of the captain or the three soldiers. The incident with Bratak's man had rattled him and he tried to convince his imagination that everything was okay and that the men were concealed within the stables, doing exactly what he'd told them to do. Unfortunately, as soon as he turned and entered the stables, he knew that he'd been mistaken and something was very amiss.

Standing with their backs to him was a group of perhaps six or seven men in civilian clothes. Several of them were kicking and stamping on something and it was only when they parted slightly that Jeral could see that it was Trooper Otix. His face was bloody and swollen and even his mother would have had trouble recognising him. The captain was sat on a bale of hay whilst a brute of a man held a knife close to his throat as he enjoyed the spectacle before him.

Jeral realised that if he was to be able to help his men he had to make the element of surprise work in his favour and that meant acting quickly. His right hand reached across for his sword but ended up grasping nothing but thin air. Cursing his own order to leave their swords behind, Jeral glanced around looking for a substitute weapon, his gaze finally falling on a pitchfork leaning against a railing to his right.

Trooper Otix had stopped groaning his mind finally succumbing to the hail of blows being inflicted on his body. Jeral hoped the soldier was just unconscious, but feared the worst. Quietly lifting the pitchfork with both hands Jeral thrust the twin points deep into the back of one of the men who had been kicking Otix.

The man made no noise and for a few seconds none of his comrades seemed to notice what had happened to their friend until finally, the one holding a knife to the captain's throat saw the two prongs sticking out of his friend's abdomen. Bright red circles were rapidly spreading around them. He instinctively pointed at their stricken comrade with the hand holding the knife, but before he could shout a warning, the captain had leapt to his feet and kneed the man in the small of the back. The man dropped the knife and arched his back, reaching behind him with both hands. In one almost fluid movement, the captain then kicked the man behind his right knee before reaching down and grabbing the knife the man had dropped. Then with all the force he could muster the captain buried the knife deep in the right hand side of the man's neck.

Whilst the attention of the remaining men had been drawn to the captain's exploits, Jeral had moved swiftly. First he used his knife to stab one man in the back before yanking another man's head back by the hair and then slicing his throat open.

Faced with an assault from both sides, the three remaining men fumbled for their own weapons whilst desperately looking for a way out. Two turned to face Jeral whilst the other one confronted the captain.

Jeral looked into each man's eyes searching for their intentions. One man was frightened witless and would do anything to save his own skin, including sacrificing his friend, but the other looked like he was prepared to fight if he had to. Jeral would go for him first. Before Jeral could make his move though, the man suddenly lunged at him, slicing his blade through the air in an arc. Jeral had not been expecting the move and although he'd reacted quickly, the blade had still traced a path across the forearm he'd instinctively raised for protection.

Both men looked at the thin line of blood that appeared moments later, one with triumph, the other with anger. Emboldened with his early success, the attacker swung wildly twice more trying to open up Jeral's throat, but the swings were wild and this time Jeral had anticipated them. The other man had started to work his way round Jeral's right side, though whether he was planning on attacking Jeral's flank or was merely trying to make a run for it, he didn't know.

A few paces in front of him the captain and his attacker were in some sort of deathly embrace and one of them had just grunted loudly with pain, though which one it had been Jeral couldn't tell.

The large man facing Jeral had changed the grip on his knife so that he was now holding it point down, clearly intending on stabbing down into Jeral's neck or chest. He was grinning, grinning like a man who thought he had the fight won, but Jeral knew he was wrong. The man's over-confidence would be the end of him.

With a speed that almost caught Jeral by surprise, the man brought the knife down in a vicious arc which had it made contact with its intended target, would probably have plunged right in to the hilt. Luckily Jeral had again reacted just in time leaning back at the last moment so that the tip of the blade whistled through the air just in front of him. Seeing that the man was slightly off balance, Jeral punched him square on the jaw with his left fist, before instantly following up with a similar blow from his left elbow. The man staggered back a couple of paces reeling from the blows, but still had the presence of mind to hold onto his knife.

Jeral's left hand hurt like Kaden. The last time he had punched somebody it had been Eryn on the day of the raid on the village. The lad had been hot-headed and desperate to immediately ride out after the raiders and the only way Jeral had been able to stop him was by knocking him out. It had hurt like Kaden then and Jeral was sure that he'd vowed never to punch anyone again for that very reason. Some people never learned it seemed.

The man wiped the blood from his broken nose and split lip with the back of his hand, a look of anger flashing across his face.

"You're going to pay for that, old man," he snarled as he adjusted the grip on his knife.

Jeral followed suit and turned sideways onto the man making himself a smaller target.

The man took one pace towards Jeral and then stopped a look of confusion on his face. His body suddenly jerked not once but twice and he slowly turned to look behind him. As he did so, Jeral could see the two red marks in the man's back where the captain had stabbed him, evidently having successfully despatched his own adversary.

Somehow the man remained standing and still had some fight left in him, much to the captain's surprise. He grabbed hold of the captain's throat with his left hand and squeezed tightly as he raised the knife in his right hand to deliver the killing blow. Jeral rushed forward grabbed the man by his long greasy hair and yanked his head back before thrusting his own knife deep into the man's right eye. For a few dreadful seconds Jeral thought that the man had survived even that, but then he felt his body go limp and released him where he crumpled to the ground dead.

"Thank you, General," said the captain massaging his injured throat and looking down at his dead adversary.

"You're welcome, Captain. What happened?"

"We had made our way discretely to the stables and were just in the process of saddling some of them, when these men came in laughing and shouting, dragging two young girls behind them. We went to investigate and save the girls and it turned ugly. I think they must have been part of our civilian levy that deserted because they seemed to recognise me. They told Trooper Otix to leave as they only had a problem with officers, but he refused, shouted for me to run and then launched into them. Bravest thing I've ever seen. They overpowered us both and the rest you know. Were they our men?"

"They reluctantly marched beside us, but I doubt they were ever truly our men. Cowardly scum is what they were." A sudden thought crossed Jeral's mind. "There were six of them; what happened to the other one?"

"He ran," replied the captain.

Jeral nodded when he remembered the second man who had been facing him and who had sidled past when the opportunity arose.

"Then we must be quick in case he returns with friends. How is Otix?"

The captain knelt down beside their fallen comrade and placed two fingers on his neck feeling for a pulse. After a few seconds he removed his fingers, looked up at Jeral and gently shook his head.

"His bravery and deeds this day will not be forgotten," said Jeral.

The captain and Jeral both whirled round when they heard the sound of footsteps behind them, but instead of another group of angry citizens, their gaze fell upon their other two comrades. The two men looked from the officers to the dead bodies scattered across the ground.

"Been making friends again, General?" said Roviliak.

The captain bristled at the impertinent way the soldier had addressed his commanding officer, but Jeral didn't seem to take offence and instead smiled acknowledging the man's humour.

"Always pays to get the locals on board, trooper, you know that."

Roviliak nodded back. "That being so, sir, I think we should..." His words were suddenly cut short as his body lurched violently forward as the point of a lance appeared from his abdomen. He glanced down at the obscene appendage, held out an arm towards his officer and then collapsed to the ground dead. Behind him the two officers could see a large angry crowd of men heading their way led by Pular Bratak.

"Time to go, I think, General," said the captain as he

handed him the reins of one of the horses they'd managed to saddle whilst holding the reins for two others.

The crowd outside was getting larger and at the rear now, Jeral could see a couple of Delarite soldiers.

"We won't all make it. You and Trooper Jared mount up and get back to the others, then get as far away from here as you can. You'll have to find horses for the others elsewhere," said Jeral.

"I'm not leaving you here, General. Quickly, mount up and we'll all go," pleaded the captain.

"There's no time to argue, Captain. You and Jared are to go now, that's an order." The captain still hesitated. "Now, Captain!"

With one last desperate look at the mob which was slowly crossing the dirt track towards them, the captain nodded to Jared and both men climbed upon the horses. The captain sat bolt upright in his horse and saluted.

"May Sulat protect you, Captain," said Jeral returning the salute.

"I leave Sulat to watch over you, sir."

Jeral nodded and then slapped the horse on the flank and it raced out of the barn followed by the horse carrying Trooper Jared. The emergence of the two horses briefly distracted the majority of the approaching mob and it gave Jeral the time he needed to arm himself. He pulled the pitchfork out of the back of the man he'd earlier run through and gripped it firmly in his right hand after tucking its shaft under his armpit. Then after pulling his knife out of his last victim's eye, trying not to gag at the sucking sound it made, he clutched that in his left hand. They were not his weapons of choice, but beggars couldn't be choosers; they would have to do.

By the time he'd gathered his weapons and readied his grip, most of the mob was waiting for him in a semi-circle in the bright afternoon sunshine, jeering and shouting because they knew they had their quarry trapped. To their left another group of men were hacking and slicing away at someone on the ground as a riderless horse bolted down the street. Jeral couldn't see whether it was the captain or Jared that had been brought down, but whoever it was he prayed that their death had been quick and painless and that the mob were now just venting their fury on a lifeless body.

Jeral smiled, adjusted the grip on his makeshift weapons and stepped out into the street to confront the mob, at the front of which stood the sneering face of Pular Bratak. If he could have just one wish at that moment in time it would have been to hold his sword one last time. The damage he could inflict on these men with the proper tools was immeasurable compared to what he'd be able to do with an oversized toothpick and a knife.

Still, I won't die easy.

Unnerved by the courage and apparent confidence of this fierce looking warrior, the mob took a step back making Jeral grin even more.

"Which one of you whoreson pieces of scum wants to die first?" Nobody moved at all. "That's what I thought. You're all cowards. Too scared to stand and face the Delarites and too scared to face me. You're nothing more than gutless latrine rats which sprung from the loins of pox-ridden one-coin whores."

"Get him," shouted Bratak, but nobody moved. "Kill him," he screamed, but when nobody moved he suddenly shoved the man to his right towards Jeral.

The man stumbled forward desperate to arrest his momentum before he got too close to Jeral, but it was already too late. With a minimum of effort Jeral thrust the pitchfork into the man's stomach, resisting the urge to give it a vicious twist lest its prongs got caught up in the man's intestines. The man dropped to the ground dead.

Taking their lead from Bratak, people in the second row of the mob began to shove those in front of them towards Jeral until eventually the mob's bloodlust was up and they all swarmed towards him. All except Bratak and his closest friends who remained standing where they were grinning and watching the much-hated general as he tried to fend off the angry mob with a cumbersome pitchfork and a knife.

Bratak wasn't surprised to see the old general make a proper fight of it despite his predicament and the ground was soon covered with several dead or injured bodies. It was only a matter of time though before sheer weight of numbers told and even as he looked on, the general was felled with a mighty roar. He hit the ground hard taking at least two other men with him and then disappeared under a barrage of blows.

Bratak waited until he was sure Jeral was either dead or at least close to it, before shouting for the crowd to stop, but even then some of them continued raining kicks and punches down on the old man's body. After Bratak and one of his friends man-handled the last attacker off Jeral's body Bratak stood looking down at his old adversary and for a moment felt a pang of guilt. The man had been, *was,* a hero to his country. He'd also been a thorn in Bratak's side for years.

Jeral was still alive Bratak could see, though the shallow rise and fall of his chest suggested that he had perhaps only moments to live. His eyes were closed, his face and body a mass of cuts and abrasions. In his left hand he still clung to the knife with which he had despatched or wounded several of the mob. It was fitting that he should die with a weapon in his hand and Bratak would not deny the man that one small grace.

Smiling and taking out his own knife, Bratak crouched down beside the barely breathing general.

"Well, General, it looks like I win this one and all your threats on the night of the village meeting in Lentor, came to nothing. Don't worry though, me and the boys will take good care of your precious village, once we've slaughtered your friends, the other village elders. We're going to tear down everything you strove to build in that village and we're going to do what we like to who we like." He chuckled evilly to himself and toyed with his knife. He had no idea whether the general could hear him, but it cheered him to think so. "Time for you to go, General." Bratak raised his knife above his shoulder and was about to bring it plunging down, when the general's eyes suddenly shot open. He had been partially feigning his weakened state.

Quick as a flash, Jeral slashed his knife across Bratak's face cutting him from the forehead through his right eye and down into his cheek. Bratak howled with pain. Now was the time for Jeral to make his move if he had the strength, but he didn't. He had known that the arrogant little Bratak would want to deliver the killing blow but only after he was certain that Jeral no longer posed a threat, so he had deliberately feigned the extent of his injuries until such time as Bratak exposed himself. He was dying of that there was no doubt; he just hoped that whatever damage he'd inflicted on Bratak was fatal. Now he closed his eyes and lay back in the sand again and awaited death. Bratak was still howling with pain, but soon the adrenaline coursing through him would get hold and Bratak would strike back.

The faces of his old friends, Kam Martel and Sergeant Renus floated through his mind just as the first of many blows from Bratak's knife pierced his chest. Jeral only felt the first couple and after that he could no longer feel anything as he slowly floated up to the waiting embrace of his two friends.

Bratak clutched at his ruined eye and howled with pain once again as two of his friends helped him to his feet. Behind them some sort of commotion was erupting and they could hear many angry sounding voices.

"Delarites, Pular; we've got to go," said one of the men holding Bratak's arms and even as he spoke, he and his comrade were dragging Bratak away into an alley.

Behind them the commotion had developed into a minor altercation as some of the mob that had been with Bratak took offence at being shoved out of the way by the arrogant Delarites.

Bratak was no longer howling and instead was sobbing pitifully. It was all the men with him could do not to vomit such was the extent of the injury to Bratak's face. They continued to lead him away towards the tavern where they knew the town's doctor would be steadily drinking himself to oblivion. He would know what to do provided that he wasn't already drunk.

They could hear a Delarite officer shouting in anger now, clearly outraged that he had been denied the opportunity to interrogate one of Remada's ruling body and he was taking his anger out on the Remadan civilians around him. Some of them tried to fight back against the heavily armoured soldiers, whilst most were content to just try and melt away to safety. Several Remadan civilians were lying on the ground now and one of the Delarite soldiers had also been brought down and things were getting decidedly ugly. It was the chance the men with Bratak had needed and after covering Bratak's head with a blanket they found hanging on a line, they hurriedly dragged him away from the Delarites.

Either by chance or by being extremely attentive, the Delarite officer somehow spotted the three men trying to skulk away. Suspecting that these were probably the men responsible for denying him the chance to interrogate the Remadan officer, the Delarite captain began barking orders to his men to give chase. The mob took advantage of the soldiers' momentary distraction. Seeing this as their best opportunity to make an escape, some of them lashed out felling some of the soldiers including the captain before dispersing in all directions. Some did manage to escape, but others were cut down from behind as the vengeful Delarites got to their feet quicker than expected. By the time that the Delarite captain had resumed control of the situation, Bratak and his two companions were no longer in sight and the ground was covered in dead Remadans.

The Delarite captain cursed loudly then swiftly beheaded a Remadan man who had been knocked to the floor in the melee and who was only now managing to struggle to his feet. Such was the power of the stroke that the head hit the ground hard, bounced once and then rolled a few paces away. The Delarite captain grunted with satisfaction and seeing that the fight was over sheathed his sword. Then almost as an afterthought, he strode over to where the man's head lay and then kicked it as hard as he could down the street, cursing again when he stubbed his toe on the man's hard skull.

**

The Remadan captain had never disobeyed an order in his life, at least not until then. General Tae had ordered him and Trooper Jared to ride back to the men waiting outside the town and then quickly get as far away as they could without looking back. However, after Jared had been hauled from his horse just a few paces from the stable entrance and then beaten to death, the captain had ridden to the end of the street and then stopped. After finding a reasonably concealed position he had then watched as General Tae had strode out and confronted the mob with nothing more than a pitchfork and a dagger. For a minute or so it had looked like the general's bravado would carry the day, but then some fool had gone for the general and the others had followed suit. The general had fought bravely and from what he could see it looked like he had accounted for quite a few of the deserters. Eventually, however, numbers had told and the general had been brought down and killed.

The captain had yearned to ride back at the mob and try and save his general but to do so was probably futile. If he too was killed, which was likely, then the general's and the other men's deaths would have been for nothing.

The captain had been about to turn his horse around and make his way back to the rest of the men when some Delarite soldiers had turned up. He could not hear what was said and even if he could he did not speak Delarite, but he guessed that the officer was angry that he had not been given the opportunity to interrogate a senior Remadan officer. If roles had been reversed, the captain would have felt similarly aggrieved. Someone in the town had presumably told the Delarite captain about the Remadans' presence hoping for a reward. Well these men had certainly got their reward, just not the one they were looking for, because after being denied the chance to question General Tae, the Delarite officer had ordered his men to start killing the Remadan civilians presumably out of spite. Some had managed to get away, but most had been killed. To make matters worse, before the captain had left, the Delarites had started unceremoniously hanging some of the wounded Remadans. Clearly this was a ruthless and vicious officer who was intent on making his point.

Disgusted by the behaviour of a brother officer, the captain made a clicking noise with his tongue and urged his horse out into the main street. Then with a last sorrowful look down at where General Tae's body lay, he saluted and then rode out towards where he knew Captain Baradir and the remaining men were waiting for him.

Chapter 14

Brak had told Teren that the chief of the Alith who was holding them captive had been expecting the arrival of his brother in a couple of days' time. He had also told him that they were sure to be made to fight to entertain his brother's entourage, but that had never happened. Instead they had suddenly and very swiftly packed up camp and headed east. They travelled east for several days and every now and then Teren would think that he recognised a landmark from his time searching for Valla, but he was never quite sure. He estimated that they were not far now from the Narmidian border. The landscape was for the most part harsh and uninviting; vast stretches of sand with occasional lines of barren, rocky mountains. Occasionally the land would be punctuated by a pretty oasis or a small wood that had sprung up around one of the few rivers that dissected this land.

Eventually the caravan arrived at a sprawling camp situated around a large oasis. Brak informed him that it was the camp of the Oti tribe and a regular venue for fights between the two chiefs. It was not a good sign Brak had assured him as the Oti chief possessed a fighter who had never been beaten and who had won many fights. Brak did not know from where the warrior came or how many fights he had won, he just knew that to go up against him was to invite certain death.

The mood amongst the prisoners had become sullen and depressed. Those who had fought before began to worry that perhaps this time their luck was out and they'd be chosen to fight the Oti champion. Most of the newer prisoners were just petrified by the whole thing. Teren, however, was constantly planning. He'd tried to study the guard routines as they watched over their prisoners of a night, but it seemed that they had no fixed routine; some nights three or four would stand guard, whilst others there would only be a couple. Clearly the Salandori believed that the desert was the prisoners' best guard and that no one would be stupid enough to try and escape. There was after all nowhere to go except into an almost endless unforgiving desert.

Their arrogance is going to cost them one day soon, thought Teren as he watched the two less than vigilant guards who were supposed to be keeping watch over them.

The desert held no fears for Teren. After spending five years wandering the great deserts of Salandor, Narmidia and beyond in search of Valla, he was used to the heat and the thirst. No, when he escaped and he would escape, the desert would not defeat him.

One of the two Salandori guards suddenly turned round and caught sight of Teren watching them. He stormed over and tried to poke Teren through the bars of his wooden cage with his spear, but Teren was too quick for him and managed to grab hold of it and started to try and tug it through the bars towards him.

Seeing that his comrade was in trouble and terrified of what the Teah would do to them if he learned that a prisoner had disarmed one of his guards, the other guard rushed over and also tried to poke Teren. Teren tried desperately to repeat his feat of a moment ago, but he was unable to grab the other spear with his left hand. His grip on the first spear had also weakened and the guard managed to finally tug it free of Teren's grasp.

Both guards started to viciously poke and prod Teren with their spear butts until Teren finally managed to scramble back out of range. Annoyed that their sport had been cut short the guards briefly resorted to hurling insults at him in their own guttural language before suddenly stopping and heatedly conversing. Teren didn't understand any of their language despite the time spent in their country, but he was pretty sure that one of them was intent on entering the cage to continue their conversation with Teren. The other one was arguing against it.

Whilst it was a little sooner than he expected and his plans for escape weren't quite complete, Teren hoped that they would both be stupid enough to come in after him. He was willing to embrace any opportunity for freedom whenever it came. He just hoped that when the moment arrived, some of the other prisoners would join him, though he would have to keep a close eye on the Delarite unless he wanted his plans to end with a blade between his shoulder blades.

In the end common sense seemed to prevail and the two guards turned and walked back to their positions. Before he went the one who had seemed intent on entering the cage pointed at Teren and then drew his index finger slowly across his throat, the meaning clear.

Teren smiled at the two guards as they backed away, his insolence further infuriating them and suddenly became aware that someone had come to stand beside him. Teren glanced to his right and saw Brak, the tall, muscular northerner staring out of the cage at the two guards.

"What language would you like me to speak to you in from now on, Teren Rad of Remada?"

"What do you mean what language?" said Teren looking confused. "I understand you perfectly well in the common tongue."

"Then why when I tell you not to do anything to draw attention to yourself, do you do the opposite? Are you in such a hurry to die, because believe me, you won't have long to wait in this place?" said Brak harshly.

"I meant no offence to your advice, Brak, but if I am to die here it will be at a time and in a method of my choosing. I just need to know one thing. When the time comes, will you stand with me?"

Brak stared at the Remadan as he considered his question. In the short time he had been a prisoner of the Salandori, many had talked about escape, he himself harbouring such thoughts when he was first taken, but none had succeeded yet. "Perhaps."

"Good enough," replied Teren.

"I will come with you."

Both men turned to their left to see who had spoken, their gaze falling on a man in his mid-thirties, with short dark hair. He was not big built, but there wasn't an ounce of fat on him, his whole body framed by well-defined muscles. This was a man who looked like he could take care of himself. His face had a friendly, genuine look, but his eyes were hard and suggested a stern resolve.

"Who are you, friend?" asked Teren.

"My name is Garik and I come from Menith Tar on the south western tip of Remada," replied the man.

"Then when the time comes you are very welcome, Garik; it will be good to have a brother Remadan along."

Somebody behind them began to clap and they all turned to see who was mocking them. Teren wasn't surprised to see the Delarite facing them with an almost permanent sneer upon his face. "Well done, Remadan, you've got the makings of your own little revolution, confirming my belief that there are more fools in this world than people realise. You go ahead with your little revolt because there is only one thing I enjoy more than watching a Remadan die and that's watching two Remadans die." He started to laugh to himself drawing a couple of inquisitive glances from the Salandori guards outside.

Brak felt Teren tense next to him and gently grabbed the Remadan's arm, shaking his head slowly when Teren turned to face him.

"Not now, you have antagonised the guards enough for one night. The Delarite's time will come, but it is not now," said Brak as he gently led Teren away to the other side of the cage.

"Maybe not, but it will be soon," said Teren.

"As you wish. Now if you won't take my advice about not drawing attention to yourself, take this advice - get some sleep. I overheard some of the guards talking earlier and whilst I don't profess to understand their language I do know the odd word and today I repeatedly heard the word 'bantu'," said Brak. He lay down on the ground and prepared to sleep.

"'Bantu', what's that mean?" asked Teren as he settled down on the sand next to the northerner.

"Fight," said Brak as he closed his eyes, "it means fight. Some or all of us are going to be forced to fight tomorrow. Now get some sleep. Something tells me that with all the attention you've drawn to yourself, your name will be at the top of the list."

Teren stared at the back of the man's head for a couple of minutes considering everything he had just said and was about to ask another question, when Brak began to snore gently. Teren smiled and shook his head. How the man could get to sleep so quickly in such an uncomfortable environment was beyond him. Still, he himself would have to try, especially if the northerner was right about him being one of them selected to fight tomorrow. He hadn't slept well since he'd been taken captive and he didn't expect that night to be any different, especially as he would have to sleep with one eye open for signs of attack. If the Delarite didn't try and slit his throat during the night there was always the possibility that the guards would come into the cage and beat him. He laughed quietly to himself, rolled over and closed his eyes. He was soon fast asleep.

***

Ro, Arlen, Eryn and their Salandori hostage rode all night, carefully picking their way through the rough Salandori terrain. Eryn did not ask, but he was sure they were constantly heading in an easterly direction. Whether this was the direction Ro suspected the raider had gone with Tayla or whether he'd managed to pick up a trail in the dark that Eryn himself was unaware of, he didn't know; he was just glad to be shot of the Salandori village.

They were being pursued of that there was no doubt and no one in the little party had expected anything less. After all they had just kidnapped the tribal leader and unless Perok was ready to assume the mantle of tribal chief in Nestor's stead and had enough support to make that happen, they would of course try and rescue their chief. Several times Ro had raised his hand to signal for his companions to stop and each time the friends had listened in silence for the sound of their pursuers but had heard nothing. But they were there, Eryn was sure of it. Arlen had told him that the Salandori were excellent riders, were very adept at tracking people across their country and had the ability to mask their own presence.

When Ro signalled for them to stop once again, they all listened intently and for the briefest of moments Eryn thought that he heard the sound of a horse treading on some hard ground, but it was gone as quickly as it had arrived. The expression on Arlen's face and the look he exchanged with

Ro suggested that they had heard it too. Nestor had been gagged to prevent him from calling out and alerting his men to their position, but even in the pale moonlight that now bathed the plain, Eryn could see in the man's eyes that beneath his gag he was grinning. He knew that his men were there and that sooner or later, they would launch their attack and attempt to rescue him. He also knew that his captors could not kill him, not if they wanted to escape with their lives. He was their leverage and consequently they needed to keep him alive. The odds were stacked heavily against them Eryn realised.

Ro signalled to Eryn and Arlen and although Eryn wasn't totally sure what the signal meant, it seemed to suggest that Ro thought there were a number of Salandori on either side of them as well as behind. They were clearly getting ready to spring their trap and Eryn wondered whether they were being driven towards a dead end where they'd be penned in and the Salandori could slaughter them. He reached over and touched the hilt of his sword, its hard feel reassuring. He desperately wanted to draw his weapon or at least check that it was free in its scabbard, but to do so would risk making a noise and that noise could be the difference between life and death.

Ro nudged his horse forward and the others followed, though Nestor delayed his departure as long as he could and only moved when Arlen rode alongside him and pointed his crossbow at the man's groin.

So he's not entirely convinced that we won't kill him, thought Eryn.

They rode for another hour and by then the first vestiges of dawn were just beginning to show. Ro raised his arm once again and rode back to where Eryn and Arlen waited on either side of their Salandori captive.

"If they're going to try and rescue our friend here, then it's going to be soon," said Ro. "If they allow us to reach those mountains over there, their chances are diminished so they've got to make their move as we cross this plain." Ro gestured over his shoulder at the vast plain that stretched out in all directions before them. In the distance, verdant looking mountains, completely different to the rocky barren ones they had seen earlier, rose up on the horizon, a beacon of safety tantalisingly out of the reach of the three tired companions.

Arlen took a swig of water from his flask and turned to look behind him and for the first time set eyes on their pursuers. If they had tried to flank the companions during the night they had now reformed into one group and stood in a huddle perhaps two hundred paces behind them.

"What do you think they're doing?" asked Eryn.

"Probably deciding when exactly to make their move," replied Arlen.

"We don't stand a chance if they attack us out there," said Eryn nodding towards the plain they had to traverse if they wanted to make the mountains.

"We didn't stand much of a chance in their camp either, Eryn, but we survived," said Ro. "Besides, there's not as many of them as I thought."

"Unless the others who were on our flanks during the night have ridden ahead to set a trap," said Arlen.

"I don't think so; we'd be able to see them," replied Ro.

"Could they have made it to the mountains and be waiting for us there?" asked Eryn.

"No, it's too far and besides we would have heard them riding past us during the night," said Ro reassuringly. His gaze suddenly fell on the Salandori chief. "Better give him a drink, Arlen."

"Why waste good water we might need later?" asked Arlen.

"Because it's going to get a lot hotter very rapidly and he'll be no good to us as a hostage if he's dead. Now give him a drink," said Ro sternly.

Arlen seemed to bridle at Ro's tone and it was a few seconds before he responded.

"You pull his gag down, Eryn and give him a drink whilst I keep the crossbow pointed at him."

Eryn reached over and tugged the man's gag down before holding the flask to his mouth. Nestor drank greedily and Eryn had to all but yank it away from their captive. The Salandori chief licked his lips savouring every last drip as he glanced round at his three captors. Then his gaze fell on the small party of his warriors sat atop their horses a short distance away. He smiled cruelly, looked in turn at each of the three men around him and then said something in his own language which obviously amused him.

None of the three friends understood Salandori but each knew what the meaning was. He was telling them that soon they were all going to die.

Nestor suddenly shouted something over at his warriors before bursting into laughter. Behind them, Ro, Arlen and Eryn could hear the other warriors joining in with their own laughter.

"Gag this piece of horse dung quickly, Eryn, before my trigger finger tires and I accidentally release this bolt into his neck," said Arlen.

Eryn wasn't entirely sure that his friend was joking and quickly did as he was asked.

Eryn watched Ro take a large swig of water before returning his flask to his saddlebag and then checking that his weapons were readily accessible. Eryn followed suit sliding what had once been his father's sword in and out of its scabbard a couple of times no longer afraid of the sound it might make.

"Time to make our move I think," said Ro.

"What's the plan then?" asked Arlen.

"There is no plan other than live," replied Ro. "All we can do is try and make it to those mountains. If we get there I fancy our chances of being able to evade these men, better than our chances out in the open anyway."

Arlen glanced over at the plain stretching far into the distance and sighed. "That's some distance you're expecting us to cover whilst under attack, Ro."

"I know, but what other choice do we have?"

"We could stand and fight them here. It's no different to out there other than we won't be so tired and hot as we would be out there," said Arlen, clearly not relishing the prospect of more hours in the saddle followed by a near impossible fight.

"You make a good point, my friend, but it will be just as hot and tiring for them," said Ro.

"I'm not sure these dogs feel the heat," replied Arlen irritably.

"Still glad you decided to come along, Priest of the Golden Tree?" teased Ro.

Arlen smiled, easing the tension which had been building between the two men overnight. "I wouldn't have missed it for the world. Besides, who else is going to watch out for your sorry carcass?"

Ro smiled back relieved that the tension appeared to be evaporating. If he had to die this day he did not want his last words to Arlen to have been spoken in anger. "It is good to know that you are always watching out for me, Arlen. Now one last thing. If any one of us should fall whilst we cross the plain, the others must continue. To stop or turn back is to invite certain death. Do you understand?"

Both Arlen and Eryn looked shocked.

"But..."

"There are no buts, Eryn. If one of us falls, you must leave them and save yourself. Promise me."

Eryn nodded reluctantly.

"Good. Now let's be on our way and may Sulat watch over us all. Eryn, you lead the way."

Eryn nodded and nudged his horse forward towards the plain and Ro made to follow, but Arlen reached out and caught hold of his right arm.

"I get hit you're coming back for me right?" asked Arlen.

Ro smiled. "Of course. That was just for Eryn's benefit; I don't want the boy doing anything stupid."

"Yes of course, I knew that," said Arlen looking relieved.

"Good, now let's go."

"Move you," said Arlen turning Nestor's horse so that it faced the direction they were heading rather than his men following behind. When the chief saw the plain spread out before him for the first time, he seemed to freeze in the saddle, a frightened expression fixed rigidly on his face. Arlen gestured for him to move. When he didn't Arlen lowered the crossbow and pointed it at the man's groin again, but the chief never averted his gaze from the plain ahead of them. Ro noticed that Arlen and their captive hadn't immediately followed him and turned round.

"What's the problem, Arlen?"

"Our friend here seems reluctant to move even when threatened with emasculation. He seems frightened of the plain."

Ro rode up alongside the chief. "You might not understand the common tongue too well, but understand this. Either you move right now or my friend here is going to kill you where you sit and we'll take our chances making a run for it." To reinforce his point Ro pointed at Arlen then at Nestor and then drew a finger across his throat.

The message seemed to get home and the chief tried to say something but they couldn't understand him through his gag. Ro reached forward and pulled it down freeing the man's mouth.

"Alari, Alari," the chief said excitedly as he nodded towards the plain.

"What in Kaden is Alari?" asked Arlen.

"I've no idea but whatever it is he seems reluctant to enter the plain. Something's got him scared," replied Ro. "What is Alari?"

"Alari, Alari," repeated Nestor as if that explained everything.

"We haven't got time for this," said Ro reaching over and pulling the man's gag back up. Then he slapped the chief's horse on the rump and it reluctantly lurched forward closely followed by Arlen. After a last glance behind him at the small cluster of warriors, Ro followed behind them.

Eryn had travelled a fair way before he noticed that his companions were not right behind him, but were in fact some distance back although neither appeared injured. Torn between Ro's instructions to keep going no matter what and concern for his friends, Eryn halted his horse and decided to wait. He'd deal with Ro's anger later. Besides, although the Salandori warriors were following them again, they were not technically under attack and Ro's instructions were not therefore valid. He doubted Ro would interpret the situation quite that way, but that was another matter.

Ro, Arlen and Nestor took a couple of minutes to catch up with him and during that time Eryn had twice thought he saw a plume of sand or dust rising up in the direction which they were heading. Having witnessed one sand storm, he wasn't keen on experiencing another. Whether it would help or hinder their escape he did not know, but Ro or Arlen were sure to know what to do for the best. He glanced back round just as his companions rode alongside him and noted that their pursuers had also entered the plain.

"I told you to keep going, Eryn," said Ro as he pulled up alongside him.

"I know, but we weren't under attack so I thought it would be all right to wait. Besides, I didn't know what to do about that," said Eryn gesturing with his head.

"What is that?" asked Arlen whilst keeping his crossbow pressed into the chief's back. "Another sandstorm?"

"I don't think so," replied Ro.

Nestor who was still gagged was desperately trying to say something which both men assumed was the word 'Alari'.

"What's he saying?" asked Eryn.

"He keeps babbling on about 'Alari' or something," said Arlen as he glanced nervously over his shoulder at their pursuers. They too had stopped, but only after closing the gap by perhaps fifty or so paces. "It must be the Salandori word for sandstorm or something. He was probably trying to warn us."

" 'Alari'?" repeated Eryn.

"That's right," said Ro also noticing that the Salandori warriors had closed the gap. "Does it mean something to you, Eryn?"

"I'm sure I've heard my Uncle Kam mention it before. It might have been someone's name, I don't remember."

"Well whatever it is, I suggest it can wait," said Arlen. "I believe our friends are getting ready to make their move. It seems we're caught between a rock and a sandy place."

Ro glanced over at the Salandori warriors and it did appear that they were readying themselves for an attack. Either they hadn't seen the sandstorm or whatever it was or they didn't care.

"We'll make for whatever that is heading towards us and with luck we'll manage to lose them in it. Are you ready?" asked Ro as he reached over and grabbed the reins of the chief's horse. Arlen and Eryn nodded. "Then let's go," and with that Ro kicked his horse into a gallop towing Nestor, who looked absolutely petrified, behind him. Arlen and Eryn followed close behind.

Chapter 15

Teren woke to the sound of men shouting though he had been in such a deep sleep that it took him a few moments to remember where he was. When he finally came to the first thing his eyes focussed on was the smiling face of the northerner, Brak.

"You slept well for a man with so many cares, my friend," said Brak as he chewed on some less than appetising food. "A good dream was it?"

Teren slowly sat up, flexing his neck as he did so and was rewarded with a satisfying click as one of the joints freed itself.

"It was as it happens. I was in a little Lydian brothel that I was known to frequent when I was younger and was being rewarded for being a loyal customer, and when I say rewarded I mean rewarded." Teren smiled as he wiped away the saliva which had evidently escaped his mouth and pooled in his beard overnight.

"Then it is as well that I managed to grab some food for you whilst you slept; it sounds like you might need some energy," said Brak grinning as he tossed some stale looking bread and a small lump of cheese over to Teren.

Teren looked at the meagre rations before looking back at his friend. "Is this it?"

"You're lucky I managed to get that for you, but if you don't like it please feel free to complain to the cook. I believe it's that fellow over there," said Brak nodding towards a particularly mean looking Salandori scowling outside the cage.

The man's clothes were filthy and it looked to Teren like he hadn't bathed in months, suddenly making Teren wonder about his own appearance.

"Beggars can't be choosers I suppose," said Teren as he tore a chunk of the bread apart and stuffed it into his mouth desperately trying not to think what the Salandori might have been doing immediately before handing out the food rations.

Brak laughed at the faces Teren pulled as he chewed laboriously on the stale bread before hurriedly swallowing it.

"I can see that you are going to fit in around here just fine," said Brak.

"Trust me, my friend, when I say that I am now more determined than ever to escape this pig sty," replied Teren as he swallowed the last of his food. He then reached over and picked up a flagon of warm water and drank greedily.

The men in the cage suddenly all stood up as a small group of Salandori warriors slowly made their way through the throng outside towards their cage.

"Looks like you might get the chance to leave here sooner than you were planning, though perhaps not in the way you intended," said Brak as he watched the Salandori approach the cage.

The three warriors walked right up to the bars and stared at the gaggle of prisoners within, some of whom had tried to melt anonymously back into the crowd and all of whom averted their eyes. All except Teren. Teren took a step forward and stared stoically back at the Salandori warriors a small mocking grin on his face.

"What is he doing?" Garik whispered to Brak. "Didn't you tell him not to draw attention to himself lest he gets picked for the arena?"

"Of course I told him, Garik," said Brak risking a quick glance up, "the trouble is he wasn't ready to listen. Besides, if I'm not mistaken, he is deliberately doing everything he can to get picked."

"Then he has a death wish?"

"No, he has a plan."

"Then he is truly mad," said Garik slowly shaking his head.

There was suddenly an explosion of voices as the Salandori warriors who had grown accustomed to the generally timid and petrified behaviour of their captives, became indignant at the way that Teren stared mockingly in their faces. The commotion had attracted other Salandori warriors to the cage who had become equally enraged. One or two of them were now trying to prod Teren with their spear shafts through the cage bars but he was too nimble for them. When one of them decided to try and prod him with the head of his spear, Teren managed to grab the shaft and yanked it so hard that he sent the Salandori warrior crashing into the cage bars, the sudden jolt causing him to loosen his grip. Teren immediately pulled the spear into the cage and hefted it above his head and made to throw it at the men outside.

Within seconds a number of Salandori warriors had nocked arrows and were aiming at Teren through the gaps in the cage bars, whilst everyone else was screaming at him to drop the spear. Still grinning, Teren continued staring back at the men outside. Brak nervously stepped forward to stand alongside his friend, his eyes never leaving the anxious looking Salandori warriors outside, some of whom looked ready to shoot at any moment.

"I think that you have made your point, Teren. Now before they pepper us both with arrows, why don't you give the nice Salandori their spear back?"

For a moment or two Brak worried that his new friend was going to ignore his advice and provoke the Salandori into action that would only end badly for both he and Teren. Then, just when he was preparing himself for the inevitable pain that a dozen arrows piercing his body would bring, Teren turned the spear around and passed it out through the bars. The Salandori didn't immediately lower their bows and for a moment or two Brak feared that they were going to shoot anyway, but the order never came. Instead after briefly locking eyes with Teren, the warrior who appeared to be in charge, suddenly pointed at Teren and then at another man Brak couldn't see, standing at the back of the cage. After grinning malevolently, the warrior turned and strode off closely followed by the others.

"That was lucky," said Teren grinning. "For a moment there I thought those lads were going to open fire on us. I was only having a bit of fun after all."

Brak shook his head in disgust. "Your bit of fun nearly got us all killed and has certainly got you killed."

"How do you figure that?" asked Teren.

"Because they just selected you to fight this evening. Still think that it was lucky?"

"Oh, yes," replied Teren grinning some more, "very lucky. Who am I fighting?"

"Him over there," said the voice.

Teren turned and saw Garik pointing back at a dark-skinned man who was glaring over at Teren with unbridled hate.

"Who's he?" asked Teren.

"Nobody knows. The Salandori call him *Mutaki,* the wolf. He hasn't said a word since he was captured somewhere to the south. He's a fearsome fighter and has won both of his fights."

"Then it's high time that he lost one then. When do these fights take place?"

"Usually after the evening meal when it's cooler. Nothing helps the chief sleep better than watching a good bloody fight."

"I'm glad that we can be of service," said Teren. "Are the fights always to death?"

"No, not always. Depends what sort of mood the chief is in. Fights between his own men are usually just until he has seen enough blood. Fights between us and prisoners from another camp on the other hand are nearly always to the death. All you can do in either case is fight as hard and as well as you can, because if the chief is displeased with your performance or he thinks that you are deliberately holding back, he is just as likely to have your throat cut as spare your life."

Teren nodded and glanced once again at the mysterious man he was apparently going to have to fight later that evening. The man was still staring at Teren and his expression had not taken on a friendlier disposition.

Whatever you've got to do to survive I suppose, thought Teren as he turned away from the man's cold gaze.

***

The day passed slowly, giving Teren plenty of time to contemplate the fight ahead. Most of the day had been spent trying to hide from the oppressive heat with nothing to do although every now and again one or two of the prisoners would be collected from the cages and set to various tasks like cleaning the latrines, fetching water or seeing to the horses.

As the evening drew near, however, the atmosphere around the camp seemed to change as if an air of excitement and anticipation was building. Groups of Salandori warriors were hurrying about the camp talking animatedly and occasionally glancing over at the cage in which Teren stood watching them. Every now and then money would exchange hands as wagers on who would be the victor in the evening's contest were made.

Teren didn't care about any of that; all he was interested in was how he could turn the situation to his advantage and make good his escape.

"How are you feeling, my friend?" said Brak as he sidled up alongside Teren and stood staring out of the cage towards the makeshift arena which was being constructed.

"I'm fine, Brak; why shouldn't I be?"

"Because you are about to face our mean-looking friend over there; he is not known for his charm or mercy."

Teren gave an almost derisory glance towards the man he'd been informed he was fighting that night before turning back to face the centre of the camp. "I'm not worried about him, Brak and neither should you be. All I'm worried about is these other lads and how I'm going to deal with them."

"You plan on attempting to escape tonight?" spluttered Brak astonished.

"Of course," replied Teren, as if it was the obvious thing to do.

"But even if you beat our glowering friend, how in Kaden do you expect to get past all of the others?"

"I don't know yet; I'm still working on that part."

"Well you'd better work quickly as they will soon be coming for you." Even as Brak spoke a group of Salandori warriors were pushing their way through the throng towards the cage. It was a large group and the men were all heavily armed. "Sooner than you think it appears."

One of the warriors unlocked the gate to the cage and five other warriors quickly headed in and lowered their spears towards the prisoners forcing them back.

"You and you come with me," said one of the warriors pointing at Teren and the dark-skinned man.

Teren's opponent walked straight out through the gate and after a few seconds deliberate hesitation Teren followed.

"Good luck Teren Rad of Remada," said Brak as Teren passed him by. "I hope that if it is your day you die well."

"It's always my day, Brak, but I have no intention of dying I can assure you. I'll see you in a while."

After the gate was once again secured, Teren and the other man were bundled towards the centre of the camp from where a cacophony of noise was rising as men cheered, sang and banged on drums. Clearly the fights were big news and everyone was determined to enjoy themselves.

At the centre of the camp someone had made a makeshift arena, though arena was probably overstating the matter some. An area of sand perhaps twenty paces by twenty paces had been roped off and behind this rope sat dozens of Salandori warriors. Most sat or stood on the sand but others Teren noticed, presumably the chiefs and their senior men, sat on rudimentary chairs which were probably not much more comfortable than the sand, but appearances had to be maintained.

The watching crowd all began to jeer and point when first Teren and then his opponent were pushed into the arena. Teren ignored his opponent for the moment instead studying the crowd around him. On all four sides of the arena the warriors were standing approximately four or five men deep, perhaps more around the chiefs. The chiefs also had several large and fearsome looking warriors standing around them who were wearing distinctive clothes and Teren imagined that these were probably their own personal bodyguards. Whether they were to protect them from outside attacks or were protection from assassination attempts, Teren didn't know and it was something he'd have to give consideration to.

His hastily conceived plan had been to despatch his opponent as quickly as possible, but only if he couldn't persuade him to join him and then fight his way to the horses and ride like Kaden into the desert. It wasn't a very good plan and was fraught with problems, but it was all he had. At that moment in time all he could think about was escaping and going to find his son who had once again been painfully torn from his life.

Teren glanced about him at the multitude of men bearing arms and suddenly realised that the plan was not only ill-conceived and foolhardy, it was damned near suicidal. The only way he was going to escape that camp was if he had some help. He was going to have to wait, plan and recruit. In the meantime, however, he had to survive.

Two Salandori warriors stepped into the arena and dropped a shield and sword at both men's feet. The weapons and shields all looked like they'd seen better days.

"I wouldn't do that if I was you, sonny," said Teren turning to face the chief who owned him. "Because if you give me a weapon I'm as sure as night is dark, going to use it on you."

"Bold talk from a man about to die." It hadn't been the chief who had spoken, but one of the young warriors stood by his side, perhaps a son. "Besides, if you even twitch in a way we don't like, our bowmen will fill you with holes before you even move." To illustrate his point a number of bowmen with nocked arrows suddenly appeared around the arena before slowly melting back into the crowd.

Teren nodded, but was already considering the possibilities.

His opponent leant down and retrieved his sword and shield, his eyes never leaving Teren, who after a few seconds studying the other man picked his up as well.

"What do you say that we turn our weapons on these lads and have some fun?" said Teren as he adjusted his grip on the shield and sword. The other man had begun circling Teren menacingly. "It's got to make more sense than just slaughtering each other for their damned entertainment." The other man suddenly launched himself at Teren shield first before slicing down with his sword. "I guess that means no." Teren easily stopped the other man's shield thrust with his own shield and raised his sword horizontally to block the sword blow, before rolling his wrist and slicing the man across the belly and drawing blood.

The crowd roared with the effortless way the old and

scruffy looking Remadan had drawn first blood against one of the chief's fiercest slaves. They were in for a good fight.

"That's only a flesh wound, sonny, to keep the crowd happy, but if you come at me like that again I can't guarantee that the next one won't be deeper."

The other man launched himself at Teren once more, again leading with his shield before assailing Teren with a combination of cuts and thrusts all of which Teren easily anticipated and blocked. The man was trying Teren's patience.

Feinting with his sword arm, the other man suddenly swung his shield in a flat horizontal arc in an effort to slam its metal rim into Teren's exposed neck. Teren had again anticipated the move and had ducked under the swing, albeit a little slower than he would have liked. Whilst the other man was slightly off balance, Teren sliced his sword across the back of the man's left thigh hamstringing him. His opponent collapsed to his knees howling in pain, but even as he did so he took one last defiant swing at Teren with his sword which Teren swatted away with contempt.

"You're beaten, sonny, but alive; be content with that and don't push it."

The other man snarled at Teren and tried to stagger to his feet, but was unable to do so. Although he didn't understand what they were shouting Teren could tell that the crowd were baying for him to end the other man's life, but Teren wasn't into murder. Instead he turned and began to walk out of the arena as projectiles started to rain down on him from the disgruntled crowd.

Two Salandori warriors stepped forward and blocked his path lowering their spears so that their points were mere inches from Teren's face. Teren glowered at them daring them to make the next move.

"You must kill him," said one of the two warriors in broken common tongue.

"Making me fight for your pleasure is one thing," said Teren, "but I'll not murder a man in cold blood for your amusement. You better either stick me with those things or get out of my way." Even as he spoke the words though Teren's keen sense of hearing had picked up the sound of movement behind him. Someone was slowly approaching him from behind, someone with a limp.

Teren turned just as the dark-skinned man lunged clumsily at him with his sword, the first swipe missing Teren's face by no more than a few inches, the second coming even closer. Teren's actions were purely reflex and before he knew what he was doing, Teren had disarmed the man before driving the point of his short sword up through the underside of his chin through his mouth and into his brain. Teren grabbed the man's face and yanked his sword out, his hand suddenly awash with blood and gore. All around him the crowd erupted in cheers and money exchanged hands.

Teren looked around him in disgust. How these people could enjoy watching one man slaughter another was beyond him. To kill a man in battle was a terrible thing but it was understandable, justifiable even, but to kill him purely for the pleasure of it was quite another. Teren suddenly felt dirty.

The two guards stepped forward once again and without preamble took the sword and shield from Teren whilst three others dragged the dead man's body away and picked up his weapons.

It was a very disconsolate and quiet Teren who was returned to the cage a few minutes later and Brak could tell by the look on his friend's face that he wanted to be left alone. A few yards away the Delarite prisoner stared over at Teren and grinned malevolently.

***

Things were going from bad to worse as far as Arlen was concerned. What they had thought was a sandstorm heading towards them had in fact turned out to be an even larger band of Salandori warriors galloping at speed and kicking dust up. By the time Arlen and the others had realised, it was too late and they were faced with the choice of continuing to ride towards the oncoming men or turning back and riding towards their pursuers. Something about their prisoner's frightened demeanour had given Ro pause for thought though and on a hunch he had signalled for the small group to stop.

Their pursuers also immediately stopped a couple of hundred paces behind them, but the larger group continued to bear down on them at speed. Arlen had just enough time to check that his crossbow was ready, whilst Ro and Eryn unsheathed their swords. The larger group of riders were soon upon them and in a well rehearsed manoeuvre; they quickly surrounded Ro and the others. Another ten or so riders formed up in a straight line between them and Perok's group.

The warriors surrounding Ro's group stood staring at their captives for a couple of minutes without saying anything. Three of them were staring coldly at Nestor. For his part Nestor looked absolutely petrified. One of the newcomers gently nudged his horse forward his eyes never leaving Nestor. Then he slowly tore his gaze away from the chief and looked at the other three men as if trying to weigh up which one was the leader. By luck or skill his gaze settled on Ro.

"What are you doing in the land of the Alari?" The words had been spoken in flawless common tongue with an almost Remadan accent.

"We were unaware that we had inadvertently entered your lands and assure you that we mean no harm. This man held us prisoner in his camp, but we escaped and took him hostage hoping that his friends would not attack us whilst he was still alive," replied Ro. He inclined his head towards where he knew the other Salandori warriors sat nervously upon their horses watching the proceedings.

"That is the how; I asked you why you were in our lands."

Ro noticed Arlen bristle at the man's abrupt tone and prayed that the priest wouldn't do anything rash; they were helplessly outnumbered and miles from help.

"Yes, you did. We are trying to find my friend's fiancée, a young girl of about sixteen summers who was abducted by Narmidian raiders. The last we knew he was heading across this land towards his home."

"Narmidian?" asked the Salandori warrior.

"Yes," replied Ro.

The warrior spat on the floor as if the sheer mention of their neighbours' name disgusted him.

"We have not seen them."

"That is a pity," said Ro still smiling and trying to maintain a calm exterior, "but your lands are vast and they may have slipped past you in the night."

"Nobody slips past me," said the warrior straightening himself in the saddle. "They have not come this way."

"Then we must try and pick their trail up elsewhere," said Ro adjusting his reins as if he were about to leave.

"Travelling through our land uninvited is forbidden," said the Salandori eyeing Ro suspiciously.

Ro held his gaze, his smile and air of confidence never wavering. "Perhaps there is something we can offer you by way of payment?" Ro had noticed how the man kept looking at their captive and it wasn't a look of friendship. "The life of this brother Salandori perhaps?"

The Salandori looked at the cowering chief and sneered. "He is a Salandori that much is true, but he is no brother to us. This cowardly dog leads the Muhabi tribe, sworn enemies of my people. Many of my fellow Alari have died at his hands."

"Then we have a deal?" asked Ro reaching over and holding out the reins of the horse bearing the chief. Nestor's eyes were wide with fright and he was babbling incoherently through his gag.

The younger Salandori glared at Nestor before glancing back at Ro. "We have a deal, Arkadian. His slow and agonising death will provide much entertainment in the camp tonight." He reached over and took the reins from Ro and Nestor began to struggle frantically until another warrior rode forward and placed a small but sharp looking blade at his throat. The chief's babbling became instantly quieter and subdued.

"What about his friends over there?" asked Ro turning to face the small group of warriors who had been following them.

"We will take care of them. None will see home again. Be on your way now and ride swiftly. I hope you find what you seek." The young Salandori warrior then turned and said something in his own language and moments later twenty of his men raced towards Perok's group with their swords drawn. Then after nodding at Ro and the others, the young Salandori and the remaining riders headed off west dragging their petrified captive behind them.

"Seemed like a nice fellow," said Arlen sarcastically as he watched them go. "Very hospitable as always in this place."

Ro smiled. "Maybe, but he made it abundantly clear that we weren't to outstay our welcome, so we'd better be on our way."

"Which way?" asked Eryn.

"East of course," replied Ro.

"But that man just said that he hadn't seen the Narmidian or Tayla," said Eryn.

"Yes, he did and we believe him. What we don't believe is that one man and a young girl can't sneak past him without his noticing. That was just the man's ego talking," said Arlen.

"All the same I suggest that we don't try his patience. Let's be on our way before his men come back from dealing with Perok and change their minds about us," added Ro and with that he nudged his horse eastwards.

Chapter 16

Kern Razak took a long drink from his water flask, the warm liquid lubricating his throat but not quenching his thirst. When he had emptied the flask's meagre contents he hung it back on his saddle and gazed out over the familiar landscape ahead of him. The land here was fertile with many rivers irrigating the verdant plains and valleys. Just over the next rise was the valley of Ashalar and once he was through that he would be back in Narmidia and not a minute too soon as far as he was concerned.

Kern stroked his beard, wincing at its unusually straggly and bushy feel; he would have to do something about that before he ran into any of the Narmidian nobility; appearances had to be maintained no matter what the circumstances.

Kern laughed quietly to himself. *No matter what the circumstances?* Well his circumstances had been harsh and untenable. In fact the whole expedition had been a disaster. If one of the old crone witches from the Caves of Lixtar had cursed his expedition it could not have gone any worse.

His entire body of men had been wiped out in a series of melees and fights. Some he had even killed himself after they mutinied against him. Kern was not overly bothered about the loss of his men as for the most part they were just hired hands, but he had also lost some good friends; men who had been at his side for years. Men like Varil.

Ordinarily Kern would have been happy with the reduction in the number of men making it back home again. Fewer survivors meant fewer men to pay which in turn meant he could enjoy greater profits. But that was the problem with this expedition. Not only had he lost the entire complement of his men but he had also returned without a single girl to sell as a slave; his client would not be happy. As he and his men had journeyed east with ever dwindling numbers, keeping a close watch on the girls had become increasingly difficult if not impossible. Some had escaped and one or two had been killed to set an example. Kern had hated doing that, not because he was averse to killing women, far from it in fact, but because their deaths meant an erosion of his profit margins. An example had to be set though and whilst finding their executions distasteful they had been a necessary evil.

Yet more of the girls had been rescued. Things had been going relatively well at that point when in a random act of bad luck, his party had stumbled into a small Remadan cavalry patrol. Outnumbered and taken by surprise, Kern had been lucky to escape with his life, taking just one of the girls with him. She was a pretty young thing and as they'd travelled further east Kern had all but made up his mind to keep her for himself and to Kaden with his client.

The journey across the accursed lands of the Salandori had been perilous to say the least and Kern had been forced to bribe, run and kill his way across the often hostile terrain. Narmidians were not universally liked by their poorer and ill-disciplined cousins, but because of their strength, the Salandori were respectful of them, at least outwardly. One Narmidian travelling on his own however was a different matter and many Salandori had tried to avenge whatever grudge they harboured against his people. They had all been sorry though and were now food for the carrion.

All except one group, thought Kern bitterly.

He had almost made it all the way across Salandor with his hostage when yet another unfortunate chance encounter had befallen him. He had been tired and not paying much attention to his surroundings otherwise he would have smelled the fire or heard the gentle whinnying of the horses, but he hadn't. Instead he had stumbled blindly into their camp. Although he had managed to pull himself together just in time and had killed two or maybe even three of the Salandori dogs, he'd been forced to cut the girl free and ride as hard and as fast as he could away from there. A couple of them had put up a half-hearted chase, but had soon returned to where he had found them, presumably to amuse themselves with their new acquisition. That more than anything had annoyed Kern as he had been saving her for himself and hadn't dragged her halfway across the known world just so a bunch of rabid foul-smelling desert dwellers could ravish her. The thought made him angry and sick to the pit of his stomach in equal proportions.

Still, he had got away alive and that was something he realised, though how long he would be allowed to continue living was another matter once his client found out that he had returned empty-handed. Worse still was the fact that the Sultan's nephew had been killed; how the Sultan would react to that news was anyone's guess. Kern suspected his reaction would not be good.

He wiped the perspiration from his forehead with the back of his right hand as he turned in his saddle and looked about him. Something had been gnawing away in the pit of his stomach for some hours now, a feeling of dread and unease which he couldn't rationalise or explain, but now as he looked about him again, he suddenly realised the cause. The land was empty. The eastern Salandori lands which bordered Narmidia were usually teeming with tribesmen looking to trade their wares with their richer neighbours. Whether out of choice or necessity the tribes which lived closest to Narmidia were allied with the Narmidians and bands of Salandori acting as border guards were normally everywhere checking out anyone heading towards the border. Not today, however. Today the land was devoid of anyone. It was an enigma and one Kern couldn't explain.

He was just about to head off towards the border with his own country when he suddenly sensed rather than heard the men approaching him from behind. Where they had been hiding and how they had managed to close on him unnoticed was a mystery, one that would have to wait. Kern turned his horse as fast as he could, his sword already clear of its scabbard by the time he was facing the riders, but he was already too late. Facing him with their lance points lowered and poised just a pace or two away from him, were half a dozen riders. Kern was surprised to find that these were not Salandori tribesmen but Narmidians. Nor were they any old Narmidians; these were Kalahaki, the white clad men of the Sultan's personal bodyguard. Kern knew that his life now hung in the balance. One wrong word or twitch and he'd be skewered out of hand.

Kern forced his warmest smile and uttered the traditional

Narmidian greeting. No one replied and despite the insult, Kern forced himself to continue smiling and to not show any offence though he was seething inside at the discourtesy.

A warrior perhaps in his early twenties finally nudged his horse forward another foot. He stopped close enough to demonstrate that he was in charge, but far enough away that he would be able to protect himself from a sudden swipe of Kern's sword, which he pointedly hadn't re-sheathed.

"Who are you and what are you doing here?" the Kalahaki asked.

Kern bridled at the man's tone. Whilst he was not high born, Kern had clawed his way up through the strata of Narmidian society until his house finally had some standing. It would never be powerful enough to challenge some of the older more established houses who looked down on him and his kind, but it was powerful enough to deserve some respect and certainly more than this Kalahaki was showing him. Still he somehow managed to maintain his smile.

"I am Kern Razak, head of the House of Razak and I am returning home." He was damned if he was going to tell this young upstart more than he needed to know. Kern studied the young man's face to see if there was any hint of recognition or perhaps even fear, but there was neither.

"Where have you been?"

"I have been travelling in the west, but now I am returning home," replied Kern.

"Alone?" prompted the Kalahaki.

"My men were all killed."

"Yet you survived. That is most unfortunate for them. I must remember to never let anyone I care about travel with you," said the young warrior, much to the amusement of his men. If Kern was seething before, he was positively boiling with rage inside now, though for the most part he managed to conceal it. "And what was the purpose of this journey to the west which was to cost all of your men their lives?"

For one brief second Kern considered lunging at the officer with his sword. He was pretty sure that the young upstart had ventured too close and that he could remove his smirking head before the man could react. He was also pretty sure that a couple of seconds later he would feel immense pain as six lances were thrust deep inside his body by the man's compatriots. Still, it had been a nice thought.

"We were on a hunting trip."

"Hunting? What were you hunting that you had to go all the way to the western lands to find what you were looking for?"

"Slaves," replied Kern bitterly. "Slaves for the House of Tarvis."

The mention of the House of Tarvis, one of the biggest and most powerful houses in all of Narmidia seemed to startle the young warrior, a look of fear briefly crossing his face, much to Kern's satisfaction. The look was soon gone though as the young warrior regained his composure.

"And where are these slaves now?"

Kern's patience was wearing thin and he didn't know how much longer he could keep up this charade. "I had a change of conscience and decided to set them all free; what do you think happened to them? They escaped when we were attacked."

The warrior laughed again, the action mimicked by his men and Kern felt his grip on his sword tighten in rage.

"So not only did you manage to get all of your own men killed, but you also managed to lose all of your slaves into the bargain; you are a formidable man indeed Kern Razak of the House of Razak and I should think that Belok Tarvis will want to reward you greatly. It is lucky for you then that you will not have long to wait until you receive your reward."

"And why is that?" asked Kern sourly.

"Because Belok Tarvis and all the other great leaders are camped over that ridge with the Sultan's army."

"The Sultan's army? What is it doing so far west?" asked Kern incredulously.

The young Kalahaki warrior stared at Kern as if weighing up whether it was worth his time and trouble to tell him what was happening, but in the end he decided there was nothing to lose.

"Whilst you have been away in the west playing at catching and freeing slaves, the Sultan has prophesised that now is the time to wipe the decadent usurpers from the face of Arkadia and claim our rightful place as the dominant race on the continent."

"Does he not know that some of the western powers are already at war?"

"Of course he does. The Sultan is all knowing. He has waited until the Remadans and Delarites have weakened themselves and is now ready to go in and destroy what is left. With two of the major powers out of the way, the rest of the continent will easily fall before his mighty army."

"And where are the Salandori tribesmen; I haven't seen any for some time?" asked Kern.

"Most have been conscripted into the Sultan's army, others have been tasked to guard our southern border. The others have fled to the north and will be punished when we return," said the Kalahaki warrior proudly. "Now come, I am sure that the Sultan will have use for a great leader of men such as you."

The young Kalahaki took his eyes off Kern for the first time and glanced over at his men as they all laughed at his joke. It was a mistake that he would not ever have the chance to repeat because Kern had had enough and had surreptitiously edged his horse ever nearer to the young warrior. In the blink of an eye, Kern had swung his razor sharp curved sword in a horizontal arc, slicing the man's head off in a spray of blood.

Transfixed by the sight of their leader's head flying through the air with a grin fixed upon its face, none of his six men reacted quick enough and by the time they managed to respond, Kern had already pushed past their lance points and had cut down another two of them and was turning to face the others.

Realising that their lances were now useless in such a close quarters fight, three of the Kalahaki threw them down and drew their swords but the fourth thinking that he had created enough space thrust his lance at Kern. Kern had anticipated the move and leant back just at the right moment, his timing perfect. The Kalahaki holding the lance grinned momentarily as he felt the point bite home, but then gaped open-mouthed when he realised that he had missed his target and instead had skewered one of his comrades. Kern took advantage of the man's momentary distractedness and thrust the dagger concealed in his left hand deep into the man's exposed neck whilst reaching forward with his right arm to block a downward thrust of another man's sword.

A sharp pain in the small of his back made Kern cry out and he swivelled painfully in the saddle to see that another of the Kalahaki had stabbed him with his sword. Almost instinctively Kern swung his sword in a horizontal swipe from front to back and grunted with satisfaction as the blade sliced deeply into the man's right side before he toppled to the ground. Kern wasn't sure if it was a killing blow but it would certainly take the man out of the fight.

Even as he had swung the sword Kern had known that it was a mistake because in doing so he had opened up his chest and made himself a bigger unprotected target for the man in front of him whose sword blow he had just parried. He screamed as the man drove his sword blade deep into Kern's abdomen, leaning forward as he did so. Kern dropped his own sword and turned to face the man who had dealt him a killing blow. Mustering strength his adversary would not have expected him to have, Kern grabbed hold of the man's sword arm as he tried to withdraw his weapon, before thrusting his already bloody dagger deep into the man's right eye. Kern instantly felt the man's grip loosen as his life escaped him and Kern pushed his body to the ground.

The pain in his back was incredible but it was the stomach wound that was going to kill him he knew. He looked down at his tunic and saw an ever widening patch of dark blood and knew that his time was nearly up. He glanced around at the seven bodies lying on the ground and spat on the nearest one. He had travelled all this way, suffered all these hardships, just to be killed on the edge of his own country by these wet-behind-the-ear dogs that had probably never fought in a real battle before. Life could be unfair sometimes. Determined to see his homeland one last time, Kern nudged his horse forward up the ridge, wincing and crying out at the pain the motion caused.

When after a minute or two he finally crested the summit he raised himself from a slumped position and gazed down at the scene below him. For what seemed like leagues and leagues all Kern could see were neat rows of tents and multitudes of men wearing the colours of just about every tribe and house known to him. It seemed to Kern as his peripheral vision began to disappear, that the whole Narmidian nation was camped out before him. The rich and decadent nations of the west would not know what had hit them. There would be glory and riches for all, but he would not be there to enjoy and share in it. He was still thinking about that as his eyes finally closed and he fell to the ground.

***

Ro, Arlen and Eryn had ridden their horses hard after their encounter with the Salandori and although none of them had admitted it, they hadn't really expected the Salandori to let them go. After all, there had been more than enough of them to kill Ro and the others and just take Nestor from them. Despite their concerns, however, there had been no sign of pursuit and by the time they reached the Forest of Antoli, they knew they were safe, at least for now.

They had found a secluded and reasonably defensible spot and had set up camp for the night and after eating what felt like the first meal in days, Eryn and Ro had soon fallen fast asleep whilst Arlen took the first watch. After three hours Arlen had woken Ro who had done his turn before finally waking Eryn and instructing him to keep watch until dawn. Still feeling very tired, the three companions had then eaten their morning meal in relative quiet, each lost in their own thoughts.

They had not picked up any sign of the raider who was still holding Tayla captive and although no one actually said so, each knew that with every passing day the chances of running into them again were diminishing. The Salandori lands were vast but not as vast as Narmidia and although he didn't share his concerns with his companions, Ro was of the opinion that once the raider crossed over into Narmidia, the girl was as good as lost. This was something that Eryn's father, Teren Rad had learned to his cost seven years earlier when he had spent five fruitless years searching the eastern lands for his wife who had been abducted by raiders. Ro would allow the pursuit to continue for another day or two at most and then he would have to raise the subject of abandoning the search and instead concentrate on trying to find Teren. Arlen would be supportive of his suggestion but Eryn clearly would not.

However, of more immediate concern to Ro had been the fact that since riding away from the Salandori horsemen the previous day, the group had not set eyes on a single Salandori warrior or trader. Whilst this was obviously beneficial for their safety, it was very curious. The tribes that inhabited these lands were known to be friendly or even allied with the Narmidians and the land was usually teeming with Salandori tribesmen on their way to or from Narmidia where they would trade their wares. Now though the land appeared abandoned and devoid of life. It was strange and the matter unsettled Ro.

They had broken camp a couple of hours after dawn and had resumed their journey due east. Both of his companions were quiet, Ro noticed, but Arlen especially seemed subdued. For some days now Ro had thought that his friend seemed distracted and preoccupied and many times he had gone to raise the subject with him, only to change his mind at the last moment. In the short space of time that he had known Arlen, he had realised that his friend was a very private person who did not feel comfortable sharing personal matters. Whether that was his nature or part of his training as a Priest of the Golden Tree, he did not know, but out of respect he had chosen to mind his own business. Now Ro wasn't so sure that was a good idea. If the opportunity arose he would ask his friend what it was that troubled him so.

Ro's attention was suddenly drawn to something on the dusty ground beneath them and he casually slipped from his horse and knelt to examine the ground, holding his reins in his left hand. Arlen and Eryn rode up alongside him and after looking at the ground and just seeing a mass of indiscernible horse prints as far as he could tell, Arlen decided to ask Ro what had caught his attention.

"What is it, Ro?"

"Horse tracks."

"Two?" asked Eryn expectantly.

"Six or seven," replied Ro without looking up.

"More Salandori to be avoided then," said Arlen suddenly losing interest.

"Maybe," said Ro distractedly.

"You see something else, Ro?" asked Arlen, his interest suddenly piqued again.

"One of the horse's tracks is deeper than the others."

"So one of the riders was fat and likes his food too much; what of it?" asked Arlen.

Ro did a little grin to himself before answering. "Maybe, or it could be because the horse was carrying two people."

"You think Tayla is with these riders now?" asked Eryn.

"It's possible, Eryn," replied Ro.

"But the last time we picked up her trail she was still travelling with just the one remaining raider."

"True, Eryn, but we have not seen their tracks for some time and this is the first clue to her possible whereabouts."

"But why would she be with these men now?" asked Eryn his anxiety levels steadily rising.

"There's a whole host of reasons why, Eryn. The raider might have sold her, she might have been taken by them or she could have escaped him and then ran into these men afterwards. For all we know they may be helping her."

"You don't really believe that do you, Ro?" asked Eryn.

"No, I don't, but like everything else, it is a possibility. I think we should follow these tracks."

Arlen took a long drink from his water flask and then wiped his mouth with the back of his hand, before re-corking the flask.

"That's something of a long shot, my friend. What if your hunch is wrong?"

"Then we are no worse off than we are right now. We're riding blindly east hoping to pick up a trail we haven't seen for ages. Besides, their trail is still heading south-east towards Narmidia, so if it is a wild boar chase, then we will not have lost too much," replied Ro displaying more confidence than he actually felt.

"If you are right, Ro then Tayla's captor is going to get away unpunished and disappear into the Narmidian hinterland," said Eryn.

"True, but you must ask yourself what is more important to you, Eryn; getting Tayla safely back or losing the chance to rescue Tayla in pursuit of vengeance."

"There is no choice in such a thing; Tayla's safety is of paramount importance to me," replied Eryn stiffly.

"Good, then our path is clear; we head south-east. Besides, Eryn, for all we know the men with Tayla now may have already killed him," and with that Ro climbed back onto his horse and trotted off in the direction which the tracks led.

"We can always hope I suppose," said Eryn out loud but to no one in particular before riding off after Ro. After a few seconds and an anxious look over his shoulder, Arlen followed his companions.

Chapter 17

Teren raised his sword and shield high into the air, the acclaim of the crowd washing over him as the blood of the vanquished ran down the sword and onto his hand and wrist. On the ground around him lay the bodies of four men, slaves of another Salandori chief forced to fight in the arena for their host's pleasure. They would never fight again though, Teren had seen to that, just like he had countless other men who had been pitted against him over the last few days. At first the chief of the Alith had made him fight various men from his own slave supply but when he realised that Teren had a real flair for killing he had started to match him against men from other tribes in the camp. More often than not he was forced to fight other slaves but occasionally the opposing tribal chiefs would order his champion or best fighter to face Teren.

It made no difference to Teren; they all died bloody. He had developed a reputation as a fierce fighter and his chief had grown very rich on the proceeds of his winnings. Success had not been without its rewards for Teren either. His food ration had increased and was of a better quality and every now and again he was taken from the cage to a tent where a slave girl or two would be waiting for him.

There were other benefits to the fighting as well. Teren had shed some weight; some of his excess poundage traded in for hard muscle the likes of which Teren had not seen in many years. He had also tidied himself up, trimming his beard and cutting his long hair. He now looked and felt twenty years younger, but the pains in his hands and lower back still troubled him.

Teren did not fear pain nor worry about the fact that one day he might come up against someone better than himself, though his ego refused to accept that was even possible. What Teren feared was that one day he would step into the arena and find himself facing his son. It was a nightmare that haunted him day after day and although he found his thoughts constantly occupied by it, he never did decide what he would do if and when he found himself confronted by that scenario.

Instead he concentrated on planning his escape. Every night he would sit and study the routines of the guards searching for openings and weaknesses he might be able to exploit. He also cautiously reached out and began talking to some of the other prisoners he thought might be willing to join him when the time came.

Brak had confronted him one night accusing Teren of having accepted his fate, but Teren had just laughed. Whilst he couldn't deny that he enjoyed the fights and the exhilaration that he felt, the thought that he had accepted his new role, was absurd. He assured Brak that he was still intent on escaping the camp and that soon it would be time to make that attempt, but Brak had appeared unconvinced.

Even now though as Teren stood on the blood soaked ground surrounded by dead and mutilated bodies, accepting the adulation of the crowd he despised, he was plotting. Over the last few days a plan had been formulating in his head and he was now more convinced than ever that any escape attempt had to be made during or after a fight; the bigger the better.

Like countless times before, Teren turned and bowed to his chief, muttering a vile curse under his breath as he did so and then lay his weapons down on the ground. Then, escorted by two Salandori warriors, Teren was led back to the cage. As usual, Brak and Garik were waiting just inside for him.

"Once again you defy the gods and live, Remadan," said Brak.

"Not my time, northerner," replied Teren smiling.

"So it would seem, but what about next time and the time after that; will they be your time?"

"I don't know and I don't care. The time to leave this place has come I think."

"We're making our move?" asked Garik excitedly.

Teren caught sight of one of the guards looking suspiciously towards them and gently led the other two men deeper into the cage and away from prying eyes.

"The next time I fight is when I'm going to make my move. Let the others know to be ready but be discrete." The other two men nodded solemnly. "How many are with us?"

"At least half," replied Garik.

"What about the other half?"

"Some will probably join us when push comes to shove, the others will stay out of our way," added Brak.

"And the Delarite?" asked Teren.

"Nobody has asked him but he knows something is happening. Whether he has got wind of it from another of the captives I do not know, but I do know that I don't trust him," said Brak.

"I will speak to him," said Teren.

"But he hates you," replied Garik somewhat surprised.

"I know, but I'm gambling he hates the Salandori even more. His choice is clear; he either joins us or he dies; I'll not risk him spilling his guts to one of the guards. Now all we've got to wait for is the next suitable fight to make our move."

"I don't think you'll have long to wait," said Brak.

"How so?" asked Garik.

"I overheard a couple of the guards talking yesterday."

"You can speak their language now?" asked Teren.

"Not fluently, no, but I am picking up more and more of it every day; I've been here a while remember."

"That could be useful. What did you hear?"

"Apparently the chiefs are expecting an important Narmidian visitor tomorrow and want to put on a show for her. I think most of us are going to be involved in a fairly big contest with the fighters from yet another tribe who are also arriving tomorrow."

"What would a Narmidian be doing here?" asked Teren.

"I'm not sure, I think I heard them say that the Salandori were being asked to guard some territory for the Narmidians. At least that's what it sounded like," said Brak apologetically.

"Why would the Narmidians need the Salandori to guard their land; it doesn't make any sense?" said Teren.

"Perhaps the Narmidians have trouble brewing elsewhere and need to mobilise all their men for that," said Garik.

Teren stroked his neatly cropped beard as he considered

the matter. "Maybe! Did you say the Narmidian visitor is a woman?"

"That's what it sounded like," replied Brak.

"Isn't that unusual? I thought the Narmidians were a male dominant race."

"It is, so I assume that she is a woman of some importance who has somehow managed to claw or bed her way to a position of prominence."

"Man or woman, makes no difference to me. This sounds like our opportunity. Spread the word to those you trust and know are definitely with us, that tomorrow we take back our freedom," said Teren.

"And the fighters from the other tribe, what of them?" asked Garik.

"They can either join us or die. There will be no neutrals in this fight. Now go and let the others know whilst I go and speak to our Delarite friend."

"If you're unable to persuade him to join us, he could tell the guards and we'll all be executed," said Brak.

"I had better turn on the charm and persuade him then," smiled Teren.

"Then truly there is no hope," said Garik.

"Careful, friend or tomorrow I might mistake you for a Salandori in all the confusion," said Teren smiling. "Better keep your distance in the morning."

"Oh I plan to don't worry. I have a feeling death is going to be all around you."

Teren laughed and clasped his friends on their shoulders before striding off to speak to the belligerent Delarite. Much as Teren despised the man, he would be a useful ally in the fight as there was no doubting the man's prowess with sword or spear. Confiding his plan in him was risky to say the least but Teren felt he had no choice. For all his other faults the man wasn't stupid and will have seen the clandestine meetings and whisperings between a good many of the captives and would know that something was afoot. He might even know the full plan so Teren had decided it was better to try and get the man on board by being honest rather than giving him the cold shoulder and hoping he said nothing. More importantly still, the Delarite would probably be fighting in the arena tomorrow and Teren needed to know that the man would watch his back rather than bury his sword point in it. Besides, if the man threatened to tell the guards Teren still retained the option of slitting his throat during the night.

Taking a deep breath, Teren straightened his shoulders and strode over to where the Delarite warrior sat with his back to the cage bars watching Teren's approach through suspicious eyes.

***

Teren woke with a start and once again it took him a few moments to recall exactly where he was much to the amusement of his watching friends. He groaned when he finally came to his senses and saw them all laughing at him.

"Another dream about Lydian whores was it?" asked Brak.

"No it wasn't actually," replied Teren stretching.

"Who was she then?" asked Garik.

"Who?"

"The woman in your dreams; you only wake up looking like that when you've dreamt about a woman," said Garik smiling.

"Or two," added Brak.

"None of your damned business! Can't a man get any privacy around here?" said Teren grumpily.

"No," the others replied laughing.

There was a hive of activity outside in the camp and Teren stood staring at it trying to work out what was happening. In the end he decided it would be easier just to ask. Brak seemed to notice everything and what he didn't notice he now seemed to overhear from the guards. He wasn't to be disappointed.

"What's going on?"

"They're erecting a bigger arena and over there they're erecting some sort of dais. Must be for their Narmidian guests, because the Salandori don't normally go to all this bother," replied Brak.

"Judging by the size of it I'd say it was going to be mass

contest rather than a series of individual fights," added Garik.

Teren nodded. "Good, that will be to our advantage. Any sign of the competition yet?" Teren stepped forward to the edge of the cage and was immediately poked in the stomach by the blunt end of a guard's spear. Laughing the man pointed at Teren and then ran a finger across his throat in an unmistakable gesture. "I'm going to enjoy killing him."

"Then probably best not to provoke them before you get the opportunity," said Brak guiding Teren away from the bars and handing him some bread and a cup of water. "Tell me, how did your conversation with the Delarite go?"

"About as well as could be expected."

"He is not with us then?"

"Seems that way."

"Will he give us away do you think?" asked Brak concerned.

"No, I don't think that he will."

"What makes you so sure?"

"I'm not; it's just a gut feeling. Oh, and the fact that I said I would gut him with a blunt knife if I even suspected that he had spoken to our captors. The man's a realist. If our plan goes well I wouldn't be surprised to see him join us," said Teren.

"And if it doesn't?"

"I expect him to stab me in the back, literally and figuratively."

"A comforting thought," said Brak despondently.

Teren laughed and slapped his friend on the shoulder. "Cheer up, friend, today is going to be a good day, I can feel it in my bones."

"All I can feel in my bones is the chill of the night air."

"Well tomorrow you sleep under the stars a free man with a Salandori woman to keep you warm."

"Now that's a comforting thought," smiled Brak.

"Good. Now let's go and speak to a few of the others and finalise preparations. The only thing that can go wrong now is that they don't select any of us to fight," said Teren as he stalked off to find Garik.

Brak thought about that possibility and then discounted it. Teren was the chief's best fighter and he himself always seemed to get selected lately, probably because of his association with Teren. So long as at least some of those sworn to help them were selected they'd be all right. He wasn't convinced but it was all he had to cling to. Trying to consign his doubts to the back of his mind, Brak set off after Teren and whatever destiny awaited them.

***

Shortly after their morning meal, such that it was, the champion of the Alith tribe and a couple of other warriors had entered the cage to address the captives. The man was either very brave or he was very stupid Teren thought and he had given serious consideration to making his move right there and then. He could have taken out the champion without too much bother and Brak, Garik and a few of the others would quickly have overpowered the man's companions. Then they could have taken their weapons, freed the other captives and set about killing the other warriors. It would have been risky and very costly in terms of lives lost, of that Teren had no doubt, but such a surprise attack could work. It also had the advantage of nullifying any treachery the Delarite might have had planned. In the end, however, he decided to leave things as they were.

With more pleasure than was necessary, the champion had read out a list of prisoner names and explained that they were to work on helping to set up the arena. Those whose names had not been called out, were the men selected to fight that evening. The champion had taken great delight in telling them that it was going to be a glorious spectacle and that those chosen to fight should pray to whatever gods they believed in as this was to be their last day on Chell.

After saying his piece and staring long and hard at as many of the captives as he could and Teren especially, the champion spat on the ground and then turned and walked out of the cage. The way he had turned his back on the prisoners as if daring them to make a move against him, made Teren wonder whether he knew that they had something planned. None of the prisoners took the bait though.

Those whose names had been read out traipsed wearily

out after him, a mixture of expressions on their faces. Some were obviously glad to be missing the contests that night, glad that their lives were to be extended by at least another day, but others were clearly disappointed.

Teren watched them leave as one of the guards locked the cage door behind him and then glanced around to see who was left. He was pleased to see that in addition to himself, Brak and Garik a number of other men who had sworn to aid him were also left behind. Interestingly the Delarite had also been selected to fight and Teren wondered whether this was a good or bad sign. Still, a handful of their allies had been taken out of the equation and Teren hoped that when the action started these men would still be in a position to help.

"Could have been worse, Teren. I make it we've lost four or five good men," said Brak.

Teren nodded solemnly. "I know, but four or five might have been enough to tip the balance."

"Do you want to call it off?"

"No. I'm getting out of here tonight even if I have to do it alone," said Teren.

"Very well. Then we must try and get as many of the other men into the fight as quickly as possible."

"Agreed. Success is going to depend on three things. One, that when the action starts a few of the others who we haven't been able to confide in join in spontaneously and two that some of the fighters from the other tribes join us," said Teren.

Brak waited a few seconds looking expectantly at Teren, but when he said nothing further, Brak felt forced to prompt him. "And the third thing? You said there were three things that had to happen."

"Oh yes. The third thing's easy; don't get killed in the arena."

Brak smiled. "I can assure you that will be my top priority."

***

The rest of the day passed slowly for the men left alone in the cage and most of them spent the time resting and trying to stay out of the blazing sun though there was little shade to be found. All day long more Salandori riders arrived in the camp and although Teren was no expert even he could tell that a whole host of tribes were represented judging by the different coloured sashes and headbands they wore. From time to time small groups of warriors would venture up to the cage and talk excitedly in their own language, occasionally pointing at Teren, the Delarite and one or two of the others. Teren would smile at them whilst muttering quietly under his breath how he was going to gut each and every one of them when the time came.

The Narmidian delegation had arrived late afternoon among much fanfare and their presence and that of the woman leading them, had become the focus of the Salandori's attention. From their position in the cage, Teren and the others had not been able to see much other than the magnificent white horses they had arrived upon. Teren thought that he caught the briefest sight of a woman's back as she was led away towards the chief's tent, but he wasn't sure. He told himself that he must be mistaken, because the woman appeared to have long auburn hair and pale skin and it was well-known that the olive skinned Narmidian women all had long dark hair.

Teren turned away and saw Brak talking to one of their Salandori guards in hushed tones. Brak had been cultivating his relationship with the guard for some time now, giving him tips on who to wager on in return for snippets of information. It was information that he was again fishing for.

Brak turned and saw Teren watching him and after surreptitiously nodding his thanks to the guard, Brak walked over to where his friend was standing.

"Our guests of honour have arrived I see," said Teren.

"Indeed. It's just a small party but with an important leader."

"The woman? Who is she?" asked Teren.

"The Sultan's wife or at least one of them. Apparently she is rapidly becoming his favourite. It is a sign of his growing trust in her that he has entrusted her with such an important mission," said Brak.

"What mission?"

"He didn't want to tell me too much, but apparently from what I can tell, the Narmidians are mustering for war and want the Salandori to guard their southern borders. The Sultan's wife is here to address the chiefs of the local tribes and persuade them to do as the Sultan bids."

"And if they don't?" asked Teren.

"Then I imagine she is here to threaten them. The Salandori have long been afraid of their neighbours. I would imagine the thought that an enormous Narmidian host gathered somewhere nearby will be enough to persuade them. Anyway, most of the tribes around here are already allied to the Narmidians; it is the western and northern tribes who have no love for their distant cousins," replied Brak.

"And just who are the Narmidians going to war with?"

"He wouldn't say and became agitated when I asked."

"Well none of our concern anyway I suppose. Our priority has to be getting out of here; we can worry about everything else later. What will the Narmidians do when the fighting starts do you think?"

"Their priority is to protect the queen. I'd imagine they'd leave and only fight if the queen herself is directly threatened," said Brak.

"Then we'd better make sure that doesn't happen then. Any idea of the numbers we'll be up against?"

"All he would say is that there are six tribes represented here and they've all brought three or four fighters with them to be used in the arena. Given what I've seen around the camp so far I would say that each tribal party consists of about twenty men. Combine that with the men of this tribe and...well you get the idea?"

"Yes, you think we're dead men," said Teren.

"Sooner or later we're all dead men, even you. I for one would rather go out fighting on my own terms than as an exhibit in the arena for these worthless dogs," said Brak.

Teren smiled broadly and reached out and clasped his friend's arm in the traditional warrior's embrace.

"Then that is what shall happen, my friend. Tonight we share a meal as freemen or as dead men in Paradise."

"So be it," said Brak grinning.

The plans were made; all they could do now was wait.

Chapter 18

There were seven of them from what Ro and the others could see six men and a girl who was tied up and slumped next to a tree, her head hanging down obscuring her face. One of the men was clearly supposed to be on guard duty, though his attention appeared elsewhere, two were asleep and the other three were playing some sort of game next to the camp fire.

"Is that Tayla, Eryn?" asked Ro quietly as he watched the small group of Salandori from their vantage point on a small ridge above the camp.

"I don't know; I can't see her face."

"Well whoever she is we're not going to leave her here with these animals."

"The bonds around her wrists and legs would suggest that if that is Tayla, the poor girl has just swapped one captor for another," said Arlen.

"So it would seem," replied Ro.

"Do you think that's all of them?" whispered Arlen.

"Seems to be. This is certainly the group we've been tracking."

It seemed that Ro's hunch to change direction and follow this group's tracks had paid off. Even if the girl hostage turned out not to be Tayla, they'd still be rescuing another poor soul from their captors.

"How do you want to play this?" asked Arlen.

Ro stared intently at the unsuspecting men below as he considered his friend's question.

"You go to the right, Arlen and come at them from those bushes and Eryn you take a position up there behind those rocks. You should be able to get at least two clear shots with your bow before any survivors run for it. I'll approach from the front and take that guard out." Even as he spoke Ro was reaching into his pouch and pulling out one of his *jemtak*. "Try and get at least one shot off from your crossbow, Arlen. As soon as you see the guard drop, both of you open fire.

Any questions?" Both Arlen and Eryn shook their heads. "Good. Keep safe."

"See, I told you he was beginning to care, Eryn," said Arlen smiling.

"Don't push it, priest," said Ro returning the smile. "Now go."

Ro gave them a couple of minutes to scurry quietly round to their positions and to ready their weapons. When he was sure that enough time had passed he adjusted his grip on the *jemtak*. His hand felt clammy and warm and he wiped it on his trouser legs before again adjusting his grip. He would only get one shot at the man. He glanced left and right at where he knew Eryn and Arlen should be waiting and although he couldn't see them, he assumed they were in position. After adjusting his grip on the *jemtak* one last time, Ro quickly stood and hurled the weapon.

The small metal star struck the guard in the left eye and he immediately dropped his weapon and howled with pain, instantly drawing the attention of the men who were crouched down playing a game. They hurried to their feet and started to reach for their curved swords, but before they could do so, one was struck in the throat with a crossbow bolt, another in the chest with an arrow. Both men collapsed to the ground dead.

Unsure whether to face the adversary to his front, left or right, the third man hesitated and a few seconds later an arrow and a crossbow bolt ended his dilemma and he too collapsed to the ground dead.

The two men who had been asleep were woken by the commotion and although clearly groggy from whatever alcohol they had been consuming all evening, they managed to stagger to their feet and stood brandishing their weapons trying to decide what to do next. A tall western warrior with a huge sword had appeared from behind the ridge to their front and had quickly despatched their comrade who had been wounded in the eye. Now he was bearing down on them.

Even as they reluctantly stepped forward to meet his challenge, one of them caught a glimpse of movement out of the corner of his left eye. He turned at once and saw another

Arkadian, this one dressed in strange clothes, hurrying towards them with his sword drawn. The man shouted a warning to his friend and stepped forward to meet this new threat, but his friend who clearly didn't relish taking on the Arkadian with the huge sword turned to his right and prepared to run. All too late he noticed the third attacker, a young boy emerge from behind the rocks to his right and by the time he had fully registered the danger, an arrow was lodged deep in his chest. He turned round to face the man approaching from the front and instead walked straight onto his sword point. As the warrior collapsed he could hear another man yell out in pain and knew instantly that the strangely dressed Arkadian had just killed his brother.

"That went well I thought," said Arlen wiping his sword blade on the dead man's tunic.

"Well enough I suppose," replied Ro.

"Nice throw by the way to hit the fellow in the eye from that distance."

"Not really. I was aiming for his throat." Ro whirled round at the sound of someone approaching form his left but it was only Eryn. "You okay, Eryn?"

Eryn nodded as he glanced around at the dead bodies. His gaze suddenly fell on the girl tied up below the tree. "Tayla!"

The girl didn't reply, her head still hanging between her knees and Eryn found himself wondering whether it really was Tayla. The weight of expectation and disappointment suddenly felt like it was going to crush him. He glanced nervously at his two companions and Arlen smiled reassuringly and flicked his head towards the girl indicating that whoever she was, Eryn should go to her. Slinging his bow over his shoulder, Eryn cautiously approached her.

When he was but a few paces away from her she suddenly looked up as if she had only just become aware of their presence. When she saw the young man slowly coming towards her, she instinctively clasped her legs tightly to her chest and buried her face once again.

It had only been the briefest of glimpses, but lurking under the lank disshevelled hair and the grimy face, Eryn was positive he'd seen the girl he loved and one day planned to marry. He knelt down in front of her and quietly spoke her name, but the girl offered no reaction. He glanced again at his two companions for reassurance and this time they both smiled and nodded their encouragement as they too quietly drew nearer.

"Tayla, it's me, Eryn." For a moment or two the tension in her shoulders seemed to ease and Eryn thought that she was going to uncoil from the tight ball she had made herself, but she flinched violently when he reached out and touched her right shoulder. "I'm here to take you home, Tayla, home to see your mother and father. They'll be so pleased to see you."

Eryn withdrew his hand and moved back a pace sitting down on the ground and assuming the most unthreatening of poses he could. Nothing happened for a minute or so but then very slowly the girl started to uncoil and slowly lift her head until a bloodshot and tired pair of blue eyes fixed themselves on Eryn.

"Eryn, is that really you?" The voice was gentle but faltering, as if unsure of itself.

"It's me, Tayla. I've come to take you home."

Tayla's whole body seemed to relax and she dragged herself to her knees and stared at Eryn for what felt like an eternity. Then as if a dam had broken the tears flooded down her face. Eryn took out his knife and gently cut her bonds. Tayla stared at him again as if not truly believing that she was free and then she threw her arms around his neck and hugged him tight. Eryn hugged her back unsure what to say or do. He had dreamed of this moment for weeks but had never really planned what he would do when it arrived. In the end he decided to just see what happened.

Tayla's body was convulsing with huge sobs and Eryn's face and neck were wet with her tears. He was relieved when he felt her vice-like grip around his neck loosen and gently eased her away from him, holding her at arm's length and smiling.

"Tayla, I'd like you to meet my friends Ro Aryk and Arlen Meric. They have helped me to track and rescue you," said Eryn.

Tayla wiped at her tears with the back of her hand and tried to adjust her hair, suddenly very aware of how rough her appearance must be. She was so overawed by what had happened though that all she could do was smile sweetly at both men, the words she wanted to say stuck in her throat along with a million others.

"It is a pleasure to finally meet you, Tayla," said Ro bowing slightly.

"Indeed it is," added Arlen. "Eryn has told us much about you and I now see why he was so desperate to get you back." The priest smiled when the girl blushed at the compliment. "Are you hungry? Of course you are. I'm always hungry. Let's see what I can find for you to eat," and with that Arlen strode off to where their horses were tethered to fetch some food from his saddlebags.

"I'm going to get some more wood for that fire before it dies down. I'll leave you two to get reacquainted," said Ro as he too walked off suddenly feeling awkward around the two young lovers.

Eryn and Tayla watched him go and then burst into laughter before hugging and kissing.

"I'm so glad you found me, Eryn."

"I'm so sorry I wasn't there to protect you that morning, Tayla, I..."

"It doesn't matter, Eryn, you came looking for me and that's what really counts."

Arlen was leading their horses back towards the camp when he ran into Ro going in the opposite direction.

"How are our two young lovebirds?" asked Arlen smiling.

"Getting reacquainted. I left them to it whilst I went looking for some unnecessary firewood. You might want to take the long route back to camp with the horses to give them some time alone," replied Ro smiling.

"There'll be time enough for that when they're married. Right now the poor girl's starving I expect; I know I am. Food, my friend, must always come first."

"And they say romance is dead."

"And what would a former Captain of the Royal Bodyguard know about romance then?" asked Arlen mischievously.

"Not much. What about a Priest of the Golden Tree?"

"Oh, I know plenty, don't you worry."

"I thought members of your Order were forbidden to have relations with women?"

"We are. Doesn't mean we didn't though, not all of us," said Arlen smirking.

"Tell me more," urged Ro.

"Oh, I will, I will, when the time is right."

"The time never seems to be right though does it? Don't think that I've forgotten that you still owe me an explanation as to how you come to be in Remada in the first place. One day I'm going to hold you down until you tell me your whole story. Something tells me it will be most intriguing."

"Perhaps it is and one day I will tell you, I promise, but today is not that day. Today must be about Eryn and Tayla."

"Yes, I suppose you're right, Arlen," said Ro though he couldn't help but feel that he'd been outmanoeuvred by the priest yet again. "Come let's head back and see what you've found to eat."

"Before we do, Ro, I need to ask what happens now?"

"What do you mean?"

"I mean we've found Tayla so do we head back to Remada with Eryn and Tayla or do we now turn our attention to finding Teren?"

Ro absentmindedly scratched at the stubble forming on his cheeks as he considered his friend's question. It was a dilemma he had been silently wrestling with for some days now without resolution.

"In truth I don't know, Arlen. It doesn't feel right just heading home and leaving Teren to whatever fate has befallen him, especially after what he did at Vangor. Neither does it seem prudent to send Eryn and his young lady back through Salandor and then into war-torn Remada also to an uncertain fate. What are your thoughts?"

"I have the same mixed feelings as you, Ro. We promised to come after Eryn and Teren to help them find Tayla and we've done that. The fact that we have lost Teren along the way was not to be known. He would want us to get them safely home I'm sure. Besides which he may already be dead. However, the big man saved my life at least once at Vangor and I do not forget my debts lightly as you know. I think we should set Eryn and Tayla off on the safest path we can conceive and then go looking for Teren."

Ro nodded. The priest had just given voice to his own leanings.

"Then that is what we will do then."

"Just one more thing, Ro."

"What's that?"

"Eryn is going to want a say in all of this. He's stubborn and pig-headed," said Arlen.

"Of course, but I can't imagine where he gets it from."

The two men started to laugh and after slapping Ro on the shoulder, Arlen began to make his way back to the camp followed by Ro. After a few paces Ro stopped and hurriedly looked round for something that could be used as firewood. Shaking his head slowly and smiling to himself he hurried after Arlen.

Whilst Ro had dragged the bodies of the dead Salandori out of sight, Arlen prepared something to eat and although it wasn't much, Tayla had gulped it down as if she hadn't eaten in weeks. They had spent the mealtime making small talk, trying to avoid the subject of raiders and killing, but eventually the subject had to be faced and surprisingly it was Tayla who raised it.

"My mother and father are they...still alive?"

Ro and Arlen of course had no idea having not been to Lentor, so all eyes turned to Eryn.

"They're fine, Tayla. They were distraught about losing you when we left, but other than that they were unharmed," said Eryn.

An almost visible tide of relief washed over Tayla's face as the news that her parents still lived sunk in, but then something Eryn had just said gave her cause for concern.

"We? You said when 'we left'. Who came with you and where are they?"

For a few seconds Eryn couldn't meet her gaze as the painful memory of his best friend's death became all consuming. Just as Ro thought he was going to have to answer the question for the boy, Eryn seemed to pull himself together.

"When I asked the men of the village for help, the only person apart from Jeral Tae to step forward and say they'd come with me, was Tav Rhem. Even when the Council of Elders banned Jeral from accompanying me, Tav never faltered."

"And where is Tav now?" asked Tayla, though she dreaded the answer. Like Eryn, she was one of very few people in the village who treated Tav as an equal, even though the lad, who was in his early twenties, had a mental age of someone much younger.

"He died a hero defending the city of Vangor from the Delarites," said Eryn proudly. The tears weren't far away now. The barely suppressed thoughts about his uncle's and best friend's deaths, the exhilaration at finally finding Tayla alive and sheer exhaustion, were all threatening to overwhelm him.

"I'm sorry, Eryn, I know Tav was your friend," said Tayla.

"He was my only real friend in the end," replied Eryn bitterly.

"Well now it seems you have new friends in Ro and Arlen."

Eryn looked over at the two men and smiled. He wanted to say something to corroborate what Tayla had just said, but he feared if he tried to speak he would end up opening the floodgates. Instead he just nodded.

"Much has happened since you've been taken, Tayla. Remada and Lydia have been invaded by the Delarites and Cardellans and for all we know others might have joined in since. Your home village lost a lot of good people so Eryn says, so they will be delighted to see you back I am sure. It is of this we need to talk, Eryn," said Arlen.

"How so?" replied Eryn, glad for the change of subject.

"Ro and I set out from Vangor to help you and your father rescue Tayla," began Arlen.

"Kam Martel is out here too?" asked Tayla excitedly.

Eryn shook his head. "No, my real father, Teren Rad. Uncle Kam was killed defending the village. Like Arlen said, there is much you don't know, Tayla." Before she could ask anything further Eryn gestured for Arlen to continue.

"Like I said, we left Vangor to help you and Teren find Tayla and I am delighted that we were able to do so. We now feel that it is imperative that you get Tayla safely home as quickly as possible."

"What about you two?" asked Eryn not liking where this was leading.

"We both owe our lives to Teren and cannot in good conscience just turn our backs on him now when he needs us. We plan to track him down and bring him home."

"He may be dead," said Eryn.

"Yes, he may be, but until we know for certain what has happened to him, we cannot return home," said Arlen.

"Then I must come with you; he is my father," said Eryn more belligerently than he intended.

"Yes, he is and Tayla is your fiancée and has been through much. Your duty is to get her safely home. That is not going to be easy, Eryn. You are a long way from home with nothing but hostile country between you and Lentor. Nor do you know what will be waiting for you at home. This task is not an easy one and we would not suggest that you attempt it unless we thought you were capable of pulling it off," said Ro.

"But I cannot abandon him," said Eryn.

"You are not abandoning him, Eryn; you will be doing what he would want you to do. Don't worry, we'll find him and bring him safely home," said Ro.

Arlen winced at his friend's glib promise. They would certainly look for Teren, but with each passing day the likelihood of finding him alive was slowly diminishing. To let the lad think otherwise was foolhardy.

Eryn studied the two men for a few moments and then looked over at the tired and anxious face of his fiancée. Perhaps they were right. Perhaps his priority should be to get Tayla safely home to her parents. After all, Teren was a fearsome warrior; he would not die easy.

"Very well, I will take Tayla home, but you two must promise me you won't go getting yourselves killed without me there to protect you."

"We'll do our very best, Eryn," said Arlen smiling. "Besides, Ro owes me, so I know he'll be looking out for me."

"I thought you said I did not owe you anything?" said Ro.

"I did, but then I also said that I was getting used to having someone watch my back if you remember; that hasn't changed," replied Arlen smugly.

"You see, Eryn, you have no need to worry about us," said Ro.

The four companions laughed and then settled down to finish their meal. As they ate Ro had told Eryn that his best chance of making it back to Remada was to head south and then try to enter Remada from the south east. If as he hoped, Jeral Tae had rallied their troops and launched a counter attack, the south and south east would still be in Remadan hands. The route was much longer than going straight across Salandor and into Remada from the same direction they had left it, but Ro believed it would be safer and Arlen seemed to agree. When they'd left, the whole of the north and much of the east of Remada had been under Delarite occupation with their armies thrusting west and towards the hinterland. The south had still been under Remadan control and Ro hoped that was still the case.

Eryn had listened to his friend's advice and although he did not relish such a long journey, he could not fault Ro's reasoning and agreed they'd set out for home first thing in the morning. Ro and Arlen would then head due east and hope to pick up news of Teren's whereabouts.

Before they'd finally settled down to get some sleep, Eryn had raised the subject of her abductors with Tayla. Her face had gone deathly white and looked as if she was about to break down into floods of tears. Eryn instantly regretted his insensitivity, but then she seemed to get a hold of herself, at least enough to be able to answer his questions. She told them how the group of raiders had been large at first but had then gradually been worn down, first by the mutiny within their own ranks, then when the Remadan cavalry patrol had rescued most of the girls and then finally due to all the little attacks they had endured. She described how for the last few days or so it had been just her and the leader, Kern Razak, but how even he'd eventually been forced to release her when they were attacked by a group of Salandori. She told them that as far as she knew, Kern Razak had made good his escape and was probably by now already in Narmidia.

When she finished Tayla had rolled over and closed her eyes. Whether that was to get some sleep or to mask her tears, Eryn didn't know. All he knew was that he wanted his revenge on this man Razak. He wanted him dead.

Eryn looked over at Ro and without saying anything; Ro understood what he was asking and merely nodded in acknowledgment. Arlen gently rolled his eyes in despair. Whilst he understood the boy's desire for revenge, the chances of them running into this Kern Razak were about as good as their chances of finding Teren Rad alive.

The number of near impossible promises Ro was making were starting to mount up.

Chapter 19

A huge roar reverberated through the camp from the makeshift arena and although from his position in the cage he couldn't see what was happening, Teren knew that another man had just lost his life. Whether it was one of his fellow prisoners or a fighter from another tribe, he couldn't tell.

"How many is that now?" asked Brak as he came and stood alongside Teren.

"Five," replied Teren without turning to face his friend. He despised the Salandori. How they could enjoy watching one man maim or kill another just for their amusement was beyond him. There was no honour in it.

Well I'm going to make them pay for every man who has died just for their entertainment.

He wondered whether the watching Narmidians were enjoying the show, particularly the woman envoy. Whilst Narmidians weren't much different in looks and customs to their poorer cousins Teren had always considered them more noble and civilised. Now he began to wonder whether he'd been mistaken. If what Brak had heard was right and the Narmidians were there to ask for Salandori help, then they probably had no choice but to endure this spectacle and pretend they even enjoyed it. Not to do so would have been discourteous and would have offended the Salandori making them less inclined to help despite any threats the Narmidians might be able to bring to bear.

Two Salandori warriors were approaching from the right and Teren watched as they dragged a man's body behind them by the ankles, unceremoniously dumping it a few paces from the cage. Teren breathed a sigh of relief when he realised that he did not recognise the man meaning that Garik had won his contest.

More men were approaching the cage now. A number of Salandori warriors with Garik at their front. Garik was covered in blood, but he did not appear to be wounded apart from a gash on his upper right arm. His opponent had apparently died bloody.

One of the guards unlocked the cage and roughly shoved Garik in and both Teren and Brak reached out to catch him as he stumbled towards the ground. Then the guard and a few of his comrades entered the cage whilst the others remained outside.

"Your friend fought well and gets to live a little longer, but for the rest of you it is time to die," said the leader of the guards grinning maliciously. The man was missing a couple of front teeth and Teren had an overpowering urge to remove a few more. "On your feet and follow me." The man turned his back and made to leave.

Teren, Brak, Garik and some of the others had been working on a plan to escape for days now and everybody knew his role. Other men had been briefed as well just in case one of the main conspirators was killed in the arena before they had a chance to launch their escape attempt. The plan had been simple. Those who survived the individual contests and who were selected to take part in the mass contest at the end, would attack the guards just as it begun whilst another two men would attempt to set the others free. There were a lot of things wrong with the plan and much could go wrong, but it was a plan and the plan gave them hope.

The success of the plan depended on whether the opposing fighters would join their rebellion or would simply slaughter Teren and his comrades when their backs were turned. It would also depend on whether Brak and Petr could get to the cages and set their comrades free before they were killed.

Teren and his small band of men were hopelessly outnumbered even if their opponents joined them and would soon be cut down if no help arrived. However, if the men in the cages could be set free, there would be enough panic and confusion in the camp to give Teren and his men a chance to succeed. Even if some of the men in the cages decided not to join him, their mere presence would be enough to distract some of the Salandori.

As he watched the guard turn his back on them, Teren

could feel his rage come to boiling point, yet was powerless to prevent it. Before he could stop himself, Teren had leapt on the man's back, wrapping one arm tightly around his neck whilst the other grabbed hold of his head. He twisted it violently to his left and there was a sickening crack before the man went limp in his arms. Teren let go and the man's body dropped to the ground.

For the briefest of seconds nothing happened. The guards stared at Teren and Teren stared back whilst the other prisoners looked on aghast. Then Teren roared and launched himself at the other guards. Suddenly all Kaden broke loose.

The startled guards tried to back out of the cage and lock the door, but the majority of other prisoners were soon upon them, punching, kicking and gouging until their quarries were brought down. Teren had picked up the dead man's sword and handed the dagger to Brak and after cutting and slicing their way past the guards they were soon busily freeing the men in the other cages. Most of the prisoners immediately spilled out and joined in the killing, but others remained in their cages perhaps expecting the rebellion to fail and fearing reprisals.

Teren didn't have the time nor will to try and persuade them otherwise, as the first few minutes of the rebellion would be critical. After opening the last cage Teren glanced around him and saw that some of his men were now armed, but not enough. Most of the Salandori warriors were over at the arena as were the Narmidian escort for the Sultan's wife. Even now their leaders would be organising their men ready to launch a counterattack. Teren knew that he would have to overpower them before they had chance to get organised. He hoped that the fact that so many Salandori tribes were there would work in his favour. If they were unable to agree who was in overall command as he hoped, Teren suspected that each tribe would seek to protect its own chief and there would be no cohesive defence. If that happened he knew that they would be easier to pick off. With another mighty roar, Teren charged towards the centre of the camp and the makeshift arena. He did not look behind him to see if the others followed he just prayed that they would. If the freed prisoners lost their nerve now and tried to make a dash for it, they'd all be killed for sure.

One of Teren's main fears with his original plan had been the Salandori archers lining the arena; any sign of trouble and they were under orders to cut everybody down. It could have been a massacre. When the guard had turned his back on Teren, instinct had simply taken over and he had seized the opportunity to escape. By attacking in the manner he did and by causing so much mayhem and confusion, he had virtually neutralised the Salandori archers. Now, instead of all being in a compact space and easy meat for the archers, his men were spread out all over the camp. If they fired now they would risk hitting some of their own men, though he suspected one or two of the chiefs wouldn't have a problem with that if it meant saving their own worthless carcasses.

The scene around the arena was better than Teren could have hoped for. Unable to agree on a unified strategy against the rebels, isolated groups of Salandori were gathered around their respective leaders and trying to make it towards their horses.

Teren, Brak and a few of the other armed men slammed into the first thin line of Salandori, Teren leaping into the air just before he came into contact with them. He crashed heavily into one of the warriors and sliced clean through the neck of the man next to him before pushing on deeper into the throng of Salandori.

Teren was instantly surrounded by three warriors, but he was in a killing haze now and knew no fear. Within a matter of seconds two of the men were dead and the third lay on the ground wailing with the pain and trying to stem the flow of blood from the stump that was all that was left of his right arm.

Teren stopped briefly and looked around searching for his next target. There were still many Salandori around him, but most looked terrified and keen to avoid the mad Remadan who was already soaked in their comrades' blood. Many had seen Teren fight in the arena; none wanted to see him fight up close.

Brak appeared at Teren's side with another two men and was grinning.

"We've got them on the run already, Teren."

Teren's gaze had suddenly fallen on the chief of the Alith which had been holding him captive. He was surrounded by about a dozen men who were trying to smuggle him to his horse. Almost as if he possessed a sixth sense, the chief suddenly turned to face Teren, their eyes locking briefly. He said something to one of his men and the other man also turned to face Teren.

"What do you say we finish this, Brak?" said Teren grinning.

Brak followed Teren's gaze and then also started to smile. "Let's do it."

Teren's group suddenly raced as one towards the chief and his entourage. These were the chief's personal guards and his best fighters and to their credit they stepped forward to intercept Teren and his men. The chief, however, did not. He had panicked when he saw Teren's group and had hastily tried to mount his horse keen to get away. His horse, however, had other ideas and disturbed by the noise and pandemonium around him, it had become skittish. Whilst the chief was in the process of mounting him, it had taken it upon itself to bolt and had sent the chief tumbling to the ground with a thump.

The chief's bodyguard were good fighters and brave men, but they were no match for Teren and his band. With a burning desire for revenge and with absolutely nothing to lose other than their lives, they had smashed into the Salandori warriors with an almost reckless abandon. It had not taken the Salandori warriors long to realise that they were up against men who didn't fear death and their enthusiasm for the fight soon waned. One or two started to try and disengage, but as soon as they took their eyes off the man in front of them they were mercilessly cut down.

Teren had despatched three of the chief's bodyguard himself and soon he had cut a path through the warriors and found himself staring at the chief who was in the process of scrambling to his feet. Teren pushed him back down and then held him in place with a foot on his chest, his sword point coming to rest at the man's throat. The battle was still raging all around him and with his attention solely focussed on the chief Teren knew that he would be an easy target, but he trusted the men around him to watch his back. Besides, he had waited a long time for this moment and he wanted to savour it.

"I told you one day it would end like this," said Teren staring down at the petrified looking chief.

The chief was babbling something in his own language which Teren didn't understand. Teren pricked the man's skin with his sword point drawing the first sign of blood. The chief took the hint and immediately stopped speaking, though the look in his eyes conveyed the terror he was feeling.

Teren was suddenly aware that someone had sidled up alongside him and glanced to his left where the big northerner Brak now stood panting from the exertion of the fight.

"It's nearly done, Teren. Most of the other slaves have joined us. Some of the Salandori have got away, but most are dead. Some are throwing down their arms and trying to surrender."

"How's that working out for them?"

"Not good. The men don't seem willing to forgive and forget," replied Brak.

"Can't say that I blame them."

"The Narmidians are putting up a better fight, but we'll soon have them."

The Narmidians.

Teren had clean forgotten about them in all the excitement. He had questions for them. In particular he was curious to find out who the Arkadian woman was, especially as she was supposedly the Sultan's queen. He had only caught a brief glimpse of her once or twice and even then her features had been masked by a veil, but she was still somehow alluring and he longed to know more about her. His intention had been to let the Narmidians go, but now that the opportunity to perhaps question one of them had arisen, he was not about to turn it down.

The Salandori chief had started babbling again when Teren's distraction had led to an easing of the pressure from the sword point. Whether he had thought that he'd have more luck appealing to Brak, Teren didn't know.

"What's he blathering on about?" asked Teren nodding towards the stricken man beneath him.

"He says that he has many jewels and valuables in his tent and that we can take them all if we spare his life," said Brak.

"Really? That's very kind of him. Tell him that we're going to take him up on his offer with one little modification. We're going to kill him and then take his jewels. Then we're going to share his wives out among our men."

Brak smiled and after a few moments began to disjointedly pass on Teren's message in broken Salandori.

"On second thoughts, don't bother," said Teren as he drove his sword point deep into the chief's throat, before twisting and then withdrawing the blade. Brak looked at Teren in surprise. "You were taking too long. Get somebody you trust to go with you and secure those jewels before the mob get their hands on them."

"Where are you going?" asked Brak.

"I'm going to see who our Narmidian queen really is," and with that Teren jogged off towards the only place where the sounds of battle still dominated.

Teren had only run thirty or so paces when he came across one of the former slaves fighting three Salandori warriors. Another two Salandori were lying dead on the ground nearby. Teren nodded his approval and was about to run over and aid his comrade when he saw that it was the Delarite who was fighting. There was no love lost between Teren and the Delarite and there had been many a night when Teren thought the man would make an attempt on his life, but he never had. When Teren had approached him about joining him in the breakout he had laughed in Teren's face and called him all sorts of things and Teren had come very close to ending the man's life there and then. Now it seemed the Salandori were going to do the job for him.

Teren turned and was about to leave the Delarite to his fate, when a cry to his left drew his attention. Teren turned just as the Delarite ran one of his three remaining attackers through with his sword and shoved another back onto the ground with his foot. The third one was quicker than the Delarite anticipated though and he thrust forward with his sword piercing the Delarite in the left side. The Delarite cried out in pain before bringing his sword down in a powerful arc which the other man only just managed to block. The force of the blow knocked the man staggering backwards and the Delarite stepped after him intent on delivering a killing blow.

The Delarite had fought well and was obviously a man to be respected, but he had just made a possibly fatal mistake. By following through on the man he had just sent staggering backwards, he had turned his back on the man he had earlier shoved backwards with his foot. This warrior was now on his feet again and closing in on the Delarite's back. Without thinking, Teren raced across the ground as quick as he could, his sword drawn back ready to thrust when he was close enough.

Although he couldn't see it, Teren heard a man scream and knew without a shadow of a doubt that the Delarite had just despatched the man in front of him, but was completely unaware of the one about to run him through from behind.

It was going to be close. Teren was not as fast as he once was and the Salandori was close behind the Delarite. He could have shouted a warning to the Delarite, but to do so would have alerted the Salandori to his presence. He started to run faster.

The Salandori had just raised his sword when with every last bit of strength he had left, Teren thrust his sword into the man's back. Whether it was just coincidence or some sort of sixth sense, the Delarite turned at that precise moment, a brief look of fear and surprise crossing his face. He instinctively tried to raise his sword, but the Salandori warrior was too close. Suddenly a pained expression crossed the warrior's face and the Delarite stared as a sword point suddenly emerged from the man's abdomen, before disappearing again back into his body. The sword dropped from the Salandori's grasp as both his hands reached for his wounded stomach. Then without uttering a further sound he collapsed to his knees before finally toppling face first into the sand.

The startled Delarite stared at the dead man before looking up and seeing Teren standing where his adversary had been just moments before. Slowly he lowered his sword, his eyes never leaving Teren.

"You're welcome," said Teren breaking the silence.

"Why did you do that, Remadan?"

"Because if I hadn't you'd now be the one lying dead on the ground."

"And why would that bother you?"

"I didn't say that it would."

"So why did you help me?"

"Because as you've clearly decided to join us I couldn't very well stand by and watch these boys butcher you could I?"

"And what makes you think I've decided to join you?" asked the Delarite.

"Why else would you be killing these men then?"

"I might just have been killing them because they got in my way as I tried to make my escape."

"And were you?" asked Teren.

The Delarite stared at Teren for what felt like ages before finally speaking.

"No."

"That's good, because you're a handy lad to have around. Now follow me, there's still plenty of work for your sword I think."

"One thing, Remadan."

"Oh and what's that?" asked Teren.

"This doesn't mean I like you."

Teren laughed heartily.

"That's good, lad, because I wasn't planning on holding your hand any time soon anyway."

The Delarite did his best to disguise the small grin that was starting to appear on his face. Despite what he had said and the way he had acted, he had started to grow to like the Remadan. He also respected the man's strength and leadership abilities, not that he intended on telling him so. Worse still he now owed the man his life and he would be unable to go home until that debt was repaid. One way or another his fate and that of the Remadan were bound together, at least for now.

Teren turned again and started to make his way towards where he knew the Narmidians would be. The delay helping the Delarite might have cost him his chance to find out who the woman was, but at least he had made himself a new ally, though not one he could fully trust.

The fighting was all but over now, although here and there isolated duels continued. The balance of power, however, had swung drastically in favour of the former slaves who now outnumbered the remaining Salandori. The ground was littered with the dead and as Brak had informed him, the men were showing their former masters no mercy. Soon the former slaves would have satiated their blood lust and their attentions would turn to enjoying the victors' spoils, which in this case meant jewels and the many women who were even now screaming and running around the camp terrified.

Teren finally arrived at the spot where the Narmidians were trying to make their escape from, but he was too late. Even as he forced his way through the throng of his men he could hear the sound of horses galloping off. He stopped when he reached the front of the mob and watched as the woman, flanked by just two men turned and galloped away. Her veil had come undone in the struggle to get away and Teren had managed to catch a fleeting glimpse of her face before she left, her long red hair trailing in the breeze.

Teren stood and watched her go, his mind and heart racing.

It was impossible, it couldn't be her.

But there was no denying it, the woman had been the spitting image of her, if a few years older than he remembered.

If it was her why didn't she try and escape, there were only two of them?

"The camp is ours, Teren," said Garik coming alongside Teren and slapping him on the shoulder. "Teren?"

Teren finally turned to look at his friend and was about to reply when his gaze fell on the last remaining Narmidian warrior who was on his knees and about to be gutted by at least four former slaves.

"Hold!" bellowed Teren. Three of the men immediately took a step back, but the fourth either somehow didn't hear Teren's command or was of no mind to heed it. He raised his sword to strike the petrified looking Narmidian, but Teren quickly stepped forward, grabbed the man's wrist and shoved him backwards. "I said hold."

Teren slowly stared at the semi-circle of armed men, each of whom was looking at the Narmidian with hate-filled eyes. Teren let his gaze linger daring any one of them to challenge his authority. Brak, Garik and the Delarite had come to stand behind Teren in a show of support.

"Why do you spare this man, Teren?" asked a disembodied voice in the crowd.

"Who says I have? I just want to question him first," replied Teren.

That thought obviously hadn't crossed their minds and it seemed to appease the majority of the crowd. Teren wasn't sparing the man merely giving him a stay of execution.

When he was as certain as he could be that none of his own men were going to stab him in the back, Teren turned to face the Narmidian.

"I've two questions for you, Narmidian," said Teren.

"Why should I tell you anything? You're going to kill me anyway," the man spat back.

"No, I'm not," replied Teren.

"Then you're going to get those dogs to do it for you," sneered the man and nodding towards the mob behind Teren.

"I promise you that if you answer my questions honestly neither I nor they will kill you. Do we have a deal?" Teren ignored the mutterings of discontent from behind him.

The Narmidian's eyes narrowed in suspicion, but then the first glimmer of hope flashed across his face. "Very well."

"Good. Firstly, why are the Narmidians massing for war and who are they preparing to attack?"

"Our great Sultan has amassed the largest army the world has ever seen and all will tremble before it."

"I didn't ask for a propaganda speech, sonny, I asked why he's put together such a big army and who he is planning on attacking."

"He is going to wipe all of you decadent usurpers from the face of Arkadia so that the Narmidian people can take their rightful place as the dominant race. All will fall before his might and kiss his feet," replied the Narmidian grinning.

"Probably not going to happen that way actually, but

whatever gets you through the day I suppose. Tell me, if the Sultan has such an indestructible army why does he send emissaries to the lowly Salandori asking them to guard his southern borders?"

"Because our enemies in the south have been crossing into Narmidia and harassing our trade routes. With the might of the Sultan's army elsewhere, they might feel bold enough to try an armed incursion. The Salandori are a means to an end and will be dealt with another time."

"Sounds like your Sultan's got it all worked out. Trouble is I don't think he'll find the west ready to just bend down and kiss his feet. I think they'll send your little Sultan back with his tail between his legs and crying for his mother. I'd say father, but he probably doesn't know who that is right?" The Narmidian was bristling with anger at the insults being heaped on his great Sultan by this Remadan. "You didn't like that did you? Well you weren't supposed to," said Teren laughing.

"Laugh now Remadan, but your time is coming."

"We'll see. Now last question. The woman with the red hair who was with you; who was she?"

"She is our queen."

"You mean the Sultan's wife?" asked Teren.

"He has many wives, but only one queen."

"And what is this queen's name?"

"What is it to you, Remadan?" said the Narmidian sneering.

Quick as a flash Teren brought his sword point to rest on the man's forehead applying just enough pressure to draw forth the first drops of blood.

"I ask the questions, Narmidian, not you. Understand?" said Teren, his face a mask of pure rage. The Narmidian nodded. "Good. Now again, what is her name?"

"Surita," replied the Narmidian.

"Surita? That's a Narmidian name."

"She is a Narmidian queen, fool."

Before the man could even think about moving out of the way, Teren had sliced his sword tip across the man's left cheek leaving a nasty looking gash that was already bleeding profusely.

"Don't get an attitude with me, boy, or you'll find my good nature only stretches so far."

Behind him and out of earshot Garik leaned closer to Brak and whispered in his ear. "Does he even have a good nature?"

"Let's try that again shall we? Surita is a Narmidian name, yet the woman is clearly of Arkadian descent. What is her name and where did she come from?" asked Teren sternly.

The Narmidian stared up at Teren with unbridled hate, his eyes burning with fury.

"She was brought back from the west as a slave some years ago and placed in a nobleman's house. They say that one day whilst the Sultan was visiting the nobleman he saw her and instantly became transfixed by her beauty. He took her back to his palace and soon after made her another of his wives. She resisted at first, but then began to warm to him until eventually she became not only his wife, but also one of his most trusted advisers. When Queen Arixa died a year or so ago, he made Surita his queen."

Teren was beginning to feel sick and his heart was in his mouth when he asked the next question.

"How long ago did this happen?"

The Narmidians eyes narrowed again as he considered what the Remadan was asking him. He was showing an awful lot of interest in someone he had presumably never met before, unless there was history, in which case there might be something he could exploit to his advantage.

"About six or seven years ago." The Narmidian watched the muscles on the Remadan's face twitch. Something he had said had clearly unsettled the man.

"And the woman's real name?" asked Teren.

"I can't remember," said the Narmidian smiling suddenly feeling that he had something over the Remadan, perhaps even a bargaining chip. All he had to do was figure out how best to employ it.

Once again Teren moved his sword quickly, letting the point come to rest under the man's chin.

"How about now?"

"Vella, Vara, Va..."

"Valla?" finished Teren.

"Yes, that is it; Valla."

Teren suddenly felt sick and couldn't concentrate. His legs had started to tremble. Could it really be true? Had he stumbled across her after all this time only to see her ride away out of his grasp once again? So close yet so far. Teren's world was spinning. People were speaking to him, but he couldn't hear them, didn't want to. For the briefest of moments Teren thought that his legs were going to give way. He couldn't afford to look weak in front of the men whatever happened. He had to get control of himself.

"You know this woman I think, Remadan. I see it in your eyes." The Narmidian was smiling enjoying the sudden advantageous turn of events.

"Shut your mouth," snarled Teren.

"Yes, she means something to you. Perhaps she was..."

"I said shut your dirty mouth," shouted Teren as he spun round and sliced the man's head off with such force that it flew through the air, hit the ground hard and rolled some distance before coming to a halt.

Everybody stared at Teren in awe. Only the Delarite was smiling though even he tried to conceal the fact.

Brak stepped forward and addressed the men and told them to gather all the weapons and search the camp for any valuables. Other men were to catch and corral all of the horses. They would rest there tonight and move out in the morning. Guards were posted, but Brak doubted that the Salandori would be back, at least not yet. He didn't think that the Narmidians would return either unless their army was considerably closer than Teren had thought.

One of the men had asked about the women and after glancing over at Teren for guidance, but receiving none, his friend lost in a world of his own, Brak had told them that they were spoils of war. A mighty roar went up as the men spread out in every direction searching for whatever took their fancy, valuables or women.

Brak watched them go and shook his head in pity. He hated the thought of what the men were about to do to the women, but in truth whether he had approved it or not, it still would have happened. It always did. To the victor the spoils and in this case it meant the many young women inhabiting the camp.

Brak turned to face Teren who looked suddenly gaunt and weary.

"What troubles you, my friend is it that woman because if it is there are plenty more around the camp, though you'll have to hurry if you don't want to be at the end of the queue?"

Teren looked at Brak, Garik and the Delarite and nodded.

"Who is she?" asked Garik.

"Her name is Valla," replied Teren.

"That much I heard, but *who* is she?"

"She's my wife," replied Teren before slowly walking off into the darkness.

Garik went to follow him, but Brak grabbed his shoulder.

"Let him go. He needs to be on his own right now to think it through."

"How did his wife end up the Narmidian queen?" asked Garik.

"Teren told me his story one night in the cage. Seven years ago he was in the army and was away dealing with a rebellion in the north. Narmidian raiders attacked his home village killing and taking some women prisoners, among them his wife. When he returned from putting down the rebellion he left his children with his brother and spent the next five years searching the eastern lands for any sign of her. He never found her. When he came home he couldn't handle his guilt and went to live high up in the mountains turning his back on the world and his children."

"Didn't he say that before he got captured by the Salandori he'd been searching for his son and his fiancée after they were taken by raiders?" asked Garik.

"He did. He found his son and was searching for his fiancée when they got caught. Even now he doesn't know what has become of his son," said Brak.

"And now he's just discovered that his wife is alive and well and living with the Sultan of Narmidia. Bad luck stalks this man it seems. It is too much for one man to bear."

Brak nodded.

"So what do we do?" asked the Delarite.

Brak shrugged his shoulders. "We wait I guess. Then whatever he decides to do, I will follow. I owe him that much at least."

"I also," said Garik.

Both men looked over at the Delarite.

"I still don't like him, but honour dictates that until I can repay my debt, I will go where he goes."

"So be it," said Brak. "Let's go and see what's left in the camp and whether there's anything to eat; killing Salandori has given me a fierce appetite."

Smiling the three former slaves strolled into the camp to await Teren's return.

Chapter 20

It had been three days now since Eryn and Tayla had set off on their own whilst Ro and Arlen had headed east looking for Teren. Neither man had relished the prospect of sending the two youngsters on a perilous journey on their own, but if they were to find Teren it had to be done. Eryn had done his best to reassure them, but they could see in his eyes that he was scared. The prospect of a long journey through hostile country with no one there to help them if they got into trouble had not been an enticing one.

Ro and Arlen had sat upon their horses and watched until the two young lovers had disappeared over the southern horizon and even then they had been reluctant to move off in the opposite direction. Although they never admitted it, both had been hoping that the other would lose their nerve and suggest that they ride after their young friends. Neither had though and when there was clearly no point in sitting there watching the empty horizon any longer, they had turned and headed east, intent on resuming their search for Teren.

It was just after the morning meal on the fourth day of their search that they had seen them in the distance heading straight towards their position.

"What do you think; Salandori?" asked Arlen shielding his eyes against the rising sun.

Ro didn't answer immediately, taking a few extra seconds to study the small group of men riding towards them.

"Probably. I don't know who else would be this far into Salandor."

"Traders perhaps on their way home to the west?" asked Arlen hopefully.

"No, I don't think so, they're moving too fast."

"Do you think they've seen us yet?"

"I doubt it. We're two stationary dots in the distance whereas they're a larger fast moving group kicking up a dust trail," said Ro.

"Then what do you suggest; hide and wait for them to pass?"

"No, I suggest we stay right here and try to speak to them; they may know of Teren's whereabouts. Besides, there's nowhere to hide."

Arlen glanced nervously about him. His friend was right. They were in the middle of a dusty plain and there was literally nothing for miles, not even a rock to hide behind.

"Well let's hope they're the chatty kind then rather than the slit your throat and ask questions later kind," said Arlen loosening his sword and loading a bolt into his crossbow.

The riders were fast approaching and although they hadn't changed direction at all, it was clear that they had finally seen Ro and Arlen, as some of them were now readying weapons as they raced towards them.

"They're the strangest looking Salandori I've ever seen, Ro," said Arlen as he studied the men rushing towards them. None were wearing traditional Salandori attire and instead appeared to be wearing a variety of civilian clothes. If anything they looked like they were from the lands of the west.

"No, they're not, they're probably bandits or mercenaries," replied Ro as he unsheathed his small sword and held it over his shoulder. Arlen moved his horse slightly away from Ro's so that both men would have more room to fight if necessary which seemed increasingly likely. "Let them make the first move, Arlen."

Arlen nodded his acknowledgment if not his agreement.

Within thirty seconds the two men were surrounded by a group of nine riders all of whom had their weapons drawn. It was time for nerves of stone and Ro hoped that his friend wouldn't panic and loose a crossbow bolt or they were both doomed. One of the riders nudged his horse nearer to Ro than the others and studied the two men. Ro for his part met the man's gaze and held it. Ro was no expert, but the man looked like a Lydian, but the men with him seemed to represent a number of nationalities; they were a curious bunch.

Arlen too was studying the men around him, but not so much out of curiosity as worry. These were all hard, battle-scarred men who clearly knew how to fight and Arlen figured that Ro's guess about them being mercenaries was probably right. Arlen did not fancy their chances in a fight against such men, especially not when outnumbered four to one. He suddenly found himself wishing that these men were Salandori tribesmen after all.

"What do we have here then?" asked the man who had edged forward as he eyed Ro warily.

"My name is Ro Aryk and this is my friend Arlen Meric; we are searching for our friend," said Ro.

"You won't find any friends out here, Ro Aryk, just a lot of Salandori, although their numbers are dwindling as we speak," replied the man laughing. His men joined in on what was obviously a private joke. "It was very careless of you to lose your friend though."

"What can I say he's headstrong and reckless," replied Ro trying to keep the conversation light.

"Why do I think I know the name Ro Aryk?" asked the man thoughtfully.

"I don't know," replied Ro.

"I do," said another man edging his horse forward. He was quite small but had a hard look to his eyes and was clearly a fighter. Ro noticed the tattoo on his left forearm which he instantly recognised as the mark of the 4th Ligara, Jeral Tae's old command. "Captain Aryk commands the Royal Bodyguard of Remada. My suspicious friend here is Kale Hoteb and I am Garik Nard formerly of..."

"The 4th Ligara; yes I saw your mark. They are a steady and dependable force the 4th. I am pleased to make your acquaintance Garik, although I regret that I no longer carry the title of Captain of the Royal Bodyguard," said Ro.

"You're a long way from the Royal Palace, Captain Aryk," said Kale.

"Like I said, I'm no longer attached to the Royal Bodyguard. It seems to me that you men are a long way from your homes as well. I see Lydians, Remadans, a Cardellan and even an Angorran. How does such a motley group of nationalities come to be out here and together?"

"Not out of choice that's for sure. We were all taken prisoner by the Salandori at some point or other and made to fight for their entertainment, but now we've escaped and are on our way home," said Kale.

"Made to fight whom?" asked Arlen, his interest piqued.

"Each other or fighters from another tribe," replied Garik.

"To the death?" asked Ro.

"Usually," replied Garik.

"Barbarians!" said Arlen shaking his head.

"Does he have a name this friend you're looking for?" asked Garik.

"His name is Teren Rad," said Ro.

Garik and Kale exchanged glances.

"You are friends with Teren?" asked Garik.

"We are," replied Arlen.

"Of course, that's where I knew your name from. You were both with Teren at the battle for Vangor," said Kale.

"We were. You know Teren?" asked Ro.

"Put your weapons away, lads, these are friends," said Kale glancing round at his men as he sheathed his own sword. "Yes, we all know Teren. He was taken prisoner by the Salandori as well and eventually ended up in our camp. He was made to fight like the rest of us and was damned good at it. It was he who led the breakout and earned us our freedom. Every man here owes him."

"Where is he now?" asked Ro.

"After we rebelled and took the camp we held a meeting to decide what to do next. Some wanted to satiate their revenge on the Salandori and others like us just wanted to go home. Teren, however, said that he was going to look for his son. He was with him when Teren was captured but he didn't know what happened to him. He fears that he may be being forced to fight for one of the other tribes. Teren rides with the other men attacking Salandori camps, searching for his son and setting other captives free. It is a bloody business and the Salandori will be paying a hefty price for ever crossing Teren Rad."

"But his son, Eryn was with us and is now heading home," said Ro.

"So he wasn't taken prisoner by the Salandori then?" asked Garik.

"No, we got to him before that could happen," replied Ro.

"Then he searches in vain."

"How long ago did you last see him?" asked Arlen.

"What, four or five days ago?" replied Kale. Garik nodded his agreement.

"In which direction were they headed?" asked Ro.

"I don't know I'm afraid," replied Garik.

"He could be anywhere by now then," said Arlen feeling discouraged.

"Just follow the trail of Salandori bodies and you'll find him soon enough. The men with him were in no mood for taking prisoners," said Garik.

"Is one war not enough for him that now he has to wage war on Salandor almost single-handedly?" Arlen said turning to face Ro.

Ro smiled at his friend's attempt at humour.

"The Narmidians have struck then?" asked Garik.

"What do you mean?" replied Arlen.

"You asked if one war was not enough and I assumed you were referring to the war with the Narmidians."

Ro and Arlen exchanged a worried look.

"How long have you been away from your homelands? The war I refer to is the one with the Delarites who have invaded Lydia and Remada," said Arlen.

The men behind Garik suddenly started heatedly discussing what they had just heard which was evidently news to all of them.

"Some of us have been prisoners for months, some only days. Your ability with a sword or spear dictated how long you lived. So Delarite has invaded Lydia and Remada? How fares the war?" asked Kale.

"Not well," said Ro, "if you're a Remadan or Lydian. But tell me, what did you mean about a war with the Narmidians?"

"The night we escaped we were meant to take part in a large scale display of fighting in honour of some Narmidian guests," said Garik.

"Narmidians! What were they doing in a Salandori camp? They despise their neighbours," said Ro.

"I know, but they were there to persuade or cajole the Salandori into protecting the Narmidians' southern borders as the entire Narmidian army was massing to the west. We managed to take one of the Narmidian soldiers escorting the queen alive and Teren questioned him. Apparently the Narmidians have gathered a huge host and are planning on invading the whole western continent."

"That explains why we haven't seen many Salandori around for the last few days," said Arlen. "They've mostly gone south."

"But why?" asked Ro.

"Because their Sultan wants to reclaim the land that was once theirs and cleanse the land of all decadent usurpers; his words not mine," said Garik.

"And this was four or five days ago you say?" asked Ro.

"Yes."

"Then the army could be anywhere in Salandor by now?"

"Yes, but it won't be too hard to find; they say it's the biggest army the world has ever seen."

"If true, only the combined forces of the west might be able to stop it," said Ro.

"Except that they're not unified are they? They're too busy slaughtering each other," said Arlen.

"What happened to the Narmidian queen?" asked Ro.

"She managed to escape with a couple of her escort. She's probably rejoined her husband by now," said Kale.

"That's the other thing," said Garik. "The Narmidian queen, Teren knew her."

"Teren knew the Narmidian queen. How?" asked Ro.

"Apparently she is his wife, the one who was abducted some years ago."

"Valla?" asked Arlen incredulously.

"Yes, I think he said that was her name. Now he searches for his son and his wife."

"Then we must find him and tell him that his son is alive and heading home so he has one less thing to worry about. Then he can decide what he wants to do about Valla, though it sounds like he doesn't need to search for her as the Narmidians are coming to us. You must each ride to your respective countries and tell the people in charge what you know. We don't know where the Narmidians are but a small group travelling light should arrive ahead of their army," said Ro, his mind a mass of conflicting thoughts.

"And what if they don't listen or don't believe us?" asked Kale.

"You must make them believe you; all of our lives depend on it. If the warring nations unite, there is a chance, but if they continue to fight amongst themselves we will all be picked off one by one. Old animosities must be forgotten if we are to confront this new threat. Garik, you must seek out Jeral Tae. He is on the Council of Generals running the country now," said Ro.

"What happened to the king?" asked Garik surprised. Much had changed since he'd been away it seemed.

"He's been deposed. It's a long story and unimportant right now. Seek out General Tae and tell him that you ran into us and Teren. Tell him everything you know. He will believe you."

"And what will you do?" asked Kale.

"We'll try and find Teren and his men before they wipe out the Salandori nation and before he single-handedly tries to rescue his wife from the Sultan's tent," replied Ro.

"Very well, I wish you both good luck; you're going to need it," and with that Kale turned his horse and rode off due west closely followed by his men.

Garik waited behind briefly.

"When you find Teren, tell him that I hope he gets his wife back."

"If there's one thing I've learned in the time that I've known Teren it's that when he sets his mind to something it usually happens," said Ro smiling.

"Maybe, but the lady's got to want to be rescued in the first place."

"What do you mean?" asked Arlen.

"If she'd really wanted to I think she could have escaped from the two men left with her at the end; they were more intent on saving their own necks," explained Garik.

"You think there's a chance she might want to stay with the Narmidians?" asked Ro incredulously.

"I don't know, maybe. Perhaps she is no longer the same woman she used to be seven years ago and this is one hornet's nest that shouldn't be kicked," and with that Garik nodded and rode off after his companions.

The two men watched Garik leave each lost in their own thoughts.

"Do you remember when life used to be much simpler, my friend?" said Arlen.

"No, I don't actually," replied Ro.

"Me neither," replied Arlen grinning. "So all we've got to do is find Teren and his band of vengeful slaves in this vast wasteland, whilst avoiding the biggest army ever seen. Then help Teren rescue his wife from the heart of said army, that's if she even wants to be rescued, then ride home through hostile territory and prepare for yet another war, a war which by all accounts will make the last one seem like a picnic?"

"Sounds about right," said Ro smiling some more.

"Sometimes I long for the simple life of a priest," said Arlen.

"No you don't."

"No, you're right I don't. So where to now?"

Ro wiped the sweat from his brow as he considered his friend's question.

"Well those men said they'd last seen Teren four or five days ago to the east. If you were Teren who would you go looking for first, your wife or your son?"

"Well he knows that his wife rides with the Narmidian army and that shouldn't be too difficult to find by all accounts, so I would go after my son, though where I'd start I don't know," replied Arlen.

"I agree. However, if Teren still thinks that Eryn is a prisoner of the Salandori and knows that most of them are heading south, then I would have thought it likely that he too would head in that direction."

"Makes sense to me. So we ride south?"

"So it seems," said Ro and after taking a much needed drink, they turned their horses and headed south.

Chapter 21

Eryn had promised Ro and Arlen that he would travel south and then enter Remada as far down its eastern border as he was able in an attempt to avoid the Delarite army. The plan had seemed a sensible one to Eryn and although he was annoyed that it would take much longer than just heading due west from their starting position, he did understand the reasoning.

Nobody had expected the journey to be easy, but it had turned out to be much harder than any of them had envisaged. The further south Eryn and Tayla travelled the more Salandori they were running into, forcing them into several unwanted changes of direction. Luckily for them the terrain also became more accommodating, providing them with a plentiful supply of places to hide whenever they spotted any Salandori heading their way. Had they have run into so many Salandori on the open plains from which they had started out, they would not have got far.

Bands of Salandori were not their only problem however. Several days after leaving Ro and Arlen they had run into yet another sandstorm, which not only delayed them, but also caused Eryn to lose his bearings. He was not a natural tracker like Ro and apart from knowing that the sun rose in the east and settled in the west, he was devoid of any real sense of direction. He now found himself wishing that he'd paid more attention to his Uncle Kam when he'd taken him out on trips and had tried to teach him such things.

As Eryn rode sullenly along he couldn't help but feel that circumstances were conspiring against him, doing their best to prevent him from returning safely home with his fiancée. When they woke up on the sixth day to a cloudy sky with not even the sun to help guide him, he was sure of it.

Panic had threatened to overwhelm him then. He had no idea which direction they were supposed to be heading and he feared that they might even end up retracing the route they'd taken to get there. When he had seen the frightened look in Tayla's eyes he knew that he had to somehow keep it together and be strong for the both of them. After packing up camp he had made a great show of studying the terrain before reassuring Tayla that he recognised several of the landmarks around. He knew exactly where they were he had told her and that they'd soon be home. She hadn't looked convinced, but to her credit she didn't say anything and dutifully followed him without complaint.

On the rare occasions when he and Tayla had not been chatting Eryn would ride along and marvel at the countryside around him. That a single country should contain such a widely diverse terrain was a surprise to him. He had always thought that Salandor was nothing but dusty plains and rocky, barren mountains. To find some parts of it fertile and full of rivers and wildlife, yet punctuated with the occasional stretch of sand, was a pleasant surprise. Every change in landscape brought forth a multitude of new smells.

It was not a journey though during which Eryn could relax. He was acutely aware of how precarious their situation was and he was constantly on the lookout for riders heading their way. Of a night he would have to find the most secluded spot he could and hope that they were sufficiently well hidden that any passers-by were not able to spot them. Camp fires had to be kept small and were only kept alight long enough to cook the evening meal, meaning that they were often cold during the night. It had been Tayla who had suggested that they snuggle together and share body warmth. Eryn had been only too willing to do just that, but it did not help him sleep at all, the closeness and soft warmth of Tayla's body causing pleasant stirrings that denied him sleep.

The following night he had made his excuses and they had slept apart. Tayla had thought it was because of the argument they had had earlier in the evening, but Eryn had all but forgotten about that. He just wasn't sure that he could trust himself another night sleeping that close to her alluring body.

It hadn't been so much an argument as a judgement, Eryn had thought. He had told Tayla about everything that had happened since he had left Lentor and she had listened attentively. Maybe he had sounded proud of the fact that he had killed so many men and she hadn't liked it; he didn't know. The truth was that he wasn't proud of what he'd done but he was proud that he was still alive and had helped his friends when they needed him. His courage had not failed him and he had not let his father or his new friends down. Whilst she clearly marvelled at the transformation from boy to man in such a short space of time, he could see in her eyes that she hated what he had become; a killer of men. She had judged him and he had been found wanting.

He had wanted to make her proud, but all he had done it seemed was drive a wedge between them. It had been his soft and gentle nature that had attracted her to him in the first place she had said. Now she claimed not to recognise the boy in front of her. With a last disgusted look she had rolled over and turned her back on him.

Hurt and confused, Eryn had turned away from her too, not wanting her to see the hurt in his eyes, hurt that soon gave way to tears.The next morning after barely sleeping at all, Eryn had not been concentrating as diligently as he had been and they had run straight into a small group of Salandori. Eryn had panicked and drawn his sword, but the old man leading them had just smiled warmly and spread his arms in a gesture of peace.

The old man and one of his sons spoke enough broken common tongue for them to be able to communicate with each other and Eryn had learned that the group were outcasts belonging to no tribe and who hated the Narmidians. Over a meal of bread, cheese, olives and a meat Eryn had never tasted before, the family had told him how most of the Salandori were being driven south to protect the Narmidian border. The Narmidians he learned were going to war with the peoples of the west.

Eryn had thought that he had either misheard or misunderstood the man or that perhaps the old man had got his facts wrong. Maybe he had heard there was a war to the west and instinctively thought that his traditional enemy, the Narmidians were involved. Eryn didn't know for sure, but one thing the old man said was right and that was that all of the Salandori Eryn had seen had been heading south or south-east. At the time he had just thought it was because that was where the more arable country was, but now he wasn't so sure.

After thanking the man and his family for their hospitality, Eryn and Tayla had set off a little after midday. Eryn had asked the man how far south he and Tayla now found themselves and the old man had looked surprised. He then told Eryn that they were some way from the south and were in fact now not very far from the western border with Remada. Eryn had been shocked that he had managed to wander so far off track, but hearing that the Remadan border was not that far away was also heartening news. If they now headed due west, they would enter the country exactly where Ro had wanted them to avoid as it was likely to be under heavy Delarite occupation. To head south, however, with all the risks that involved, when they were so close to home, didn't make any sense either. No, Eryn decided, they would head west and take their chances. Perhaps Jeral Tae had led a counter-attack and the area was back under Remadan control.

***

It was a couple of days later after they had just crossed into eastern Remada that Tayla had fallen ill. At first she had turned very pale and complained of a terrible headache. Then she'd developed chronic stomach cramps and was unable to keep any food down and it was all Eryn could do to get her to sip some water. Frantic with worry he had thrown caution to the wind and headed to a town he could see in the distance. He would worry about whether it was full of Delarites later after he'd got Tayla some help.

As they had neared the town Eryn had begun to realise with a sinking feeling that he recognised the odd landmark here and there. Although the old Salandori traveller had told him that he was nowhere near as far south as he had thought, Eryn couldn't believe that he had got so badly lost that the first Remadan town they came across was this one. When they finally arrived on the outskirts of town and he recognised the town for sure, his spirits slumped.

Ederik.

By his estimations they should have been much further south than they actually were and he could only imagine that in their first few days in Salandor they had practically been going around in circles.

Ederik.

He had hoped that after his brief and unhappy visit to Ederik with Tav, he would never have cause to visit there again, but it seemed he was wrong. Only minutes after arriving in the town last time, Eryn and his friend Tav had visited a tavern to get something to eat and drink. After satiating their hunger, Eryn had stood up in the tavern and made a speech about the quest they were on and had called on the men of Ederik to join them. They for the most part had laughed at and ridiculed the two boys and in a spat of anger Eryn had called them scum and cowards. The place had erupted and both he and Tav had taken a beating. They only got out with their lives because Ro and Arlen, who they didn't know at the time, had come to their aid, as had the tavern keeper and his wife, Mad Maryke.

Eryn didn't know whether anyone there would remember him, but he had no reason to believe that his welcome would be any warmer this time, whether they did or didn't. Still, he had no choice. Tayla had taken a decided turn for the worse and Eryn was scared. He was going to have to visit the town and try and find a doctor to help her or she was liable to die.

He glanced over at Tayla just as she was about to drop from her saddle and quickly grabbed her arm to steady her. She was very pale and gaunt and looked back at him with dull sunken eyes. Eryn wished that he knew what was wrong with her so he could help her in some way, but he was no doctor and was therefore powerless to ease her suffering. All he could do was get her into town and hope that somewhere in that den of scum resided a doctor.

After checking that she was going to be able to remain seated after he let go of her and receiving a small smile in return, Eryn gently nudged his horse forward towards Ederik, leading Tayla's horse by the reins. His instincts were screaming at him to ride as hard and as fast as he could to try and find help, but he knew that if he did so Tayla would fall from her horse for certain.

The outskirts of the town were pretty much as he remembered them although this time in daylight he could see that many of the houses were in a dilapidated state and in dire need of work. The streets were fairly empty, the few people that were around looking at him suspiciously before scurrying indoors or down an alleyway and out of sight. There was something different about the people this time Eryn realised. Last time the streets had been bustling and although they had regarded him and Tav with suspicion, they had not reacted in the same manner as the people he'd seen so far. It was as if they were terrified of everything and everyone.

Eryn led their horses down a street bearing off to the left and instantly recognised the town's high street with its mishmash of shops and houses. There were a few more people abroad down there, but there was no sign of the laughing and cheerful faces from last time.

Eryn briefly locked eyes with a man sat in a rocking chair off to his left, sure that the man was familiar somehow. When it became clear that the man wasn't going to break his stare Eryn looked away only to look back again a few seconds later. The man had gone the only sign that anyone had ever been there was the gentle motion of the rocking chair as it maintained its lonely vigil. Eryn thought it was strange that the man should disappear like that, but decided not to dwell on it. Still, he was sure that he recognised him from somewhere.

A few dozen paces further on Eryn and Tayla came to a stop outside a building Eryn recognised. It was the building where on his last visit he and Tav had met several scantily dressed young ladies who had seemed keen for them to come with them into the house. As always though, Tav had been keen to get something to eat and an older woman who was also under-dressed in Eryn's opinion, had told them to get lost in no uncertain terms. Eryn had no idea why the woman had become so offended when they'd declined the girls' invitation, but they'd moved on as asked ending up in the tavern where they'd eventually met Ro and Arlen.

Ro and Arlen. I wonder where they are. Perhaps they're with my father and on their way home. It was a comforting thought.

Eryn tried to recall the name of the young girl who had spoken kindly to him and Tav last time and told them where to go for something to eat and drink. He could visualise her face but couldn't remember her name. He did, however, recall how pretty she was.

He was still thinking about her when the building's door swung open and a pot-bellied man in his late forties with a balding head walked out adjusting his clothes. He looked at Eryn and Tayla for a moment and then strode off without saying a word. It seemed to Eryn that the town's residents had not become any friendlier since he was last there.

The door opened again and the girl he had just been thinking about stepped out into the bright afternoon sunshine.

"Eryn, is that you? What's happened?"

"Lily!" said Eryn suddenly remembering her name when he clapped eyes on her.

Lily walked over to his horse and smiled up at Eryn. Then her gaze turned to Tayla and her expression turned to one of concern.

"What is wrong with your friend?" asked Lily.

"I don't know," replied Eryn honestly. "She suddenly became very sick and now can't eat and barely drinks. I've brought her here in the hope that the town has a doctor who can help her."

"Oh, we've a doctor all right, it's just that he's useless when he's drunk, which he often is. You'd be better off pushing on to Briden or somewhere else. Anywhere else! This place is like Kaden on Chell, Eryn."

Eryn glanced over at Tayla whose eyes had closed and was swaying in her saddle. He put a gentle hand on her arm trying to steady her.

"You are probably right, Lily; I have not forgotten the welcome we received here last time, but I cannot move her anywhere else as she just won't make it."

Lily nodded knowingly.

"Can you help us, Lily?" Lily glanced over her shoulder at the house from which she had emerged as if she was worried somebody might be watching or listening to their conversation. Eryn remembered the fierce older woman who had told him and Tav to beat it and shuddered. "Your mother doesn't have to know."

"My mother?" Lily laughed. "You think that old hag's my mother?" She laughed some more and had to clamp a hand over her mouth to save drawing unwanted attention to them. "She's not my mother, Eryn, she's my...employer. You really are from the country aren't you?"

Eryn had no idea what she meant by that as he'd already told her he was from a country village.

"So will you help us or not, Lily?"

"Of course I will. You must go and hide down that alley and keep out of sight and I'll go and speak to the tavern keeper and see if he's got a room free upstairs for you."

Eryn smiled as he recalled how the tavern keeper at the *Wild Boar* had helped him and Tav. He had also told them never to return.

"I don't think that's a good idea, Lily. Too many people will remember me. I'll never be able to just walk through the tavern without incident."

"I wasn't planning on you walking through the bar, Eryn; we have back doors in this town. Now you stay here out of sight like I said. If you thought the town was rough and unforgiving last time, I can assure you that compared to the men running it now, they were nothing."

That worried Eryn.

"Are there Delarites here, Lily?"

"Not at the moment as far as I know. They usually pay us a visit when they come into town, but I haven't seen any in a while. There are worse people than Delarites in this town."

"There was a man sitting in a rocking chair back down the road when we rode in. I'm sure that I know him but I can't place his name. When I turned to have another look he had disappeared."

Lily did not know who Eryn meant, but the fact that the man had gone scuttling off could not be a good sign. In all likelihood he had gone running off to tell the vile man who now was the self-proclaimed leader of the town, about the arrival of the strangers.

"I don't know who you mean, Eryn, but this town is full of strangers now, more so than usual. It's run by a group of army deserters who in return for their safety, run the town for the Delarites," said Lily.

Eryn shook his head in disgust. Deserting was bad enough but to then start working for the enemy was another thing altogether. The sooner he could get Tayla fixed up and get away from there the better. All he could do was hope that one day whoever these men were that ran the town for their Delarite masters, would get what was coming to them.

Tayla groaned and then vomited.

"We need to hurry, Eryn, your friend does not look very good to me at all. I will speak to the tavern keeper and if he will take you in I will come back for you. In the meantime I'll ask the tavern keeper to send his son to discretely fetch the doctor, though what state he'll be in I don't know; it is past midday after all. Now hurry and get out of sight as best you can. I'll be back soon," and with that Lily turned to leave.

"Lily!" Eryn called after her.

She turned to face Eryn once again.

"What is it?"

"Thank you," said Eryn.

Lily smiled. "You're most welcome. I hope that your friend makes it," and this time she turned and hurried away.

Eryn had done what Lily had suggested and had led his and Tayla's horses down a nearby alley and out of sight of all but the most inquisitive of eyes. Even so Eryn had felt that his departure had been eagerly watched.

Tayla was looking worse by the minute and Eryn did his best to comfort her whenever her body was suddenly wracked with stomach pain. The minutes had dragged like hours until eventually Lily had returned. She did not say whether the tavern keeper was happy about it or not, but either way he had agreed that Eryn and Tayla could stay in the small back room at the top of his stairs.

One look at Tayla told Lily that in the short period of time she had been gone, her condition had worsened and although she didn't say as much, Lily held out little hope for his friend's survival. She had seen this illness before, ten years ago and then again just the previous year when the illness had returned to claim her younger sister.

As quickly as they were able, Lily had led them through the backstreets of the town towards the *Wild Boar*. Despite their ponderous route, Eryn still felt like their every movement was being watched. On at least one occasion he had spun round and thought that he caught a glimpse of somebody melting back into the shadows behind them.

When they passed by another alleyway the other end of which seemed to come out in front of the town stables, Eryn came to an abrupt stop as he peered down the alley trying to make out what it was that looked so out of place. After a few seconds he could see that there were two or three things hanging outside the barn.

"What are those?" Eryn asked Lily.

Lily followed his gaze but knew instantly to what he referred.

"A warning."

"What do you mean a warning?" asked Eryn.

"They're a warning to the rest of us that if we don't do exactly as we're told that we'll end up the same way," said Lily bitterly.

"You mean they're bodies hanging there?" asked Eryn but even as he spoke he could make out that the bloody and torn rags hanging several feet above the ground had once contained men. "Who are they?"

"Remadan soldiers from the army that was beaten in a big battle just north of here. They retreated here and found that some of the men who had deserted their ranks had taken refuge in the town. They tried to arrest them but were killed. If it's any comfort they were dead long before their bodies were strung up."

Eryn's eyes were wide with indignant rage. He was starting to hate this town more and more with every passing minute.

"Did these soldiers have names?" asked Eryn.

"I only know that one of them was a general called, Jeral Tae," said Lily.

Eryn stared at her open-mouthed, momentarily unable to speak as the news sunk in.

"Jeral Tae is dead?"

Lily nodded. "Did you know him?"

"He was from my home village."

"I'm sorry, Eryn, I didn't know. He was fighting right up to the minute they overpowered him. He was a brave man. They all were."

Eryn nodded. "Who did this, the Delarites?"

"No, the deserters, although some Delarite soldiers then started killing the mob when they found that they'd killed a Remadan general before they'd had chance to interrogate him. The soldiers pulled out soon after. Now come, we must get going. I think we are already being followed."

"I know we are," said Eryn, "but now I'm going to do something about it. You take Tayla to the *Wild Boar* and get her safely upstairs and I'll be along presently. I know the way from here."

"What are you going to do?"

"I'm going to find out who he is and then I'm going to kill him," replied Eryn.

Lily made to persuade him otherwise, but the look in his eyes told her that she'd be wasting her time.

"Be careful."

"I will," said Eryn as he showed Lily his knife and skulked away to find a hiding place.

Not long after watching Lily lead Tayla and the horses away, whoever had been following them, suddenly came into sight and Eryn wasn't surprised to see that it was the man from the rocking chair earlier.

The man was either extremely cautious or very perceptive, because he stopped in virtually the same place they had and looked round suspiciously as if he knew that now he was the one being watched. After a few seconds he made to move on when Eryn suddenly leapt at him from his position of concealment.

Despite his vigilance, Eryn had still managed to take the man by surprise and sent him sprawling to the ground beneath him. Eryn wasn't the biggest physically and knew that his best chance of success was to strike fast and hard whilst the man was still recovering. Eryn quickly knelt on top of him and began pummelling his face with his fists, weeks

239

of rage being let loose. At first it looked like Eryn's plan had worked as the man lay there unable to evade the beating Eryn was giving him, but then he seemed to recover his senses and punched Eryn in the kidneys.

Eryn yelled with pain, his own assault immediately ceasing and his opponent seized on the opportunity and managed to roll over and dislodge Eryn from on top of him. Both men got to their feet and the man who had been following Eryn reached into his tunic and produced a knife. He grinned evilly at Eryn clearly thinking he now had the upper hand, but his grin soon faded when Eryn produced his own knife.

The two men began to circle each other warily until all of a sudden the other man slashed his knife horizontally, intent on carving Eryn's abdomen open. Eryn had somehow anticipated the move, however, and had leant back and drawn his stomach in just at the right moment and the blade hummed harmlessly through the air.

Undeterred the other man now swung his knife back towards Eryn's face with a backward thrust but again Eryn managed to comfortably lean out of reach. Frustrated by the fact that the boy wasn't turning out to be such an easy target after all and clearly had some skill of his own, the man launched into a ferocious, but crude assault slashing his knife this way and then that in an attempt to catch Eryn by brute force. The evenings Eryn had spent practising with Arlen had not been wasted though, and he found himself anticipating the man's cuts and thrusts before he'd even made them. All he had to do was be patient and await his opening.

That opening came sooner than he had expected. Clearly demoralised at the fact that he had not already killed the boy, his attacker was now looking for a way out and kept glancing over his shoulder trying to weigh up whether he could outrun his opponent. The man's attacks were fewer now and almost half-hearted as if he was just going through the motions for the sake of appearances.

When the man made his next wild swing towards Eryn's face, Eryn merely swayed out of the way and waited for the man's momentum to leave him unsteady. When as expected the man stumbled forward a pace, Eryn briskly stepped forward and kicked him behind the right knee, dropping him instantly to his knees. Quick as a flash Eryn then kicked the man's right wrist making him drop his knife before moving in and placing his own blade under the man's chin. His left hand grabbed the man's hair and yanked his head back exposing his throat.

"You have just five seconds to tell me who you are and why you've been following me, before I cut your throat," Eryn hissed in his ear.

"I wasn't following you," said the man unconvincingly.

Eryn dug the knife point in just far enough to break the skin and draw forth the first drop of blood.

"Are you really sticking to that answer? Now who are you and why are you following us? Lie to me this time and this conversation is over. Understand?" Eryn dug the knife in a little more for emphasis and the man nodded enthusiastically.

"My name is Calib Haliver. Pular pays me and some of the others to let him know when strangers enter the town. I was following you to see where you went. That's the truth I swear."

"Pular?" asked Eryn. The sheer mention of the name made his blood boil. "You don't mean Pular Bratak?"

"Yes, Pular Bratak. He runs things around here."

Eryn suddenly felt sick to the pit of his stomach. Pular Bratak, the lowlife from his home village who had done everything he could to undermine his plans to rescue Tayla and the others. His mind briefly flashed back to the altercation in the village hall the night after the raid on the village. Bratak and his cronies had baited him and Jeral all night long until it looked like it was going to turn violent. When one of Bratak's cronies had come at Eryn with a knife, the village blacksmith, Rom Tagral had stepped in and blocked the man's way forcing him to back down although the man swore that it wasn't the end of the matter. Calib Haliver had been that man.

"So Pular Bratak is in town?"

"Yes," replied Haliver. "He and a number of others deserted the army the night before the battle just north of here and this is where we ended up. He now runs the town with the Delarite's blessing."

"And what of the town's people? What do they think about Bratak and the rest of you?" asked Eryn.

"Some have joined us and the rest are terrified of us and do what they're told otherwise they end up like those soldiers swaying on the end of a rope."

"I remember you now," said Eryn menacingly. "Are you one of them that hung Jeral Tae and the others?"

"No, I swear I had nothing to do with that. I'm just trying to survive that's all."

"Maybe, but now you've given me a problem. I can either kill you here and now and live with that on my conscience, or I can let you live and trust you won't go running to tell Bratak that I'm here. I want that to be a surprise."

"You can trust me, son, I won't tell a soul," pleaded Haliver.

For a minute Eryn almost believed him, but it was the almost imperceptible glance towards the alleyway to his left and the brief look of joy that swept across his face that gave him away. Without even looking Eryn instantly knew that someone was approaching him from that direction and from their stealthy movements they were not coming in peace. When whoever it was inadvertently trod heavily on a dry twig, Eryn's fears were confirmed.

Saying a silent prayer that it was not Lily coming back, in one fluid movement Eryn dragged the knife across Haliver's throat before hurling the knife at the newcomer who had emerged from the alleyway with his sword poised to strike Eryn.

Haliver collapsed to the ground clutching his torn throat, a gurgling sound escaping his mouth as thick red blood oozed through his fingers and down his tunic. To Eryn's right the man with a sword had stopped dead in his tracks and stared at the knife that was protruding from his chest as if he was trying to work out what had just happened. Then with a look of disgust he pulled the knife out and threw it to one side, wincing as the blood from his chest began to flow freely.

He looked up and saw Eryn watching him and with a roar that Eryn feared might attract the whole town, he ran towards Eryn and swung his sword wildly at his head. Eryn managed to duck well below the swing and after drawing his own sword he swung low catching the man just above the left knee, the blade digging deep into the man's flesh and muscle. Eryn yanked his blade free and immediately rolled away out of striking distance before turning to face his opponent again in a crouched position.

The man had howled in pain and stumbled to one knee but was incredibly struggling to his feet again, a look of murder in his eyes. He advanced on Eryn waving his sword from left to right in front of him trying to unnerve and intimidate him. Eryn slowly rose to his feet, but remained in a hunched position becoming as small a target as he could. His eyes never left those of his opponent, trying to gauge what the attacker's next action might be.

The man was tiring, the loss of blood making him sluggish, but one lucky swing or one lapse in concentration by Eryn could still end up costing him his life. He hadn't come all this way and gone through everything he had, just to die in some filthy alleyway in that cesspit of a town.

With a speed that Eryn thought the man no longer capable of, he suddenly swung first for Eryn's head and then for Eryn's lower legs before suddenly turning his sword around and thrusting at Eryn's stomach. The first swing Eryn had easily ducked beneath and the second he had nimbly jumped over, but the thrust had almost caught him unawares and he had felt the tip of the man's sword pressing on his leather waistcoat, but it had not pierced his skin.

Eryn could see in the man's face that it had been an all or nothing attack and that he was now spent. With as much strength as he could muster Eryn brought his sword crashing down onto the other man's weapon, which was still extended towards Eryn, knocking it clean out of his hand. Then before the other man could even consider his next move Eryn drew his sword arm back sending his elbow crashing into his opponent's jaw. Eryn felt the contact and heard the crunching sound as his elbow smashed into bone, teeth and flesh.

Still the man did not go down. Eryn swung his sword in a reverse swing and caught the man in his right side. The sword's blade bit deeply into flesh and Eryn heard the man cry out. He pulled the blade back and struck again and again. By the time he had pulled his sword out the fourth time, the man had slumped to the ground dead, his body a lacerated and bloody mess. Eryn too was covered in blood.

He looked down at the man's ruined body and remembered seeing the man before; this had been one of the three men who had started the fight with Eryn and Tav on their last visit. He and two of his friends had literally bumped into Eryn and Tav when they had entered the tavern on their last visit to Ederik. They had shoved the boys back out into the road and left them lying in the mud. Then later on when Eryn had been making his speech and trying to enlist the help of some of the men of Ederik, the three men had re-entered the tavern and started heckling. Eventually they had provoked Eryn too much, he had said something to offend them and then all Kaden had broken loose.

Well I bet you wish you'd never crossed us now, thought Eryn bitterly. He didn't like what he had become. He didn't like what the war and other people were turning him into. He'd never wanted to kill anyone, but now it seemed that he had no choice. Suddenly feeling slightly ashamed he sheathed his sword. It was a good sword and had belonged to his father Teren Rad and had no doubt killed a great many men.

Well now it's killed another one.

Shaking his head in disgust he glanced around to make sure nobody was watching and then hurried off towards the *Wild Boar* to see Tayla and Lily.

As Eryn strode off a third man stepped out from his place of concealment and watched him go. He should have gone to the aid of his two friends, he knew that, but he had decided not to and as he looked at their lifeless bodies he congratulated himself on making the right decision.

He had recognised the boy instantly. He had only seen him once before and that had been some weeks ago. He had been with another young lad in the *Wild Boar* trying to persuade some of the town's men to go with him on some fool rescue mission. Lukan had baited and heckled them throughout the meeting and eventually the lad had bitten giving Lukan and the others the excuse they needed to give the boys a beating. Everything had gone to plan at first, but then two strangers had come to their aid. When that fool of a tavern keeper and his lunatic wife had weighed in as well the boys and the strangers had managed to make their escape.

He had seen then that the boy could fight but tonight he could also see that in the intervening weeks that boy had turned into a man. He had no wish to take a further beating or worse and that is why he'd decided to remain concealed when first Calib and then Lukan had tried killing the boy. They were fools and had paid a fool's price. The man smiled. Besides with them out of the way there was only him left to tell Bratak about the boy's arrival and he wouldn't have to share the reward with anyone.

He didn't know what that reward might be; the level of generosity showed by Bratak very much depended on what sort of mood the man was in on any given day. It might be a monetary reward or it might be some extra time with one or more of the girls at the brothel. That was appealing. He had his eye on that little blond girl who always looked at him with disgust as if he was something she'd trodden in down the street. Well if Bratak ordered it she would have to lie with him and then he'd teach her. He'd teach her some respect and that was for sure.

Yes, if Bratak was in a good mood when he told him the news, he'd ask for some time with the blond. He smiled at the notion and quickly turned back down the alleyway. The sooner he told Bratak, the sooner he'd get his reward.

Chapter 22

"They're ready for you, Teren," said the man grinning.

Teren tore his eyes away from the body strewn ground and looked at his comrade.

"How many?"

"Three."

Teren grunted; it would have to be enough. He followed his comrade back through the battlefield to where three Salandori men, one more ornately dressed than the other two knelt with their heads bowed.

"The one with the blue headband is the tribal leader," said the man who had fetched Teren. "We don't know if any of them can speak the common tongue, Teren."

"Then they'd better learn quickly."

The other man smiled knowing what Teren was implying.

Teren walked up to the man kneeling on the right and stood before him. Sensing his presence, the Salandori slowly looked up and met Teren's fierce gaze. There was no fear in the man's eyes Teren noted admiringly. A little fear crept in though when Teren slowly and meaningfully drew the long sword that was slung over his shoulder.

"I have just one question for you. On your travels have you seen a young western boy with blond hair about eighteen summers old?" The Salandori warrior just looked at Teren blankly. "Well?" Teren could not tell whether the man was refusing to answer him or just didn't understand. Nor did he much care.

Whether deliberately or not the man made no attempt to answer Teren and a few seconds later his headless body toppled to the ground.

Some of the man's blood had splattered his comrade kneeling next to him and the terror on his face when Teren came to stand before him was almost palpable.

"Same question to you. Have you seen a young western boy held captive by any of the other tribes you've run into?"

The warrior glanced nervously from Teren to his blood

stained sword and back again before he started babbling in his native language. Teren had no idea what he was saying and although Brak had a rudimentary understanding of the language, the man was speaking too fast and in a strange dialect that he could not understand.

"Anything, Brak?" asked Teren.

"Sorry, Teren, I can make out the odd word but nothing that makes any sense or is of any help."

"That's what I thought," said Teren has he swiftly cleaved the man's head from its shoulders to the cheers of the other freed slaves. Teren stepped in front of the last remaining Salandori, the one wearing the blue headband, which Teren's men believed to be the tribal chief. "What about you, chief? You seen the boy or do you want to go the same way as your men here?"

For a moment it didn't look like the chief was going to reply, but then he fixed Teren with a stare and spoke in the common tongue. "We have not seen this boy you speak of, nor have I heard anything about him. If he is truly a prisoner of the Salandori and is not already dead, he will be travelling south with his tribe to guard the Narmidian border."

"And why didn't you speak up and say that a minute ago? It might have saved your men's lives."

"I doubt that, Remadan. Besides, my interfering would have shamed them. To each man his destiny."

"Well yours doesn't look too clever either if you can't help me," said Teren smiling.

"I cannot tell you where to find something I have not seen."

"True, but that also means you are of no use to me."

Before the man could say anything further Teren had removed his head as well, before striding off to the cheers of the other men. Brak watched him go. Teren was becoming increasingly ruthless with each passing day.

The day after Teren had led the break out against their Salandori captors, he had held a meeting with all of the freed slaves who had not melted away during the night. Teren had told them that each man was free to do as he chose. Teren was to continue the search for his son who he feared had been taken prisoner by the Salandori.

Some of the men chose to try and find their way home and drifted off in small groups during that morning, but most remained behind unsure what to do. Some burned for vengeance against the people who had enslaved them and made them fight for their entertainment.

Teren had proposed that those who sought revenge would best be served by accompanying him. He promised them that they would spend every waking hour hunting down the Salandori and making them pay for what they had done. Teren promised them that he would lead them until such time as he found his son.

Then the slaughter had begun. Camp after camp was ruthlessly and mercilessly attacked. Every man and boy old enough to bear arms was killed out of hand. Brak had tried to persuade Teren against the slaughter, but he would not listen. He needed the men and the men needed revenge. The killing would go on.

At the end of every raid several prisoners would be taken and questioned about his son's whereabouts. Regardless of whether they didn't understand him or simply didn't know anything about Eryn, all were beheaded. None were spared. At first it had seemed to Brak that Teren felt guilt for the atrocities he was committing, but now he knew his friend felt nothing; nothing but contempt and hate. The man no longer had a conscience.

Brak had considered leaving on several occasions like Garik, but he owed the man his freedom and perhaps even his life. He therefore chose to remain at Teren's side, but with each passing day he grew to hate what Teren was turning into. Worse still he was beginning to loathe himself for letting it happen. Those who did nothing to stop the slaughter were surely as guilty as those who wielded the blade.

The majority of the men who rode with Teren loved the man and what he was doing. Together they were getting the chance to exact their revenge and to get rich. Despite their poor appearance and nomadic way of life, some of the Salandori, especially the chief and his inner circle, were very rich and their tents were full of jewels and treasures. They were also full of young wives and these too had pleased the men following Teren.

With every raid on a Salandori camp Teren's group grew stronger. Not every Salandori tribe kept slaves for fighting, but many did and every time they liberated some they were given the same choice as the original men; return home free men or ride with Teren and seek revenge. Most chose to join Teren and his band of followers was growing larger every day.

The lightly armoured and poorly disciplined Salandori were no match for the hardened fighters that followed Teren and casualties in his men were often light and negated by the number of new men who joined their ranks. By comparison, all the men in the Salandori camp were killed, either in battle or as part of Teren's almost ritualistic interrogation of those unfortunate enough to be taken prisoner. None ever claimed to know anything about Teren's son and Brak was starting to wonder whether the boy was even in Salandor.

"Another bloody day, Brak," said the voice to his right, breaking his train of thought.

Brak turned and saw the Delarite standing there observing him.

"They are all bloody nowadays."

"True, but until our friend finds what he is looking for, that is how it has to be."

"And what if what he seeks is no longer here, Delarite? What happens to the Salandori then?"

The Delarite shrugged his shoulders. "I don't know, but every dead Salandori is a good Salandori as my people would say."

"I've heard that your people say that about every nationality."

"Also true, but that is just because we are superior to everyone else," replied the Delarite smirking.

"Ever thought about becoming an emissary or ambassador for your country when your sword arm is no longer able to bear arms?" asked Brak.

"No," replied the Delarite after brief consideration.

"Good, because I don't think that you'd be very good at it."

The two men locked eyes and then after a few seconds began to laugh.

"I grow to like you northerner," said the Delarite.

"That is just as well; I hear that those you dislike don't always wake up," said Brak.

"So it is said."

"What is your name, Delarite?" asked Brak.

The man's face seemed to cloud over for a second. "Delarite will do. My name is my business," and with that he turned and stalked away leaving a bemused Brak staring after him.

A few minutes later, Brak found Teren sitting alone cleaning and sharpening his blade. He briefly considered leaving the man to his thoughts but in the end decided that the matter couldn't wait; what he wanted to say needed to be said.

"I am sorry that your son was not among them, Teren."

Teren glanced up at his friend and grunted his agreement before resuming work on his sword.

Brak undid his sword belt and slumped to the ground next to the Remadan. They sat there in companionable silence for a few moments, Teren apparently lost in his own thoughts and Brak deliberating whether or not it would be detrimental to his health to say what he had come to say.

"I have lost count, my friend, how many camps and tribes we have attacked without any sign of your boy. I think it is time for you to face the possibility that he may no longer be alive, Teren."

Teren stopped cleaning his blade and a dark look flashed across his face as his entire body tensed. Brak's hand surreptitiously slid towards the hilt of his own sword lying next to him, though he truly doubted that he would reach it before Teren had removed his head. The angry look passed and Teren again began to sharpen his blade.

"He's not dead."

"I truly hope that he is not, Teren, but you must at least consider the possibility," pleaded Brak.

"No, I won't, because I know in here that he's not dead," said Teren gently tapping his chest above his heart with his right fist.

"There are other possibilities."

"And what are they?" asked Teren.

"That he escaped the Salandori and perhaps is no longer in the country or was maybe never caught by them in the first place."

That caught Teren off guard because he hadn't even considered either of those possibilities.

"Unlikely. A young lad on his own in a strange country with so many Salandori warriors wandering about, wouldn't stand much chance."

"Well there are a great deal fewer of them now," said Brak bitterly.

"And their numbers will continue to dwindle."

"How long is this killing going to go on, Teren?"

"Until I find my son."

Brak sighed. He was right back to the beginning of the argument. An uneasy silence fell over the two men, neither wanting to make the simmering bad feeling between them any worse than it already was. It was Brak who eventually spoke.

"So where do we go now? I think we've wiped out every Salandori for hundreds of leagues."

"South," replied Teren.

"But virtually every Salandori still alive is converging on the south," said Brak suddenly alarmed.

"Exactly, so that's where we need to be," replied Teren.

"Attacking isolated groups of Salandori is one thing, but attacking a horde of them is quite another. The men are good, Teren, but not that good."

"I'm not proposing attacking the whole Salandori nation, Brak, just going where they are. We'll find their weak spots and attack them there. They won't be expecting an attack from behind as their gaze will be firmly fixed to the south. Sooner or later we will run into one of them who knows of my son's whereabouts."

"And all the rest of us have got to do in the meantime is to try and stay alive?" said Brak.

"You're free to leave anytime, you know that, Brak."

Brak nodded. "I know, but my place is with you, at least for now."

"Good, then please go and tell the boys to enjoy themselves tonight because tomorrow we ride south."

Brak held Teren's stare for a few moments before turning and striding off towards the camp where already the sounds of drunken revelry were filling the night air.

***

They had headed south straight after the morning meal the next day. As usual, most of the men rescued from the latest camp to be attacked had opted to join Teren's group. A few though had decided to take advantage of the lack of Salandori roaming around to try and make it back to their homelands.

They did not see a single Salandori warrior for the next couple of days although early on day three they were forced to take cover when some of the scouts Teren had sent out had come racing excitedly back. No more than two leagues away and just over a small ridge topped by a few sparse trees, was the entire Narmidian army moving westwards.

The scouts had been very excitable and the numbers they used to describe the Narmidian army were ridiculous as far as Teren was concerned and could not be trusted. At their insistence, however, he, Brak and a couple of the others rode back with one of the scouts to see for themselves.

After giving orders for their men to take cover as best they could, Teren and the others had ridden to the small ridge and after securing their horses below the skyline, they had crawled their way to the top of the ridge.

Teren tried to hide the surprised look that swept across his face, but he saw it reflected anyway in the faces of all the other men. The scouts had indeed been telling the truth about the size of the Narmidian army and Teren wasn't even sure that there was a number to describe such a host.

One of the men suddenly shook Teren's shoulder and pointed at a group of twenty horsemen who had broken away from the main force and were now heading their way. For a moment Teren worried that their presence had been spotted, but before they reached the slope of the ridge, the riders suddenly changed direction and began to ride parallel to the main column.

Teren and the others breathed a collective sigh of relief. Obviously the Narmidians felt so secure in their numbers and in the fact that no usurpers were likely to be that far to the east that they had not bothered sending out any scouts. If they had, Teren and his men would have been found for certain.

"I think we'd better be getting back to the boys to make sure they stay hidden," said Teren. The others all seemed relieved at the suggestion and nodded eagerly. "Raul and Burat, you two remain here and observe them. If there's any change in their movement or you think our position is likely to be compromised, you hurry back and tell us, understand?"

Both men nodded but looked worried about being left alone so close to such a powerful enemy.

Thirty minutes later, the two men returned to where they knew the rest of their comrades were hidden and reported that the Narmidian army had moved on and whilst their rearguard was still in sight, it would be safe for Teren and the others to now move on in the opposite direction.

Nodding his thanks, Teren gave the order to ride out and the column of freed slave fighters continued south.

Teren felt his heart and soul ripped in two. The unsuspecting war torn west was about to be hit by an army the likes of which the known world had never before seen. The Narmidians might not be the strongest and most heavily armoured foe, but they certainly made up for that in numbers. Whilst the nations of the west were locked together and slugging it out, they would suddenly be hit by such an overwhelming force that they would simply be rolled over. The only way they would survive was if they immediately stopped fighting one another and united against the common enemy, but to do that, someone had to firstly warn them of the coming danger.

Teren's head told him he should ride with all haste to Remada and warn Jeral Tae and the others what was coming, but his heart told him something completely different. Some would not believe him of course, but Jeral would and one way or another he would cajole the others into believing. But if Teren was to ride west to warn his friend of the coming catastrophe, he would be abandoning his search for Eryn. If Eryn truly was a prisoner of the Salandori as Teren feared, then by leaving him on his own he was practically consigning the lad to death.

He had put duty before family once before and look what it had got him; a lost wife, a dead daughter and an estranged son. He would not abandon them again, not this time. To Kaden with Remada, this time it would have to save itself; his son needed him more.

Teren's thoughts suddenly turned to Vangor and he found himself wondering what had become of Ro Aryk and his friend Arlen Meric. Did they stay and defend the city or leave in the end? Had the relief column arrived to help? He hoped they were okay. Ro had promised that when they were sure that the city was safe or no longer defensible, that he and Arlen would come looking for Teren and Eryn and help them find Tayla. Teren had smiled and thanked Ro, not for one moment expecting it to happen. Ro Aryk was a good man and Teren had no doubt that his word was good and that his intentions true, but with everything else going on Teren had not really expected Ro and Arlen to follow them east. Duty was a harsh mistress and whilst he no longer held a rank, Ro Aryk was the kind of man who would still answer the call of his country.

If they had indeed escaped or survived Vangor they would more than likely be driven deeper into Remada rather than east towards Salandor. It was a pity, Teren reflected, because they were handy lads to have around.

After one last glance westwards towards home and the call to battle, Teren turned his horse and headed south. Maybe today would be the day he'd find Eryn.

Chapter 23

Ro and Arlen had spent several days riding between one battle site and then another, though to Arlen they seemed more like slaughter houses than battle sites. In every location the Salandori had seemed to come off worse, their bodies littering the ground, food for the carrion. By comparison the bodies of their dead attackers had been neatly stacked and then burned on a pyre, though it was plain to see that their losses had been considerably fewer. Of more concern to Arlen had been the fact that at every battle site there seemed to be evidence that a number of Salandori had been lined up and then beheaded in some sort of execution.

"There's another three who've been beheaded over there," said Ro as he walked back towards Arlen.

Arlen grimaced. "What's going on here, Ro? Is this truly Teren's work?"

"It must be. I understand the desire even the need for revenge, but why they are executing some in every camp is beyond me," replied Ro.

"Unless they're trying to send a message to the Salandori," suggested Arlen.

"I think the sheer fact that they are wandering around the Salandori homeland killing their men with impunity is sending out a big enough message," said Ro.

"True, but what madness possessed him to come down here into the south where they know the Salandori is massing?"

"He must figure that where the Salandori are, so too must Eryn be. It's madness."

"I'm more interested in what madness has persuaded you to lead us down here after them. I've lost count of how many times we've had to hide from Salandori patrols, not to mention the little matter of the entire Narmidian nation passing by just a stone's throw from us," said Arlen.

"Yes, that was a close one wasn't it?" said Ro smiling.

"Too close. Do you not think our duty lies to the west

warning the leaders that an even bigger threat than the Delarites is bearing down on them?"

"Probably, yes, but I gave my word that we'd come and find Teren and judging by the freshness of these bodies I'd say we're the closest we've been for some time," said Ro.

"Closer than you know I think," replied Arlen. His sword hand slowly travelled towards his weapon as he stared at something over Ro's shoulder.

Ro spun round drawing his sword as he did so. Lined up behind him were a dozen heavily armed men of various nationalities and more were coming, seemingly appearing out of nowhere. Before they knew it, the two friends were surrounded by about forty hard faced and battle scarred men.

A tall dark haired man with a muscle bound torso stepped forward, leant on his axe and then stared at Ro and Arlen for a few seconds.

"And what do we have here then; a couple of western slavers doing the Salandori's bidding?"

"My name is Ro Aryk and this is Arlen Meric and we are no slavers; we're searching for our friend, nothing more."

"I didn't ask who you were but what you were," said the man Ro had already decided by his dialect if not his attitude was a Delarite. That was not going to endear him any further.

"He's the man who's going to end your life prematurely if you don't show him some respect, stranger," said Arlen.

The Delarite stared at Arlen with contempt. "Is that right, fat man? Maybe I should quickly kill him and then take my time with you. I could carve you up like a boar; the lads haven't had much meat lately and there seems to be plenty of you to go around."

A few of the men with the Delarite started to chuckle, though some looked uncomfortable.

"Like you said; you'd have to get past me first and I don't fancy your chances of doing that," said Ro smiling. He and Arlen were in a truly precarious position, but to show weakness now would be foolhardy perhaps even suicidal.

Still it would have been better if Arlen had bitten back his threat, thought Ro.

"Let's put that to the test shall we?" said the Delarite standing straight and hefting his axe.

Ro stepped forward and took up a defensive stance and the two men began circling each other.

"Hold." The voice boomed out and cut across the cheers and jeers of the watching men.

The Delarite maintained his posture, but risked a quick glance at where the voice had come from.

"I don't take orders from you, Brak."

"Maybe not, but I think it would be very unwise of you to risk harming two of Teren's friends."

At the mention of their friend's name both Ro and Arlen glanced over at the newcomer. He was also tall and well-built, with blond hair and striking blue eyes. Ro guessed that he came from one of the northern kingdoms though he didn't know which one.

"What do you mean friends of Teren's?" asked the Delarite suspiciously.

The northerner ignored the question and looked over at Ro. "You said your name was Ro Aryk and this is Arlen Meric?"

"That's right," replied Ro still not relaxing his defensive posture.

"Teren has spoken of you many times and will be pleased to see you both. Please come with me." He then glanced back at the Delarite. "Put your toy away, Delarite before you hurt yourself."

More chuckling from the gathered crowd this time at the Delarite.

The Delarite cursed under his breath but did as the northerner suggested. Ro and Arlen brushed past him on their way to join the northerner.

"Another time then," said the Delarite as they passed him.

"I shall look forward to it," said Ro.

"You too, fat man. We'll have our day."

Arlen stopped, turned back around and came to stand virtually in the Delarite's face. The man was grinning, happy that he had apparently succeeded in provoking the stranger.

Arlen smiled. "Why wait?" Before the Delarite could react, Arlen had head butted him sending him staggering backwards clutching at his broken and bloody nose.

Arlen reeled backwards as well holding his aching

forehead. He had never done that before and quietly vowed to himself that he would never do it again. He wasn't sure who it hurt more, him or the Delarite.

Whilst the Delarite was still clutching at his face, Arlen raced forward and punched the man on the jaw before swiftly kicking him behind the right knee. The Delarite dropped to his knees and as he did so, Arlen spun round and kicked out, his foot making perfect contact with the side of the man's head. The Delarite dropped to the ground unconscious in front of a stunned crowd.

Ro had watched first in admiration and then in trepidation, unsure how much authority over this rabble the big northerner had. If it was limited, he and Arlen might be about to find themselves in a very ugly situation. Thankfully the crowd seemed to just admire the way the newcomer had despatched what was presumably one of their finest fighters.

"Making friends again I see, priest," said the familiar voice to their right and everybody turned to face the speaker.

Staring back at them with a stern look upon his face was Teren.

"The hospitality of your camp leaves a bit to be desired, Teren," replied Arlen.

"Oh, don't worry about the Delarite; he's like that with everyone," said Teren breaking into a broad grin. "By Chell it's good to see you two boys. I didn't think you'd come." Teren strode forward and gave them both a hug.

"I said we would," said Ro.

"That you did, lad, but not everyone keeps their word, however well-intentioned. I should have known better in your case than to doubt you."

"We have much to talk about, my friend," said Ro solemnly.

"That we do, lad. Ah, where are my manners. Come, follow me, I've got some fine wine we've liberated from these fellows back in camp. We can share the wine and the news." Teren turned and started to walk away and then almost as an afterthought turned back the other way. "And somebody clean that up," he added nodding towards the stricken Delarite.

"Seems like a nice fellow," said Arlen.

"Ah, he's all right once you get to know him," replied Teren earnestly.

"Really?"

"No, he's a treacherous and vicious dog, but out of some misplaced loyalty he's sworn to remain with me until he can repay his debt," said Teren.

"His debt?" asked Ro.

"I saved his life."

"Ah, I see."

"I might have to free him from that bond in exchange for him not slitting your throat during the night."

"That's a comforting thought," said Arlen sarcastically. "Now where's that wine?"

***

Teren had led them back to his camp and the three friends had talked for hours, stopping only briefly for something to eat. Ro and Arlen had told Teren about the terrible moment they had realised that the mass of men closing in on Vangor wasn't the relief column, but another Delarite army. They explained or perhaps tried to justify their decision to leave the city defended only by wounded men and a handful of volunteers, but Teren appeared to agree with their decision.

"You did the right thing, lads, saving as many people as you could. We should have all got out whilst we could after we won the battle; to linger was to invite certain death. Nobody expected us to bleed the enemy as much as we did. The prefect stayed you say?"

Ro nodded. "Captain Matalis too."

"Brave lads. Stubborn, but brave. And then you travelled east you say?"

"We initially headed south but then turned east whilst Queen Cala went west to try and rendezvous with some of her men. Several days into Salandor we ran into Eryn."

Teren's face seemed to automatically brighten up at the mention of his son's name and he urged Ro to continue his story.

Ro started to recount everything that had happened from the moment they had run into Eryn hiding in the woods after

Teren and he had been ambushed. When Arlen felt that his friend was omitting a piece of vital information, he would jump in with more details.

When Ro had finally got around to describing the preceding twenty four hours and their eventual meeting with Teren's men, Teren leant back and started to consider everything that he had just heard.

"So the last time you saw Eryn was a couple of weeks ago when you sent him and Tayla off to the south?"

"That's right. We thought the further down the eastern border that they emerged into Remada the greater the chance of them running into Remadan troops rather than Delarite," said Ro.

"It's still damned risky," said Teren fixing Ro with an icy stare. "Why didn't you let them come with you?"

"Because we didn't know how or when we were likely to find you and the girl had been away from her family long enough," snapped Arlen. He was tired of people questioning their choices when they hadn't even been there at the time. The man should just have been grateful that his son was alive and not a prisoner of the Salandori as he had feared.

Teren seemed to baulk at the priest's tone, but then his expression softened.

"Then you probably did the right thing."

Probably, thought Arlen. *Will he never fully admit that the other person was right all along?*

"By now he should be safely inside Remada," said Ro trying to dispel the awkwardness that had developed between the other two men.

"Remada certainly, but safely is another matter," said Teren.

Ro could tell that Arlen was seething with indignation at the man's apparent lack of gratitude and once again an awkward silence descended over the small group. Once again it fell to Ro to break it.

"Anyway, that's our tale, Teren, but I should imagine you have an interesting one of your own to recount."

Teren nodded. Both Ro and Arlen were looking at him expectantly; clearly they wanted the full details of his own adventures over the last few weeks.

After helping himself to another large cup of wine and then refilling the others' cups, Teren sat back again and started to tell his own story, leaving nothing out. The others listened attentively until it was clear that he had finished.

"So you've got your own personal army now?" asked Ro.

"I wouldn't say that. They follow me for now whilst the killing is easy and the plunder even easier, but the first time we taste defeat most will disappear."

"And you, what do you get out of it?" asked Ro.

"The strength to be able to go where I like in this land and to question who I like. It's a marriage of convenience I guess you'd say," replied Teren.

"And the men missing their heads?" asked Arlen.

Teren looked at Arlen. "Who?"

"The Salandori warriors missing their heads; we saw a few at the site of every battle your men seem to have won."

"They didn't have the right answers when they were questioned," replied Teren. There was a definite absence of remorse Arlen noticed.

"So now you'll head back to Remada and try to find Eryn I suppose?" said Ro. "Remada's going to need every one of her sons to fight off the Narmidian storm that is bearing down on her."

"Remada is going to have to do without me this time; I've paid my dues," said Teren suddenly looking downcast.

Ro and Arlen exchanged a quizzical look.

"Surely you are joking? You have spent all this time and killed all these men in a quest to find your son in this Sulat forsaken land and now when we tell you he is back on home soil, you lose interest in the task," said Arlen.

"Careful, priest; you assume too much in our friendship."

"I assume nothing, but I have earned the right to speak my mind. We risked our lives to come and find Eryn and you and we're happy to find you both alive and well. Eryn wanted to ride with us and search for you but we persuaded him otherwise for the reasons we have already spoken. We had to promise him that when we found you we would all return home immediately and try and meet up with him. Are you now going to make us break our word?"

"It is not that simple, Arlen."

"And why is that exactly?"

"Because I have found my wife, Valla."

"We heard," said Ro. "We ran into Garik and some of the others a short while ago and he told us about Valla."

Teren nodded, pleased to hear that his former comrades were safe.

"I am sorry, Teren, to spend all that time looking for her only to find that she is now a willing guest of her former captors, must be soul destroying," said Arlen.

"Don't be sorry, lad, I'll soon get her back. Besides she's not a willing guest, but a prisoner."

Arlen looked at Ro as he recalled what Garik had said about her making no attempt to escape and seemingly leaving with the other Narmidians of her own free will. Teren needed to be told, but Ro shook his head warning the priest not to mention it.

"You plan on going after her?" asked Ro.

"Of course! Why wouldn't I? Eryn is too far ahead of me and is at least out of this Sulat forsaken country. Besides, having seen the size of the Narmidian army, they shouldn't be too difficult to find should they?"

"I can think of about a hundred thousand reasons why and they all ride horses and have nasty curved swords – they're called his army," said Arlen.

"One man, a thousand, a million, it makes no difference to me. She is my wife and belongs by my side."

"This is madness. Tell him he's mad to even consider it, Ro."

"Your mind is set then?" said Ro.

"It is," replied Teren.

"Please don't say what I think you're about to say," pleaded Arlen looking at Ro.

"Then I will accompany you for as long as I can," finished Ro.

"What did I just say?" said Arlen exasperated.

Ro turned to face his friend. "You do not need to come on this one, Arlen. You have done more than enough already."

"I know; saving your life has become a habit. Started in that woods all those weeks ago and never seems to end, so I guess I'll have to come with you."

"No man ever had truer friends," said Teren grinning.

"Nor so many fools," added Arlen wryly.

"What about your men, Teren, what will they do now when you tell them you no longer need to travel this land searching for Eryn?" asked Ro.

"I don't know that will be for each man to decide. Hopefully some of them will still want to come with us, others will go home. They're a handy bunch of lads to have at your back for the most part."

"What about that delightful Delarite chap; will he be joining us do you think?" asked Arlen.

"He claims he owes me a debt of honour so probably yes, but I will try and get him to accept his release from the bond. Knowing him as I do though, he will probably want to come with us anyway," replied Teren.

"This just keeps getting better and better," said Arlen rolling his eyes.

The other two men laughed.

"Come I will address the men now," said Teren. "Then in the morning we can make an early start west towards home and destiny."

Ro and Arlen raised their half full cups of wine in salute. "To home and destiny."

Arlen wasn't quite sure what that destiny would be, but he was pretty sure that it wouldn't be uneventful.

Chapter 24

After concealing the bodies of the two men he had just killed, Eryn had hurried through the backstreets to the *Wild Boar*. He suspected that in a town like Ederik the occurrence of dead bodies lying on the street wasn't that unusual, but it had still felt like the right thing to do.

After checking that no one was watching, Eryn had entered the tavern via the back door and made his way cautiously up the rickety wooden stairs to the top floor and the room at the end of the landing. He listened outside for a few seconds to make sure he'd got the right door and then quietly entered the room.

Tayla was lying on a small bunk in the middle of the room and around her stood Lily, the tavern keeper and an older man whom Eryn didn't recognise but assumed was the doctor.

Eryn closed the door quietly behind him after first checking that nobody had followed him up the stairs. Then he walked over and extended his hand towards the tavern keeper.

"It is good to see you again, sir," said Eryn smiling.

The older man regarded him for a few moments and then shook the young lad's hand returning the smile.

"And it is good to see you again, young Eryn, despite what I said about never returning here."

"Yes, I am sorry about that, but I didn't know where else to go. Is this the doctor?"

"Closest thing that passes for one round here that's for sure," replied the tavern keeper.

The doctor looked up from where he was bent over examining Tayla and gave the tavern keeper a fierce scowl.

"If you think you can do any better, tavern keeper, you go right ahead and take over," sneered the doctor.

"Sadly his bedside manner is no better than his medical skills," said the tavern keeper smiling.

Eryn smiled too. Despite the venom in each man's words,

it was clear that the two men were friends and enjoyed baiting one another.

"How is she, doctor?" asked Eryn.

"How does she look?"

"Ill, very ill," replied Eryn somewhat abashed.

"Well then you have your answer young man; she is very ill." Apparently his rudeness wasn't reserved just for friends.

"Do you know what ails her?" asked Eryn.

The doctor glanced towards Lily who surreptitiously shook her head. She had already told the doctor not to mention that her sister had died of the same disease the previous year. "Not a clue. I have not seen this type of ailment before. Have you been travelling?"

"In a manner of speaking, yes. We've just come back from the east."

"Ah, well that probably explains it then. She's contracted some foul sickness from over there, perhaps from the water or even an insect bite," said the doctor.

"Is she going to be all right?" asked Lily.

"I've no idea, but I've done everything I can for her. She is burning with an extremely high temperature and appears delirious. The medicine I've just given her is the most powerful in the known world, but I must caution you that she is extremely ill and I can offer no guarantees. Her fate is in the lap of the Gods now. The best thing you can do is let her rest. I'm sorry, young man; I wish I could do more. I hope she pulls through."

Eryn didn't answer. He had heard the doctor's words but his brain was refusing to accept them. Surely he hadn't spent all this time, killed all those men in the process of rescuing her, just to have her snatched away again because of an insect bite or some foul polluted water?

"Thanks for trying, doctor. Tell Maryke I said you could have as many free drinks as you like tonight," said the tavern keeper.

"That is kind of you, Trey, but somehow I don't feel like drinking now," said the doctor glancing over at the girl laying on the bed and the young man kneeling by her side trying desperately to hold back the tears that needed to fall.

The doctor had done what Lily asked and hadn't told them

the full truth. It was true that he had given her the most powerful medicine he possessed and that in most cases it would cure the patient. What he hadn't told them was that he had seen this illness twice before and that on both occasions the patient had died very quickly despite the medicine. One of those patients had been Lily's younger sister, Elor, a sweet girl snatched from them so cruelly. He hoped that this young girl, Tayla, would be the exception, but he doubted that would be the case. After nodding at Lily and Trey, the doctor slipped quietly out of the room and down the stairs not giving the bar and the free drinks a second thought.

Trey walked over and put a hand on Eryn's shoulder.

"You heard the doctor, Eryn, best to let her rest awhile. When did you last eat?"

Eryn slowly stood, his eyes never leaving Tayla as he watched the shallow rise and fall of her chest.

"I don't remember."

"Well that's something I can help with. You come with me and I'll get Maryke to fix you something to eat. Lily here will stay with the young lady won't you, Lily?"

"Of course I will. If there's any change I'll come and find you, Eryn."

The door behind them swung open and Eryn's hand automatically travelled to his sword hilt, but it was only Trey's son.

"What is it, Bran?" asked the tavern keeper.

"Trouble," replied the boy.

"What?"

"Some of Bratak's thugs are here. They know about Eryn and want us to hand him over. They're already starting to rough up a few of our customers."

"What's your mother doing?"

"Looks like she's about ready to take them all on," replied Bran grinning.

"If I could just get that piece of scum Bratak on his own I'd rid this town of him once and for all."

"You'd have to join a very long queue, Trey," said Eryn.

"You know him?" asked Trey surprised.

"Oh, yes, we have history, which is why he's so keen to find me now."

266

"Then you must hide and let me get rid of these men."

"Not this time, my friend," replied Eryn. "This one's mine."

"There are many of them, Eryn," said Bran.

Eryn smiled. "I'm kind of getting used to that, Bran."

"Most of the people in this town hate Bratak and his men, but are too scared to do anything about it; I'm not," said Bran.

"My son has your fighting spirit, Eryn and would take them all on," said Trey.

"If the town's people feel like that why haven't they done something about Bratak and his men?" asked Eryn.

"Like Bran said, most are scared and nobody wants to be the one to make the first move in case nobody else steps forward to help them. But believe me most in this town do hate them. They've killed, robbed and raped with impunity and strut around as if they own the place because they can count on support from the Delarites if need be. Bratak and his men save the Delarites from having to leave a garrison here."

Eryn nodded his understanding. "Whatever happens just promise me you'll do your best to look after Tayla?"

"You have my word," replied Trey.

"You can't go down there, Eryn, they'll kill you," said Lily.

"And if I don't they're likely to come up here killing even more on their way. I don't need that on my conscience as well, Lily."

The sound of shouting and arguments carried up the stairs from below.

"Bran, go and tell them that I am just securing Eryn and that I'll be bringing him down in a minute," said Trey. Bran nodded and hurried away to do as his father requested. From downstairs the sound of people shouting and furniture being knocked over grew louder. "You must hurry down the back stairs, Eryn and pray that they haven't stationed men there."

"You are a good friend, Trey, but I told you I'm not running. Stay up here until it's over," and with that Eryn started towards the door, but it swung open before he got there. Eryn's sword was out in a flash, momentarily startling the newcomer.

"It's all right, Eryn, this is Rak, one of my regulars; he hates Bratak as much as we do. What is it, Rak?" Trey asked the frightened looking man.

Rak tore his eyes away from Eryn to look at the tavern keeper.

"It's Bran, Trey. One of Bratak's men...he's stabbed him."

For a moment it didn't look like the news had sunk in, but then Trey's face clouded over and he barged past Rak and hurried down the stairs closely followed by Eryn.

When Trey was no more than eight steps from the tavern floor, he stopped and looked down. Bran was laying in his mother's arms a pool of blood spreading around him. The commotion had stopped and everyone, Bratak's men and the tavern's patrons were all stood in a semi-circle a couple of paces away from Bran looking up at Trey.

When Trey finally stepped all the way down, the crowd took a pace backwards, but one man who was holding a bloody dagger was shoved forward into Trey's view. Trey knelt down and stroked his son's head, but his son was already dead. He looked into his wife's face and saw for the first time since the day Bran had been born, tears streaming down her face. He leant forward and kissed his son tenderly on the forehead. Then with a speed that few would have thought him capable of, he leapt up and grabbed the wrist of the man holding the dagger and forced it up into the man's throat and under his chin half a dozen times. By the time he had finished and eventually let the man's body fall to the floor, Trey was covered in blood.

He stared about him at the mixture of Bratak's men and customers. He had hoped that the snake Bratak was here but as usual the coward had sent other men to do his bidding. Everyone's gaze was on Trey. Some looked on in awe, others in terror. Some clearly did not want to be there.

"Those of you who are afraid or want no part of what is about to happen should leave," said Trey. Nobody except Maryke, who came and stood by her husband's side, moved. From somewhere inside her apron she produced a vicious looking knife of her own.

"I don't know what you're planning, tavern keeper, but you need to think this through. Any harm comes to us and

Bratak will see to it that you're all killed," said a man whom Trey recognised as one of Bratak's lapdogs. The man and his comrades had raised their weapons and were starting to back their way towards the door. They looked terrified.

There was a squealing noise from behind them and the man who had spoken risked a glance over his shoulder. Two burly and hard faced looking men who were not part of Bratak's gang, had bolted the front door and now stood barring the way. They too had drawn their weapons. Swallowing hard with nerves, Bratak's man turned back to face Trey and his wife.

Trey fixed the man with an icy stare and then smiled.

"Kill them all."

By the time the leader of Bratak's men had registered what Trey had just said, Maryke had already plunged the dagger deep into his abdomen and was now biting into his throat with her bare teeth. The man fell to the floor screaming as all around him those known to be Bratak's men were overpowered and butchered by the townspeople. Within a couple of minutes it was all over and all eight of Bratak's men lay dead either from stab wounds or beatings; one man's throat had been ripped out.

It had all happened too quickly for Eryn to intervene and he felt somehow guilty at not having taken part seeing as Bratak's men had been there for him in the first place. Only two of the tavern's customers had been killed in the brief melee and another had received a nasty gash on the upper right arm.

Eryn went and knelt by Bran's body and brushed the boy's eyes closed with his fingers. When Trey came back over Eryn looked up and met the tavern keeper's eyes.

"I am truly sorry about, Bran, Trey. This is all my fault; I should never have come here."

"You are not to blame, Eryn."

"But if I hadn't come back in the first place none of this would have happened."

"Maybe, maybe not, but it has happened and there's not a thing we can do about that to change it. There is only one person responsible for my son's death and he is going to pay for it," said Trey bitterly.

"When Bratak hears about this he's going to come looking for you," said Eryn.

"I'm counting on it. Besides, I won't be hard to find because we're going to look for him aren't we?" said Trey glancing towards his wife. Maryke had fresh blood all around her mouth where she'd bitten into the throat of one of Bratak's men. It wasn't a pleasant sight but it was a terrifying one, Eryn decided.

"Yes we are," Maryke replied brandishing her wicked looking knife.

"I think it's about time we took back our town, boys, what do you think?" asked Trey.

Every single occupant of the tavern punched the air or waved a weapon.

Trey realised that when Bratak heard that some of his men had been killed he would send for help from the Delarites. They had to act quickly. There was no turning back now.

"Where will Bratak be?" asked Eryn.

"This time of night they're probably at Ellie's whorehouse. We've got to get to him before he can send for help," replied Trey.

"Then lead on," said Eryn.

"This isn't your fight, Eryn."

"Like I said, Bratak and I have unfinished business."

The steely look in Eryn's eyes told the tavern keeper the point wasn't up for discussion as far as Eryn was concerned.

"Then let's finish it." Trey looked about him and began giving orders to some of the men dividing them into smaller groups. They were going to try and rid the town of Bratak's men once and for all. "Flush them all out, boys and leave none alive. Let's clean up our town."

A great roar went up and after the door was unbolted the men began to disperse out of the tavern towards their designated targets. Trey gathered eight men about him and together with Eryn they set off for Ellie's whorehouse. Maryke made to go with them, but Trey smiled, put his hand on her shoulder and told her to stay with their son; he would handle it. She clearly wasn't happy, her own desire for revenge not yet quenched, but she did as her husband bade.

As they made their various ways throughout the town and

word began to spread, more men who had been aggrieved by Bratak's gang or perhaps just resented their presence, joined their ranks. It was soon pretty clear that the town's people prepared to make a stand greatly outnumbered those loyal to Bratak.

Here and there word filtered through to some of Bratak's men and those with any sense mounted the nearest horse whether it was theirs or not and headed out of town as quickly as they could. Some made to rally with their leader whilst others, whether out of a sense of bravado or just simply underestimating the numbers of men opposing them, made a stand, but these were quickly overpowered and killed. Some when they realised their mistake threw down their weapons and tried to surrender, but it did them no good and every one of Bratak's men that was found was put to the sword. Soon their bodies littered the streets. Women and girls who had been raped or assaulted by them started to come out and kick or spit on their dead or dying bodies. The town was turning ugly and vengeful.

Eryn, Trey and the other men gathered outside the whorehouse. Whether Bratak and any of his cronies inside had heard the commotion, was debatable. If they had or if someone had got to them first and warned them, they could be waiting inside with swords drawn or even crossbows, although that was unlikely Eryn thought. Of more concern to him was the possibility that Bratak had been tipped off and had already left town. That thought made Eryn feel sick. He wanted revenge for what he'd done to Jeral Tae so bad that he could almost taste it.

Trey was still discussing the layout of the whorehouse with a couple of the men who frequented the premises, when the front door flew open. Several armed men, a couple of whom Eryn recognised from Lentor, came bursting out. For a moment or two they caught Eryn's group by surprise and managed to take out two of their number with sword thrusts, one dead and the other taking a wound to the side. Led by Trey, however, the town's people rallied and after backing them into a tight group with their backs against the wall, they began the bloody business of cutting Bratak's men down. Again one or two suddenly dropped their swords and tried to surrender including the man Eryn had been fighting. Eryn hesitated, unwilling to kill an unarmed man in cold blood.

Sensing that there was a chance he could make it out alive, the man began to plead even harder as Eryn gradually lowered his sword. His words were suddenly cut short, however, when Trey thrust his own sword point deep into the man's throat.

"We can't let any live, Eryn, not after what they've done to this town and its people," said Trey.

Feeling foolish and weak, Eryn nodded and then looked around. All of Bratak's men were laying dead but only one of Trey's men, although three had sustained wounds of varying degrees of severity.

"I don't see Bratak," said Eryn.

"Neither do I. The maggot's either fled or he's still hiding inside like the coward he is," replied Trey.

"Let's go and get him then," said Eryn, but even as he made to move towards the open door he caught a flicker of movement from that direction. Slowly Bratak began to emerge from the doorway. He had his left arm around a woman's neck and held a knife to her throat. He was grinning. Eryn recognised the woman as the one who had asked him and Tav to enter her house the last time they'd been there and had then got unpleasant when he and Tav had refused. Now he understood why. This was presumably Ellie; Lily's employer.

"Well, well, well, Eryn Martel, back from his quest. I hear that didn't go too well," sneered Bratak.

Eryn made to attack the man but he just grinned some more as he pressed the knife closer to Ellie's throat.

"Not so fast, boy unless you want to see how much blood there is inside this stuffed pig." Eryn took a couple of paces back. "That's better. Now why don't you all back away nice and slowly so that I can pass. Then me and the whore are going to mount those horses over there and ride out. When I think I'm far enough away, I'll set her free – maybe. If I so much as get a sniff that any of you are following me, I'll..."

A pained expression suddenly crossed Bratak's face followed by one of surprise. Ellie felt Bratak's grip around her neck loosen and immediately reached up and grabbed his restraining arm before sinking her teeth into it as hard as she could. Bratak instinctively let go of Ellie but as she moved away he swung wildly with the knife trying to slash her back but missed by several inches. Realising that Bratak was off balance Eryn seized his chance and quickly stepped forward and thrust his sword deep into his abdomen.

"That's for Tav you miserable worm," said Eryn as he twisted the blade viciously, "and that's just because I don't like you," he then said as he twisted it equally as viciously back the other way. Eryn pulled the sword from Bratak's body and stepped back.

Bratak stared open mouthed at Eryn for a moment, the knife dropping harmlessly from his grasp. Then he dropped to his knees before falling face first into the dirt. A couple of paces behind where Bratak had been standing stood a young scantily dressed girl with ginger hair. She had a swollen lip and a nasty looking bruise developing on her right cheek. Eryn glanced down at Bratak's body and saw the small knife protruding from between his shoulder blades where the girl had plunged it just moments before. Presumably Bratak had been enjoying her services before Eryn and the others had arrived. It also looked like he enjoyed giving the girls a beating as well. This one, however, had struck back and given Eryn the opportunity to kill him.

Eryn was still thinking about that when Ellie walked up to Bratak's lifeless body and spat on his back before giving him a hefty kick in the ribs. After a few seconds deliberation she gave him another one, even harder this time, before placing an arm around the girl with ginger hair and leading her back indoors, locking the door behind her.

"That should be an end to it, Eryn, so why don't you go back and see how your young lady fares?" said Trey. "Me and the lads will go and see how the others are doing, but I suspect the only men loyal to Bratak left in town now are dead ones."

"Thanks, I will," said Eryn nodding. He wiped his sword clean on Bratak's tunic and turned round and headed back to the *Wild Boar.*

The moment he walked into the tavern bar, Eryn knew that something was wrong. Lily had promised to sit and watch over Tayla yet here she was sat downstairs. The doctor was also back and he was talking in hushed tones with Lily and Maryke when Eryn walked in. They stopped talking the moment they saw him and glanced at one another as if silently debating who was going to tell Eryn.

"Lily, why aren't you with Tayla?" asked Eryn.

Lily stood and started to walk over to him. "I'm sorry, Eryn, there was nothing anybody could do."

Eryn stared at her for a couple of seconds trying to comprehend what she was trying to tell him without actually saying it. Then as realisation dawned, he bounded upstairs taking the steps two or three at a time. By the time that he reached the room he was out of breath and panting hard. He stopped in the doorway and stared in. The bed in which Tayla had been placed still had an occupant but that occupant had now been covered by a sheet. Eryn walked slowly over and stopped by the bedside. Prepared for what he knew he'd find he reached down and gently pulled the sheet down exposing Tayla's head and neck. He thought the tears would come then, hard and fast, but instead he found himself just staring silently at his dead fiancée's body.

It had all been for nothing; the journey, the battle at Vangor, Tav and the travel eastwards, all pointless. He had failed. Tav was dead, his sister Keira was dead, his father was missing, probably dead and now his fiancée had been stolen from him again and this time there would be no rescue.

His legs began to tremble and then the tears started to flow. He felt someone come and stand to his left and take hold of his arm, but he didn't bother to look. He imagined it was Lily, but he didn't want to look at her and see his own shame and failure reflected in her eyes.

"I'm so sorry, Eryn. Not long after you went she began coughing violently and her temperature seemed to soar even higher. With Bran dead I had no one to send for the doctor so I had to go myself and by the time we got back she had already slipped away. I really am sorry."

"You left her alone? She died alone?" The news was heartbreaking for Eryn.

"I had no choice, Eryn."

"She did the right thing, lad," said the doctor who had

also followed them upstairs. "She was frightened and didn't know what to do. It all happened really fast."

"Was she in any pain?" asked Eryn.

"No. I'd given her a powerful pain suppressant before I left. She hadn't been in any pain for some time."

Eryn nodded and bent down and kissed Tayla on her forehead. The sound of running footsteps coming up the stairs startled him though and he spun round reaching for his sword thinking that one of Bratak's men still drew breath. Instead it was Trey who stopped when he entered the room and sighed.

"Damn it. I'm so sorry, Eryn."

"After everything she'd been through, the kidnap, the journey, the attacks, after all that it's some damned disease that kills her. Life isn't fair," said Eryn bitterly.

"That it's not, lad. I know you're hurting and need to grieve, we all do," said Trey, his thoughts suddenly straying to his own son's body lying covered under another sheet downstairs, "but a rider has just arrived with some news. I think you ought to hear it; all of you."

"Is it good news?" asked Lily.

"When is it ever?" replied Trey, before turning and heading downstairs followed by Eryn and the others.

When they emerged onto the street, it seemed to Eryn that virtually the whole town had gathered and were now eagerly milling around waiting to hear what the rider had to say. Trey had instructed the man not to tell anyone else the news until he had brought Eryn and the others out.

"Listen everybody," began Trey. "Bratak and his thugs have all been dealt with and ordinarily that would be a cause to celebrate, but a rider has arrived from the east and brings news you all need to hear." Trey gestured for the rider to begin.

"I live on a farm to the east at a place called Yurathni, on the border with Salandor; some of you may know it. Yesterday morning when my brother and I were ploughing one of the fields we heard a tremendous thumping noise coming from the other side of the hills which lay to the east of our farmstead. The noise was getting louder and louder. We rode up to the top of one of the hills to investigate." The

275

man paused whether for dramatic effect or because the news he had to impart was truly terrible, Eryn didn't know.

"Go on," urged Trey.

The man took a deep breath. "The plains to the east of the hills were full of soldiers heading west; tens of thousands of them."

"Where are the Delarites getting all their men from?" one man in the crowd shouted out.

"That's just it," said the rider. "They're not Delarites; they're Narmidians."

"Narmidians! How can you be sure?" asked another man.

"Because one of their outriders stumbled across me and my brother and tried to raise the alarm. My brother jumped him but was killed. I killed the Narmidian with this knife," said the rider producing a clearly blood stained knife.

"So whose side are they on?" asked a woman at the front of the crowd.

"I've no idea," said the rider, "but not ours that's for sure. I think it's an invasion of the west – all of it."

"What can we do?" another man shouted out.

"I don't know what you're going to do, but I'm going to ride as far west as I can as quickly as I can. There's no army in the known world that can stop a force that large. I suggest you all pack up and leave as soon as possible because they're headed this way and they're not that far behind me." His message duly imparted the man pushed through the crowd, mounted his already exhausted horse and sped out of Ederik heading west.

People began to panic and shout, unsure what to do until Trey raised his voice and ordered them to shut up.

"It looks like we've got two choices friends; pack and leave or stay and face an uncertain fate. If our friend disappearing in the distance is telling the truth and judging by the terrified look on his face I would say that he is, then I think we should leave and head west. That's what Maryke and I are going to do, right after I've seen to my boy. Any who want to travel with us meet back here in one hour."

The crowd immediately began to disperse talking animatedly amongst themselves. The majority of the town it seemed had decided to flee.

"What will you do, Eryn?" asked Trey.

"Once I have taken care of Tayla I too shall head west, at least for now. We need to let whoever is in charge of the country know what is coming. It sounds to me like the only way we could resist these Narmidians is by uniting the western nations and making a stand, but what hope there is of that I don't know. Still, we have to try and convince them."

"Well if anyone can do it, I'm sure you can. We'll see you back here in an hour then?"

Eryn nodded and watched Trey walk away with his arm around his wife's shoulders. Everybody had already lost so much and now an even worse and more powerful enemy was heading their way. Eryn momentarily closed his eyes and wished that his father, Ro and Arlen were there; they'd know what to do. They weren't though and he was going to have to take responsibility himself he realised. He suddenly became aware of Lily staring at him.

"Would you mind very much if I tagged along with you?"asked Lily. "I've no one else."

"What about the other girls at Ellie's?" asked Eryn.

"They'll be all right. I'd rather be with you."

Eryn thought about it for a moment and tried to figure out how he'd feel if Lily tagged along. After a few seconds deliberation he realised that all he felt was pain, bitterness and anger.

"I don't think it's a good idea, Lily; everybody who travels with me ends up dead or missing like Tav and Tayla."

"Neither of those were your fault, Eryn," said Lily reaching out and touching Eryn on the shoulder. She quickly withdrew her hand when he flinched.

"They were both my fault. I should never have let Tav accompany me and I should have taken better care of Tayla," he bit back.

"Tav was where he wanted to be, with his best friend and there was nothing you could do about Tayla; that could have happened to anyone."

"Yes, but it always happens to me. I'm bad news to be around."

"I know how you're hurting, Eryn, but now you're just being childish."

"You've no idea how I'm hurting," snapped Eryn, his eyes wide with anger. "How could you?"

"I'll tell you why, because I too have lost friends and family." Eryn just stared at Lily unsure what to say and still struggling to contain his anger. "What, you think you're the only one who has suffered? I've lost my entire family; it's how I came to end up working at Ellie's in the first place."

"I'm sorry, I didn't know," replied Eryn slightly abashed.

"I know. It's right that you hurt, Eryn and it's probably right that you're angry with the world; Sulat knows I was. But it's not right that you just give up; Tayla wouldn't have wanted that I'm sure." Eryn nodded begrudgingly. "Now can I tag along with you or not?"

Eryn shrugged his shoulders. "If you want, though I will not be the best travelling companion."

"Thank you. Any company is better than none."

"As you wish. Now come, there is much to do before we leave," and with that Eryn turned and walked off to see to Tayla's body. He wasn't sure what the future held for him now. His heart was telling him to head back east and search for his father and friends, though that would be an almost impossible task. His head, however, said that his duty was to find someone on the ruling council, someone like Stil Lordik from his home village and tell them about the Narmidians. With a heavy heart he started to climb the steps to where the body of his dead fiancée lay.

Destiny would have to wait.

Lightning Source UK Ltd.
Milton Keynes UK
UKOW04f1107230615

253974UK00001B/6/P